# YES, I KILLED HER

# YES, I KILLED HER

HARRY FISHER

This edition produced in Great Britain in 2022

by Hobeck Books Limited, Unit 14, Sugnall Business Centre, Sugnall, Stafford, Staffordshire, ST21 6NF

www.hobeck.net

A CIP catalogue for this book is available from the British Library.

ISBN 978-1-913-793-67-8 (pbk)

Cover design by Jayne Mapp Design

Printed and bound in Great Britain by Clays Ltd, Elcograf S.p.A.

# ARE YOU A THRILLER SEEKER?

Hobeck Books is an independent publisher of crime, thrillers and suspense fiction and we have one aim – to bring you the books you want to read.

For more details about our books, our authors and our plans, plus the chance to download free novellas, sign up for our newsletter at **www.hobeck.net**.

You can also find us on Twitter **@hobeckbooks** or on Facebook **www.facebook.com/hobeckbooks10**.

*In memory of*
*Alice, Jean and Phyllis*

# CHAPTER ONE

EDWIN FULLER RECKONED he had less than twenty-four hours before the police arrived to tell him they'd discovered his wife's body hanging upside down in a dense tangle of undergrowth; *better get a move on*, he thought.

He slid from the bed and snapped off the condom. He'd never been a fan, but Rachel had refused point-blank to entertain the pill. He dropped it into the bin where it lay, perched on a fold in the translucent polythene liner. Normally he'd have disposed of it in the bathroom, but tonight he was happy to leave it where it lay.

The top pane in one of the room's two sash and case windows rattled in its frame as the storm battered against it. An accompanying squall sluiced against the glass, followed hot on its heels by another, repeating so frequently that individual drops didn't stand an earthly. The news for days had warned of severe weather for Edinburgh, in fact the entire east coast of Scotland from Berwickshire to Caithness. This storm, eighty mph winds with all the accompaniments, was due to hang about for thirty-six hours if the forecast was to be believed.

Edwin looked out onto the street, but the rain blurred the image. And despite being framed in the window, it was unlikely he'd be spotted; even if someone was crazy enough to be out on a night like this, they'd have their shoulders hunched up around their ears, head down and eyes fixed on the ground.

But loitering wasn't a luxury he could afford. He stretched up and hauled down the two top panes until they jammed, exposing about a foot of fresh air on either side. Instantly, the right-hand curtain billowed into the room, flattened against the panes then flopped back to neutral. He dropped to one knee, twisted the radiator thermostat to zero then returned to the bed.

He sat, side-saddle, studying his wife. She lay on her side on top of the duvet, facing away from him. The light filtering through the rain-spattered glass picked out the smooth contours of her hip, waist, and shoulder; a scattering of moles across her back resembled isolated rocks on a pale Hebridean beach. He leaned over and gently kissed the soft triangle of flesh in between her shoulder blades. 'I'd love to cuddle up beside you, darling, but I have so much to do.' He glanced past her to the bedside table and the luminous green display.

21:27. Bang on schedule.

He sighed, moved her hair to the side and slid his fingers under the PVC coated cable that was tight against her throat. With his other hand, he slipped the knot. The white pillowcase that had formed a makeshift hood contrasted with a lock of her hair, damp due to their recent exertions. It had ridden up, so he lifted her head, and tugged the cotton material down until it fitted neatly across her scalp. He retightened the ligature and let her fall back onto the bed. Her hair had to stay in place, for now at least.

2

'Well, Rachel, time to get you cleaned up and dressed.' Edwin shivered from the howling gale blasting through the open windows and winced as another slash of wind-driven rain battered into the front of the house. The roof tiles rattled and groaned under the onslaught. 'I know it's a shitty night, but sorry to say we'll be going out later.'

He opened a deep drawer in the base of his wardrobe and lifted out a sizeable bundle of mid-grey clothing: two hooded sweatshirts and four pairs of joggers. Same brand, same material, same colour. He pulled on one set and threw the other four garments onto the bed, then disentangled her underwear from the pile of clothing she'd stripped off less than half an hour earlier.

'Come on, then. Can't have you lying there all night. Things to do, places to go.' He smiled. 'Bodies to dump.'

He grabbed his wife's feet and dragged her corpse onto the floor. He knelt next to her, exhaled, then the bell dinged to signal the opening round of the one-sided wrestling match that would end half an hour later with Rachel in the boot of their car.

# CHAPTER TWO

Twelve Hours Later

Friday 08:15

'HELLO, Detective Inspector Cooper. So pleased you're free to join us on this beautiful January morning.'

The officer sporting the latest line in soaking wet Day-Glo is PC Dave Devlin, pound for pound one of the best beat cops in the business. We've worked together on many a case so I know that telling him to piss off will be even more rainwater off this particular duck's back. 'Thought you'd have things all tied up by now, Dave. I mean, how long is it since the shout? Half an hour?'

'That's correct. 07:46.'

As he says, 07:46, and here's the story. About quarter of an hour ago I was making my usual mess with the mascara brush when my phone began belting out one of those horrendous Christmas tunes my kids stuck on the bloody thing when my back was turned. My sidekick's face appeared on the screen. This is Detective Sergeant Andrew Young, and don't make the mistake of shortening his first name – he'll hit you with one of his best raised-eyebrow expressions. I had been about to head into the office, but his call diverted me to a double row of lock-ups that sit at right angles to Powderhall Lane. It runs along the south edge of St Mark's Woods, next to the local crematorium. Ten lock-ups, formed in two rows of five, facing each other across an eight-metre strip of shattered tarmac, gravel and muddy puddles. This is my patch: North Edinburgh and Leith, and that's why I've been dragged out on this bastard of a morning.

Dave does the decent thing and helps me struggle into a white Tyvek cleansuit but leaves me to pull on the overshoes myself. The whole get-up can be a pain but it's vital we don't compromise the forensic integrity of the scene by depositing particles or fibres, while the overshoes have *Police* stamped in raised letters on the soles to distinguish our footprints from those of the villains. Once we're both fully togged out, a uniformed PC signs me into the scene, and Dave raises the police tape so I can duck underneath.

I glance around. As locations go, this one's as miserable as sin although, to be fair, the weather doesn't help. As if on cue, the wind blows my hood back, and the rain spatters off my forehead. Why the hell am I not a beautician? Or a plumber? But then I wrinkle my nose when I consider where plumbers have to put their hands. 'So, Dave, who do we have on site?'

'DS Young, as you already know, the crime scene guys are getting themselves organised, and the Crime Scene Manager's here too. Chap by the name of Greg Brodie.'

'Brodie? New one on me.'

'Well, now's your chance to get acquainted. Here he comes.'

Two men, both decked out in cleansuits, are picking their way carefully along a narrow taped-off corridor in front of the left row of lock-ups. They're using plastic stepping plates to keep their size tens clear of the surface and safeguard any forensics. Truth is, a herd of buffalo could rampage through here without causing any further harm to prospective evidence because there's precious little chance of anything useful surviving this bloody awful weather.

Andrew hops off the last plate. 'Lovely day for it, Boss. Apologies for dragging you out in this.' He doesn't give even the slightest impression of being sorry, but it was gentlemanly of him to say. We form a huddle of four. Andrew gestures towards the man in white. 'DI Cooper, this is Greg Brodie, Crime Scene Manager. He was already on site when I arrived.'

Greg sticks his hand out in my direction. 'Morning, Detective Inspector.' He pauses. 'Or may I call you Melissa?'

Now, I'm no stickler for rank protocols but usually we kick off relatively formally and relax that fairly quickly. Just not normally this quickly. But I don't have time to bristle before his eyes crinkle behind his mask. 'It's been a long time. Lovely to see you again, shame about the circumstances.'

I blink. Hesitate. Peer at his face, or as much as I can see of it behind the mask. I obviously have *Nope, no idea* stamped across mine. He smirks. 'I'll leave that with you for a while.' The amused expression vanishes as if it's been turned off by a switch. 'Let me bring you up to date.' He indicates a concrete wall about three feet high, pebble-dashed at one time but what still adheres to the surface more resembles giant acne. The wall forms a border at the end of the strip that's farthest from the lane. 'She's on the other side.'

I join him, careful to steer clear of a hatched section of police tape on our right. He points over the wall, which drops about six or seven metres on the other side. I peer down into a tangled mess of drab, decaying undergrowth mainly comprising rhododendron, ivy and bramble, and can't possibly miss the vivid blue sole of a training shoe; about two, three metres away and facing me. Still to be confirmed, naturally, but I'll be surprised if this woman ended up there of her own volition.

I follow the line below the shoe to an exposed calf and concertinaed grey casual clothing. Now I see her other leg. I'm pretty certain a raindrop hasn't navigated its way to my spine, but the sensation is similar. This leg is impaled by a rusty spike. A relic, it's one of a few surviving iron bars still embedded in the original retaining wall. My eyes track further down and now I can pick out the pale skin of her lower back, more grey clothing, and arms hanging. Her head and upper body are enveloped in a sagging bundle of quilted coat. The colour is on trend right now; burnt orange, I think they call it. And the whole macabre scenario is wrapped up in a jungle of tree, bush and bramble. Particularly bramble, the devil's own work.

'This is an absolute pig of a site,' says Greg. 'It'll take more than five minutes to free her from all that mess.'

As he's talking, I check him out again, but I still haven't a clue when, where or even if we've met before. I cup my hand across my brow in an attempt to stop the driving rain blinding me. The dense foliage runs for several metres along the wall to left and right. In front of me, if an Olympic swimmer dived out from here, he just might touch the far edge. Shredded supermarket bags are snagged by the branches, alongside a maelstrom of assorted garbage. Clearly the lock-ups' owners don't list recycling among their top priorities.

The nearest building in view is easily fifty metres away, and that's because the Water of Leith flows down below. This river staggers its way in a series of kinks and corners from the Pentland Hills, through the city of Edinburgh before spilling out at Leith Docks, a few streets from our HQ. I peel my glasses off my nose and smear the raindrops away. Pointless exercise. 'So, Dave. Do tell. Which particular model of exercise junkie had a bit of a shock before they'd even had breakfast?'

'A runner. With her spaniel. She called it in.'

I shake my head; this is precisely why I'll never let my kids have a dog. 'What else have you done to preserve the scene?'

He points across the river to the Water of Leith Walkway; there's no path on this side. Just upstream, towards the city centre, the river bends away at a right angle. A PC is standing there, his back to us. A woman appears, jogging towards him, wearing ridiculous pink Lycra. She veers to pass the constable on his left, but he sidesteps smartly and sticks out an arm. He leans in close to speak to her, and her immediate response involves furious arm-waving and gesticulating, both at him and at the walkway. But even from behind, our man exudes *Thou shalt not pass* in spades. She gives in and jogs off, retracing her route.

Dave nods, a silent *Well done that man*. 'I have another PC stationed downstream,' he says. 'They were the first two on site, and they did a damn good job.' Dave's familiar with how I work. He knows to keep talking; I'll only ask questions if necessary. 'They went to where the woman was waiting but realised straight away they were on the wrong side of the river. So they told Control to send a car up here, pronto, in case whoever dumped the body had stuck around. We couldn't be *that* lucky but at least the site's secure.' He glances up, grimaces, pulls his collar in a bit tighter. 'Fat lot of good it'll do us, mind you.'

'Gave us a fighting chance though,' says Greg.

I take another quick look at him but still the bells are silent. He's Scottish, definitely, but with a twang. Spent a number of years south of the border by the sound of it. I'm back on Dave. 'What's the runner's story?'

'Passes here every morning on her way to work. A pet shop,

hence the spaniel. Told the uniforms she was coming round that bend when she spotted the body. At first she thought it was bedding that had been tossed over the wall but when she got closer she could see what it was.'

I hear voices below, catch a glimpse of white. I'm about to ask how Greg's team gained access when he explains. 'With this particular location, it's definitely better if we work from below. Items might've fallen out of her pockets, or the perp could've dropped something.' He points way over to the right. 'We managed to drop a ladder down from a garden over there but all that did was give us access. We need a much easier route to move personnel and equipment in and out and, eventually, to extricate the victim. As it happens, I have a contact in the Engineers over at Redford Barracks and I've been in touch to ask if they can build us a temporary crossing. They should be here in about ...' he checks his wrist, 'twenty minutes or so.'

I nod. Scan the wider area. Focus in on the far bank. Lift my gaze. Then I groan, sling a few swear words in that direction, and turn to Andrew.

He shrugs. 'There's not a lot we can do about them, I'm afraid.'

Hugging the path, no more than a few metres on the far side, is a block of apartments. In common with other urban settings, these developments have sprung up along the Water of Leith. This one has three levels, at least half a dozen properties on each, and two penthouses lording it over the lesser wealthy below. Typical riverside theme: all decking, powdered metal balconies and hanging baskets. And virtually every window has a face peering out. I can see arms raised in what might once have been considered an unnatural position, but not these days. Phones, therefore cameras, therefore social media. A couple have donned waterproofs and are braving the elements, elbows leaning on railings. I feel like giving them all the finger but going viral has never been my thing.

'Could be a double-edged sword, Boss,' says Andrew. 'We'll canvass the residents, maybe one of them saw something.'

In most circumstances, when we have a body we erect a shelter. For three reasons: to keep prying eyes away, to preserve the victim's dignity, and to protect the scene. But like Greg commented earlier, this is a pig of a location. And then some. I turn to him, but he's read my mind. Again.

'I spoke to the Engineers about that too. We'll rig up a hanging shelter that'll keep the rain off.' He nods towards the apartments. 'We'll do our best to spoil their fun too.' He adjusts his hood. 'I have to get back; they'll need help down there.'

I say thanks, and then a glimmer flits across my memory. Something about him. Or what he said? Or the way he said it? Or his expression? No. Whatever it was, it's gone. *Damn.*

I glance down, Greg's colleagues have begun to clear the lower foliage. We know these guys as Crime Scene Examiners, or SEs. They're specialist police officers, not civilians employed by the police as they are in many other countries, where their collective term is CSIs. One is on his knees, working his way methodically over the ground. Another has wedged a narrow aluminium ladder into a natural chimney below the body. He's snipping away the vegetation and passing it, branch by tangled branch, to yet another white clad SE. This one is slighter. They're inching towards the orange quilted coat but really, there's nothing for me to see yet.

I'm turning away when a fourth person in white appears as if from nowhere. This one is tiny, about half the size of even the smallest of the others. You'd be entitled to ask: what the hell's a kid doing, working a crime scene? Andrew's beside me; I shut my eyes, keep them like that for a couple of seconds.

We both speak at the same time: 'Klaudia.'

# CHAPTER THREE

It's NOT that I dislike Polish people; I have two Polish friends who run a deli on Leith Walk. My son and I often pop in there. Spend a fortune. Since Conor was nine, he's been part of an extra-curricular group for kids gifted in languages. He can converse happily in Spanish, Italian and Greek, he's recently taken up Mandarin, and for a couple of years he's been studying Polish. So, when we're in the deli he does all the ordering and gabbles away to Izabella and Elwira. I've no idea what they're talking about half the time, so I just smile and nod a lot, hopefully in all the right places.

Doctor Klaudia Grześkiewicz hails from Kraków. I can't take to her at all, and the fact I can't pronounce her surname has absolutely nothing to do with it. Although my team practically need oxygen every time I try. Klaudia is the tiniest adult you ever met in your whole life, way short of five feet and lucky, very lucky, if she's seven stone carrying a brick. Black fringe that could have been cut with gardening shears, button nose, glasses. And although she could be any age between twenty-five and forty-five, she's probably asked for ID whenever it's her round.

But it's her expression that does something to me. It's like she's been caught in freeze-frame. In the four or five months I've known her, not a glimmer of emotion has ever altered that face. Not anger, not sadness, not excitement: nada.

She clambers up Greg's ladder and I walk over to meet her. We're outside the crime scene now, so I can take off this flamin' mask. 'Detective Inspector Cooper,' she says.

I never get DI, or Mel, or anything apart from the full formal bifta. 'Klaudia. What can you tell me about this woman?'

'In these times, I must be careful how I reply to your question, Detective Inspector Cooper. Because while I can confirm the deceased appears to be of the feminine form, I cannot say for certain until I have concluded my examination.'

Many, many responses are beating each other with sticks, desperate to be first to launch themselves off the tip of my tongue. Regrettably, none of them are even remotely appropriate in professional situations. Even for Klaudia, that statement was a belter, but I know I'll have to play her properly or this discussion will go nowhere fast.

'How did she die?' I say.

'There are marks on her neck and throat that are consistent with a ligature, but I—'

'Yes, Klaudia, I get it. You'll confirm later.'

She blinks. Once.

'Did she die there? In that position?' I say.

'The wound in her leg, a lateral puncture caused by the spike on the railing, has not bled. Therefore, no.'

'Time of death?' I wonder how much breath I wasted with that one.

'In relation to the post-mortem interval, there are many variables—'

*Enough!* Jeez, this woman's turned obfuscation into an art form. 'Klaudia. This is almost certainly a murder investigation.' I glare at the good doctor, challenge her to debate the point. She blinks again, but I charge on. 'I need to move extremely quickly so all I want is your best estimate, and I promise I will take it at face value. So don't worry, I'm not going to publish a paper in the bloody *Lancet*.'

For a second I think she'll actually respond to that, but she jams on the anchors. She's probably dying a slow death as a result.

'I estimate,' she says, as if the word will choke her, 'between 23:00 yesterday, that is Thursday, and 03:00 today. But I will be able to give a more accurate—'

'Thank you, Klaudia.' I smile at her. Just a down payment.

———

I WALK BACK to the wall. Greg's soldier buddies have showed up and they're making short work of bridging the water below. It'll make the Scene Examiners' jobs easier and put us much closer to the scene.

Then I hear a call. 'Boss!'

It's Andrew. He's several puddles away, waving something polythene in my direction. I totter back across the plastic block highway and move in close. We turn our backs to the rain, huddle together to form a human shelter so I can examine two evidence bags. One contains a car key with a Ford fob; the other holds a keyring with four or five different keys. Definitely domestic in nature.

'One of the SEs found them in her left coat pocket,' he says. 'Nothing else on her at all.'

'No phone? Unusual.' But then, maybe not so unusual when we're talking about a corpse.

'Could be in her bag if she had one. But if she did, why would she carry two sets of keys in her pocket?'

I can't help him there.

He jerks a thumb over his shoulder. 'I've been out into the lane and beeped the key a few times but no sign of her car. I'll go over to the Ford dealership to see if they can tell me the reg of the vehicle it belongs to. Then we should have an address for her, or at least for the car's owner.'

'Smart thinking, my boy. I'm off to see how Isambard Kingdom Brunel and his team are getting on down there.'

As the crow flies, the bridge they're building is only about forty metres away, but I'll have to drive the long way round then walk back along the towpath. As I head for my car, I wonder how much this woman suffered during her last few minutes on earth, and hope to God we catch her killer quickly, before he develops a taste that needs to be satisfied.

# CHAPTER FOUR

'GOOD AFTERNOON, sir. Are you Edwin Fuller?'

The man framed in his doorway two steps higher than us is frowning, probably wondering *who on earth are these two drowned rats?* He folds his arms. 'I am. May I help you?'

I show him my ID. 'I'm Detective Inspector Cooper, and this is Detective Sergeant Young. Could we come inside, sir? It's rather wet out here.'

We're in the Trinity area of Leith, one of the more affluent parts of town. Most of the houses are sandstone, the majority dating back to the mid-nineteenth century. Edwin Fuller's property is in a conservation area so that gives you an idea. It's a two-storey end-terraced, with bay windows to either side of double storm doors. He's only opened one door so is practically filling the entire space. The stone lintel above is keeping him dry, but we're forced to stand back to avoid the mini waterfall that's slashing off the leading edge.

He starts to speak but interrupts himself and opens the vestibule door into the hall. We squeeze through the gap, shuck our coats off in a valiant attempt to leave the moisture outside.

There's a bit of toing and froing while he clicks the storm door closed behind us then leads us past a staircase with a dark wooden banister and into a decent-sized living room. He offers us the sofa and stands with his back to the fire. It crackles and spits as a log settles. Above, a clock that's been carved out of a shard of polished driftwood declares it's bang on half past two.

'Would you mind telling me what this is about?' he says.

'Before I answer that, Mr Fuller—'

'Just Edwin, please.'

'I'm sorry, Edwin, but I need to check a few facts first. Do you own a Ford Focus?' I read out the registration number. As I'm speaking, Andrew flips open his PDA and taps the screen with a stylus. For most operational police officers, notebooks are a thing of the past and we now use Personal Data Assistants while we're in the field. I'm happy Andrew's taking notes; he's way faster than me.

'Yes,' says Edwin, 'that's our car. Has Rachel had an accident? Where is she? Is she hurt?'

His voice breaks on that last syllable: *hurt*.

'Where is your car, sir? We couldn't see it outside.'

He's shifting feet from side to side, any faster and he'll be hopping on the spot. 'Officer. I do understand you have a process to follow but I'm beginning to panic now. Has my wife had some sort of accident? Is she okay?'

I show him the evidence bags. 'Are these your wife's keys?'

He examines them. Gives a jerky nod. 'Please tell me.'

I take a pause. 'At this stage, sir, we can't be certain. But what I can say is we're investigating the discovery of a woman's remains this morning at the Water of Leith near Warriston Crematorium. These keys were in her pocket.'

He covers his face with both hands. When he moves them away, his eyes are brimming. 'Is it Rachel?'

'The woman has nothing on her person to identify her,

apart from the keys.' It doesn't seem to occur to him to ask how we found his address. And I don't intend to tell him. 'When was the last time you saw your wife?'

He doesn't answer. Instead, he leans down and lifts a mobile from the arm of a chair, stabs at the screen a few times then puts it to his ear. 'I'm phoning her.' He half turns away, and a few seconds later, 'Rachel, darling. It's me. Call me please. Right away. It's urgent.'

He holds the phone down by his side. Rubs his eyes. Holds them tight shut for a couple of seconds. He swipes the sleeve of his shirt across his cheek.

'Again, Edwin, when was the last time you saw your wife?'

'Last night.'

'And where was that?'

'Here.'

'At what time?'

'It was about,' he checks his wrist, 'ten o'clock.'

'And that was when she left the house?'

'That's right.'

'Did she say where she was going?'

'No, but I assumed she went to her friend, Lisa's. They're ... em ... best pals. We had an argument, you see. Actually, more than an argument, a blazing row.' He hesitates. 'I'll try her.' He stabs at the phone, bristling with tension. 'Lisa, hi. Listen, sorry to bother you at work but have you seen Rachel today?' A pause. 'Oh. Did she come over to your place last night, some-time after ten?' He glances at me. 'Thanks. No, nothing. Sorry, can I ring you later? Okay, will do.'

I don't need to ask.

'Rachel's sister's in the Lake District but I'll see if she's heard from her.'

Same result, only it takes longer for him to end the call.

17

'Edwin,' says Andrew. 'Apart from just now, have you contacted your wife since she left here last night?'

'No.' He checks the clock. 'I'm expecting her home at some point this afternoon. I was planning to take her out for dinner.' He stands taller. 'No. What am I saying? I *will* take her out when she gets home. I'll ring her again.'

I edge forward on the sofa, steady my voice. 'Sir, we have to slow down here for a moment. When your wife left the house last night, what was she wearing?'

He doesn't take time to think. 'Casual. Tracksuit bottoms and a hoodie. Grey. She put them on just before she went out.'

Curious. 'She changed into casual gear before she went out?'

'Em ... no. She didn't change. She wasn't dressed at the time. We had been ... you know ... having sex.'

Well, now he's grabbed my attention. A couple, they're having sex, they fall out, she leaves the house. It's painting all sorts of pictures. 'Did she put on a coat?'

He nods. 'Burnt orange padded thing. A Christmas present, from me. Hasn't been off her back since.'

Andrew closes his PDA; I stand up and fasten my jacket. 'I'm incredibly sorry, Edwin, but it's imperative we establish whether the woman we've found is your wife.' He doesn't move, doesn't speak, just stares at me. 'So, would you be prepared to come with us to the hospital mortuary to conduct a formal identification.'

He doesn't move a muscle. 'Oh my God. Seriously? Do I ... does it have to be me?'

'It's normally the next of kin. Perhaps there's someone you can call to accompany you?'

He hesitates. Then, 'I'll ask Lisa. She's a strong person.'

———

AND IT TURNS out that Lisa McCafferty is indeed a strong person. Which is just as well, because when we meet her and her husband at the morgue Edwin Fuller falls to pieces. Says he can't do it and drops it right on her. Tells her she'll have to make the identification.

The woman is stunned, suggests they go in together. He refuses, point blank, and marches off towards our car. Andrew follows him and blips the locks. She gives me a look, shrugs, and we both go inside.

Five minutes later, we're back in the car park, and I walk over to Andrew to tell him what Lisa said in there.

# CHAPTER FIVE

When Andrew and I return with Edwin to his house, he fusses around then goes into the kitchen. It's an L-shape off the living room and I can see most of the space from where I'm sitting. He fills the kettle but doesn't switch it on. Then he opens a cupboard door, closes it without taking anything out and does the same with the fridge. We'll die of thirst at this rate, so Andrew goes through, takes over, sends Edwin back to me.

He positions himself in an armchair, carefully and precisely, and now I see why. Tucked part way under a cushion is a petite, coal black cat. Edwin strokes its head with the back of his forefinger, but it doesn't open its eyes. It definitely wasn't here earlier. I'm not that keen; sneaky little blighters, cats.

I study him. The man's had a hell of a jolt, and his face shows it. Bloodshot eyes and an expression like a partially melted waxwork. Apart from that, he's neat enough. Fair hair, slightly on the long side. Foppish, one might say. His dress style is casual outdoors, suitable for a forest walk or a day in town.

Sturdy but soft shoes; Timberlands, or something of that ilk. He's two or three inches off six feet, and I'd say he takes a decent amount of exercise.

The room is tidy too. Just on the worn side of comfortable but nothing left lying about. A couple of magazines are lying on the top of the unit under the TV. One features a mountain bike propped up against a rock, snowy peaks in the background, improbably blue sky. I can only see the title of the other one; it concerns men's welfare. My husband, Callum, subscribed for a while but cancelled because the content was so repetitive. Sex, pecs and six-packs, according to him.

Andrew comes back balancing three different mugs. As Edwin adjusts his position to take his, the cat unfurls, performs a brief calisthenics routine then wanders off. Seconds later, a cat flap rattles. Edwin picks up his phone. 'I have to contact people, tell them what's happened.'

'I do apologise if this sounds harsh,' I say. 'But we need to move ahead with our investigations as quickly as possible, it's our best chance of catching whoever did this. You'll be able to make your calls as soon as we've finished.'

Let's be clear, at this point Edwin Fuller is a potential suspect. Nothing ruled out, nothing decided. A long way to go.

He leans over, sets his mug down on the coffee table, rotates it a few degrees. 'I'm sorry, I can't stomach coffee. Not right now.'

I lead straight into my questions; it's hard to tell how long he'll remain stable. We double-check that Rachel drove away from the house at 22:00. We know what she was wearing but not if she was carrying a bag. I push him on this.

'Honestly, I wouldn't know. She charged off down the stairs, I heard the front door slam, the car door, and that was it.' He stands up. 'But I'll find out. Hang on.' He's back in a few seconds holding a burgundy and fawn canvas backpack, and a handbag that dwarfs it. Black, silver detail, shoulder straps. It's open. He lifts a phone from a pocket on the front, holds it out. He stares at me but doesn't speak.

Andrew fishes a pair of latex gloves from an inside jacket pocket and snaps them on. He doesn't keep anything in the outside pockets; he only recently admitted that they're still stitched down – helps him maintain the GQ man look. He takes the phone, taps the screen with his stylus. Nothing. He presses the power button until the screen lights up. He glances at Edwin. 'Do you know the access code?'

'No. I'm afraid I don't.'

I wonder, is that normal? Why wouldn't he know it? Don't couples normally share their passwords? Is she the secretive type? Is he? I choose not to read anything into it, but I do take note.

Andrew produces an evidence bag. Drops the phone in. Scribbles on the front. Asks, 'Would she normally go out without her phone?'

Fuller doesn't reply, just spreads his hands. Another curiosity. We'll come back to it.

'What's her number, please?' says Andrew.

Edwin consults his own phone and reads out the number. While Andrew records it, I ask, 'Is her purse in the bag?'

'She doesn't use a purse; she keeps her cards in a tan leather wallet.' He tilts the bag towards the light, rummages inside. 'It's not here.'

'So, she had bank cards with her, she had the means to pay if she'd needed to.'

He nods. 'I suppose.'

Andrew comes in again. 'We've been searching for your car but no luck so far. We know it's a two-year-old silver Ford Focus, but does it have a built-in app?'

Edwin stares at him.

Andrew is patient. 'Some cars have apps that allow the owner to connect remotely, check it's locked, find out when the next service is due, that sort of stuff.'

'If it has, I've never used it.'

My turn. 'If she didn't go to Lisa's after she left here, is there anyone else she could have stayed with?'

He stands up, takes a few steps away, stops, half turns. 'Quite a few people, I suppose. She has lots of friends—' He interrupts himself. 'Sorry, I'm beginning to feel light-headed. I need some liquids.'

He walks into the kitchen and moves off to the right, out of my line of sight. I hear a clink of a glass, a tap running. A pause. The tap runs again and now he's back, sipping from a full tumbler.

'You asked where else she could have gone,' he says. 'There are three women in particular, they've been friends for ever, but I don't have their contact details.' His expression hardens. 'Truth is, I can't stand them. Bloody witches' coven. When they're together I keep out of the way. She does have other friends but after Lisa, those three would be the best bet.' Then he puts his head in his hands. 'Oh God, how on earth will I tell everyone? Her friends, her family – what will I say?'

His eyes are a bright pink now. I give him a few seconds to compose himself then I move on. 'You said earlier that you didn't try to contact her after she left last night. But did she get in touch with you?'

'No. This has happened before, once, and she didn't call then either.' His voice lacks any spark. He studies the carpet.

'Mr Fuller, I'm struggling here. After you and your wife had, to quote your words, "a blazing row", she left the house in a foul temper. So, she's angry, she's driven off on her own, into a hell of a storm, you have no idea where she's gone, where she'll

23

spend the night ... and you make no attempt to confirm your wife is safe?'

'Look, I know that sounds bad, and on my *life* I wish to hell I had phoned her, but I didn't.'

No, I don't like this. Fair enough, take the easy option sometimes, but what he's just described strikes me as being a stretch. I'll let it lie for now, but the alarm bells are deafening. I lean back and observe Edwin more closely as Andrew picks up. 'This argument you had, what was it about?'

He draws in a deep breath. 'That was later in the evening, but it had been bubbling under since I came home from work. She was in a shit mood.'

'What time was that?'

'About half four, twenty to five.'

'And did she say why she was in that mood?'

'No. I didn't ask. It's not unusual. Anyway, I was making dinner, she started picking faults, nagging. So, I stayed quiet, didn't react. I know it pisses her off but ...' He makes a decent fist at smiling but it's at the watery end of the scale. 'I made her a G&T and she disappeared off upstairs. I shouted up when dinner was ready. She came down, she was fine, as if nothing had happened.'

'Is that normal too?'

He nods. 'That's just Rachel.'

That's just Rachel? Have you no backbone, man? Why didn't you stand up for yourself? Then I remember why we're here and wonder, not for the first time, if that's actually what he has done.

'You said you made dinner,' says Andrew. 'What did you have?'

'Leftover lasagne with salad and bread. I'm not much of a cook. We had it in here with some wine then we went upstairs to eh—'

I don't have time for fannying about. 'So, when you got home she was in a foul temper, but after a few drinks, dinner, you had sex.' I leave the paradox hanging.

'Gin has that effect on her.'

Let's not tell my husband that. 'DS Young asked you about the argument.'

'It was something stupid. Nothing, really.'

Nope, doesn't work like that. 'I'm sorry to be so blunt, Edwin, but it's almost certain your wife was murdered so it can't be nothing. I need you to tell us.'

He goes quiet. Wipes a hand across his eyes. The tears spring up again. It seems they're never far away. I can wait but not too long. I have sympathy with him, of course I do, but time's ticking on here. He draws in a breath. 'I'm sorry. It's just that I don't normally discuss our sex life with other people. But let's just say things weren't going particularly well – for me, you understand. And afterwards, I just wanted to get out of bed, but she told me to stay where I was. I had things to do, work stuff I wanted to finish. She went off on one. Started shouting. Screaming. About how I was a typical man, fucking Neanderthal, screw the wife then into the man cave to watch football. I just laughed, pretended to beat my chest. It was meant to be funny, but she didn't see it like that. I tried to apologise, climb back into bed, but she wasn't having any.'

'Did she say any more before she left?'

'She made a comment about going off to find someone a bit higher up the evolutionary scale.'

'Did you think she meant it or was it simply a throwaway line?'

He shakes his head. 'She wouldn't have meant anything by it. Like I said, that's situation normal. She bandies insults about then calms down as if nothing's happened, even if she knows she's hurt my feelings.'

And here we go again. This woman, Rachel Fuller, was she really that harsh? That insensitive? She insults her husband, hurts his feelings then doesn't seem to care. Or at least, care enough to apologise or even acknowledge she's been guilty of these things. I'll never be able to ask her, more's the pity.

'Okay, let's go back in time a bit.' Good lad, Andrew. We often catch people out by switching timelines. Sometimes a suspect will trot out what is no more than a well-rehearsed speech, but they will often come unstuck if we force them to dot back and forth along the timeline. 'Yesterday, Thursday,' says Andrew, 'what did you do during the day?'

'I was at work. I'm a school teacher at Morton Street Primary, down by The Links.'

Ah! My old school, or at least the building is. When I went there it was Leith Academy Primary. Then in 1991, the school moved to a new campus a few streets away. I was coming up for eleven, and our family moved house, so I changed schools. Before I fall into a well of happy reminiscence, another thought drops into my mind that solves one puzzle from first thing this morning.

Meanwhile, Andrew's repeated an earlier question. 'And you arrived home when?' The type of question that's always worth asking twice, just in case. But if Fuller notices, he doesn't react. A point in his favour, I'd say.

'About half four, twenty to five. I cycle to and from work. You saw the weather; I was absolutely soaked so I dried off my bike and took a shower. When I came down, she was sitting here, watching a quiz show on the box.'

'Which one?'

He makes a face. 'No idea.'

Jeez. The Fullers had an odd relationship to say the least. I decide some context would be handy. 'How long have you been together?'

'Coming up for twenty-two years.'

'How did you meet?'

And for the first time in this interview, Edwin Fuller looks downright uncomfortable.

# CHAPTER SIX

Twenty-two Years Earlier

THROUGHOUT HIS SCHOOL years and all the way through university, Edwin was liked and respected. 'A great lad. A gem'. That's what people said. Back then.

In social and sporting settings, he was often the butt of his friends' humour but they all, including him, knew perfectly well they didn't mean it. He joined in as often as not. In his final year at school, he had one long-term girlfriend but when she went off to university in Southampton that was that. Neither even considered the possibility of a long-distance relationship. She had to move; he didn't want to: game over. But the split was amicable because that was what he was like. 'Hey, that's life,' he said, but all his friends, male and female, could see he was gutted. So, they took the piss even more and that cheered him up.

Then he met Rachel. Although *met* was the understatement of the century; they collided head-on like two fully laden trucks on a country road.

He was in his second year at the time, out on a Friday night with four of his mates. They were squeezing single file through the swing doors of a crowded pub, a student haunt on Edinburgh's Southside. The five lads leaned into the wall as a larger group came barging out. Rachel was at the tail end. Wild hair, black tee shirt under a black top, and curvy even back then.

Edwin caught her eye and threw her a hopeful smile. She looked him up and down then pushed past. He stayed where he was, gawping after her. His friend behind thumped the heel of his hand into Edwin's shoulder-blade. 'Shift yer arse, man. There's beer in here to be drunk.'

Edwin turned away then heard, 'Oi. Handsome boy!' Rachel had stopped, she was holding the door open with her bum. She crooked her finger; he stood stock still. She took a couple of steps towards him, gripped his sleeve and hauled him outside.

His mates were on their second round when he joined them at the bar. He was all over the place. They bugged the life out of him until he ran up the white flag and told them what had happened in a lane right next to the pub. And all at her instigation, too. 'Jammy bastard', they said, laughing. He didn't know what to think.

For days on end, she camped out in his head. Edinburgh is a sprawling city, but it can also be a village. Students tend to congregate in the same venues: wherever drink was cheap. Several weeks later he was in a different bar, it too was mobbed, music bouncing off the walls. One of his friends yelled in his ear. 'Over there. By the side of the bar. Isn't that the lass who interfered with you outside the St Andrew's a few weeks ago?'

Edwin squinted across the room, had to wait while a couple of tall lads carrying three pints each shuffled past. She came back into view. He nodded. Yelled, 'I'm going to speak to her.' Then remained rooted to the spot.

His friend prodded him in the small of his back. 'Well, make up your mind, Mowgli. We're about to move on.'

As Edwin watched, Rachel threw the rest of her drink down her throat, thumped her empty glass down on the bar and flipped up the collar of her denim jacket. Three other students made similar movements. Edwin galvanised himself and set off across the bar to intercept Rachel before her group reached the door. He just made it. Reaching out, he tapped her arm, twice.

Vaguely registering the touch, she attempted to focus on her sleeve then turned a glassy-eyed stare on him. 'What?'

He hesitated. 'We met. Before. I mean, a few weeks ago.'

She checked him out, swayed a little. 'So?'

*This is a bad idea. How do I get out of this?* But then she nodded, twice. The movement seemed to take an effort. She raised her arm halfway, indicated the door. Her bag slipped from her shoulder, but she managed to catch it before it hit the floorboards. 'Oops.' She lifted it over her head, so the strap ran diagonally across her chest. It caught in the collar of her jacket, but she was oblivious. 'Goin' home.' She staggered, put her hand on the wall. 'You comin'?'

Edwin glanced over at his mates, but they weren't paying him any attention, so he trailed after her and out of the pub. She stopped on the pavement, debating left or right – but slowly. It appeared as though her eyes weren't rotating quite as fast as her head. She nodded again then weaved off to the left. 'This way.'

He fell into step beside her. In the first few metres she twice bumped shoulders with him before beginning to sober up. They trudged along for about a mile without exchanging a word. He would have preferred some sort of conversation but couldn't think of anything to say and she behaved as if she were on her own. They zig-zagged through a series of streets before she slowed to a halt at a tenement door that had been painted red at one time in the dim and distant. Her flat was on the second floor. As they climbed, she raked about in her bag, tilting it up and to the left each time they passed a stair light. She surprised him by sliding her key smoothly into the lock first time.

Inside, she dropped her bag and jacket on the floor and pulled him into her bedroom. They had sex. It was quick, and instantly forgettable.

'I'm on an early shift at the café,' she said. 'You have to leave.'

'But—'

'Fuck off. I need sleep.' Then, as she was hauling off the rest of her clothes: 'Give me your number.'

———

THEIRS WAS the very definition of a one-sided relationship. Edwin was now officially obsessed, but to Rachel, most of the time he was simply wallpaper. They say love is blind: he wasn't. He knew exactly what was happening, but he couldn't prevent it. Mainly because he didn't want to.

Gradually he became disengaged from his friends with the exception of his long-time pal from school, Niall. He spent all his free time either with Rachel or waiting for her to summon him. And he came a-running, every single time. If they were out socialising, it was with her friends or people she knew. He met Lisa and her boyfriend, Jack, who would later become her husband. They were neither friendly nor hostile to him. The four of them were definitely three plus one. Then there were the three women whom he'd eventually christen 'The Coven'. One night Rachel phoned him and told him to come to the pub. The coven were there. They didn't quite look him up and down and carry on with their conversation as if he didn't exist, but they might as well have done. And the trouble was, Rachel mimicked their behaviour. He bought them drinks, they hardly said thanks, and he was on the fringes of the conversation all night long. But when he finally decided enough was enough and said he was leaving, Rachel snapped at him. 'No you're not. We're going back to my place later'. Because she never stayed over at his house. Later that night, as on many other occasions, after they had sex she threw him out.

And then, Rachel had the accident.

Lisa called him: Rachel was in hospital. She'd been crossing a road near her flat when a motorcycle came hammering round a corner and took her out. He flew into a row of parked vehicles and smashed his right arm and shoulder. She suffered multiple fractures to her left leg: femur, patella and tibia. When she was eventually released from convalescence, no one else could put her up because they all lived in flats. But Edwin owned a house he'd inherited from his parents. So, he took her home, and she never left. He waited on her hand and foot; she forced herself to be mildly appreciative.

Even while she was still recuperating from her injuries, Rachel continued to treat Edwin like a slave. Someone to go shopping, to cook, and to clean up after her. Someone to bring her home from the pub ... unless she had a better offer. Someone to have sex with, and the only difference was she couldn't throw him out afterwards.

Edwin had long since become disenfranchised, heading towards desperate and trying to figure out how to extricate himself. Then she dropped a bombshell. 'We should get married.' But instead of running a mile in the opposite direction he bit her hand off. And that was that.

The ceremony was functional. There was no one there from his side, not even Niall. Rachel decreed that Jack should be his best man. *Grudging* was a kind word for Jack's reaction to being lumbered. The party in the pub afterwards – no one could ever have called it a reception – was nothing short of a debacle. The coven did their best to out-bitch each other, while Jack and Lisa fell out after she slapped him. He left, she stayed. Edwin sat with her for a while, did his best to console her, but she was intent on drinking herself into oblivion. It didn't take her long.

At one point he couldn't find Rachel. After nearly an hour he was bouncing off the ceiling. Then she sauntered in the door, two guys in tow he'd never seen before, and high as a kite. He tried to pull her aside, reason with her. She was having none of it. 'This is *my* wedding and I'm going to fucking enjoy it.' He complained, and all she said was, 'Sod off, Edwin. Get used to it.'

She lived in her husband's house, but Rachel was a wealthy woman in her own right. Compensation from the accident had netted her a healthy six-figure sum. But Edwin never saw a penny.

On at least three occasions, heavily fortified by alcohol, he made moves to end their relationship. And every time she rebuffed him without any discussion. 'No, I'm staying right where I am'. His only recourse was to walk out. But this was his family home, where he and his sister had grown up. His parents had bequeathed it to them so there was no way on earth he was leaving Rachel in the house on her own. There was no telling what she would do – and who she would do it with. Then things would settle down and he'd feel better, but it wouldn't be long before something else blew up, and he'd be back to square one and feeling worse than he did the time before. Eventually the intervals in this soul-destroying pattern were becoming so short they were in danger of merging into one another.

That was when he began to study himself more closely. At work he was fine, more or less. He loved his job and interacted effortlessly with the kids as he'd always done. He was able to lose himself in their world and devote all his energies to their education and wellbeing. But out of school his personality was markedly different. He knew he'd changed. He'd become pessimistic, morose, and disengaged in most social circumstances except for the gym. He didn't class any of the instructors or the people who worked out alongside him as his friends because most of the time they just did their own thing with only superficial communication between them. Nobody disturbed the status quo. So his main interests were solitary, in particular when he was out cycling, which was most days.

There was no doubt who was to blame: Rachel. Her behaviour, the way she treated him had dragged him down. He was no longer the same Edwin Fuller. He couldn't see how he would be able to return to the old Edwin, or anything like him, while she was in his life. He was trapped. No way out, not by conventional means at any rate.

That was when Edwin finally accepted he'd had enough and began to fantasise about killing his wife.

# CHAPTER SEVEN

The Present Time

'WHAT DOES your wife do for a living?' I say. I've been maintaining fairly solid eye contact with Fuller so far, but I relax a little, let my gaze drop away. I wince as I spot a clod of mud a few inches to the side of my right boot. Trust his carpet to be oatmeal. Don't people fit swirly Axminster any more? I tune back in to Edwin.

'She ...' He winces. 'She was an account manager for an advertising company. Sold space in newspapers and magazines. Her patch was the Central Belt, so mainly Edinburgh and Glasgow. But up as far as Stirling too, I think.'

This is progress. Up until now I've deliberately been referring to Rachel Fuller in the present tense because, through experience, deciding precisely when to switch into past tense can be tricky. Most people who are bereaved in tragic or violent circumstances don't want to hear it, so I have to judge when to alter my language. Stops the partners or relatives from freaking out too much. One of the keys is when they switch over and Edwin's just done that. 'Who was she employed by?' I ask.

He leans forward and scratches his knee. Pauses. 'The company changed its name recently; they were taken over. I'll find out for you.'

'Thanks. So did she work from an office?'

He angles his head. 'Through there, spare bedroom. She worked from home most days, but she visited clients' premises too. Met people for coffee, lunch, you know?'

'What were her movements yesterday?'

'I couldn't say.'

'What about her diary, did she use paper or electronic?' His face says he has absolutely no idea. 'What about access to her PC? Do you know the password?'

'No. There's never any need. We each have our own PCs.'

'I'd like to examine her office before we leave. And we'll have to take her PC too.'

He waves a hand. 'Of course, whatever.'

'Yesterday, did you talk about your day?'

'Rachel never did, said print advertising isn't exactly sexy. Sometimes I do, but not yesterday. Like I explained, she was in a mood.'

'What was it about her behaviour that told you that?'

He snorts. 'Believe me, when Rachel was in that frame of mind you weren't left in any doubt.'

'So, after she left the house, what did you do for the rest of the evening?'

He gives out a short, harsh laugh. 'After that, I couldn't be bothered working so in the end I did sit and watch football. Ironic, isn't it?'

'A Thursday night?' I say. Andrew's not interested in football but with a husband and teenage son at home, I don't have much choice. 'What was on?'

'Match of the Day highlights from Saturday. On catch-up.' I wait. Edwin smiles. Mentions a few games and scores but they were played last weekend so not exactly a secret.

'You didn't go out?'

'Did you see the weather?'

That's a fair point, I suppose. I move on. 'So, when you woke up this morning did you still not consider calling her?'

Edwin's chin wobbles. 'I know I'm sounding like a stuck record, but no, I didn't.'

I have to admit I can't make head nor tail of this man. Was his attitude to his wife staying away overnight driven by how she's always treated him, or by the fact he knew damn fine she was never coming home? Is he genuinely a bereaved husband or is he a murderer? At this stage, both options are up for grabs. I'm beginning to think I won't get a definitive answer here, but we still have a fair chunk of the story to explore.

'And what about today?' I ask. 'Were you at work?'

'No. I only do a four-day week. A probationary teacher takes my class on a Friday. It helps her, it benefits the pupils, and I have a day off.' He shrugs. 'Everybody wins.'

I don't ask the probationer's name; we'll be talking to Edwin's colleagues at the school.

'So what did you do?'

He gazes up at the cornice, lets his eyes wander along it. 'Cycled over to the gym, spent a couple of hours there, had my breakfast in a café down at Newhaven, came back here, finished off that bit of work I mentioned earlier. Then in the afternoon I tidied up a bit, tinkered with my bikes, pottered about.'

'And what should your wife have been doing today?'

'You'll have to look at her calendar. Sorry.'

I struggle to stop a great heaving sigh and just about manage it. How many times now has Fuller said he doesn't know? I can appreciate their relationship wasn't exactly sweetness and light, but doesn't he care at all? I don't live in my husband's pocket, but I do have a rough idea what he's up to most days.

'Edwin,' I say. 'Were you not concerned even in the slightest when your wife didn't come home? Did you not imagine she'd need a change of clothes, make-up, things to do with her work?'

'No. I'm afraid I didn't. She knows I go to the gym every Friday morning, and I just thought she'd take the opportunity to pop home while I was out.' But he can't hold my gaze.

'And when you arrived back here after your breakfast did you actually check to see if she'd been home?' My question is answered by his silence and the expression on his face.

This time I can't stop myself, but I keep my tone relatively even. 'Let's see if I've got this right. She stayed away overnight, you haven't spoken to her for almost eighteen hours and, to cap it all, you didn't even notice if she'd been home?' He stares at me, an expression like a dying fish. I have his attention now and I don't intend to let him off the hook. 'You need to explain why not, Mr Fuller, because, yet again, that strikes me as more than a little bit odd, if you don't mind me saying.' Truth is, I don't give a shit whether he minds or not. And this time I want a better answer than, 'Oh, you know, that's just Rachel'.

He doesn't respond but I'm prepared to wait. Andrew relaxes in the sofa, lays his PDA on the arm, makes a microscopic adjustment to his shirt cuffs. Then Edwin says, 'I'm not entirely stupid, I can imagine what you're thinking.' He fidgets in his seat, addresses the floor. 'I know our friends say things like, it's easy to see who wears the trousers in that house. They probably imagine I don't know their opinion of me, but I don't actually care. Rachel has always been ... what's the best word for it ... domineering, and up to a point it didn't bother me.

Maybe I should have been more assertive, less acquiescent, but if I was going to do that, to be that way, then I'd have had to do it years ago. But if I had, she wouldn't have stayed with me. Married or not, she'd have dumped me and moved on. And I didn't want that.'

He pauses, gazes at each of us in turn. 'So, I swallowed my self-respect and put up with it. When she did these things, walked out or whatever, I didn't push it. I never have. And that's just the way we are.' He takes out a tissue and blows his nose. Settles himself then says, 'Were. The way we were.'

He started off this so-called explanation by saying he wasn't stupid. Well, I wasn't born yesterday either. I'll take what he said with a handful of salt because I still don't get it. But I'll put that aside for now because, after all, the poor man's wife's been murdered.

I move about on the timeline again. 'Going back a bit, I'm still extremely surprised your wife left here last night without her phone. I mean, horrible night, driving alone?'

'Oh, Rachel could be scathing about people being over reliant on their phones. "Glued to them", she would say. Or "How on earth did we manage before mobiles?"' Now his eyes are fixed on me. 'In fact, if she was staying home to veg in front of the TV – which recently was most nights – she would usually switch her phone off. So her not having a phone was far from being a showstopper.'

Hmmm, quite a tirade. There's no doubt certain elements of his wife's behaviours and attitudes really pushed his buttons. Interesting. Andrew and I exchange a quick glance. We're left with the killer question. I leave it to my sidekick.

'Edwin. I apologise for asking this but is there any possibility Mrs Fuller was having an affair?'

Edwin pushes himself upright. He takes his time about it. I watch him closely, wonder what's coming. For the first time there's an edge to his voice although that's in stark contrast to his gaze, which appears to be in soft focus. 'My wife and I may not have got on all the time. Yes, sometimes she was tough to live with; I imagine I was too. But I've never been unfaithful and, as far as I know, neither has she.'

I guess the key phrase in there is, 'As far as I know'. But we don't react, there's no need. I bend down, pick up the mud and drop it in a metal log bin by the fire. Edwin doesn't appear to notice.

We spend some time in Rachel's office, half workspace, half spare bedroom in the back corner of the house. The desk is an old kitchen table; files and folders stand vertically on shelves up to the right. There's a decent quality swivel chair in front, arms tucked under the leading edge of the desk. A few photos, all of Rachel with girlfriends, none of her and Edwin. He explains the women are Lisa and members of the coven. The only oddity is a heavy blue glass jar that contains about fifty pens and pencils, with a twelve-inch wooden ruler lording over them. If she doesn't keep a paper diary, I wonder what the hell she needs all those for.

'Would you mind if we had a quick tour around the rest of the house?' I say. His eyes narrow but I keep talking. 'It helps us gain a sense of the person if we can see where they live, sleep, stuff like that.' Fair to say that wasn't total bullshit, but it wasn't far off. He'd have been perfectly within his rights to refuse but that would have told me a lot more than I actually expect to find.

He takes a second. 'Yes. Sure. Anything that might help.'

We'll make this seem like a casual scout around. If Fuller is involved in his wife's murder, I'd prefer not to alert him in any way. Of the rooms we haven't seen, the ones that interest me most are upstairs: their bedroom and bathroom. We pass the bathroom first, so I click the light switch and walk inside. They have one of those jazzy walk-in showers with a screen, no door and a rainfall shower head, which, as far as I'm concerned, is simply an opportunity to flood a bathroom floor. The room is clean and tidy, nothing untoward. I glance inside a cabinet but stop short of hauling stuff out.

We follow him into the bedroom. It's a decent size, with an expanse of cream carpet between the foot of the bed and the opposite wall. Edwin is clearly domesticated; this room is as neat as the rest of the house. Bed made, duvet smoothed out, contrasting throw arranged on top. There's a cycling magazine, folded open, on the left-hand bedside table. On the right, a radio alarm, a small fat jar of expensive hand cream and a couple of novels. Sweeping sagas, you'd call them. As I turn away, Andrew catches my eye and holds my gaze for half a second. Whatever he's spotted isn't urgent but clearly it's worthy of mention. He'll tell me in the car.

Back in the corridor, I spot one more door; it's towards the rear of the house. I glance at Edwin. 'My office,' he says, flipping his hand over to indicate I'm free to go in. I click the light on and take a couple of steps inside. The room has two windows, one a tall narrow Velux set in a sharply sloping ceiling – so clearly this is a conversion. There's a desk with a PC, loaded bookshelves on the three vertical walls, and a curved bamboo coat stand that's swamped with a rainbow of biking and outdoor gear. Leaning against the base is a laptop bag. It has several zipped compartments, many of them open, jammed with folders, notepads and a crimson aluminium water bottle. On the floor to the right of the desk is one of those grey metal four-drawer filing cabinets that probably came from an office clearance sale. It's a relic from at least the eighties and, bizarrely, there's a key in the lock. I scan the shelves above his desk; most of his books are related to teaching – both technical and behavioural – although there are a couple on Microsoft applications. Overall, my impression is I'm in a functional home office where Edwin can work undisturbed.

As I turn to leave, I'm faced with a framed photo of the Flatiron Building; that instantly recognisable, impossibly triangular construction on Manhattan's Fifth and Broadway. During that hedonistic and footloose period fondly remembered as BTK – Before The Kids – Callum and I spent a glorious week in New York and, at his insistence I might add, we traipsed around the borough for hours to find the building. But while he stood there in open-mouthed awe, the only thing in my head was *I need to pee*.

Before we leave the house, I ask Edwin if he'd like us to appoint a Family Liaison Officer but without much consideration he says no. Maybe he saw the question coming. He gives us Rachel's email address and promises to send me as many of her friends' contact details as he can find. We ask about social media, he says she was active on Twitter but not on any of the other platforms. Andrew takes note of her handle.

Andrew puts Rachel's PC in the boot then we take a walk round the side of the house. We're sheltered from the worst of the weather, so we take the opportunity to fasten our coats. The house is on the end of the terrace, so we're hit by a belt of rain as we pass the back corner. My colleague's wearing a calf-length waxed coat, bottle green I think although it's hard to tell in this light. The rain bounces off like it was a force field. Naturally, I'm soaked through. One of these days I'll take the time to sort out my winter gear properly.

We stop by Edwin's side fence. It borders a lane, which disappears behind the garage. On the other side of the lane is a city garden with black wrought-iron fences and locked gates. A small brass plate about the size of a postcard declares it exclusively for residents' use. A paved drive with slabs and stone chips leads to the garage, standard concrete build with a scuffed white up-and-over door. I scrunch up my face as we use the flashes on our phones to peer over a chest-height trellis fence into Edwin's garden. Typical layout: path up the middle, drying green on one side, earthen borders, and refuse bins arranged like guardsmen on either side of the back door. The light's still on in the kitchen but the blinds are drawn.

I point at the window. 'You were in there, what was it like?'

I'm not surprised by the answer. 'Sparkling.'

I nod, and we stride off down the drive, back into the lee of the gable end. 'I did wonder. The whole place is like something out of *House and Home* and it's hard to imagine that a man who's murdered his wife would keep it like that all night and the following day. Doesn't seem realistic.'

'But if he's a neat-freak, maybe it would come naturally.'

In the car, I swivel in my seat. My colleague runs his fingers through his hair; it's completely unaffected. How annoying, compared to my rats' tails. 'What did you spot in the bedroom?' I say.

'A condom. In the bin.'

'Used?'

He crinkles up his nose, which mildly amuses me. 'Used, in that it had been worn. But it didn't appear to contain ejaculate.'

'I suppose that's what he meant by things not going partic-ularly well. And because it wasn't, that's why they argued, and as a result the sex ground to a halt?' I pause, ponder that for a second. 'No, can't be. Who the hell argues during sex?' I shake my head. It's an odd one but surely not much more than that.

'But his response to whether his wife might be having an affair was interesting. Neither a yes or a no, the way I heard it.'

I nod. 'Likewise. Maybe things will become clearer once we've spoken to their friends.' I change the subject. 'Okay, my boy. Apart from that, general thoughts so far?'

Andrew turns on the engine; the wipers kick in straight

away and sluice rainwater off to the sides. 'If his description of his wife is even reasonably accurate, it sounds like she was hard to handle at times. He let her rule the roost, either because he preferred the easy life or—'

'Because he's a bloody doormat.'

'Maybe. But this country's known a few doormats who've murdered their wives.'

'At this stage, I'm certainly not ruling that out.' I pause. 'What about all the times he said he didn't know what she was doing, or the code for her phone, or the password for her PC? Is that not weird?'

'Possibly. But I know a few couples who've been married for years, and they still keep all their finances separate. Possibly that's just the way the Fullers lived. Or maybe she had something to hide so she was secretive about stuff like that.'

'Well, I'm not sure about Edwin Fuller yet so, personally, I think your suggestion about her being secretive is far more likely.' I click my seat belt. 'Right, driver. Time to visit Lisa and Jack McCafferty, and on the way I'll call in to find out what our esteemed colleagues have been up to.'

# CHAPTER EIGHT

EDWIN CLOSED the storm doors on the two police officers then he ran upstairs, slowed as he entered the bedroom and stood where he could see their car. They would snoop around, he knew that, but it still took an age before they appeared on the pavement. The car's lights came on, but they sat for a minute before pulling away.

Back in the kitchen, he lifted a bottle of vodka from the booze shelf in the bottom of a pine Welsh dresser. He trailed his fingertips across the warm surface, feeling all the little dents and dinks that had accumulated over the years. Like a number of items scattered throughout the house it had belonged to his parents, but this piece in particular reminded him of his mother. She had been the first to go: oesophageal cancer, caused by those damned cigarettes. Time after time after *time* she tried to stop but never lasted longer than a week. She had a scant three months from diagnosis to deceased. On the day they buried her, his father's life ended – metaphorically speaking. Twelve months later, Edwin and his sister became orphans. They were a year either side of twenty.

He carried the bottle over to the worktop next to the sink, hacked a wedge off a lemon, threw ice in a glass and sloshed a healthy measure of the clear alcohol across the top. He fished a litre of Coke from the fridge, gave it a shake, set it on the work-top, cracked open the cap and allowed the sticky froth to dribble down the side and onto the previously gleaming surface. He poured the same again into his drink then took a stiff belt. 'Wow!' *That* made his eyes water. He picked up the rest of the lemon, rubbed juice into his fingers and tossed it into the corner of the worktop. Then he washed his hands in freezing cold water, a ritual he expected to repeat several times over the next few days.

He ran a quick appraisal of his conversations with the two police officers. He thought he'd come through it, maybe not ahead but level on points. Naturally, he would still be a suspect in Rachel's murder because, in the beginning at least, the husband is always the prime suspect. He was relaxed about that because if all his plans worked out, and he was confident they would, he wouldn't remain a suspect for long. He'd had no idea what calibre of investigator would take the case. He'd been hoping for the equivalent of dumb plod but had always known that was unrealistic. And so it had proved. Cooper and Young were two sharp cookies who had asked him all the questions he'd rehearsed, plus a few he hadn't. That's when he'd resorted to tears and mock upsets. If they'd noticed, that was unfortunate; there would be plenty more of those along the way.

His cheeks warmed when he recalled saying he'd been tinkering with his bikes. He'd slipped up there, no question. Fortunately they hadn't delved any deeper, probably because it was a fairly humdrum thing to do with his time and not worthy of further discussion. But there was every possibility the subject would crop up again and he'd be ready, his story all primed. And he'd just have to deal with anything that came out of it.

He sighed and sat down quickly. The rush that had kicked in when the doorbell rang had fallen off the edge of a cliff. In different circumstances he would have said he was exhausted, but drained was a more appropriate term. The ups and downs of the past twenty-four hours had finally taken their toll. During the previous night he'd experienced a range and scale of emotions that were way beyond anything he'd suffered before. Plus he'd expended a combination of extreme mental and physical energy that were considerably higher than the sum of their parts.

And it had been a late one; well past midnight when he returned home. The weather had made his journeys arduous, especially cycling into the teeth of the storm as he worked his way in an extended series of lefts and rights to a row of scruffy shops near the abandoned gasworks at Granton. Only a chip shop and a Chinese takeaway had still been open, but neither were selling food in that weather. Despite that, he was virtually certain his bike wouldn't remain in the concrete vennel where he'd left it for longer than it took the antennae of the local hoods to kick in. Then he'd trudged back to the house, following similarly circuitous routes to avoid detection. And despite being certain he wouldn't sleep he'd gone to bed; any form of rest was better than nothing.

Edwin thought it through one more time. All things considered, the initial stages had worked out as well as he could have hoped.

The cat flap lifted part way and a tiny pink nose poked in. The fur that followed on was white with ginger blotches. This was Chilli. Once he sussed out the coast was clear he completed his entrance, sat right down and began cleaning his fur. Edwin knew not to pick him up until his pet had finished.

He'd learned the hard way that offering the ginger tom any affection had to be entirely on the cat's terms.

He made himself another drink, with less of a kick. This time he deliberately poured a pound coin-sized pool of the tea-coloured mixer on a different part of the worktop. He laid his glass on top and slid it back and forth. Then he lifted his knee and rested the glass on his trousers, halfway down his thigh. The material was a light khaki and stained easily. Then he chose a clean area to leave another mark.

He glanced around the kitchen. Pale surfaces and a teak laminate floor. The table and four leather chairs in chromium frames toned in with the units. Leaving aside the mess he'd made, the place was spotless. But that was about to change. He took two steps to the swing bin; it was only half full. He hauled the bin liner out, being deliberately careless. Slivers of salad and a few breadcrumbs from the previous night scattered on the floor. He stamped on them then opened the back door. The landfill refuse bin was due for collection the following Monday, but he wouldn't be putting it out. He dropped the half empty liner next to the bin and lifted out a full bag. In the kitchen, he untied it and crammed it into the swing bin, being none too careful. He spotted a polystyrene container that held the remnants of a red sweet and sour sauce. He ripped off the lid, a couple of spatters hit the toe of his shoe and a larger dollop slapped onto the floor. Again he stepped in it, then dipped a finger into the semi-congealed sauce and dabbed it on his tee shirt.

He assessed the effect, decided that would do for now although he would make more rings on the coffee table as the evening wore on. He sat down, took another slug and held the glass up to the light. 'One more, and that'll do. Now it's time I ruined some people's evenings, methinks.'

Edwin was certain the police would be scrutinising his

call patterns, so he'd already worked out a logical order to contact people. He rang Rachel's sister first; she lived in the Lake District. Susannah was a stoic woman but even so, she broke down when he told her, in deliberately halting language, what had befallen Rachel. He paused to give her space, even offered to phone back later, but Susannah recovered, and they were able to speak on a reasonably even keel. She admitted that when he'd called earlier she'd known instantly there was something disastrously wrong. Several times she'd been on the point of phoning him but had forced herself to sit tight. Edwin reckoned Susannah had a soft spot for him, as if she empathised that he had to put up with Rachel. Susannah had said more than once that if Rachel had been a friend and not her sister, she'd have dumped her years ago.

They discussed telling Rachel's mother, who lived in Sussex. Their father had been killed in an industrial accident when Rachel was preparing to go to university. Susannah said she'd make the call but when Edwin tried to convince her it was his responsibility, she dug her heels in, leaving him no choice but to agree.

He would have loved to be a fly on the wall when the mother was told. He'd never liked the old bag. No matter who Rachel offended, or how nastily she behaved, her mother would pat her on the head and coo the equivalent of: naughty Rachel, you mustn't do that.

As they were signing off, Susannah offered to drive north to see him, but he thanked her and said no. Explained he still had lots of calls to make, which was true, and that he was exhausted. Then he turned on the waterworks. But Rachel's mother wouldn't be able to stop herself travelling to Edinburgh from the south coast, and Susannah wouldn't be put off forever. If he were to succeed, these were challenges he'd have to face.

He intended to act pathetic and overcome, and he was certain he could pull it off.

Since the police first showed up at his door, he'd been surprised to find he didn't have any difficulty sounding emotional – especially on the phone. But then, he had murdered another human being. Although, he thought, he had been remarkably calm since he'd arrived back home in the early hours of the morning with his list of tasks accomplished.

He'd had a few tricky moments while he was with the police during the day, but they'd all been justified by the circumstances. In fact, he saw these as periods of release – when he could let go, be himself. In private, it wasn't long before any tears dissolved into laughter. *I'm going to get away with this. I just know I am.*

He refreshed his drink then rang his own sister, Hayley. She was divorced with two kids and because she would, 'Never let that complete tosser back into my life', she'd reverted to Fuller. She lived in Glasgow, and Edwin had never known anyone who was quite so resourceful. 'I'll be with you in a couple of hours,' she said, not batting an eyelid at the prospect of dumping her kids on someone at that time of night with zero warning.

He sighed. It was a battle that wasn't worth fighting but he'd be sending her home to Glasgow as soon as humanly possible.

Then he phoned Jack, who asked in the briefest terms how he was before putting Lisa on.

'How are you, Edwin?' Her voice wobbled. 'My God, I can't believe this is happening. Can't take it in.'

'I know, Leese. It's ... it's surreal.' He stopped there. His strategy was never to lead a conversation if he could get away with it. He reckoned if all his responses were reactive, he'd find it easier to sound more like the grieving husband and be less likely to trip himself up.

'What are the police saying?'

'Not a lot. Asked loads of questions as you'd expect.'

'Do they know where she went after she left the house? And how she came to be at the Water of Leith?'

'No, they don't.'

'I guess they'll be working on all that stuff now.'

'I suppose so.'

Silence.

'Listen, Edwin. If there's anything we can do. In fact, do you want us to come over?'

'No. Thanks for offering but Hayley's on her way.' Lisa started to say something, but he cut across her. 'I'll have to go. I still have a list of people to call, including the school.'

'Can I help? Would you like me to speak to the girls?'

He paused, as if he were considering her offer. 'If you wouldn't mind, that would be great.'

'I'll do that.' Then she hesitated. 'Is it okay to tell them ... shit, I mean explain the police think Rachel was ... ?'

Edwin smiled. *Murdered, Lisa? Oh yes, it's definitely okay to pass on that juicy little titbit. Especially to the bloody coven. Bitches!*

When Edwin hung up he briefly considered having one for the road because Lisa was probably the one person he'd actually wanted to speak to. But he desisted on the drink front. He was determined not to let the demon take a hold although he didn't imagine anyone would blame him, especially not at this stage.

The next name on his list was Rachel's employer. Despite telling the police he would have to search for their details, he knew exactly how to contact them. So he would *somehow* find the information and ring them Monday morning. He scribbled on the sheet of paper, 'Look them up – tell police – phone Monday'. This was solely for effect; he might leave the paper lying around for Cooper to *find*.

His boss, however, was far more straightforward although he deliberately skipped his line manager, his department head, and went straight to the head teacher: Selwyn Bierman. Edwin would get a big kick out of this one too; Bierman was a nasty man whose colossal ego demanded the world should worship at his feet. All the teachers, and possibly some of the pupils, called him The ELF. Evil Little Fucker. Well named, and not only because he was shorter than a few of the older kids.

Edwin knew Bierman would freak out about the negative publicity the school would attract and it would hardly cross his mind that that one of his staff had suffered a personal tragedy of unimaginable proportions. Bierman marched about the place as if he'd not only purchased every brick and slate but lugged them to the site on his own back, before building the school himself. He strode around as if he had a snooker cue rammed up his arse and addressed everyone in tones that suggested he was so *so* tired of spending his time with beings who clearly were inferior.

As Edwin anticipated, the conversation was brief. A cold war secret agent making a Mayday call to his handler to say the Russians were knocking his door down would have spent longer on the phone. Bierman's solution was blunt. 'Take next week off, and then we'll see where we're at. And don't worry, your classes will be covered.'

Edwin wanted to scream down the phone, *I've just murdered my wife, you arrogant cretin. Why the fuck should I worry about whether my classes will be covered or not? And a week off? Cheers.*

But he had no intention of returning to work, at that school or anywhere else. He would sign off with stress then simply disappear quietly. He could afford it.

Then he contacted some relatives and finished up by speaking to his one true friend: Niall.

Niall's response was typical of the man. 'What can I do to help, mate?'

'Nothing.'

'Okay, but I don't like to think of you sitting in that house on your own. Will I come over?'

'No. It's fine. My sister's on her way.' And then Edwin promptly and completely fell to pieces and genuinely could not continue the conversation.

'I'm glad to hear Hayley's coming through,' said Niall. 'But I'm here when you need me and if I don't hear from you by tomorrow evening at six, I'll be ringing your door bell.'

Once he recovered enough to stand up without his knees buckling, Edwin did have another drink, then several more after that.

# CHAPTER NINE

Ten Months Earlier

FOR EASILY A COUPLE OF YEARS, Edwin Fuller had seriously contemplated murdering his wife. At certain times, usually when she was being a total cow, the idea consumed him.

And the only thing that stopped him was the prospect of being caught. Because, in essence, he was a coward. He'd watched TV documentaries about prisons. Terrifying places, particularly American penitentiaries where inmates with shaven heads and pneumatic muscles flaunted tattoos like sports' insignia. No way was he going inside, definitely not.

So, he'd thought about it. Plenty. But until he came up with the perfect plan, all he had was the dream.

Then, one evening while Rachel was out, he was spread out on the sofa marking essays from his class of eleven-year-olds. The topic was, 'I woke up one morning and a space monster was eating its breakfast in my bedroom'. He hadn't laughed so much in a long time. While he was reading, the TV was on, set to a Sky music channel.

As soon as he'd finished his work and tidied up his papers, he switched away from the music and onto his list of favourite channels. A scheduled programme was playing; it had started a few minutes earlier. He paid it no attention. He was on his phone, checking messages and roaming around various sporting websites. Then something that was said on the programme caught his attention. It was a true crime documentary, reporting on a series of murders that had taken place in Essex several years previously and filmed from the viewpoint of the police officers and experts from various fields of forensic science. He scrabbled around for the remote, pressed rewind at twelve times speed for several seconds, and replayed what had just been said. And there it was. 'In most circumstances criminals are almost always caught through a combination of ...'

He listened to the detective speaking for a few seconds then rewound again.

'Caught through a combination of CCTV, biological or digital forensics, or their electronic footprint'.

He let the programme play on. He was enthralled. It was precisely what he'd been searching for – not how to commit a crime but how to get away with it. It was only ten past nine and he watched it through to the end.

Rachel came in part way through, clearly the worse for drink. 'What're you watching?'

He muted the sound as if he were being polite. 'Don't know, just something that's on. I'm not really all that interested.'

'You coming upstairs?'

He shook his head. 'Not yet. I'm not tired.' *Tired? Jeez, I've never been so awake.*

As she headed for the staircase she tossed over her shoulder, 'Suit yourself.'

When the documentary ended, he played it again from the

start. It was episode two of three, and although he was desperate to watch the others, he sat and pondered. CCTV, digital and biological forensics, electronic footprints. That's where criminals slip up. Those words would be his mantra. But how on earth could he commit murder without falling foul of one or all of these? It was a complex puzzle, and he liked solving puzzles, so that's how he would treat it. Nothing more than a puzzle. Now he was buzzing.

After thirty-odd years in education and academia he understood his preferred methods of learning, how to study and how best to retain information. And that was by taking notes, having points of reference, and constantly reviewing 'til it stuck. Murdering Rachel would be an intricate puzzle, with multiple strands. He would have to log everything, write things down. 'Electronic footprint'. So that ruled out his PC and his phone; he didn't possess a tablet.

As his mind wandered, touching on an overwhelming array of ideas and possibilities, a key question hit him – hard. Could he do it? Could he actually murder his wife? A living, breathing, human being? And leaving aside all those bad times, all the arguments, all those occasions when she'd treated him like shit, this was a person with whom he'd laughed, made love and shared dreams. He was sure if you asked anyone if he was capable of murder they'd laugh the idea out of court. Edwin? Kill someone? Are you mad? No way on earth. He's too ...

*Too what?*

Too nice. Too soft. Too much of a doormat.

First things first – take notes. And find a way to keep them hidden. But how? They had to be on paper. *A notebook, maybe? Yes, everything in one place.* He smiled when he pictured his school notebooks; he always gave them a title. This one would be *Killing My Wife – A Plan by Edwin Fuller.* He would keep it handy for logging ideas or solutions. *But where?* He sat, thinking, but nothing came to him.

*Well, Edwin my lad. Until you come up with a rock-solid solution to problem number one, you're stuck.*

He discounted all the rooms on the ground floor. No privacy at all, had to be his office. He crept upstairs. Their bedroom light was off. He paused at the doorway, leaned against the jamb. If Rachel was awake she'd speak to him. Steady breathing. Dead to the world.

His office was to the rear of the house, a box room he'd made larger and brighter by knocking through to a closet and installing a Velux window. He pushed the door to and clicked on the desk lamp. Soft light illuminated the desktop and the two bookshelves on the wall behind his monitor.

He swivelled from side to side in the chair. Examined his desk, rifled through a tray of papers, opened and closed a few drawers. Nothing. He turned his attention to the bookshelves, trawled back and forth. Textbooks, schoolbooks, reference books. He came up with a couple of options but torpedoed them as quickly as they surfaced. He spun the chair and scanned the room. More shelves holding novels and travel guidebooks, his collection of LPs, photograph albums. The four-drawer filing cabinet might have been a possibility, but the bare metal runners screeched so much they'd waken the dead; no use if he needed access while Rachel was in bed.

*Come on, man. There must be something.*

Returning to his books, this time he worked methodically along the rows. *Nothing even remotely suitable. How can that be?* Then he remembered something and realised he was searching in the wrong place. He slipped downstairs to Rachel's desk. There it was, a yellow and black paperback with an instantly recognisable logo. He flicked through the pages. *Just the job.*

Back at his desk he smoothed out the book with his palm. Rachel had bought it a few years previously for a specific work project, but he'd heard her complaining it was now out of date and she might as well throw it in the bin. Now, if she noticed it was gone he'd make some excuse about borrowing it, but the chances were she'd never miss it. The two open pages were typical of the series' content and layout: brief explanations in text, supporting diagrams, lots of white space. It was perfect. He'd already figured out how he'd use it to record notes so even if someone did read his scribblings, it wouldn't be obvious what they meant.

He grinned. *A murderer's handbook. Brilliant.*

Although no one ever went in there, especially Rachel, he decided he should hide it – in plain sight was a saying he'd always liked. He stood up and rearranged the shelf, so his new handbook was second top in a small stack of similar sized books. Then he selected a few others and laid them right next to his keyboard, as if they were the ones he referred to most often.

He took a step back, happy with the overall effect.

Sleep wasn't an option, so he padded back down to the kitchen. He stood with his back to the gas hob, the heels of his hands resting on the edge of the worktop. He forced himself to revisit the priority question: could he kill his wife? Edwin was an intelligent man, and logical with it. He was practical, he could follow a plan. As a teacher, he had to be creative too. He was methodical, thorough, paid attention to detail. So yes, on all counts, he was convinced. But there was a secondary consideration; he had to make certain he would never be caught. Because, no way on earth was he spending the rest of his life in prison. What would be the point in that?

That led him directly onto the second key component of

what was beginning to feel like a monstrous concept: what method would he use to kill her?

He part filled the kettle and made himself a cafetière. Waiting for the coffee to brew he realised he would have to prove to himself that he could take the life of another human being. Because if he couldn't do that, all the dreaming, all the scheming was a complete waste of time and emotional energy. Plus, his life would continue along the same lines, and he couldn't stomach that prospect. He'd probably end up topping himself. *And that would be pretty stupid, wouldn't it?*

So, mentally, he toughened up. He had the motive: he loathed her. He would have the opportunity: they lived in the house on their own after all. And now the crime documentary had given him the means. Or, at least, the beginnings. He had to build on that, not allow the momentum to drop off. He had to focus on hitting *Yes* at all the binary choices on the 'Kill Rachel' flowchart.

He stood with the steaming mug of black liquid cradled in his hands, staring into middle distance. If he found a spider inside the house he gathered it up carefully and popped it outside, and if it was raining he would simply shoo it away under a piece of furniture. Crazy really, you can't drown a spider. Even wasps. He wasn't scared of them, but he was wary, he had a healthy respect for them. His view was that wasps had an unjustly bad reputation. So, he ushered them outside too.

Now he had a task for the coming days. He had to get past being squeamish. Could he kill insects, small animals, even birds, and feel nothing. He wondered how far he'd have to go to prove it to himself. How far up the food chain? A dog? He snorted: don't be ridiculous. A cat? Possibly. A couple of toys lay on the floor. Could he? One of his own pets, that he'd cared for, played with and doted upon since they were a few weeks old? It would certainly prove a point – beyond any doubt.

Just then, he felt soft smooth pressure wrapping around his shin. He smiled, laid his mug on the table, bent down and hoisted the little black cat up until they were face to face. His pet bopped him softly on the nose.

Edwin chuckled. 'Well, Pepper, enough of the theory. Time for me to start putting things into practice.'

# CHAPTER TEN

The Present Time

SOMETHING IS MOST DEFINITELY AMISS HERE. I glance at Andrew. All that comes back is a flicker of an eyebrow. But that's enough, we're on the same wavelength. 'So, Lisa,' I say. 'You've said that Rachel's personality changed when she started uni. Can you tell me a bit more about that, please? In what way did she change?'

There are four of us sitting round the table in Lisa and Jack McCafferty's dining kitchen. Lisa possesses an air of vitality that surrounds her like a body sized halo. She's wearing a white tee beneath a red tartan shirt; her dark brown hair falls shy of the collar. Her husband is significantly larger in all dimensions. Powerful, but something tells me he doesn't go to the gym. More like an ex-rugby player who'd rather spend time in the bar than run about for eighty minutes. They live in the Canonmills area of Edinburgh, not much more than a mile from Edwin Fuller's place. If I had to guess, I would say Andrew and I have arrived in the middle of a domestic. I don't know if it was already simmering before I called to say we were on our way, or if the palpable tension is because we're here. Asking them questions.

Lisa's gaze bounces about all over the white melamine table top before she begins to speak. 'Rachel and I were classmates, all through school. She'd always been quiet. Shy, I suppose. When we were kids, I was a bit of a tomboy. Rachel was the opposite. In secondary school, things were more or less the same. I had my first boyfriend when I was about fifteen but Rachel ... she didn't even notice boys existed. And to be fair, they didn't pay her much attention either. She was more interested in revising, passing her exams, making sure she got into uni.'

I watch as she stretches out a hand, nudges a wooden pepper mill 'til it's hard up against a matching salt grinder. She flicks a black crumb off the table. 'Then, in sixth year, we both had acceptances for Heriot Watt to study business management.' Lisa glances up at me. 'And that's when Rachel's dad was killed.' She stops there, as if unsure how to continue.

I prod. 'What happened?'

'An industrial accident. He worked in a company that made steam turbines, or something. He was caught up in some machinery.' She hesitates. 'Terrible injuries, rushed to hospital. He didn't pull through.'

'How did that affect her?'

'Not in the way you might think. It was as if an enormous weight was lifted off her.' She sighs. 'I'd never noticed, or I never asked, and Rachel didn't volunteer, but reading between the lines, I think her dad was ultra, ultra-strict with her. And always had been. Compared to him, her mother was a real mouse and as soon as Rachel was off the leash, well, she went crazy.'

'Define crazy,' says Andrew.

Lisa points at Jack. 'All three of us, first year uni, living in halls, parties every weekend. The whole sex, drugs and rock 'n roll thing. Rachel behaved like a woman possessed.' Again, she hesitates. 'Unfortunately, she didn't have any boundaries and she became incredibly ... how can I put it—'

'Experimental,' says Jack, with a dry laugh.

I turn to him. 'Meaning?'

He fixes his gaze on me. 'You name it.'

Lisa rushes in. 'Her behaviour led her into some bad situations and one in particular definitely had a huge impact on her.'

'In what way?' I ask.

She doesn't answer straight away. But I can see she will, so I wait. 'She stayed on at a guy's flat, alone, after a party. I knew she'd had far too much to drink so I pleaded with her to come home with me, but she wouldn't. Told me she was a big girl, and I should piss off and leave her.' I don't react and she keeps talking. 'When I left it was only her and the guy, but then a few of his mates ...' She does the air quotes thing. 'Turned. Up.'

There's a heartbeat of silence. 'And what happened?'

Lisa spreads her hands. 'She never told me, and I never found out. But from that day on she had a *huge* downer on men, all men, and basically treated them like shit.'

'Including Edwin?' says Andrew.

'Especially Edwin.'

I glance at Jack, who's studying something fascinating on a wall behind me.

Andrew prods her further. 'Can you elaborate? Give us examples?'

She leaves the table and walks to the sink, pours herself a glass of water and drinks some before rejoining us. 'They'd been going out for about a year, then, for some strange reason, she started calling him Ed. Or Eddie. He hated that; it bugged the hell out of him. Said his mother named him Edwin and it wasn't up to anyone else to shorten it. His mum had passed away, so that made it worse. Anyway, he asked Rachel several times to stop but she wouldn't. She was being deliberately cruel, and she didn't care.'

My face is obviously saying *Is that it? Seriously?*

'I can see what you're thinking,' she says. 'But she knew damn fine how much it annoyed ... no, hurt him. And she could twist the knife every day in life if she felt like it.'

'And what did he do? How did he react?'

She waves a hand around. 'Oh, like with most things Rachel did, or said, he tried to laugh it off. Pretend it didn't bother him. But it did. You could see it in his eyes.' She paused. 'I could give you lots more but the worst one was their wedding.'

Jack snorts at that, and she hits him with a ferocious glare. He goes back to staring at the wall, while Lisa continues with her rant. 'Once he figured out what she was like, Edwin should have dumped her and got the fuck out. He certainly never should have married her. On their wedding day she was an absolute horror, totally out of order. Flirting with complete strangers—'

'Aye, and not only flirting.'

'You don't know that, Jack. So shut it.'

Hmmm. Now this is becoming interesting. Lisa's in full flow now. 'She'd stay out all night, not tell him where she'd been. Go away for weekends, wouldn't contact him at all. She bashed his car once, didn't even mention it 'til he noticed. He was livid, but she said something like, "What's your problem? It's insured, isn't it?"'

Jack comes in at this point. 'Edwin admitted to me once, after we'd both had a few, that even if Rachel behaved really badly towards him, he had no sanctions to come back at her with. "I'm powerless," he said. And he was right, because what could he do apart from physically throw her arse out on the street?'

There's a brief lull in the conversation while I formulate my next question. 'Did their relationship simmer along like that all the time or did things become worse recently?'

Lisa leans forward, palms flat on the table. 'Wait a minute. Are you saying what I think you're saying?'

Before I can answer, Jack jumps in. 'If you imagine Edwin was responsible for what happened to Rachel, you must be out of your tree. The man's too weak to do something like that.'

I eyeball them both. 'Is it fair to say you don't like him?'

'That's right, we don't,' says Jack.

'You mean you don't,' says Lisa.

Jack holds up his hands. 'Okay, okay. It's not that I dislike him. We go for beers every now and again, just the two of us. The football occasionally. And when Rachel's not there, he's fine. But it's incredibly difficult to have respect for a man who lets himself be treated like dirt, by his own wife, in front of people like us, their friends. As Lisa said, he tried to laugh it off but all that did was drive Rachel on. Sometimes we were cringing with embarrassment.' He pauses for a breath. 'And that's my problem with Edwin. He's a bloody doormat.'

The room falls silent while we each consider Jack's tirade, probably all from different perspectives. Andrew takes us along a different line, a crucial one. 'Did you ever see him bite back? Insult her in return. Shout at her. Maybe even raise his hand.'

They glance at each other. 'Absolutely not,' says Lisa. 'Never.'

I move on to clear up a few facts. I ask, did either of them see or speak to Rachel or Edwin the day she left the house? Did Rachel come here last night after she stormed out? Did either of them see or speak to Edwin today? Their replies are all no.

Then I ask if they knew of anyone who could have been

responsible for Rachel's death, or who might have had a motive for hurting her. Jack runs a finger round the inside of his tee-shirt collar before saying, 'Definitely not.' And Lisa nods along in unison.

'What do you do for a living, Jack?' says Andrew.

Jack sits up straighter. 'I have my own business. Plumbing. Just small. I employ a time-served plumber and an apprentice. And before you ask, I dropped out of uni part way through second year. I don't even know why I stayed that long; it wasn't for me. I didn't want a job, so I enrolled in one of those government sponsored apprenticeships and when I finished that, I set up the company and became my own boss.'

'And why plumbing if you don't mind me asking?'

He shrugs. 'I'm pretty good with my hands and I'm usually working inside, not much more to it than that.'

I switch my attention to Lisa, but I don't have to ask.

'I'm deputy leader of Edinburgh City Council.' Then adds, 'I did finish uni.'

I didn't see that coming, but I certainly didn't miss the dig at her husband. And neither did he by the look on his face. There's more, possibly much more, to this pair than meets the eye. But that's for another day. I move on to my final question. 'Do either of you know for certain if Rachel was having an affair, or indeed ever has had an affair?'

Which produces yet another interesting reaction. Lisa sneaks a quick glance at her other half. He drops his gaze to the table. She says, 'No,' but even that single syllable has a break in it. And Jack doesn't reply at all. He simply shakes his head. Once. And the movement was barely perceptible.

To quote a word I used earlier: interesting.

There's no on-street parking at the McCafferty's flat so we have to walk a couple of streets to our car. It's still raining but the wind seems to be backing off. I'm fed up with my hood, so I push it back. Andrew says, 'They weren't entirely convincing when they said Rachel hadn't ever had an affair.'

'No. They weren't, were they?' I ponder while we cross a road. 'Probably a question we should ask other people.' My phone buzzes. I ferret around in my bag, read the display. 'Steph,' I say.

I listen while she speaks, then turn to Andrew and perform a mini fist pump. 'That's brilliant, Steph. Where was it found?'

She tells me.

'We'll be there in five.'

# CHAPTER ELEVEN

Six Months Earlier

As THE MONTHS PASSED, Edwin was ticking off the more important elements of his plan. He'd asked himself dozens and dozens of questions, some hypothetical, some all too real. He didn't yet have all the answers, but he'd made significant progress with every detail logged methodically. He closed his handbook and laid his propelling pencil down. That was one of the finer points, he didn't ever record anything in ink.

In his mind, he reviewed what he'd accomplished, steps he still had to achieve and problems he was still puzzling over. Since day one, a key component had stood in his way as if it were Cerberus, the multi-headed dog from Greek mythology that guarded the gates of the underworld to prevent the dead from leaving. In simple terms, would he be capable of killing? That was his Cerberus, and eventually he would behead the beast.

Over a period of a few weeks, he systematically disposed of ... no, he forced himself to use the correct term, *killed* a variety of small creatures. At first, he was squeamish. They hadn't done him any harm; they were all entitled to their time and place on this earth. He told himself to get over it. This was a means towards an end.

He used objects as instruments of death. A brick to crush a spider; a spade to cut a worm into slices; the sole of his gardening shoe to obliterate snails and slugs. He hadn't considered it necessary to include insects but then a bee wandered into his kitchen. Edwin loved bees. A worldwide popularity promotion was under way because the species was perceived to be under so much threat. He captured it in a jar, apologised, then filled the jar with water and poured it down the drain.

One day, his ginger and white cat brought a fledgling into the garden. A blackbird. It wasn't long before Chilli became fed up tormenting the poor creature and sloped off to sleep in the sun. The bird was hopping in tight circles around the grass, dragging its wing behind him like a mother with a sulky toddler. It was time for Edwin to take the next step up the food chain. He watched it for a minute, chirping in distress, parents sitting in a tree screeching their heads off. He knew what he had to do, and he also knew he'd better move quickly or there was a good chance he would chicken out. He grimaced at both the task ahead and his unintentional choice of words. He marched over, swiped the injured bird off the ground, and twisted its neck. He both heard and felt the crunch. The bird's head flopped over. It twitched, stopped, and he didn't throw up. He stepped over to the bin and dropped the carcass in.

Rachel spoke from inside the kitchen. 'What was that?'

'Dead bird. The cat got it.' He swiped his fingertips across his throat.

'Which one?'

'Why do you care? You've never bothered to tell them apart and they're different colours.'

69

It was a rare flutter of defiance that she didn't even register.

'Little shits,' she said. 'Don't know why you put up with them.'

In the following week he set mousetraps and crushed the rodents with the heel of his hand. He built a box with a hatch and a cord, left a few nuts inside and captured a grey squirrel. Cute, but doomed. Although had it been a red, he'd have released it unharmed. He put on a leather work glove and stuck his hand into the trap. The creature tried to bite him, but he tightened his grip. He almost managed to shut out its squeals of pain and terror, but they haunted him for days afterwards.

He imagined that was enough but found himself questioning: was he satisfied? No, not quite. There was one final step he had to take. A few days later, he was sitting outside enjoying a beer in the late evening sun, when Pepper appeared over a wall. The cat trotted over and bounced up on his lap, stamped her claws a few times, turned a couple of circles then positioned herself – paws on Edwin's chest, eyes closed, purring. He stroked her soft black fur, running his fingertips along the cat's spine. This was an acid test. Could he? He thought so, but he had to make certain. He scooped Pepper up in his arms and kept a firm but gentle hold to prevent her from squirming from his grasp. He crossed the grass, walked into the garage and kicked the door shut behind him.

———

A FEW DAYS later he felt able to consider the next major question. It was standing directly in his path – chest out, arms folded, an evil scowl on its face. What would be his preferred method for killing a human? He drafted a list of nineteen options on a piece of scrap paper that he later ripped into tiny shreds and flushed down the toilet. He rejected a few right off the bat. An accident had too much potential to go wrong or to not be fatal. And he wouldn't kill her in a public place either, which ruled out running her down.

No, she had to die by his hand. Then she would recognise what was happening, even if only for a few moments. And maybe she'd wonder why. Would she? He doubted it, she'd be fighting for her life. Most of the remaining options, like shooting her, failed the test because he would have to source a weapon. So, although he was amused by the idea of blasting her head off with a sawn-off shotgun, it too bit the dust. And as soon as he matched any of these possibilities against 'biological forensics', if they resulted in her bleeding all over the place, he discarded the option.

Eventually, from his list, he settled on strangulation. By that method, he calculated he'd be able to commit the murder using standard household items that could be found in every home in the land, while leaving no incriminating blood or gore behind. Perfect.

But at that point, his thinking, his planning, his dreaming, crashed to a halt. *Do I really want to do this? Will I be able to handle the guilt afterwards? Will I transform into a blubbering wreck as soon as the police apply the merest pressure? Isn't there anything else I can do?* That was his first major wobble, the seeds of self-doubt sprouted like weeds on a roadside verge. But then, that very same evening, he and Rachel were out with friends, and her behaviour towards him was demeaning to the point he almost punched her. She couldn't have known it, but that night sealed her fate.

Edwin was now watching any relevant police documentary he could find on TV: but live, never recorded. And live through the aerial, not via his Sky box. He was sure the provider would habitually gather consumer data for marketing purposes but, thinking logically, he couldn't imagine how his TV watching habits could be tracked through terrestrial channels coming through the aerial. That was when he realised he needed to gain even more knowledge about electronic footprint and the IT world in general. Google searches were a complete nonstarter, so he had to find another solution.

One weekend, he cycled into town. He wore a helmet, luminescent yellow jacket, a buff covering his lower face, and sunglasses. Just another cycling clone. He visited a chain retailer that stocked a wide range of magazines. He left his helmet locked to his bike, but used the buff to cover his hair, and kept the sunglasses on. It took a while, but finally he stopped worrying that his fellow shoppers would think he was a poseur. After all, he was far from the only Al Pacino lookalike wandering about the mall.

Poring through the computing section in the store he came across a fortnightly magazine. It was issue 623 so clearly it had legs. The index covered a range of topics, general stuff, not specific to any of the behemoths like Apple or Microsoft. He found regular columns on computer security, warnings about scams, and best buys on all manner of hardware and software. While he stood there, engrossed in the content, a shop assistant was working his way along the shelves replenishing the stock from a cage on wheels. Edwin had already decided he'd buy the magazine but spotted a bundle of new issues in the cage. So, he pretended to pore through the photography magazines until the young man had moved on then picked up the later issue and bought both copies, paying by cash.

Back home, he leafed through the issues in order. Similar to some of the documentaries he'd watched, the articles explained how to protect his IT, prevent scams and maintain security. All he had to do was spin things round, examine them from the opposite angle and translate all this positive information into criminality. He wondered if the editor had ever considered he might be done as an accessory after the fact.

But his purchases that day brought yet another issue into sharp focus: money. Since he'd begun planning his wife's demise he'd been skimming cash from their accounts. It had been ridiculously easy because Rachel never paid that much attention to their finances. And if she had ever questioned what he was spending cash on, he was ready with an excuse. He was forever buying spares and accessories for his bikes, from the only independent shop in Leith. Since long before Edwin's time it had been situated in a lane off Bowling Green Street. A veritable Aladdin's Cave of the bicycle world, every spare inch of floor and wall space was blanketed in all things bike, and the proprietor appeared to be permanently coated in a thin layer of 3-in-one. He also preferred cash transactions, but he was mightily surprised one day when Edwin, apparently on the spur of the moment, paid £550 cash for a second-hand Cannondale mountain bike. Edwin told Rachel it had cost £1100; she didn't bat an eyelid.

Also, during the same period, Edwin paid cash to tradesmen for jobs around the house, and claimed they'd cost significantly more than they actually did. Rachel paid no attention; it was his house, his money, he could do whatever he liked. Eventually, his cash kitty passed £3000. And counting.

He was well aware there were certain purchases he could only make online. Yes, buying from a store was a possibility but that would expose him to CCTV. And any credit purchase meant a card, which had to be tied in to a bank account, and both would need an address.

He didn't panic because he was beginning to enjoy solving these riddles although this one was the trickiest so far. He'd been throwing ideas about but hadn't yet come up with an answer.

Then, one evening he picked up the latest copy of his computing magazine. He'd bought it earlier in the day but had jammed it in his backpack without opening it. It had a headline plastered across the front cover that screamed, 'DARE you explore the DEEP, DARK Secrets of The Internet?'

*What the hell's this?* Intrigued, he flicked through to page fifty to find out. The feature article was eight pages long, chock-full of information that astounded him, but littered with jargon and technical terms, most of which were alien to Edwin. But every issue included a glossary of computing terms, so Edwin grabbed another magazine and reread the article side by side with the glossary. He was utterly astonished by what he learned and, by the time he'd finished it for the second time, he knew the bulk of his remaining issues were about to vanish as if they'd never existed. He could now see clearly how he'd be able to circumvent the big three, his collective term for digital and biological forensics, CCTV surveillance, and electronic foot-print. Because if he could do that, he would definitely get away with murdering his wife.

Edwin spent the rest of the evening logging information in his murderer's handbook, and half the night tossing and turning before eventually he gave up on the idea of sleep, went back to his desk, and began working on the finer details of his plan.

# CHAPTER TWELVE

The Present Time

I'VE JUST BEEN TOLD that two PCs found Edwin Fuller's silver Ford Focus in St Mark's Woods, less than a mile from his house and only a few hundred metres from where his wife's body was discovered. The main parking area is a rough circle bordering a clearing about the size of a couple of tennis courts, and there are three much smaller loops off the outer perimeter. The Focus is in the second of these loops, in a bay on the far side. Apart from our vehicles, the place is empty. It's still raining, but it's not quite so relentless and the wind has dropped away although the odd gust still rattles through the trees.

The main area is taped off at the entrance, and a marked path leads to the car. A couple of uniforms are stationed where two trails enter the car park, to stop people blundering into the scene. Fat chance in this weather, dog walkers and crazy joggers aside.

The car is cordoned off too. As Andrew and I approach, wearing fresh cleansuits, a PC steps forward and logs us in. We duck under the tape then hang back. Greg Brodie is standing a few feet behind the car; the hatch is open and there's a white-clad bum sticking out. A second SE is standing off to the side, tablet in hand. He notices me, his eyes crinkle so I return the smile. I might know him, I might not.

Greg glances over his shoulder, mutters something to the bum then comes over. I'm not surprised to find him here. Same crime, but multiple locations – his job is to coordinate activity at all of them and form the link between the SEs, the labs and the operational units.

'Ah,' I say. 'It's little Gregory Johnston. What gives?'

He bursts out laughing and holds his hands up. 'You got me.' Andrew's clearly wondering if I've gone round the twist. 'Maybe you should explain, Melissa,' says Greg.

I turn to my sidekick. 'We first met when we were five, we started school together. But *Gregory* left when he was about, what, ten?'

'Yeah,' says Greg. 'You probably won't remember this, but my dad died suddenly when I was about seven.'

Shit! That caught me out. 'I'm sorry, Greg. I don't remember.'

He flaps a hand. 'Ach, no worries, we were just kids. I was kinda lucky because it happened right at the start of the summer holidays, and I became very adept at dodging questions. Anyway, my mum remarried, hence my change of surname to Brodie, and we moved over to Fife. When did you suss me?'

'I twigged when Edwin Fuller told us he's a teacher at our old school. Only it's called Leith Primary now. But we should leave the reminiscing until we've got a couple of drinks in front of us. So, tell me, what have we got here?'

He gestures towards the car. 'The driver's door was pushed to, but not closed properly, so unlocked. No keys either, obviously. No sign of any struggle, no obvious blood. But we need to get a covering over it before we can open it up fully ... ah!'

Two SEs hove into view lugging huge navy-blue bags bedecked in Police Scotland logos and, in no time at all, the car is tucked neatly beneath a canvas shelter. They tie it down and we all edge in bit closer.

Greg points at the ground. 'As you can see the Focus is jammed right up against a tree on that edge of the bay so there's space for another vehicle on this side. It could be they parked driver's door to driver's door, but it probably doesn't matter because with the area being awash with puddles there's little chance of finding much.'

I curse the weather again and another squall blows in, tearing at the roof of the shelter and bending in the side nearest us. I screw up my face then ask, 'What's the story with the car?'

'Not a lot.' He extends an arm. 'Feel free.'

I lean down, peer in the driver's door. Some cars are full of rubbish, but the Focus is neat and tidy. Reflects what we've seen of Edwin, I suppose. A few coins and a Biro with a blue lid are sitting in slots in the centre console, a yellow windscreen cloth and a Cellophane pack of tissues in the driver's door pocket, and a few maps and guidebooks over in the passenger door. I check out the back seats. Apart from a pair of women's wellies – dark blue with multi-coloured dots all over them – the upholstery and the carpets are in showroom condition. But then, the Fullers don't have kids so it could be the rear seats are rarely used.

We move to the back of the car. One of the SEs is moving stuff around, while the other records information on a tablet, and takes photos where appropriate. A sturdy white plastic box, about two feet square, is secured to the side of the boot with a bungee cord. It seems Edwin Fuller is prepared for driving in a Scottish winter. I can see a partly used container of screen wash, a can of de-icer, windscreen scraper, colourful microfibre cloths, a pair of work gloves, a hat and a green tartan blanket.

We step back to make space for a third SE, who's carrying a large evidence crate and a healthy supply of bags. She places the crate by her colleague's feet. One by one, the SE lifts all the items out of the white box and places them in evidence bags. The other two note everything, and seal, mark and scan the bags to ensure Chain of Evidence is intact, before placing each bag in the evidence crate. They do the same with the white box and the bungee cord, then close the crate. Now the boot is empty, the SE takes a lint roller from an equipment case that holds the tools of his trade, runs it over the carpeted floor in a linear pattern before bagging that too. He lifts the carpet. As you'd expect – spare wheel, standard tools, all in pristine condition.

'There's a transporter on the way,' says Greg. 'Once the car's at the lab we'll take it to bits properly. Check it for prints, DNA, all that good stuff. But as far as here is concerned, the rain's forecast to go off in the early hours, so I'll have people come back then and see if we can recover anything from the ground. I have to say, though, I'd be surprised. In the meantime, we've closed off the car park and our uniformed colleagues will keep the scene secure.'

I hang about for a few minutes longer then when I'm about as cold and wet as I can be, I walk over to where Andrew is chatting to yet another SE while she packs away her equipment. 'Right, my boy,' I say. 'Let's go and see what our esteemed colleagues have been up to all day in the dry and warmth of our office.'

# CHAPTER THIRTEEN

It's a sad but inescapable reflection of our times that crime in Scotland is on an escalating curve, and the capital city is far from immune. My boss, Jeff Hunter, was recently promoted to Detective Chief Inspector and placed in charge of the three existing Major Investigation Teams, or MITs, which cover the city. But the increase in serious crime meant Edinburgh needed an additional MIT so the Division was reorganised, I moved with Jeff, and I now lead MIT4.

Last year, a great hole appeared in our chain of command when our Detective Chief Superintendent, a slimy weasel called Mark Thornton, was relieved of his duties. That's the polite version; he was bent. In political terms that gave Police Scotland, 'A tremendous opportunity for invigorating new growth', or some such bullshit, and the upshot was Jeff became DCI. I moved up to DI, while my sidekick, Andrew, earned his promotion to DS; richly deserved, and not a minute too soon.

I didn't fancy licking a completely new or inherited team into shape, so I *suggested* to Andrew that he come with me. He pretended to think about it then said yes. And no way was I leaving the other key member of my team behind so DC Steph Zanetti came along too.

One of the personal reservations I've always had about being promoted to DI is that, unlike certain TV dramas which feature police detectives of all grades and ages traipsing around the countryside chasing after the bad guys, the reality in modern police life is somewhat different. Officers at my level should be managing investigations and coordinating resources, not scraping mud off our smart suits or perish the thought, breaking a heel while chasing villains.

I've been working with Jeff for nigh on ten years and we rub along just fine. He doesn't mind when I challenge him on police issues as long as I can back it up, but I rarely overstep the mark. I'm acutely aware that if I do, he won't miss and hit the wall. So, we struck up a deal that I wouldn't be imprisoned behind a desk with a mouse welded to my palm. I would still be able to keep my hand in by concentrating on key suspects and witnesses, but I'd leave the bulk of detecting to Andrew and the other DS who was drafted into my team.

Unfortunately, that DS – chap by the name of Lawrence Ratcliffe – isn't exactly my cup of tea. Just a few days ago I had to pull him aside following what I saw as a clear lack of respect for one of his colleagues. Now, I'm a big fan of reasoned internal debate but that definitely does not stretch as far as shouting, swearing or using the phrase, 'You stupid bloody woman'. So, and admittedly I'm speaking euphemistically here, I gave him the rest of the week off to allow him the opportunity to reflect on his indiscretion, and to stop me taking his head clean off at the shoulders. The next day he phoned in a request to use up the remainder of his holiday entitlement in one fell swoop – a day short of three weeks. I was only too happy to grant it because the bottom line is, he's worse than a man short. Steph can easily slot in, she's more than capable.

Andrew and I are on our way back to HQ on Queen Charlotte Street, deep in sunny Leith. A fantastic three-storey ashlar sandstone building almost two centuries old, it was originally designed as Leith Town Hall. Later incarnations included a prison block, a courtroom and now, a cop shop. Until recently our offices were scattered around the building, which still boasts a grand central staircase and ceremonial meeting rooms. I'd always dreaded being shipped out to a centralised regional building but the powers-that-be authorised the capital investment and built a huge extension to the rear of our building; a glass and steel monstrosity immediately christened the 'Fish Tank'. Thankfully it has solar control glazing so we're not boiled alive while we go about our detecting.

I'd phoned ahead and asked the team to congregate in the incident room, and as I walk towards it I'm amused to see Steph and my boss standing just inside the doorway, head to head. Little and large have nothing on them; Steph's about five four and Jeff's the guts of a foot taller. Her blonde ponytail bobs about as she talks. One of the great things about any conversation with Steph is she gives it to you straight, and Jeff will be perfectly fine with that.

As I move through the group I spot the man I've been keen to meet all day long. He's average height, a tad overweight, and black. This is Tobias, pronounced Toe-Bee-Ass. A native of Cologne, Tobias worked with us for a couple of months last year, principally on the case that resulted in the professional demise of our ex-Chief Super. Tobias was on secondment from our German colleagues and when he was transferred away from my team, dead against my wishes I should add, I thought that might be the last time I would work with him. But he contacted me about six months ago to explain his girlfriend was moving to Edinburgh to take up a position with Heriot Watt University, and to ask how he would go about effecting a permanent move to Police Scotland. One brief conversation with Jeff and the deal was done. Tobias isn't due to start 'til Monday, but he's been going through induction today. Makes sense for him jump in on the ground floor with this investigation so I invited him to join us.

I tap Jeff's elbow on my way past and he joins me at the front of the room. Everybody else takes the hint, and their seats. Jeff stays standing and addresses the team.

'Evening all. Apologies for keeping you here so late but this is the first chance we've had to bring the whole team together since this morning's events. You all know me, so all I'll say by way of introduction is that although I'll be SIO on this investigation, Mel here will lead and keep me in the loop. I'll join you for as many briefings as I can but, having said that, I might have to slope off before we finish tonight. I have a function to attend.' He grimaces, and the people who know him well have a chuckle at his expense. Then he hands the floor to me and sits off to the side where he can take in the whole room.

'Before I start, folks,' I say, 'the cheerful gentleman wearing the leather jacket that looks like he rescued it from a skip is DC Tobias Hartmann, a new but old member of the team. Tobias is rejoining us permanently from next week. Say, Willkommen, everyone.'

Andrew gives Tobias a wave, and Dave Devlin sends a thumbs-up from the far side of the room. Steph performs a virtual high-five then pretends to glower at him when he doesn't reciprocate. There are two other officers in the room, junior DCs who are part of the MIT pool and who have been allocated to Andrew for as long as we need them. They're both female, a welcome sign of the times as far as I'm concerned.

I pick up a remote control and press a button. The lights dim and the wall behind me illuminates. Our four new incident rooms, one for each MIT, are kitted out with technology that Tom Cruise would kill for. The focal point is a wall-to-wall interactive whiteboard, which duets with a SmartTable; a futuristic wonder with a surface like a giant iPad, two metres by one. Using it as the interface I can project all manner of images and documents on to the wall then move them around, resize, annotate them, and draw connecting lines in any colour or style that takes my fancy. We can use electronic flipchart pens to add notes, which are translated by the wallboard and added to the file. And I can pull up interviews and statements that we've uploaded from our PDAs. Beats sticking pins in a corkboard, I can tell you.

But there are too many of us in the room to crowd round the SmartTable so I'm working with a tablet, and with a couple of taps I paste an image top and centre on the wall. 'Rachel Fuller. Wife of Edwin Fuller.' I paste Edwin's image directly below. 'Her remains were discovered at 07:46 this morning. Already deceased, Mrs Fuller had been thrown over a wall into dense undergrowth from behind a row of lock-ups off Powderhall Lane. The lock-ups overlook the Water of Leith.'

Next I pull up images of each of these locations then I add the icing to this particular cake. I show a short video of the scene, taken by one of Greg's team. When it finishes, it zooms out and morphs into an interactive 3D reconstruction, viewed from above. It was compiled by our Forensic Multimedia Unit using technological wizardry that I don't even pretend to understand. But the advantage is my team, or anyone else who's involved, can be transported back to our crime scene instantly, without needing to leave the office.

I leave all the images on the board, give everyone time to study them. In response to a couple of questions, I tilt and rotate the reconstruction then once everyone's seen enough, drag them off to the side and stack them. Next, I bring up a map covering all the points of interest, connected by solid red lines. The Fullers' house in Trinity, the row of lock-ups, and the car park in St Mark's Woods where the Fullers' car was found.

'Here's what we know so far. Rachel drove away from the family home last night at approximately 22:00. Her husband has stated he and his wife had been arguing. Immediately prior to that, they'd been having sex.' My colleagues are too experienced to gasp but hardly an eyebrow remains in place.

Jeff raises a finger. 'What's your take on the husband, Mel?'

'According to the man himself, and backed up by two of their closest friends, his wife ruled the roost. Sounds like he was seriously under the thumb. We have no evidence nor even any suggestion that he was involved in her murder. But, early days. He says when she left, he remained in the house. And again, we have no evidence to refute that. There was no one else present at the time.'

'Just as well, Boss, if they'd been having it away,' says Steph. In other circumstances, in other professions, her comment may have earned her a rebuke but for all emergency services personnel, black humour is rarely far beneath the surface. It's our way of coping with all the horrific stuff we have to deal with – day in, day out.

'Thank you for that image, Steph. Now, you've been checking out the Fullers. Either of them on our systems anywhere?'

'No, Boss. Nothing.'

I nod. Expected that. 'Okay, key questions: where did she go, and what route did she take when she drove away from the house last night?' I look over to my left. 'Dave?'

I've heard other MITs can be a bit sniffy about who they

include in their ops briefings, and some keep our uniformed colleagues at arm's length. To me, that creates an unnecessary barrier and we are on the same side. So, I don't give a tinker's about what rank an officer is; if they can help me, they're part of the team. PC Dave Devlin is here to liaise between detectives and uniforms. His colleagues have already contributed a lot to the investigation, and we'll be relying heavily on their input, especially in the early stages.

'We canvassed the neighbours, but no one actually witnessed her driving away,' says Dave. 'Nobody was out and about, they all had their front curtains closed, some were already in bed. Hardly a surprise given the foul weather and the time of night.' He pre-empts my follow-up question. 'The house diagonally opposite has CCTV, but it only catches a corner of the Fullers' drive. We have a few seconds of the car pulling away but no clear view of the driver.'

I move on to explain that Rachel left the house without a phone, and ask the rhetorical question: who does that, these days? It's unusual, possibly even suspicious, but relatively speaking it means little. If they were arguing, and she shot out the door, it's conceivable she simply forgot to pick it up. The upshot is we have no means of tracking her movements.

But the car's a different matter and I turn to Steph again. I'd tasked her to work on this while Andrew and I were with Edwin. There are several remote controls scattered around the room, she has one in her hand. The map is still on the wall and now she's spinning circles on the Fullers' address with a bright green laser dot before she moves it in a short straight line. 'Their street exits onto Craighall Road, and I was able to pick the car up, a silver Ford Focus, at 22:02. It travelled due south, four hundred metres to the junction with Ferry Road.' She's referring to a poker straight road that begins in Leith and runs for four miles east to west through North Edinburgh. She moves the green dot to the right. 'The Focus turned onto Ferry Road, heading west. Then, no further sightings but that's easy to explain. Had it continued west, it would have passed CCTV here, at the junction with Inverleith Road.' She jumps the dot a few hundred metres to the right. 'So that suggests it actually turned south again, off Ferry Road, towards Warriston Crematorium and into the car park at St Mark's Woods, where it was found.'

'And you've checked CCTV on streets to the north of Ferry Road in case it doubled back?' The question is overkill, but it has to be asked.

She uses the pointer to indicate alternative routes the driver could have taken. 'There are cameras here, here and here. Nothing on any of them.'

'What about CCTV at the crem?'

'On the buildings, yes, but a good distance from the road. And screened by trees and high bushes.'

I pause to think. 'What about NESTS?' Tobias sits back. His eyes say *What the hell is NESTS?*

I explain that *North Edinburgh – Security Through Surveillance* is an initiative that's kicked in during the past year. Although this part of Edinburgh has St Mark's Woods, there's also Inverleith Park which has extensive recreation areas, plus the Royal Botanic Garden and several rugby and cricket playing fields. But the area, and we're talking several square miles, also has its fair share of expensive old-money houses, many of them hidden behind high sandstone walls and mature trees. The residents were fed up being burgled so they amalgamated their neighbourhood watches, and NESTS was devised: a network of domestic security cameras that they manage internally. We don't have access carte-blanche to their footage, but MITs and the wider police service can usually gain permission from the administrators in minutes.

But Steph reports the Focus wasn't captured on any of the NESTS' cameras. Therefore, she's almost certainly confirmed its route – it drove the shortest possible from the house, directly to the woods.

My turn with the green dot. 'Right, let me tell you what I'm thinking. Thus far it's reasonable to assume two things: Rachel drove directly from her house to St Mark's Woods, and she drove there alone. But why would she drive to that particular location, at that time of night, in that weather? Did she go there simply to give herself time and space to calm down? If so, she met her killer by chance. Alternatively, she arranged to meet someone, and that meeting resulted in her death.'

So far, no disagreement. I move on. 'Doesn't matter which one it was, she met her killer in the car park, or somewhere between there and the lock-ups on Powderhall Lane. Maybe she walked to the lock-ups of her own accord, but I doubt it, given the terrain. I mean, why would she? Her shoes and clothing appeared to be relatively clean, so I can't imagine she tramped along a woodland path that would have been a sea of mud. Greg's analysis might say differently but I can't see it.'

'Important question, then,' says Jeff. 'If she died in that car park, how did she end up three hundred metres away at the Water of Leith?'

'There are only two options; she was carried, or she was transported there. Now, the autopsy will confirm her weight, but I've seen her, and I'd be surprised if she's less than nine and a half, ten stones. Carting a body that distance, at night, along muddy paths would be no easy task. And incredibly risky. Yes it was late, yes it was raining, but there's no guarantee he wouldn't have met someone.'

I'm back on the map. 'So I'm betting she was driven. Which brings up another issue, there's no direct route by road between the two locations. You all know the area. Because of the way the river twists and turns, to drive from A to B would mean going down one side of the river, about half a mile, crossing the bridge at Canonmills, and returning along the other side.'

'And you're convinced this would have been in the killer's vehicle?' says Steph.

'Well, it wasn't in hers. The floor mats and the carpets were spotless, not even damp. It's inconceivable that another person got into her car, killed her, drove her to the lock-ups, dumped her over the fence then reversed the journey. No, Rachel left her car where we found it. But let's check it out, Steph. See if you can track down any footage showing the Focus or indeed any other vehicle travelling that route.'

'Will do,' she says, and leaves quickly. Steph wouldn't be caught dead using TV clichés like *I'm on it.*

'Thinking about the husband for a minute,' says Jeff. 'Under the thumb or not, do you have any sense he killed her? Could he have driven their car away from the house with her inside, possibly already deceased?'

'Can't discount the possibility, but like I said earlier, we have no evidence to support that. However, no matter what the car or the autopsy throw up, we'll definitely be talking to him again.'

He nods. He knows as well as I do how often men kill their wives, no matter which one wears the trousers. I click my fingers. 'Actually, Andrew. Anything from Klaudia about the autopsy?'

'I'm afraid she had a backlog to deal with today, but we're first on the list tomorrow morning.'

Jeff's fidgeting in his seat. 'Sorry to sound like a dog with a bone, Dave. The neighbour's footage of the Focus exiting the driveway, is there any way we can tell if the driver was female?'

Dave wears a moustache from time to time and today it's

gracing us with its presence. He smooths it down before saying, 'I sent the images to one of the techs but there's nothing to enhance. It was still teeming down, and the driver wore a hoodie.'

I scan the case notes. 'Rachel was wearing a hoodie when she was found. Mid-grey in colour.'

Andrew pipes up. 'There's one question that's been bothering me all day. Where she was found, tangled up in all those bushes, why would the killer drop her there of all places? I mean, it certainly wasn't to hide her. Even without the bright orange coat, she was in plain view from the walkway on the other side of the river. And someone using the lock-ups would only have had to glance over the wall; she was right there.'

I shrug. 'Who knows? There's no indication he was in a panic, so maybe it was planned. He deliberately put her in a place that was easy to see but hellishly difficult to get her out of. As for why – well, who knows. But speaking about the lock-ups, have we tracked down the owners?'

Andrew defers to the younger of his two DCs, Crissi. She's Bangladeshi with a strong Scottish accent, has glossy dark hair, and if there was a competition for the most amazing eyes in Scotland, she'd be seeded straight through to the final. She reads from her notes, hardly glances up – takes her work extremely seriously, does Crissi. 'Ten lock-ups, but only eight owners – one gentleman owns three of them. Six of the eight owners haven't been there since before Christmas. That leaves two. One chap had his motorbike out for a run last weekend but hasn't been back since. The other owner was there the day before yesterday, Wednesday. He knew this storm was coming so he was there to fix a leak in the roof.'

'No joy there, then.' I guess a Scottish January isn't the best time of year to spend your leisure time pottering about in an unheated concrete block. 'It occurs to me we should also find out if any of the owners have any connection to the Fullers.'

Andrew leans to the side, murmurs to his colleague. Crissi nods, takes a note, gives me a single twitch of a smile and before I can draw breath, she's gone. I see Andrew turn half sideways, phone to his ear. Then, to me: 'That was Greg. The Focus is on its way to the lab.'

'That's good news, here's hoping it has some juicy secrets to give up. Now, moving on, we know Rachel had bank cards with her. Andrew, any activity on her accounts last night? And, supplementary question, any unusual transactions recently?'

'Ella's been looking at this, Boss.'

Ella is the other pool DC. Four or five years older than Crissi but with similar seniority, having joined the police in her late twenties. Tall and rangy, Ella is a fell runner in her spare time. She told me all about it one day, while we were having lunch; sounds like the ultimate form of masochism as far as I'm concerned. Ella's far more confident than her younger colleague, though, and her voice rings out across the room. 'Mrs Fuller didn't use any cards yesterday at all. Last time she used her credit card was five days ago, Monday. Bought a variety of items from a chemist on Elm Row. Her debit card, Tuesday, a coffee shop on Shandwick Place. I'll go and visit both places first thing in the morning. Now, re her finances, in addition to her current account she also has a savings account, a cash ISA, and a stocks and shares ISA.' She holds up a finger. 'But here's the interesting thing. The current account balance is just over £400 but the total balance in the other three accounts is not a kick in the backside off half a million pounds.'

Even if the incident room was fitted with shag pile carpet, a pin dropped right then would have sounded like Ginger Baker on cymbals.

I stare at her. 'Half a bloody million?'

'Well,' says Andrew. 'We'll definitely be paying Mr Fuller another visit.'

'Damn right, my boy. Thanks, Ella. But you know what's coming next.'

She laughs, holds up her PDA and stylus at eye height and pretends to tap the screen. 'Action Ella ... contact Mrs Fuller's bank ... discuss account balances.'

'Got it in one,' I say. 'But don't forget to include the word *immediately*.'

Five hundred thousand? This might put a different spin on things. Then Steph says, 'Boss, I know he's not currently a suspect but are we entitled to look into Edwin Fuller's accounts?'

I deliberately don't glance at Jeff while I consider the question; he'll expect me to make the call. 'This is a murder case so it would be both justified and proportionate to carry out financial checks on Edwin too. As you say, he's not a suspect but that amount of money is no small beer, and he doesn't have a corroborating alibi for the period covering the estimated time of death.' Now I check with my boss. 'Agreed?'

He sends back a firm nod. 'Agreed.'

'Will I cover that too?' says Ella.

'Yes. And ask Crissi to help you. Okay, one more thing. Dave, did anything come out of the canvass of the riverside apartments?'

'No. At that time, between seven and eight am, residents were up and about, getting ready for work and suchlike. But it was still dark outside, so no one saw anything. It was only when they spotted our flashlights on the other side of the river that word spread like wildfire, and they all started pressing their noses against the windows.'

Just as Dave stops speaking, the door swings open. It's

Greg. 'Sorry I'm a bit late, Mel. Just finished tidying up over at the car park.'

'No worries. Find anything exciting?'

'I hope so,' he says, holding up two evidence bags as he crosses the room.

# CHAPTER FOURTEEN

ONE OF GREG's evidence bags holds a leather wallet. A closer examination suggests it probably is tan, but it's soaked through, so it appears significantly darker. I point at the wallet. 'In the undergrowth?'

'Yes,' says Greg. 'It had fallen into a puddle.'

'And it's booked in?'

'It is.' This wallet is a piece of physical evidence – an 'exhibit' or a 'production' relating to our case. With all productions, it's vital we are able to state accurately where they've been at any time between when they are discovered and when they are brought to court as part of the prosecution's case against the defendant. We also need to be able to state who had the production in their possession at any point in time. The Scene Examiner's first task after discovery, therefore, is to log the item into our Productions Store, where it might even remain, safe and secure, throughout the investigation. Our store is managed and controlled by dedicated officers. If the item is unaccounted for at any point, the defence would argue it could have been tampered with and its veracity will be questioned. For example, could we confidently state the accused's DNA on the bloody knife was there when it was pulled from the victim's back? This is known as the 'Chain of Evidence' or CoE.

But Greg needed to bring it here, to enable us to investigate it further. So having just booked the wallet into the Production Store, he will immediately have booked it out again. Now we have it, we will complete a CoE, thereby accepting responsibility. And if we pass it on to someone else, they will do the same until eventually it's booked back in to the Production Store. At some point soon, we'll take photographs of the cards inside, meaning they don't have to be handled again.

I take it over to Ella. 'While you're speaking to Rachel's bank, can you check if any of the cards in here are linked to her accounts.' She reaches out, accepts the bag from me and updates the CoE. In days gone by, this meant completing never-ending forms, but Police Scotland are trialling a new system involving a phone app, with Quick Response, or QR codes printed on all our evidence bags. Ella uses her phone to scan the QR code on the bag, the app talks to a server in the Production Suite, and the server recognises from Ella's profile that she is now in possession of the evidence bag containing the wallet. Her phone beeps, and the CoE transfer from Greg to Ella is recorded.

Then Greg hands me the second evidence bag. Inside is a black smartphone, on the neat side, suggesting it isn't new. 'From the car?' I say.

'Yes. Hidden in a sock, inside one of her welly boots.'

'Prints?'

'One set. The points of similarity indicate they are highly likely to be Mrs Fuller's, but as we know, that can only be classed as opinion. Informed opinion, but opinion nevertheless.'

Greg's making a clear statement here. In recent years, doubt has been cast on the reliability of fingerprint evidence following several high-profile cases including one right here in Scotland involving a police officer whose misidentified print was *found* at a crime scene she had never entered. Partly as a result of this case, prints are now regarded by the courts as opinion rather than scientific fact.

The phone itself has seen better days, it's a bit bashed around the edges and has a hairline crack snaking diagonally down the screen from the top left corner. I grip the phone through the bag, hold the power button. When it finishes loading it goes straight to a security code, a job for the experts.

I turn to Ella again. 'Could you take this downstairs, please. I think Bob's on shift now. Explain I need to see what's on it; hopefully it won't present too much of a challenge.' Then I add, 'While you're there, ask where we are with Rachel's personal phone and her PC.'

'Righty-ho.' She picks up her phone again and taps the CoE app. When it beeps, she excuses herself and leaves the room.

*Downstairs.* When Jeff brought all the MITs into the Fish Tank, he moved heaven and earth to secure our own lab facilities for electronic comms and cybercrime detection, amongst other things. His argument was that by the nature of the crimes we investigate – and the clue is in the word *Major* – it would hardly make sense to have our analytical requirements battling for supremacy with all the other cases the Division handles. So, the sub-basement was gutted out, remodelled and all the latest toys were installed. The denizens, meaning our IT techs, come out in hives if they see daylight so they're happy as pigs in shit. And if we're in a hurry, we can always nip down and lean over their shoulders.

We have a bit more chat, but nothing new comes up. I'm

winding up the meeting when Ella comes back in with the burner. 'Jeez,' I say. 'That was bloody fast, even for Bob.'

'Not really. The security code was set to 9999.' That catches me by surprise but let's not count the teeth in a gift horse. 'Bob says to tell you Mrs Fuller's phone and PC have been fast-tracked so we're at the front of the queue. They'll do what they can tonight but realistically, it'll be tomorrow. And, re the burner, you've to pop down for a chat before you knock off.'

I thank her, then Jeff motions to say he's leaving, putting his hand to his ear in a *Phone me* signal. I nod, and he heads for the door. The phone is a Tesco Pay-As-You-Go, almost fully charged, with only a few icons on the home screen: Phone, Contacts, SMS, and Settings. I tap Contacts. I don't fall off my perch, there's only one listed. It's been named 'J', and I assume it's a person's initial.

I'm tempted to tap it, but I desist. Better if I do that under controlled conditions and preferably while I have access to our systems. I speak up. 'Right, folks. It's way past your bedtimes so let's call it a night. I'm off to check if Steph's found any interesting CCTV, and to see what Bob makes of this phone. Can we reconvene at 08:00 sharp, please? It's been a long day and tomorrow might be the same, so no going out clubbing. Okay?'

# CHAPTER FIFTEEN

'Night, Steph,' I say, as she slings her jacket over one shoulder and pushes the button to open the door. I have to say I'm surprised. She's just told me she checked CCTV all along the circuitous route from St Mark's Woods to Powderhall Lane and no vehicles made that specific journey between 22:00 last night and 06:00 this morning. *None?* I rationalise my disappointment. It was a terrible night, and the route's an unusual combination of quiet streets and changes of direction that few motorists would be in the habit of following, especially at that ungodly hour.

I trot downstairs and use my swipe card to access the mysterious world that is our Computer Crime Unit. Given this part of the building was once a jailhouse, the ceiling's only about two feet above my head. The room is lit only by desk lamps and the glow from about thirty monitors. There are only three techs still working, two on one side of the room and Bob over to my left.

As I pick my way across the floor, baulked at every turn by

assorted computing paraphernalia, Bob peers round the side of a monitor about the size of a plate glass window.

'Evening, Mel. Did you hire a diving bell to bring you all the way down here?'

I laugh. Bob's my go-to tech and fortunately for me, seems to be on shift no matter what time of day, or night, I need IT support or advice. I wheel a chair in and drop a viper's nest of cables onto the floor before parking my backside.

'Cheeky cow,' is the best I can come back with. But hey, I've been working for fourteen hours straight. Roberta Summers, Bob to everyone, is at least twice the average age of the rest of her IT team but what she doesn't know about digital forensics and computer related crime you could stick in your eye without experiencing the slightest discomfort.

Bob's a redhead, with not a tinge of grey. She swears blind she doesn't use hair dye, and if that's true I hate the woman. Unfortunate as, outside of my family, there's no one I'd rather spend leisure time with.

She pushes back and stretches her arms above her head. 'You'll be here about the burner. Have you tried the number yet?'

'Nah. I thought I'd wait 'til I was with you. Oh, by the way, I hear the access code had been set to 9999.'

'It was, and that's a bit odd. This is a fairly cheap phone but still, it does have the option to increase the number of digits in the code to six, including capital letters and special characters like exclamation marks. And if whoever set it had done that, we'd still be trying to break in halfway through next year.'

'Oh, well,' I say. 'Lucky us.' Then I lay the phone on the desk, tap the 'J', and listen to the number unobtainable tone. I cancel the call.

'Is there a "J" involved anywhere?' says Bob.

'The Fullers have a friend called Jack.'

'Is he a suspect?'

I waggle my hand. 'Not so far. But there could be some history between him and the deceased, let's just say.'

Bob angles one of her smaller screens; there are five, including the behemoth in the centre. 'As you would expect, the phone hadn't been used much. No calls listed, just some SMS. Beginning on Boxing Day, messages were exchanged between this burner and the contact, "J".' She clicks an icon. 'This is the full list. There are only twelve. I've coded them "J" for the contact, and "A" for the burner because it was in Rachel's car. And I've grouped the messages into what look like related exchanges. They're all incredibly brief, I have to say.'

26/12 _ 17:03 _ A (Burner) messages J (Contact) _ 'home, meet tonight @ 9?'
26/12 _ 18:26 _ J replies to A _ 'yes'
26/12 _ 21:07 _ A messages J _ 'ICI'

10/01 _ 16:42 _ A messages J _ 'tomorrow @ 9?'
10/01 _ 16:50 _ J replies to A _ 'yes'
11/01 _ 20:58 _ A messages J _ 'ICI'

17/01 _ 16:38 _ A messages J _ 'tomorrow @ 9?'
17/01 _ 16:47 _ J replies to A _ 'yes'
18/01 _ 21:09 _ A messages J _ 'ICI'

24/01 _ 16:42 _ A messages J _ 'tomorrow @ 9?'
24/01 _ 16:50 _ J replies to A _ 'not sure. tell you tom'

25/01 _ 16:19 _ A messages J _ 'can you make it tonight?'
25/01 _ 16:28 _ J replies to A _ 'no'

25/01 _ 21:59 _ A messages J _ 'must see you now. smw.
emergency!'
25/01 _ 22:02 _ A messages J _ 'ICI'

BOB TAPS the screen with the tip of her pen. 'To save you the
bother of working it all out, all the January messages, strangely
enough, are on Wednesdays and Thursdays.'

I scan the list. 'So, 10th and 11th, 17th and 18th, 24th and
25th. And it's always Rachel who kicks off the conversations.
An affair?'

'If it is, how come there are no emojis, no frivolities, no,
"Can't wait to get my hands on you, lover". Not exactly lust's
young dream, are they?'

'I suppose not. But then again, predictive text often throws
up the same words. I always put, "Homeward bound xxx".
Never change it, no need.'

'Three kisses? Jeez, romance isn't dead after all.' She hits
me with a sardonic expression then immediately brightens up.
'By the way, what's "smw"?'

'St Mark's Woods. It's where we found her car.' I run my
finger down the list. 'One oddity is that Rachel's Thursday
texts always finish with "ICI". Any idea what that is?'

'It could be text-speak, like LOL. But if it is, I've never
heard of it.'

'Me neither. I'll ask the young ones tomorrow. But what
can you tell me about locations?'

Bob clicks to pull up a map. Three red icons are pulsing on
the screen. They're numbered one, two and three, running
north to south. Her pen is back in action. 'As you said, Rachel
starts off every conversation, and cell mast triangulation
suggests they're all from her house – which is icon one. And,

now you've told me that "smw" is St Mark's Woods, that'll be icon two.'

'So, she texts him from her house, and the meeting place is the woods.' I point at icon three. 'Is that where his replies come from?'

'It is indeed, and it's a strange one. I know triangulation can't place a phone at a specific location, but it does seem to suggest the replies were sent from a point close to the Water of Leith.'

She zooms in the map, and I lean in closer. 'But that's an open area,' I say. 'As far as I know, there are no houses or other buildings nearby.' Bob switches to street view to prove the point. I turn to her. 'That is a bit weird.'

'As you say. But there's more. Because the time difference between her asking, and him replying is always the same. Eight or nine minutes.'

I stay quiet, while I marshal my thoughts. Always eight or nine minutes. Why?

I talk myself through some of the messages on Bob's list. 'In the afternoon of the day she was killed, she asked if he could meet her that night but he just replied no. Then she sent another message, from her house, at 21:59, saying it was an emergency. But he didn't reply. Then she sent the ICI thing from the woods, but he didn't reply to that either. So, the last message he actually sent her was at 16:28, and all he said was no.'

'Correct. And, once more, the phone signal for that message was triangulated to the same location, near the Water of Leith. That was thirty hours ago, and as far as we can tell, the phone's been switched off ever since. But I've put a trace on it for you. If or when it's switched back on, the Control will be alerted with location data, and your phone will be pinged simultaneously.'

'Thanks. Being honest, I didn't expect anything else.' I rub my eyes, I'm desperate for my bed.

'Now, regarding Mrs Fuller's personal phone, as you might imagine that took longer.' Bob reaches across her desk and hands me a sheaf of papers, held together by a bright pink paperclip. 'I've printed off some light bedtime reading for you – calls, SMS, emails, web browsing history. I've highlighted repeated contacts, but I haven't analysed the lists in depth.' She leans over and pats my forearm. 'Thought I'd let you have the pleasure.'

'You're all heart.' I yawn. 'And her PC?'

Bob points at a workbench that runs along the longest wall in the room. The entire surface is littered by heaven knows how many items of hardware, many of which are plugged into trunking that has every connection type known to man. I don't know which PC is Rachel's, and I'm struggling to care. 'All her devices are up in your office,' says Bob. 'I've copied what I need onto a clean hard drive, and I'm running file and data analysis routines that'll take several hours. Maybe more, depending on what they find. When are you back in?'

'Eight. But I'll have to tell Callum to kick me out of bed.'

She smiles. 'I'll be here by then. I'll give you a shout as soon as I have anything firm.' I make a huge deal of checking my watch, which causes her to laugh. 'You may well mock my attendance patterns, my dear, but fortunately I have eternal youth on my side. Now be off with you and give that gorgeous hubby of yours a big smacker from me.'

She examines me over the top of her glasses. 'Assuming you can stay awake that long.'

# CHAPTER SIXTEEN

Saturday 09:05

THE WOMAN STANDING in Edwin Fuller's doorway regards Andrew and me as if we were the last two morsels on her dinner plate and she's figuring out which one to spear with her fork. It's just after nine am. She's wearing a lilac zip-up fleece over blue and white checked pyjamas, and her dark hair is scraped back off her face. Her arms are tightly folded.

'I'm DI Cooper, this is DS Young. We need to speak with Edwin.'

'My brother's resting.'

Well, that answers my question about who she is, although Edwin didn't mention a sister last night. 'I can understand that, but I'll have to insist, Mrs ...'

'It's Ms actually. Fuller.'

Clearly, she'd love to tell us to take a hike but instead she shows us inside. We go into the living room, and she disappears off upstairs. I hear an exchange in low tones. The room isn't anywhere like as tidy as it was yesterday. The TV remote is upside down on the carpet and there are sticky rings on the coffee table. But, bonus: there's no sign of the little black cat. I take a few steps towards the kitchen, clock a half-empty bottle of vodka in the corner of the worktop. I wonder if our man tied one on last night.

Then, light footsteps descending. 'Edwin will be down in a couple of minutes.' She glances around, can't settle on anything. 'Listen. I apologise if I was rude when you arrived, but you know, he's my brother ...'

'Don't worry, Ms Fuller. We understand. This is a terrible situation, but I'd prefer to keep things as informal as possible.' I leave out *For the moment*. 'I'm Mel, and this is Andrew.'

She smiles for the first time but doesn't put any enthusiasm into it. 'Hayley. Edwin's younger sister. Can I offer you tea? Or coffee?'

We both say no to that. I ask, 'Will you be staying with him?'

She shrugs. 'I'm not sure. I don't want to leave him on his own, but he's made it pretty clear he doesn't want me here.'

Before I can ask why, the man himself appears. He hasn't changed his clothes; I wonder if he slept in them. He's unshaven and whereas yesterday he was neat and tidy, his tee shirt and trousers are stained in a few places, although I'd be surprised if he's eaten anything since we last saw him. He drags the back of his hand across his mouth. 'Need a drink.' Hayley begins to rise out of her seat, but he waves her away. He comes straight back, popping the ring pull on a can of Coke. Full fat. He takes a couple of swallows, burps, apologises, and clanks it down on the coffee table. He doesn't appear to notice the mess.

There's no question I'd rather speak with him privately, but this is a delicate balancing act. He's not accused of anything, we have no evidence he's involved in his wife's murder, and, in truth, I haven't any grounds to fuel my inherently suspicious nature. If Hayley doesn't butt in, I'm happy enough for her to stay while we talk.

'Edwin, you didn't call us with the name of your wife's employer,' says Andrew.

'No.'

If my colleague is surprised by Fuller's blunt response, he doesn't show it. 'We've gained access to files and emails on her PC. Does she work for Belvedere Advertising Ltd?'

He takes a second. 'That's right, yes. They bought out the previous lot.'

Andrew taps away on his phone. He'll be messaging Steph to ask her to contact Belvedere. Then I ask Edwin, 'Did Mrs Fuller make a will?'

He blinks at the lightning change of subject. 'We both did, at the same time. Why do you ask?'

'Who's your wife's main beneficiary?'

'Split between me and her sister. Again, why do you ask?'

'There are significant amounts of cash in her savings account and in her ISAs. Were you aware of that?'

'Of course. Most of it is the compensation payment from her accident.'

Hayley snorts at that. I glance over. If she folds those arms any tighter, she'll break a rib.

Edwin ignores his sister. He goes on to explain that Rachel's compensation claim against the biker's insurance company turned into a saga after there was an issue with her blood alcohol test. They claimed she'd been under the influence and thus had contributed to the accident by stepping out in front of their client. But Rachel had called on several witnesses who testified she'd only drank one glass of wine, and a small one at that. After the insurer's claim was thrown out they appealed, lost, and appealed a second time. It was six years before the case was finally settled in Rachel's favour.

'There's been a development,' I say. 'We've found your car. It was in the car park at St Mark's Woods. Do you know of any reason why she might have gone there?'

Edwin shakes his head. 'No. We've walked in those woods a few times. One of the paths takes you down to the Water of Leith.' He stops, covers his face with his hands. When he pulls them away there are tears streaming down his cheeks. 'Was she ... was that where she was ...?'

Hayley moves quickly, kneels beside his chair, takes his hand in hers. But he snatches his arm away. Her face falls and she pushes herself slowly to her feet. It's only a couple of steps to her chair but she turns her back on him. The dynamics are certainly interesting.

'We don't know,' I say. 'The car's at the lab but it'll be later today before I see their findings.'

Andrew slides an evidence bag out of his pocket. Shows Edwin the phone. 'Is this familiar to you?'

Edwin leans forward. Studies it. 'No.'

During this exchange, I'm distracted for a few seconds. I catch a hint of something in the air. I can't place what it is, but it seems incongruous to the time and place. I scout around, twitch my nose. No. Whatever it was, it's gone. I listen as Andrew explains the phone was in the car, hidden in her Wellington boot.

'You think it belongs to Rachel?' says Edwin.

Andrew doesn't answer that. He produces a piece of card. 'What about this mobile number, do you recognise it?'

Edwin takes the card, places it on the arm of his chair, pokes away at his phone. 'It's not one of my contacts.'

I glance at Andrew. We both stand up.

'Wait,' says Edwin. 'You haven't really told me anything. I mean, what happens now?'

I zip up my coat. 'I'm sorry, sir, but I have nothing concrete

to offer you. And until that changes I'm not prepared to speculate. But I'll keep in touch.' I pause. 'You declined my offer to
bring in a Family Liaison Officer, have you changed your mind
on that?'

He slumps back, appears to shrink into himself, and shakes
his head without looking at me.

I catch his sister's eye, jerk my head towards the door. As
we reach the outside, I stop and turn. 'Hayley, did you and
Rachel get on?'

She sighs. 'There's no point in sugar-coating it just
because the woman's dead. Rachel was an aggressive, egotis-
tical cow. She treated my brother like shit, and she's never
given a toss about me or my kids. They're her niece and
nephew but they might as well not exist. So, no. We never
even came close to being friends.' Her lip is trembling. 'But
no matter how she behaved, or what she did, no one deserves
to be murdered. So I hope you catch whoever did it. I
really do.'

'When was the last time you saw or spoke to either of
them?'

'I speak to Edwin most weeks on the phone, but I haven't
seen them since Boxing Day. They came to my place to give
the kids their presents, but they wouldn't stay for dinner. For
the kids' sake I wanted them to, but she said they needed to go
home. God knows why, they were going back to an empty
house. But that's how she was. Whenever they came to see us,
which wasn't often, she always found an excuse to escape as
quickly as she could.'

'And how were they that day?'

She makes a face. 'Normal. There was always a wee bit of
tension, she was never totally relaxed when we were all
together. Possibly jealous of me because I'm Edwin's sister, but
who knows.'

'And when you were speaking to your brother on the phone, how did he seem?'

'Fine. But when it's only the two of us he usually is.' She glances over her shoulder. 'Not right now, obviously.'

And as we walk along the path I can't help but wonder if there's something else going on between the two of them.

# CHAPTER SEVENTEEN

'HAYLEY,' said Edwin. 'There's nothing you can do here. You should go home, be with the kids.'

She loomed over him; arms folded. 'Have you seen yourself in a mirror this morning?' She bent down and picked the remote off the floor. 'And this place is a mess. I know you're not the tidiest person on the planet, but you can do better than this.'

'I'll tidy up when you go.'

Her lips formed a straight line. 'Fair enough. I get the message. I'll make you something to eat before I head off.'

'I'm actually not that hungry.'

She glared at him. 'I'm making you a meal. Whether you eat it or not is entirely up to you.' Despite Hayley's harsh words, she was desperate to give her brother a hug, but he'd thrown up the shutters. 'Edwin, please, why do you want rid of me? Listen, I can stay 'til tomorrow. The kids will be fine, they love sleepovers.'

He hesitated, then reached out and gently took her hand. 'I just want to be on my own, sis. I'll be fine. Honest.'

Those were the words that came out of his mouth. But in his head, he said *Because I've got things to do today to make damn sure I'm not done for murder, that's why.*

# CHAPTER EIGHTEEN

As we pull away from the kerb, I say, 'Is it just me, or is their relationship a bit odd?'

'I was wondering about that,' says Andrew. 'Maybe they're not all that close but then again, it looks like as soon as he told her about Rachel she dropped everything to be with him. Now it seems he doesn't want her here.'

'But why wouldn't he? Especially as she's the only close family he has.'

'Might be worth asking him, I suppose.'

We both fall silent before I remember I have a question. 'Incidentally, did you notice a faint aroma in the room?'

'Well, he hadn't showered.'

I tut. 'Not that type of aroma, fool.'

'What then?'

'It's hard to say. It was ... something.'

Andrew slows down for a roundabout, checks right, then accelerates. He clicks off the indicator. 'I've begun to realise we have these conversations quite often. Or, to be more accurate, you have them with me. And the only problem is, I usually have absolutely no idea what you're on about.'

I'm tempted to nip the skin on his arm, but a crash would be more than a tad embarrassing.

'What's next on the agenda?' he says.

'I'm heading back to the Fish Tank. Time to contact the lovely Klaudia, and call Greg about the forensics.'

We stay silent for a while, which gives me time to ponder. My jury's still out on Edwin Fuller but, being fair to the man, there's nothing to suggest he's involved. And based on the brief chat we had on the doorstep with his sister, Rachel's personality and her relationships with a range of people do seem to be consistent. Hayley appears to be pretty straightforward but Edwin's attitude to her is a little off. Clearly there's something behind that, I just don't know what it is. Yet.

We turn into Queen Charlotte Street; our HQ is on the corner. The road surface here is constructed from cobblestones, and I've always found the rumble as a car moves over the blocks to be strangely comforting. They make a completely different sound when it's wet but still, it makes me feel at home. In one way, we're fortunate that a decent number of Edinburgh's streets have retained this surface, but I grimace as I recall being a front seat passenger in a high-speed chase on a drizzly night up in the New Town. My colleague totally misjudged a corner leading onto Great King Street and we slid all the way across the junction on glistening cobbles with zero traction. There was nothing we could do apart from brace ourselves and wait for the metallic crump as we smacked sideways into two parked cars.

As Andrew pulls up, Steph comes out of the station and crosses the pavement towards the car. She sweeps the passenger door open with a flourish and performs the worst curtsey I've ever witnessed. 'You'd have made a terrible butler,' I say, clambering out. 'Where are you off to now?'

Steph hops into the passenger seat. 'I've lined up interviews for Andrew and me with three of Mrs Fuller's friends, the ones Edwin calls the coven. Then the school to meet his colleagues. I'll keep you posted.'

As they move away, my phone beeps. A message from Bob.

*Finished with the PC. Gimme a shout ASAP*

ASAP? That sounds intriguing. I ping an immediate response.

*Be right down*

# CHAPTER NINETEEN

EDWIN WAS GLAD WHEN EARLIER, Hayley had finally relented and returned home. The drive would take her the guts of an hour; she promised to text, to let him know she'd arrived safely. She'd made him lunch, which he regarded with distaste but as soon as he closed the door behind her, he hurried into the kitchen and wolfed it down. He left one salad tomato that he cut in half then picked it up and squeezed it. The juice and a few seeds squirted across the surface of the table; a splash landed on the hem of his already stained tee shirt. He smeared his thumb through the mark, satisfied he'd made it worse.

He stood up, leaving the remnants of the meal where they lay then stepped out into the hall and stood in front of a full-length mirror. Unshaven, unwashed and untidy. Precisely the effect he was aiming for. He sniffed his left armpit, there was a definite whiff. The right one didn't seem so bad. *Give it time*, he thought. *Give it time.*

His phone buzzed in his pocket. *Niall.* When Edwin had ended the call with him last night, he'd instantly felt guilty for lying to his oldest friend. Now Edwin considered not answering but Niall would likely show up at the door. 'Hey, man,' he said, and left it there.

The conversation, if it could be called that, lasted no more than three minutes. Niall asked how he was; Edwin said okay. Niall asked if there had been any progress; Edwin said not really. Niall asked if he should come over; Edwin said probably not.

Edwin wasn't blunt or rude to his friend, he simply batted back all the questions in the same dull tones. But when he sensed the call was coming to an end he brightened up and said he'd be pleased to hear from Niall the following day. But he wasn't to come over. 'Sorry, but I wouldn't be good company.'

So, yes. He did feel guilty, but once all this was over, he'd pick up with Niall again and eventually, Rachel and his marriage would fade into the past.

That was his plan.

Such a pity that plans don't always come to fruition.

# CHAPTER TWENTY

'I'M GUESSING from your message you've found something interesting,' I say.

Bob takes her glasses off and smiles up at me. 'Depends what you mean by interesting.'

'Oh, I don't know. How about a video of the murderer confessing?'

'Ah, that would be a stretch. But we did find this.' She lifts a sheet of A4 and lets it float across the surface of her desk.

I pull up a chair. The paper contains text. Two paragraphs, about a dozen lines. I read it. It's a bit of a ramble. I reread it, take my time.

*I don't even know why I'm typing this, maybe 'cos what happened earlier was so bloody ridiculous, so strange, so stupid, so risky, so lots of things. Screwing in the back of his truck, in a car park, at my age, what was I thinking about? ANd it's a bloody pigsty, he could at least have cleaned it up a bit, 'cos it's not as if he didn't know it was going to happen, WE ... didn't know it was going to happen. 'Cos he's been angling for it for years, ever since he tried it on before, at that party, in the kitchen, when everybody was rat-arsed. THen dear old Eddie staggered in, and threw up in the sink, one minute later and we'd have been caught. 'Cos I wasn't stopping him, no way, I was too far down the road.*

*Two weeks later, Screw 2, the sequel, just as good, just as exciting as the first time, but this has got to stop. After the next time, 'cos there will be a next time, I'll tell him enough's enough, these things only end one way, badly. So, three screws and you're out. Ha! I'm so funny.*

'Wow!' I glance up. 'Can you tell when this was written?'

Bob spins her chair and points at her wall-planner with her pen. 'It's a Microsoft Word document, and the file data indicates it was saved twice, on two different dates. Working back, the second date was a week past Thursday, the 18th. And the first date was one week earlier, the 11th. In my humble opinion, considering how it's worded, it's reasonable to assume she wrote para one after the first time she hooked up with this guy, and para two after the second time. Oh, and guess what?'

'Go on, then.'

'The document's filename was only one character: "J".'

My eyes widen. 'The same as the contact on the burner?'

'Give that girl a coconut.'

'So, all I have to do is find this contact, it's likely he's "J", he's the person she's written about and texted from the burner, and probably the last person to see her alive. Find him, and I'll have my murderer.'

Bob laughs. 'Yeah, if only it was that easy.'

'As you say, if only.' I read the two paragraphs again. 'What's with the two capital letters at the start of some of the sentences?'

'It's probably because she's held the shift key down a shade too long while she's typing, ends up with two caps instead of one, and doesn't bother to fix it. There's a setting in Microsoft Word that stops it happening, but I checked her PC; the setting's turned off.'

'Intentionally?'

'Impossible to say. But, I do know she deliberately hid the file on her PC.'

'Why, what did she do?' I regret the question as soon as I ask it.

She smiles. 'Bless you, my dear. I haven't even started to explain, and you look terrified already. Do you know what a jpeg is?'

I scoff. 'Of course I do. It's an image file, a photo.'

'That's right. There are other image file types but jpeg's the most common.' She points at the paper. 'But that's from a Word document so it *should* have a filename ending .docx. That's called the file extension. She altered it to .jpg then moved the file into a folder with all her other photos. All she had to do when she needed access to it was change the extension back to .docx and Word would be able to open it.'

I close my eyes. Think. 'I'm struggling to understand. If this was in a folder, with loads of other jpegs, what made this one stand out?'

'One of the things our analytics look for is a file whose content doesn't match the extension. This file didn't contain any pixels.'

'It wasn't all that well hidden then.'

'To be fair, your average computer user would probably never have found it. But we have the technology, as they say.'

'Good spot. Anything else?'

'No. Her PC has a standard system, similar to most you'd find in any homeworking environment. It only has one specialist piece of software, which allows her to access files and databases on her company's servers. The hard drive holds all her personal files: photos, music, all that good stuff. She doesn't store anything in the cloud.'

'Nothing? Is that normal?'

'Yeah. Most people are Luddites. They don't understand the cloud, and don't back up their data – even in this day and age.'

'Thanks, Bob. You're a star.' I grab the paper and stand up. 'But you know that.'

She waves me away and turns back to her screen, the one that's half the size of China.

And I head off to find Tobias.

———

MY GERMAN COLLEAGUE has his gaze fixed on Rachel Fuller's PC, immersing himself in her personal and business lives. On the desk beside him are her phone and the burner. He knows the drill: sift through her calls, SMS, emails sent and received, social media, and her browsing history for anything noteworthy. Tobias is concentrating on this week, and Thursday in particular.

'How's your girlfriend settling in with her new job, Tobias?'

He takes off his glasses, knuckles his right eye. 'This is only the third week, but it is going well so far, I think.' He grins, perfect white teeth against a dark skin. 'One evening Nathalie said to me, "Tobi, what is a bloody part-timer?"' Then we both have a chuckle while he explains about the presenteeism culture in Nathalie's department, and the reaction from her colleagues when the poor dear had the temerity to shut down her PC and pull on her coat at her contracted stopping time.

'She thinks,' he says, 'they are inefficient and if they spent less time on the *Daily Mail* website they could finish their work on time.'

We chat some more then I show him the Word document and explain about Bob's theory concerning the two caps at the beginning of certain words. He'll check for this curiosity across her communications and see if he can identify any other inconsistencies. I don't think there's much he can do with the burner at this stage, but there's definitely a pattern relating to Thursdays.

I'd been planning to contact Greg, but when I reach my desk there's a message from the man himself. I make the call. 'What news from the sites, Greg?'

'And top of the morning to you too, Melissa.'

I ignore him so he blusters a bit then regains an even keel. I smile to myself; I seem to recall Gregory pulling my ponytail when we were about six. Or maybe I made that up.

Greg switches into formal reporting mode, and I let him talk. 'First, her clothes. Joggers and a hooded sweatshirt, brand and colour generic, widely available in major retailers. Underwear, Marks and Sparks, plain cotton, black. Her coat, as described by her husband, branded *Her Style*; they have a store on George Street. Shoes, casual, cream with blue soles, from the same shop. Traces of soil in the treads of both soles, consistent with samples taken from St Mark's Woods. A vertical scuff on the toe of her right shoe matches the coping stone on the wall at the lock-ups, caused most probably when she was dropped over said wall. Her jogging bottoms and shoes are clean apart from a few splashes of mud; I would say it's highly unlikely she walked from the car park to the lock-ups.'

'Could the rain have washed the mud away? She was probably hanging there for several hours.'

'Possibly from the soles of her shoes, they're synthetic. But mud stains on cotton joggers wouldn't wash away without detergent.' I stay silent and he takes that as a signal to move on. 'Going back to her underwear, early indications from the lab suggest DNA materials on her pants and her body – specifically her stomach, groin, thighs and buttocks – stem from two different people. And the gender markers indicate they are both male, one of whom is extremely likely to be her husband.'

'Two? She'd had sex with two men?'

'We can't state that. As we both know, secondary transfer can happen quite innocently so just because this man's DNA is on Mrs Fuller's body does not mean he was involved in her murder.'

'I don't suppose we know who he is?'

'No match on the national database.'

That's a pity, but rarely do we find perpetrators quite so easily. I ask Greg to move on. 'No jewellery apart from wedding and engagement rings on her left hand, and a plain gold band, right hand, fourth finger. No watch, and no other accessories. Traces of her blood on the spike that impaled her leg, and on the foliage. But I agree with Dr Grześkiewicz, only traces, so she didn't die there.'

How annoying, his pronunciation of Klaudia's surname is bang on. That's him off my Christmas card list. I sigh. 'And any evidence from the ground at the lock-ups?'

'Nothing. The whole place was completely awash. If your murderer was waiting for the ideal conditions to conceal his tracks, he couldn't have chosen a better time. The rain and wind were not our friends on this occasion.'

'Okay, Greg. Now, what about the car park?'

'Well, ditto for evidence on the ground. No footprints, no tyre tracks, no trace evidence outside the car. But, inside, we found fingerprints and DNA identifiable as belonging to both Mr and Mrs Fuller. Also fingerprints and DNA for other parties in the passenger seat and the rear seats, as you would expect in most cars.'

Greg probably hears me drawing in a breath but jumps in before I can speak. 'Sorry, Mel. The second man's DNA wasn't present in the Fuller's car.' He waits 'til I stop swearing before continuing. 'The interior, including the boot, contained nothing untoward with the exception of the burner phone you already have. By the way, was there anything interesting on it?'

'Several text conversations between it and one other contact, as yet unidentified. Replies triangulated from an open location down near Inverleith. So, short answer: no.'

Greg's silence is long enough for him to register that before he picks up again. 'The car's exterior relating to tyres, wheels, chassis, sills and lower bodywork have mud spatters that also match soil samples from St Mark's Woods. In my opinion, the amount of mud is consistent with it being driven once into that car park, while also bearing in mind the cleansing effects of wind-driven rain. But, there is no mud inside the car so that suggests Mrs Fuller exited and didn't get back in. Neither did another person. And, while we're talking about the interior, there's no evidence of heavy detergent use, or vacuuming marks on the carpets or upholstery. My interpretation is the car is normally kept in a reasonably clean condition.'

I nod to myself. 'So, considering the timings for the whole night and the condition of her vehicle, her clothing and her shoes, we can be reasonably certain she spent time in another vehicle. And she was killed in that vehicle before being transported to the lock-ups.'

'I would say so, yes.'

'And what's the current status of both sites?'

'They're still secure but I don't believe there's anything else to be found. I'd recommend maintaining security at the lock-ups for now, but we can release the car park.'

I think for a few seconds. 'Can we keep things as they are for another twenty-four hours, just in case?'

'Sure thing.'

'Thanks, Greg. Appreciated.' I pause for a couple of beats. 'Right, I'm off to consult with my favourite pathologist.'

# CHAPTER TWENTY-ONE

Now that Hayley had gone home to Glasgow and he'd put Niall off for a while, Edwin had some breathing space. It was time to move things on a stage.

Wearing a pair of yellow kitchen gloves, which he struggled to get his hands into, he opened the cupboard below the stairs and pulled out a large green canvas bag with white piping and a dry cleaner's logo. Inside was a heavy-duty polythene bag containing a hillwalking backpack. The canvas bag and the backpack had both been through a sixty-degree machine wash three times, separately. He opened the backpack inside the polythene and used the canvas bag to carry both of them out to the garage, which he accessed from the side door. He pulled the door to and clicked on the lights. From a hook on the wall, he took down a bicycle work stand and positioned it in the centre of the floor. Two bikes hung from the rafters by their rear wheels: a racer with narrow tyres and drop handlebars, and a hybrid. He missed having a mountain bike but once the Cannondale had done its job, he had no choice but to get rid of it. If everything worked out, he'd replace it in time. He lifted the hybrid down and attached it to the stand. Now it was positioned at a comfortable working height with its wheels clear of the floor.

A hybrid bicycle combines the features of a racing bike and a mountain bike and is suitable for riding over a variety of terrains. So, its tyres are not as chunky as a mountain bike, but it has a more upright riding position than a racer. Fast on the streets and pavements, yet capable of handling light off-road surfaces, it was ideal for the tasks he needed to accomplish later that day. Edwin lifted his toolbox onto the workbench and began to make adjustments to the bike, removing a few standard components and adding others that certainly were not.

Less than an hour later he was back inside the house and ready for what lay ahead. He'd stored all the equipment he would need in the backpack, which, if the police walked in now and found it, would send him directly to jail without passing go. But he'd reduced the chances of that happening by temporarily hiding it on the other side of the fence between his house and his neighbour's. Olive was well into her eighties, lived on her own and had slowed down a lot even in the past few months. There was zero likelihood of her leaving the house and only minimal chance of a visit from her daughter, a pinched-faced streak of misery who looked like a vulture and who, in recent times, had been acting like one.

He hadn't laid out thermal and waterproof biking gear; it was all to hand. But one item he wouldn't be wearing that night was his yellow Hi-Vis.

# CHAPTER TWENTY-TWO

WHEN HE WAS ABOUT TEN, my son wandered up to me while I was lounging about on the couch and said, 'Mum, what's an auto-spy?' Connor was smack bang in the middle of his James Bond period, so it took me a minute to figure out he meant autopsy. It took about the same time again before I stopped laughing, while he stood there, waiting patiently, with a *Whatever* expression on his face. So, in line with the strategy my husband and I had recently devised when my daughter, aged twelve, began asking questions designed to embarrass-her-parents-at-every-conceivable-opportunity, I explained to Conor what an autopsy was. I omitted the graphic detail, but he was satisfied with my answer and off he trotted.

But, seven years later, the memory is as clear as a bell so I'm in high spirits as I sit in front of Dr Klaudia's desk, waiting to hear the results of Rachel Fuller's *auto-spy*. If only the diminutive pathologist hadn't decided she must reread her entire report before she tells me what's in it. But today, I am the epitome of calm demeanour, a goddess of tranquillity. I too can wait patiently. Until I become seriously pissed off, that is.

Just in time, Dr Klaudia clears her throat and speaks. 'The deceased, Rachel Fuller, is female: confirmed. Age forty-two, height 168 centimetres, weight 64.5 kilogrammes. The time of her death can only be estimated at between 23:00 Thursday January 25th, and 03:00 Friday, January 26th.'

I open my mouth to speak but she sticks a palm up and states: 'Low temperatures and wet weather delay the onset of rigor mortis. High wind-chill would have been a factor but to counterbalance those, the deceased was sheltered by the under-growth, and she was wearing warm clothing.'

This time I widen my eyes. Keep going, Doc.

'Rachel Fuller died as a result of strangulation ...'

When she starts droning on about petechial haemorrhages, facial congestion and fractured small bones in Rachel's neck, it's my turn with the flat palm. 'The fact she was strangled is all I need to know, Doctor.' Now I smile, and I give it big licks. 'So, we can both save a bit of time, eh?'

Her eyes cloud over, and her brow drops an inch. As a junior DC, I gulped down all this supporting information like an osprey's chick but countless pathology reports in the inter-vening years have given me an excellent base knowledge. So, these days, only unusual or outlandish medical explanations will perk me up in my seat. I'm still smiling but it's becoming a strain. 'Did she die where she was found?'

Klaudia studies her notes, I've no idea why. 'Before she reached the locus, she had been deceased for a period of approximately thirty minutes.' Klaudia pauses. 'Would you like me to explain why I believe that to be the case?'

Bless her. I expect this will have something to do with livid-ity, but I hit her with my most encouraging expression. 'Yes, please.'

'This concerns Post Mortem Hypostasis, more commonly known as lividity. Because it is obvious that blood supply ceases to move around the body once the heart has stopped pumping, blood will settle in direct response to gravity. So, if the body is positioned on its left side, and it is on a firm surface, any blood left in the body will gravitate towards that surface and that side of the body.'

Klaudia seems to sense I'm beginning to shift in my seat but I'm not sure she's capable of speeding up. In a rare bout of generosity, I remain silent and cut her some slack, as long as her point is not simply about blood settling in a corpse.

'Lividity, as I've described it, begins to work through the deceased within thirty minutes of their heart stopping and can last up to twelve hours. But the key point here is that lividity can be altered by moving the body within, approximately, the first six hours of death. Through my examinations this morning, I have observed initial signs in the deceased's lower back, and on her left side, before finding significant and more permanent levels in her upper body. And by that I mean chest, shoulders and neck.'

I lean forward, elbows on the front edge of her desk. She edges back as if I've invaded her precious inner sanctum. 'So, to confirm, after she died it's possible that Rachel Fuller was laid on her back, then on her side for a period of up to thirty minutes, before she was dropped into the upside-down position, where she was found. Yes?'

She studies her papers before she replies. 'I am driven by science, not speculation ...' I wait to see what she says next. I hope I don't have to scream at her. 'But you have made a reasonable assumption.' She spits out the last word as if it were coated in angostura bitters.

I sit back, let my gaze wander across the wall above her head. I wonder if this might alter the timeline. 'We know she was strangled, but can you elaborate any further?'

'The evidence suggests she was attacked from behind, and from a position higher than she.'

'So, he was taller?'

'I cannot state for certain her attacker was male, but the strength required to both subdue and strangle Mrs Fuller would strongly suggest that to be the case. I also cannot state they were taller. The evidence indicates they were in a higher position. They could be taller, or standing above her on a step, or on a slope.'

'Kneeling on a bed?'

'That is also possible.'

While I think about that, Klaudia continues with her report. 'The deceased suffered three broken fingernails: left hand index, right hand index and right hand middle. There are scratch marks to her throat that are consistent with the likely positions of the same fingernails.'

This makes sense. A victim of strangulation will, in most circumstances, panic and try to free themselves by grabbing at the ligature. But by then it is probably too tight, and they are beginning to lose consciousness. A person highly trained in self-defence might have the presence of mind to target their attacker instead. Not that long ago we had a case where a would-be murderer turned up in A&E with a four-inch black patent stiletto heel pierced vertically through his instep and out through the sole of his foot. The case was a done deal when a glamorous blonde carrying the heel-less shoe limped into the station to report the attack. Moral of the story: if you're planning to strangle someone, wear stouter shoes. And, make sure your intended victim isn't an Iraqi war vet.

'The ligature, Klaudia. What was it made from?'

'An electrical cable, with a soft Polyvinyl Chloride sheathing ... apologies, I should have said PVC.' I wave a hand, pretend I knew that. 'I was able to extract a sample from beneath her right index fingernail.'

'Anything else under there? Like skin?'

'Not skin. White cotton. Your colleague, Greg Brodie, confirms it is from a bed sheet or a pillowcase.'

'You're positive about that?'

'It is Mr Brodie who is positive. The material has a high thread count, five hundred threads per square inch.'

If I could whistle, I would. 'You don't find those in every house.'

'Quite,' says Klaudia. I swear that was almost a smile.

She moves on to the next page in her report. 'Prior to Rachel's death, she had had sexual intercourse: oral and vaginal. Traces of lubricant were detected, so her partner wore a condom. Generic, impossible to determine the brand. No signs of violence, lesions or tears. No defence marks, no other bruises on her body that can be related to sexual activity.'

'Therefore, consensual?'

She looks up. 'I can only speculate but yes, I believe so.'

'Klaudia, the lab results have shown DNA materials on Mrs Fuller's body from two different men. Did your examination pick up any suggestion she'd had sex recently with two partners?'

She tilts her head, gives that some thought. 'Had there been two brands of condom, or two semen samples, then perhaps. But no.'

I stand. Walk behind my chair. Resting my palms on the hard black plastic, I conjure up a series of images. A couple having sex. He's kneeling behind her. He's taller. He loops a ligature, electrical cable, round her throat, pulls it tight. She grabs at the cable, breaks three fingernails, scrapes her skin, but her nails don't puncture the surface. Why not? A layer of material is in the way. Cotton, with a high thread density. A sheet?

A pillowcase? Yes, a pillowcase. He used it as a hood and before she could react he added the ligature. Pulled it tight over the material.

'The cotton, Klaudia, did you find traces in her mouth or in her airways?'

'Only on the gum, below her front teeth.'

I'm beginning to warm to her. We're on the same side, we're both searching for the truth and we both want justice for Rachel Fuller. 'Her husband said she drank a large gin and tonic, and wine with her evening meal.'

She flicks through her paperwork. 'Yes. Alcohol, bread, salad, meat, cheese: all present. Her meal was not fully digested, so it had been consumed in the few hours prior to her death.'

I rock my head from side to side a couple of times. 'The alcohol. It's highly likely the gin was a house measure, much stronger than would be served in a pub. Then she drank some wine and drove within two or three hours. Was she over the blood alcohol limit?'

'She was. In Scotland it is 50 mg per— Of course, I apologise, you know what it is. Yes, toxicology tests confirm she was approximately three times over the legal driving limit.'

Over the past thirty years, driving under the influence has become far less socially acceptable, but we stop and charge enough drivers to know the problem hasn't disappeared. Maybe Rachel just took a chance, maybe she was in such a state when she left the house that she didn't stop to think about it. But still, I'm surprised she was so far over the limit. 'Did toxicology reveal any narcotics in her system?'

'No.'

I reach down for my bag. 'Anything else significant you need to tell me?'

'No.'

Tell you what, my gradually thawing Polish pathologist can be a woman of few words when it suits her. 'Okay. Thank you for the moment, Klaudia. You've been most helpful.'

She moves to join me at the door. Sticks out her hand. 'Detective Inspector Cooper.'

I return her grip; remarkably firm for one so petite. 'It's Mel. Or Melissa, if you prefer.'

I smile, and as I'm turning away she says, 'g–jzesh-kee–eh-vitch.'

I swallow. Give it a go. Completely screw up that second syllable.

Now it's her turn to give out the encouraging looks. 'Keep practicing.' A pause. 'Melissa.'

# CHAPTER TWENTY-THREE

It's well into the afternoon when Andrew and Steph arrive back in the office. Perfect timing. I call everyone through to the incident room for a review of the day's events so far, but I don't disturb Tobias while he's working on Rachel's media. It's a task that will benefit from train of thought.

I power up the wallboard and dim the room lights. It's dark outside so the glass wall I'm facing appears to be solid, shiny and black. The side wall of a neighbouring building is about twenty metres away, but any windows were bricked up aeons ago. I use a tablet to open the investigation file, and all the items I logged yesterday appear on the wall in their saved positions. I tap an icon on the left, and an open field appears, which resembles a blank notebook page. At the top I type: Rachel Fuller murder – salient factors (1). Now it's ready for me to create a list.

'Okay, folks,' I say. 'In rough chronological order, here's all the information we've gathered so far. Please chip in with updates from your activities today. I'll start with some news from Bob concerning the burner found in Rachel's car, her PC, and her own personal mobile.' Then I explain about the texts between the burner and an unknown contact 'J', that appear to relate to Rachel meeting someone in St Mark's Woods on three successive Thursdays, including the night she died. This becomes the first item on the list on the wallboard. 'And before anyone asks, we've no intel to suggest "J" is Jack McCafferty. But it could be. Our problem is, this other phone is switched off so there's bugger all we can do 'til it comes back on again.' At this point I remember to ask them what 'ICI' might stand for, but all I see are shaking heads, so I don't linger on it.

'Now, as far as Rachel's own devices are concerned, Tobias is trawling through them just now. Crissi and Ella, I should explain that Tobias is a top-notch Crime Analyst, so this is right up his street.' They both smile and nod, and I move on to display the Word file Bob found. It generates some amusement, but I suggest we put it to the side for now because I know Tobias will be looking at it in more detail.

Then I describe how Andrew and I visited Edwin first thing this morning, that we met Hayley, and that their relationship seemed a little odd. Also, that Rachel's will splits her estate equally between her husband and her sister, and Edwin knew his wife's bank balances totalled mid-six figures. 'We know how often money is the motive, but, Ella, Crissi, anything new crop up in either of their accounts?'

They both begin to speak at once, so Ella defers to her younger colleague. Crissi flicks her tongue along her top lip. 'There's nothing about Mr Fuller's bank accounts that strike me as unusual. He pays the main household bills like phone, utilities, council tax and insurances. He doesn't have a mortgage; but I guess that's not a surprise as the house was left to him. He does make a lot of cash withdrawals from his current account but, on the other hand, not too many debit card payments.' She glances round the table. 'So, I suppose they balance each other out. He maintains his current account around or above the £12,000 mark, probably because he earns cashback if it stays above £10,000.' She sips from a sports' bottle. 'Moving onto his credit card, the balances over the past twelve months have all been less than £1,000, and he pays them off every month.'

'And income against expenditure, Crissi?'

'In ten of the past twelve months there was a surplus, which he transferred into a personal pension plan. He uses an investment platform known as Trident, but apart from three ISAs and the pension, he has no other investment vehicles.'

'And the balances?'

She checks her notes. 'He keeps the ISAs topped up to the maximum, so £60,000. And, as of today, he has £281,673 in his pension plan.'

I drum my fingertips along my top lip. 'So, he's not as well off as his wife but even if he did inherit half her estate, he still wouldn't be what you'd call rich.'

Crissi holds up a finger. 'On that, the house is owned jointly by Edwin and his sister, Hayley. An online estate agency recently valued a similar property in the area at just less than £600,000.'

Andrew taps his pen beside some figures he's jotted down. 'His liquid assets are about £340k. If the house was sold today, he'd pocket £300k. His share of Rachel's estate, another £300k. That's almost a million. Does that give him a strong enough motive?'

I rock my hand from side to side. 'If we suspected him, possibly. But he does seem to be quite well off in his own right. That said, at this stage I'm certainly not ruling it out.' I thank Crissi, who bats those wondrous eyelashes a couple of times and closes her PDA. 'Ella, what about Rachel's bank?'

'Spoke to them earlier. They referred back to notes from

meetings she had with their financial adviser, and everything's legit. An initial lump sum deposit from her compensation award, then gradual diversification into ISAs.'

'Only ISAs? No other investments?'

'No. Their records say other investment products were offered but declined.'

'And the bank cards from her wallet?'

'Yes. Definitely hers.'

'Hmmm,' I say. So far, so normal. 'Right, Steph. Your turn. Rachel's employer?'

No one bats an eyelid when Steph bounces to her feet. We all know she finds it impossible to sit still for long. 'Spoke to her boss at lunchtime, he's based in Newcastle. Totally shocked at the news, as you can imagine. He said Rachel was extremely conscientious, highly competent, had been doing the job a long time. He's been her manager for over ten years, and she'd been in post for a couple of years before that. They speak at least once a week, usually on a Monday morning, and they have monthly team meetings by video conference. The weekly call is just a catch-up but sounds like it's a fairly informal discussion. He explained he can read updates from their systems if he chooses to, but he prefers to chat.'

'Did he speak to her last Monday?'

'He did, and she gave no indication there was anything wrong. She kept all her appointments during the week, sent client updates on time, no undue delays to answering emails or WhatsApp, nothing untoward that he can remember. Oh, and he confirmed Friday was an admin day. She wouldn't normally have appointments unless a project had gone pear-shaped. But nothing did, it was just a standard week.'

'So, workwise, no issues at all?'

'Nothing. I did ask if she'd ever had any discipline issues. He said absolutely not. He admitted Rachel could be direct at times, but her clients thought she was brilliant. He also told me she got on well with the other members of her team although being spread all over the UK, they didn't meet up too often. He's not looking forward to telling them what's happened. Or her clients, for that matter.'

'What about Thursday, did she have any meetings?'

Steph scans through her notes. 'Yes, three. Two by video conference and one out in Livingston in the afternoon. I spoke to all three, nothing abnormal about her behaviour.'

My eyes flick around the table as I think about that. 'Edwin said she came home in a mood that afternoon.'

'Yeah, I remembered that, so I specifically asked the Livingston client how she was. They were tying up a contract, so she was definitely in good humour.'

'From memory, Edwin told us he arrived home at half four and she was already there. And grumpy. What time did she leave Livingston?'

'She was signed out of the building at 15:26.'

'So, whatever caused her to be grumpy happened in that hour.' I ponder. If she left Livingston at half three, she'd have been just ahead of the rush hour, so the timings fit in. I sigh. None of this proves anything, it's merely background data. Still, it's ticked a few boxes.

Steph drops back into her seat and crosses her legs, virtually in the same movement.

'Okay,' I say, 'what's next? Oh yes, this morning I met with the lovely Klaudia.' I look up, not quite sure which member of my team sniggered, so I give them all the evil eye. 'Anyway,' I say, labouring the word, 'my new favourite pathologist confirmed Rachel Fuller died sometime between 23:00 Thursday and 03:00 Friday. Cause of death – strangulation. The lividity in her body suggests she was moved around in the period immediately following her death, so she didn't die at the lock-ups. Klaudia believes Rachel's killer was behind her, and in a higher position when he strangled her. It appears he pulled a pillowcase over her head, then a ligature – an electrical cable with a PVC sheathing, traces of which were discovered under her fingernails. At some point in the evening, she'd had sex, which Klaudia believes was consensual. Her partner wore a condom.'

'And there was a condom in the bin in the Fuller's bedroom when we were there,' says Andrew.

'There was. And I still think that was a bit odd.' I shake my head, try to clear some space inside. 'Last thing,' I say, as I add it to the list on the board, 'is when Mrs Fuller drove away from their house on Thursday night, having consumed gin and wine, she was approximately three times over the limit.' That revelation changes the atmosphere in the room; we do not like drink drivers. 'Okay, I'll give you a rest from my dulcet tones for a while. Andrew, how did you get on this morning?'

He swipes his PDA. 'Steph and I visited the gym first, then the café. According to the people at the gym, Edwin's been a member for almost three years but only began attending regularly about nine months ago. It's an independent gym, the instructors know their customers, so they're on first name terms. They say he takes his training seriously enough but he's not what you'd call a gym bunny. He uses resistance machines and free weights, works out for about ninety minutes, usually twice a week and they can confirm he was in on Friday morning like he said. Doesn't have a regular training buddy but chats to other customers while they're working, and spots for some of them. All fairly standard gym behaviour.'

'Spots?' Not a term I've ever heard.

'It's when you act as safety for another person, usually when they're lifting a weight that's near or above their normal limit.'

I nod. 'So, he's part of their little community then?'

'Looks like it. You wouldn't let someone spot for you unless you trusted them.'

'And his behaviour on Friday?'

'I spoke to the instructor who was on shift. Said Edwin trained as normal. No difference that morning compared to any other.'

'Fair enough. And the café?'

'Across the road from Newhaven harbour. The place goes like a fair. Breakfasts are to die for, apparently.' He glances up from his notes. 'But we didn't partake, naturally.'

'What, not even a bacon roll?' If my younger colleague stood sideways behind a telephone pole, you'd struggle to spot him, which is incredibly annoying as his appetite is legendary. He places his hand flat on his chest and says, 'Not while I'm on duty, Boss.'

I shake my head. 'You'll never go to heaven, my lad.'

'Anyway,' he says, 'getting back to the point. Edwin was in the café, like he said. Sat at a table by the window, on his own. Had the full Scottish with wholemeal toast, marmalade and tea.'

'Okay, listen up. I missed my breakfast and I'm so hungry my stomach thinks my throat's been cut, so can we leave it with the food? Now, did you manage to speak to Rachel's three friends. What did Edwin call them – the coven?'

'We did. And they're well named.'

'I'm guessing you weren't impressed.'

'Let's say I can't imagine being friends with any of them and I can definitely see why Edwin isn't a fan. One is married, her husband was there. A miserable pair, they were. He contributed practically nothing 'til I asked him outright if he liked Rachel. He just shrugged, said she was all right, not his cup of tea. His missus had a sour face on; ignored him the whole time we were in the house. I asked about their relation-ship with Edwin. She would only say that he and Rachel were a bad match. But the husband told me Edwin was a bloody sap. He also said, "If she was mine, I'd have given her a kick up the arse a long time ago. Sorted her out once and for all".'

'And he didn't appreciate the irony of that statement? Nor that he'd advocated the use of domestic violence in the pres-ence of two police officers?'

Andrew flips his palm across the top of his hair and makes a *whoosh* sound. That brings a chuckle to the room. 'The next woman was divorced. In a long-term relationship but they don't live together. She was quite bitchy about Rachel. If I hadn't been told they were friends, or supposed to be, listening to her I'd have thought they were mortal enemies.'

'Bitchy in what way?'

'You name it. Rachel's job – no ambition, what was the point in having a degree. Edwin – why did she marry him; she could have had her pick. Her appearance – she didn't half let herself go recently. When I picked her up on it, she started back-pedalling liked there was no tomorrow. I asked her specifi-cally about Edwin, and all she said was he's a decent enough guy.'

'And what about her other half?'

'He wasn't there but apparently he and Edwin don't get on. I asked why, and she said they never have, so they make sure they're never in company together.' Andrew pulls a face, then carries on. 'The third one is single, and, apparently, that won't be changing any time soon. She was the only one who seemed even slightly upset at the loss of her friend, but she wasn't exactly in bits, let's put it that that way.'

'And what was her opinion of Edwin?'

'Her exact words were, "Nice enough, a bit wet, should have stood up for himself a bit more".'

'When was the last time they saw Rachel?'

'A week past Friday. They were all out for a few drinks after work, then a Chinese.'

'Let me guess. Rachel was fine, just her normal self?'

'Correct.'

'And any suggestion she was having an affair?'

'All three of them said no, without any hesitation.'

I think. Add more items to the list on the board. 'So, in a nutshell, Edwin's movements on Friday morning stack up, Rachel's behaviour recently has been nothing out of the ordinary, she didn't have a bit on the side, and if Edwin vanished from their friends' lives it wouldn't break their hearts.'

Andrew says, 'You've called that about right,' and Steph nods along.

I consider all this for a second. Nothing in there that changes the pattern at all. Most disconcerting. 'Where next? The school?'

'Yeah. Steph led on that one.'

Steph reaches behind her head with both hands, tightens her ponytail. She's a highly animated speaker and once she starts, her hair bobs about. I spot her reflection in the window behind her – she'll hypnotise me if I'm not careful. 'Three of Edwin's colleagues met us over at Morton Street Primary. First, the head teacher, Selwyn Bierman. Didn't like him.'

Steph is typically blunt today. She doesn't wait 'til I ask what this man had done to rattle her cage, just cuts straight through the crap. 'First he complained about having to speak to us at the weekend. Then he had no compassion for Edwin at all, only interested in how his classes would be covered and how Bierman and the school, in that order I might add, would be affected when the media gets a hold of the story. When I asked him anything about Edwin, I had to push him for answers. But he didn't tell me anything of real substance, too busy playing his stupid political games.'

'How hard did you want to slap him, Steph?' Deadpan from Ella.

'My palm was itching.' A pause then she moves on. 'But then I spoke to his department head. She was the complete opposite, lovely woman. Straight away she asked if she could contact Edwin to see how he was. She said he's popular with other members of staff. Never any issue with parents as far as she knows, and she keeps her ear close to the ground on that one. And the kids love him.'

'What year does he teach?' I ask.

'Primary six, ten-year-olds, he'll have them next year too. Then I had a chat with the probationary teacher who covers his class on a Friday. I'm not sure she'll be standing for President of the Edwin Fuller fan club.'

'Why not?'

'From how she spoke, it seems their relationship is a bit cool. Because they work on different days she doesn't spend much time with him and to quote her, "That suits me fine." I quizzed her on that but all she would say is she has nothing against him, but they've never hit it off. But she made sure to tell me that she knows Edwin is an amazing teacher and fantastic with the kids. And on that, if you've passed the school recently you might have seen scaffolding and building supports in the gap between the school and a derelict old church next door. I was told that structural engineers were conducting a safety assessment and discovered a subterranean corridor that connects the two buildings. All sorts of artefacts had been dumped in the corridor, many of them dating back over 150 years. Anyway, the engineers declared the corridor unsafe and sealed it off but before they did that, Edwin managed to convince them to let him recover the artefacts.

When I was leaving, the probationer showed me an exhibition that P6 and P7 pupils created, under Edwin's guidance. There are about four or five glass cases, the sort you see in museums, with the artefacts displayed. It's an amazing piece of work, and in her opinion, it doesn't half confirm how good a teacher he is.'

'Not sounding like ideal murderer material, is he?' says Andrew.

'Ah, well,' I say. 'It isn't always the husband, sadly. Anything else, Steph?'

'I'm not long off the phone to Rachel's sister,' she says. 'Name's Susannah, lives in the Lake District. She hasn't seen Rachel since early December. They met on the M74, about halfway, to swap Christmas presents. She admits they're not particularly close, but they get on well enough when they're together. She said Rachel was fine when they met.' She glances up from her notes. 'A common theme. But I'm wondering if something did push Rachel into an affair, and Christmas was the catalyst. It can be a stressful time of year for some people. Anyway, Susannah's been in touch with their mother. A family friend is driving her from the south coast up to Manchester to meet Susannah then they're heading up here. Susannah spoke to Edwin this morning after you left. She thought he was trying to put them off, but her mother insisted. Wants to see her daughter with her own eyes. Not surprising, I suppose.'

I address the room. 'Is that strange? Edwin possibly not wanting them here?'

'Maybe he simply wanted to protect them,' says Andrew. 'Save them some distress.'

'Hmmm. I'm not sure about that.' I let the idea float around then say, 'Okay. Who's next?'

Crissi lifts a hand to attract my attention. She looks like she's about to ask for the bill. 'Yes, Crissi?' I say.

'I've spoken to all the lock-up owners again, to see if there's any connection between them and the Fullers.'

'Let me guess, there isn't.'

She looks forlorn. 'No. None of them have ever heard of Mr or Mrs Fuller.'

'Okay, Crissi. It was a long shot.'

'Boss,' says Ella. 'Just quickly. I went to the two places Rachel used her cards this week. The chemist has her on CCTV, she picked a few items from the shelves, paid up then left. None of the staff recognised her so they don't think she was a regular customer. The coffee shop doesn't have CCTV, and although the staff did recognise her from her photograph, they said she only popped in from time to time so they couldn't tell me anything about her.'

'Okay, Ella. Thanks for checking.' I pause, look around. 'Everybody done? Right, a couple of things from me, then we can wrap up.' I run my finger down my notes. 'I spoke to Greg earlier. Rachel's clothes were clean, so we're virtually certain she didn't walk from the car park to the lock-ups. The under-foot conditions meant he didn't find any traces at either of the two sites. And the Focus was clean, so that wasn't where she was killed.'

Steph leans forward, elbows on the table. 'Working back, if we've ruled out the lock-ups, the car park, the woods, and the car – that only leaves the house. Because we know she drove straight from there to the woods.'

'Well, we know someone drove the car, but there's no proof it was Rachel.'

'And if it wasn't her,' says Andrew, 'it could only have been Edwin.' That makes everybody pause.

'Okay, folks, Let's take one last look at this list and shout if we need to add anything.'

Rachel Fuller murder – salient factors (1)

- Texts between burner and contact 'J' – 'J' is switched off
- Is 'J' Jack McCafferty? Possibly
- Word doc hidden on AW's pc suggests affair
- AW's will splits estate – PW and her sister
- PW aware AW is wealthy
- PW also well off – so money unlikely to be motive
- AW's work week – no issues
- AW in good mood 15:26 Thursday (client)
- AW in bad mood 16:30 Thursday (husband)
- Time of Death – 23:00 Thursday 25th, to 03:00 Friday 26th
- PW has no corroborated alibi overnight
- Cause of death – strangulation, assailant behind and higher
- Method – PVC ligature over cotton pillowcase
- AW had had consensual sex – partner wore a condom
- Condom in Fullers' bedroom bin
- AW three times over driving limit
- AW's three close friends didn't like PW
- No connection between lock-up owners & Fullers
- Colleagues mostly like and respect PW
- AW's clothes clean, she didn't walk to lock-ups
- Car and car park yield no useful forensics.

I'M JUST ABOUT to call time when Tobias taps on the door and walks in. He has a folded sheet of paper in his hand.

'Afternoon, Tobias,' says Steph. 'And by the expression on

your face, I assume you come bearing glad tidings of comfort and joy.'

He stops in the doorway, looks at her as if to say *What language is this woman speaking?* She just laughs, leans over, and pulls a chair out for him.

'Found something?' I say.

He scratches at his cheek. I'm not sure if it's that he hasn't shaved today or he's aiming for the designer stubble look. Sad to say, on our amiable German colleague, it just looks scruffy. 'I'm still working through Mrs Fuller's files,' he says. 'I thought I should tell you about the Word document Bob found.' He disconnects a spare tablet from its docking station, taps the screen a few times then looks up at the wallboard. He's opened a new window on top of my evidence lists. He gives out a delicate cough before beginning to speak. 'I discussed it with a colleague who is an expert in linguistics. I also provided sample texts, emails and other personal items Rachel had written. He was able to identify a number of consistencies that suggest she is the author of the Word document.'

Well done, Tobias. Straight to the point. About two years ago, Tobias arrived on secondment to Police Scotland from his home city: Cologne. Andrew and Steph dished out some excellent tips that made it easy for him to fit in to the team and Tobias was smart enough to listen. They told him not to faff around, give me the punchline fast then keep things rolling until I stop them to ask a question. Don't blether on, or whatever that is in German. So now he displays the text of the document on the wall and moves straight on to tell us what those consistencies are.

'The style of writing is staccato. The sentences are constructed from a series of short phrases, and she uses many commas. For example, this first sentence. "I don't even know why I'm typing this, comma; maybe because what happened earlier was so bloody ridiculous, comma; so strange, comma; so stupid, comma; so risky, comma; so lots of things". I found this style repeated in several other documents and emails. Then there are words with the two capital letters at the beginning of certain sentences. An example is "THen dear old Eddie staggered in". This is a regular feature of her writing, but only on the PC where the Microsoft Word option that prevents this error is switched off.'

'So, it doesn't happen with emails or texts on her phone?'

'No, Boss. I couldn't find any.' He pauses, then carries on. 'She also uses the word "cos" instead of "because", but she precedes it with an apostrophe. This is an old-fashioned contraction, and she even uses it at the start of a sentence. Finally, she signs off with, "Ha! I'm so funny," extensively. I was able to find it in many of her personal emails and texts.'

'Speaking of texts,' says Andrew. 'They're all brief. Just a few words.'

Tobias nods. He displays the texts sent between the two burners on the wallboard, and highlights the ones apparently sent from Rachel's burner.

Steph raises a finger. 'We were talking about this earlier – she used the term "ICI" a lot but none of us have heard of it. Is it an acronym, or SMS speak like LOL?'

'I cannot find "ICI" in any lists of popular social media acronyms,' says Tobias, smiling. 'The capital letters, I believe, are a result of predictive text. I believe this is the French word "ici", meaning *here*.'

'Random French words in texts? That's a bit weird, isn't it?' says Steph.

'Perhaps she uses it as shorthand to signify she has arrived at the meeting point. Again, I have found it in many of her texts, including to her husband.'

'So, just to clarify, Tobias,' I say. 'Our linguistics colleague believes Rachel was the author of that document'

'On balance, yes. But he cannot commit himself one hundred per cent because he says it is quite possible to replicate elements of a writing style if someone has sufficient examples to use for reference.'

'Like her husband?'

'Like her husband.'

# CHAPTER TWENTY-FOUR

Saturday 23.25

IT'S LATE, and thankfully not as wet and windy as earlier in the day. I'd been just about to turn in when my phone pinged several times in succession. While I was still groping around for my specs, it rang. A Control operative, too cheerful by half for that time of night, read out a set of coordinates; a location for the second burner. The one we know as 'J'. Unlike me, it had woken up after a long sleep. I had called Andrew, relayed the coordinates and asked him to meet me.

I'd always known the ping would only provide an approximate location; a triangulation taken from at least three masts. So all we could do was scope out the area, try to gain a sense of things, see if anything fell out. We were on Brandon Terrace, which slopes up from the Art Deco ornamental clock at Canonmills and curves left into the belly of the new town. We were standing on the bend staring across the street at four-storey tenements, stretching a hundred metres to left and right, and housing at least a couple of hundred flats. I was bemoaning our chances of tracking down the phone when I realised I was bemoaning to myself. Andrew wasn't checking out the terrace at all, in fact he was facing in the opposite direction looking over the top of a stone wall, about five feet high. An overgrown patch on the other side sloped steeply away and the first building in sight was the glasshouse at the Royal Botanic Gardens, sparkling under the crisp clear night sky. It was easily half a mile away.

Andrew had his palms on the coping stones and was gazing down, so I stood on tiptoes and tried my best to follow his line of sight. At first, all I could see was the tops of bushes and a scattering of amber street lights. Then, buildings. Like army barracks, row upon row of them, perpendicular to where we were standing. Then I got it. I clapped my hands, but my gloves muffled the sound.

'Let's go and organise a warrant,' I said. 'And drag some other poor bugger out of their bed.'

# CHAPTER TWENTY-FIVE

Saturday 23:30

THE SCOTTISH PRESBYTERIAN church on the outer curve of Brandon Terrace was no longer a place of worship. A *For Sale / To Let* sign fastened to rusting wrought iron palings leaned at a jaunty angle. The ground was pockmarked with assorted grasses and weeds, and even a couple of saplings sprouted uninvited from an area of shattered flagstones. The building is higher by a few steps, and a deep shadowed recess to the front door is guarded by four fluted stone pillars.

Edwin had laid his bike down to avoid any stray shaft of light glinting off it, although the nearest lamppost was fifty metres down the slope. He'd been hiding in the recess since he'd switched the burner on, making it accessible to several city centre masts, which had dutifully reported it's *On, but stationary* status to the network. Like the two detectives, he hadn't been able to accurately judge how it would be triangulated but his research and that of the police came from remarkably similar sources. Of course, theirs was legit and his wasn't, but on this occasion the twain had met.

He'd thought he could probably stand the frigid temperature for about another hour, so he was relieved when, well short of his deadline, two cars drove into the terrace from opposite directions. He watched as his adversaries met on the wide pavement before scanning the mostly darkened tenements on the opposite side of the street.

*Cold, detectives. Very cold.*

When the male performed a slow pirouette then focused his attention over the wall in the direction of the Royal Botanic Gardens, the corners of Edwin's mouth twitched up. *Getting warmer, DS Young.*

And when the female moved to her colleague's side and they both took an interest in the rows of housing below, he grinned. *Definitely much warmer. Verging on hot, in fact.*

He watched as DI Cooper applauded but her gloved hands were on mute. Edwin was slightly disappointed they didn't high five. Cooper made a phone call then exchanged a few words with Young before they climbed into their cars and drove off towards Leith. Edwin knew they'd be heading for the station and unlikely to return soon, but he stayed where he was for several minutes before picking his bike off the ground.

---

# CHAPTER TWENTY-SIX

Sunday 06:00

THE RAIN and wind have abated but, in exchange, God's sent us an icy cold morning with a frost so heavy the pavement crunches underfoot. I'm mob-handed today because unless I've got things hopelessly wrong I expect to be making an arrest. I yawn, my gob open so wide that if someone yelled, an echo would bounce back.

'Missing your bed, Mel?' says PC Dave Devlin. He and his three colleagues are fully kitted out, including body cams.

'Too right. I've had two bloody hours if I'm lucky.'

I'm several metres below the same wall we had looked over earlier and, beyond that, I can make out the higher floors of the tenements up on Brandon Terrace. We're in Glenogle Road, a street that takes a hairpin turn off the foot of the terrace then runs parallel to it – hence the height difference. Andrew and I are standing next to a Mitsubishi L200 pickup, and we know who owns it. It's black. Half car, half utility vehicle; four doors, with a cargo deck under a hard canopy. There are dings and scrapes on almost every panel.

He looks at me. 'Go for it,' I say.

Andrew is holding the burner phone we found in Edwin's car. He presses the *Call* icon for 'J', the phone's only contact. Nothing happens for a few seconds making me wonder if, instead of romping along the top row to the winning square, we're about to slide all the way back down one of the longer snakes, the one that deposits you on the bottom row. Then, faint but clear, comes a ringtone from inside the canopy. Andrew taps *Cancel*, and smiles.

'Right, my boy,' I say. 'Let's go knock on a door.'

---

WE'RE about a hundred metres from the Mitsubishi, in the third street in a tight rank of twelve short streets running parallel to each other. They all have the same number of houses: twenty. My mother was brought up in an area virtually identical to this, so I know the history of *The Colonies* intimately.

These are housing configurations peculiar to Edinburgh, replicated in a dozen different locations across the city. In the mid-nineteenth century, unscrupulous slum landlords ran overcrowded city-centre tenements that were among the unhealthiest in Europe. In 1861 a group of seven stonemasons formed The Edinburgh Cooperative Building Company and set out to design and build homes that would vastly improve living conditions for semi-skilled workers and their families. On cheaper plots throughout the capital, the cooperative built over two thousand colony houses and every single one is still standing today. In these developments, the houses are terraced with one on the ground level and another on the first. On each street, one side is formed by gardens that front onto the lower-level houses. The opposite side has flights of straight stone steps giving access to the upper properties, and the streets form a repeating pattern.

Dave leads the way up one of these external staircases to the front door of number eight. When they reach the landing, it splits to either side. Number ten is cheek by jowl, the doors to each house separated only by a single stone column.

Dave glances at me, I give the thumbs up, he hammers on the door and jams a gloved finger on the bell. There is no other exit from the first-floor houses, apart from jumping from the window. But we do have men stationed in the adjacent street, just in case. Most of the first floors have attic conversions and we know this is a double upper, but you'd be crazy, or desperate, to attempt an escape from way up there.

I'm still a few steps down, and by leaning back I can see all of the windows in the house. The door receives another hammering, and an upper floor light comes on, followed by a glow from the fanlight above the door. We wait, the door opens, and a man steps forward. He's wearing checked boxers and a tee shirt that might have been white at some point in its past. His hands are empty, there are precious few places he could be concealing a weapon, so I march up to him.

Before I can speak a female voice yells from the floor above. 'Fuck's sake, Jack! Who the hell's banging on the door at this time on a Sunday morning?'

He pays her no attention, he's too busy trying to take in the scene. Four burly, mean looking coppers, and a significantly smaller woman smiling up at him. My face might be familiar but with the context being so dissimilar to our last meeting, I guess he's probably struggling. So, I help him out. 'Good morning, sir. I'm DI Cooper. We've met before.'

Then I read Jack McCafferty his rights and explain our visit is in connection with the murder of Mrs Rachel Fuller.

He knuckles his eyes, blinks rapidly, probably hoping we'll all miraculously disappear. When we don't, he stammers, 'Murder? Rachel? Me?' Then he finishes with, 'What?'

I hear pattering footsteps from behind him and before the deputy leader of Edinburgh City Council can barge through, I move forward. 'Let's take this inside, Jack. Standing at the top of these stairs won't half give your neighbours a tremendous view.'

# CHAPTER TWENTY-SEVEN

Sunday 02:30

EDWIN FULLER KNEW it was imperative he held his nerve. He'd set events in motion and now he had to wait. Wait to see how things panned out. Wait for the police to contact him. Wait and hope he'd hear from Lisa.

The ride home from the church on Brandon Terrace had just about warmed him up but then he'd had to spend half an hour in the garage returning his bike to its original state, drying it off and hanging it back on its hook. He worked by the light from his head torch and despite hanging an old curtain over the window he turned the lamp down to a faint glow. Once he was back in the warmth of his kitchen, he'd stripped off his cold weather gear and ran the whole lot through a quick wash. As the machine gurgled away, he sat at the table wearing shorts, sports socks, and a towelling robe. After two mugs of herbal tea, he felt revived. He figured he'd warm up properly once he crawled under the duvet, but his brain was buzzing and showed no signs of letting up.

So far, everything was going exactly according to plan. He checked around the kitchen. The state of uncleanliness he'd created now only had to be maintained. He'd barked at Hayley when she'd started clearing up then immediately apologised. That had had some effect in that she sorted out the worst of the mess but seemed to accept she would upset him more if she went the whole hog. That morning, after she left, he'd made a deliberately half-hearted attempt to tidy up, but he left a pile of dirty dishes in the sink and didn't wipe the work surfaces clean. The floor surrounding the bin was bacteria nirvana.

He moved through to the living room and lay down on the sofa with the lights out. He thought he might drop off, but quickly realised there was precious little chance of that. The pendulum clock in the hall chimed three. In one of the police documentaries he'd watched more than once, the lead detective explained that raids on suspects' houses were often carried out before daybreak and with plenty of noise. Most people would be disoriented or confused being woken from their slumber by such an event.

Edwin tried to imagine what might happen in the next few hours. Would the police hammer on Jack McCafferty's door at five o'clock? Six? Would they have one of those handheld battering rams? The big red key, he'd heard it called. How would Jack and Lisa react? He pictured Jack's face when they found the burner. The man would deny all knowledge, naturally.

He couldn't phone Cooper, that was a complete no-no. But would she contact him to say they'd arrested Jack? Or would she wait until he was charged? How long would that take? Later that afternoon? Or the following day: Monday?

What if Cooper didn't call, what if she showed up at his door instead? He wondered how he might react, try to stay one step ahead. 'Jack? No way, there must be some mistake. He and

Rachel have been friends for years, since before I came on the scene'. *No. Overly dramatic.* Perhaps he would settle for a dull, 'Jack?'. He'd sit down, head in hands, give out a plaintive look. Ask, 'Why?'. *Yes, that sounded much better, more in tune.*

He rejected the idea of phoning Lisa, not even on a pretext. He was certain she'd ring him. Better if she did, then he'd have time to react properly to whatever she said.

Edwin thought again about the mobile in Jack's pickup. He knew the police wouldn't arrest Jack on suspicion of murder simply because they could link that phone to the burner they found hidden in Rachel's Wellington boot.

But the mobile wouldn't be all they would find.

Not by a long chalk.

# CHAPTER TWENTY-EIGHT

Sunday 06:15

'Can you confirm this is your vehicle?' I say.

'I'm guessing you already know that as we've walked straight to it,' says Jack. He's dressed in a pair of jeans and a lightweight fleece, obviously not a man who feels the cold.

'Answer the question please, sir.'

'Yes, it's ours. But listen, what's this all about?' He has his hands out, palms facing up.

'Registered to your business, McCafferty Plumbing Ltd?'

'Look. I've already told you it's ours. Why are we here? What do you want?'

Andrew is holding the burner. He shows Jack the screen. Says, 'There's only one contact on this phone. It's named "J". I'm about to place a call to that contact.'

Jack looks at him as if to say, what the hell are you on about? But when the ringtone sounds from inside the canopy, he turns so fast he's lucky he doesn't break his neck. 'What the fuck?' He stares at the burner.

Andrew kills the call. 'Open the vehicle now, please.'

Jack takes half a step away as if he'll be electrocuted if he touches it.

'Mr McCafferty,' I say. 'Open it.'

If he refuses, I'll use the warrant I have tucked into my back pocket, but I hope he consents to the search. As it happens, I don't have to use the heavy hammer. He moves round the car like he's wading through treacle, blips the locks, the tailgate swings silently upwards. We shine torches inside; tidy, it is not. Plumbing materials are all over the place. I've seen tradesmen's vans with shelving, neatly stacked boxes of components or screws or whatever, tools stored as if they were on display. With Jack's vehicle, it's more like the contents were thrown at it by a blind man standing several metres away.

'Again, please, Andrew.'

The ringtone comes from the far side, behind the cabin. I move closer so the fronts of my thighs are against the body-work, lean in and use my torch to nudge a couple of items aside. I see a screen lit with a bright green background; the phone appears to be the same model as the burner. It's connected to a USB port by a black cable. I hold up my hand, and the ringing stops. The screen is bright for a few seconds then it fades.

I turn to face Jack. Aghast would be a reasonable description of his expression. 'For clarification, Mr McCafferty, my colleague has placed a call from the mobile phone he is holding. That phone only has one number stored on it, and it has just connected to a mobile that's inside the cargo deck of your vehicle.' I point. 'Does that phone belong to you?'

'Belong to *me*? I've never seen it in my life before.' He stares down at Andrew's hand. 'Where did that one come from?'

'When we found Edwin Fuller's car, this was hidden inside.'

And now, aghast doesn't even come close to describing the expression on Jack McCafferty's face.

# CHAPTER TWENTY-NINE

Sunday 15:00

I HEAR a light rap on my office door that coincides with a smoker's cough. I say, 'Yes?' but delay looking up as I send an email off into the ether. I've always been in awe of how fast these things vanish, before they ping into the receiver's inbox, whether they're in the next room or halfway across the globe. I sigh. I can do technology, to about the same level as a six-year-old. On one of my better days.

I don't know who I expect to be wedged in the doorway, but this qualifies as a major surprise. The incredibly crumpled figure sporting the seriously hunted expression is DS Lawrence Ratcliffe, the man who should be a few days into a three-week self-imposed leave period that I was only too delighted to authorise.

'Lawrence. What can I do for you?' I smile, but it's the sort of smile a hyena would offer a three-legged wildebeest.

'I ... eh ... could we have a chat?' He flaps an arm at one of the chairs in front of my desk.

I sit back. 'Sure. Take a seat, why don't you.' He lays a meaty hand onto the back of one, and I'm so tempted to stand up and scream, *No. Not that one.* Childish, I know, but there you go. I'm so looking forward to hearing what he has to say. Hopefully it will include the words, 'I resign'.

Ratcliffe reminds me of Detective Andy Sipowicz of *NYPD Blue* fame, but at least Sipowicz was a likeable old curmudgeon. Ratcliffe eases himself into the chair, probably wishing it didn't have arms. He runs a finger round the inside of his collar; many fish suppers have swum under the bridge since he was able to fasten that top button. The brown suit's seen better days too, and I don't care to think about when his tie was last cleaned. If ever.

I glance past his head to see Steph meandering past, moving at about one third of her normal rate. She takes a casual look into my room, notices I've clocked her, but doesn't even have the good grace to blush. I touch my finger against the tip of my nose as she glides off, stage left. Ratcliffe is blissfully unaware. He removes his glasses, knuckles his eye, then jams them back on. 'So, Lawrence,' I say. 'What do you want to chat about?'

He leans to the side, pulls a far from white handkerchief from his trouser pocket, and mops his glistening pate. 'Christ,' he says. 'It's fuckin' roasting in here.'

I've never worked with him, but I've been told his mouth runs like a sewer. Clearly the man's under stress but I'm in no mood to cut him any slack. 'Mind your language, DS Ratcliffe. Now, what do you want? Because I'm busy, and the last time I heard you were on leave.'

His eyes roll up in his head. 'Come on, Mel. This is hard enough without—'

I lean forward, lay my palms on the desk. 'Everyone else on the team addresses me as Boss. There's no reason at all why you should be any different.' That's not strictly true. Andrew often uses my name, but never when protocol dictates otherwise. What this man doesn't know is Jeff offered me some advice when I was pulling my team together: 'I worked as a junior DC under Ratcliffe many moons ago. Hit him hard and early, and he'll be relatively manageable'. I believe I've just done that but how things pan out from here depend entirely on Lawrence Ratcliffe.

He holds up his hands. I'm not sure if it's an apology but it'll do for now. 'I might have been a bit hasty taking my annual leave when I did. So ...' I keep my gaze even and steady. 'So, I think I'd like to cut it short and come back to work.'

'When?'

'Oh. I suppose, well, right away.'

I lift my arm and study my watch. 'It's Sunday, and my overtime budget is taking a pasting. Plus, it's after three o'clock, you'd be over halfway through a shift. I'd have to take a day's leave off you.'

He peers at me through his glasses. 'That's fine. I'm not bothered about that. I've nothing else on anyway.'

'No. That wouldn't be fair. I'll see you in the morning.'

'But,' he says, then stops. He stands up, hoists his belt up a few inches. It slides straight back down over his belly. He glares at me. 'Have it your own way, then.'

As he turns away and marches out, I decide not to dignify that with a response. If he's calmed down by tomorrow then fair enough. But if not, his card's well and truly marked.

Andrew replaces him in the doorway. Takes a quick glance behind him, just in time to watch Ratcliffe leaving the office. 'What was that about?' he says.

'He wanted to cancel his leave, come back to work. Offered to start back this afternoon.'

'Did he say why?'

'No, Andrew, he didn't. But you're smirking. What do you know that I don't?'

He laughs this time. 'Word on the street is his missus is already fed up with him being at home. Told him not to be such a tit and get back to work.'

'Ha! I've never met the woman, but I'm already her number one fan.' I reach over the desk and lift a bundle of papers. 'Ready?'

'Sure am. Let's go and see what Jack McCafferty has to say for himself.'

# CHAPTER THIRTY

It's 15:30. Andrew and I are in an interview room with Jack McCafferty and his brief. It had struck me as odd that when we took Jack away this morning, and especially once I explained to him what he was suspected of, he didn't immediately tell Lisa to call a solicitor. I've heard many a criminal shout those words; it usually means they are guilty – or minted. Now he's here with Ralph Levinson, an impeccably dressed gentleman sitting to his right. This is the first time I've had the pleasure. I don't know whether it's the exquisitely cut suit or his effortlessly relaxed demeanour, but I'll need to tread carefully. I doubt he'll let me away with much.

Once we discovered the mobile phone in Jack's vehicle, we left well alone and closed it up. Greg would have kicked my backside halfway into next week if we'd gone anywhere near the plumbing materials in the back or even ventured into the cab in case we compromised all sorts of forensic evidence. For a couple of decades, at least, even the rawest of police recruits have it drummed into them from day one just how vital it is that the crime scene is protected at all costs. Since it was found, the phone's been fast-tracked through the lab and Greg has provided me with a comprehensive, and extremely damning, report. Andrew and I have spent the last hour poring through the detail.

I complete the formalities for the interview and make sure Jack knows he is still under caution on suspicion of murdering his old friend, Rachel Fuller. I start by asking the question that could save us all a lot of time and might mean I don't have to put Jack through the mill. 'Mr McCafferty, did you murder Rachel Fuller in St Mark's Woods during the late evening of Thursday 25ᵗʰ January?'

The colour of his complexion resembles snow on a dull day. He stays silent. I don't know if that's because Levinson has instructed him to stay quiet or if he's too scared to speak. I suspect the latter, so I ask him again.

This time, he croaks out the word, 'No.' I doubt whether he's capable of elaborating, and he's given me the answer I expected. So, I go to the top of my list, to the question of the mobile phone that was in his pickup. 'Like I told you earlier, I've never seen it in my life before.'

'So, you don't know how it got there?'

'How many times, I've absolutely no idea.'

'Because, Jack, it didn't fall in there. It was plugged into a USB charging point.' He spreads his hands at that one. I return to my notes. 'Our technicians have analysed this phone. It only has one contact, known as "A". Now, the other phone, the one we found in Rachel Fuller's car, also has one contact.' I pause. 'That contact is "J". Is that a coincidence? Two vehicles. Two phones. Two people. And the contact on each phone, is the initial of the driver of the other vehicle. "A" and "J" – Rachel and Jack.'

'I don't know. But what I'm trying to tell you is I've never seen that phone before and I have no idea how it ended up in the back of my pickup. And I definitely don't know who this contact "A" is.'

'If you've never seen it, perhaps you can explain how it happens to have your fingerprints on it.'

'What?'

It's as if I've slapped him. I move on quickly and show him a printout of the text messages. 'Are these familiar, Jack?'

He takes him an age to read them. He looks up at me. 'No.'

I change tack. 'Describe your relationship with Rachel.'

'Rachel? We were friends. Or to be more accurate, she was my wife's friend.'

'How long had you known her?'

'Twenty-odd years, I suppose. Ever since uni.'

'Did you and Lisa socialise with the Fullers?'

'Yes.'

'In what way?'

'Nights out, meals and drinks in each other's houses, a few weekends away. You know, just normal things you do with friends.'

'So, you'd known her since uni, twenty-odd years, you socialise with the Fullers as a foursome, yet you still describe Rachel as your wife's friend?'

He throws his arms in the air. 'More Lisa's friend than mine, then.'

'Was Mrs Fuller ever in your vehicle?'

'No.'

'Rachel has *never* been in your vehicle?'

'I suppose with Lisa, yes. But not with me.'

'So, she has been in it.'

'Yes, sorry, she has.'

'In the back seat?'

'I don't know. If Lisa was giving people lifts, maybe. You'd have to ask her.'

Andrew leans forward on his elbows. 'Mr McCafferty, can you describe your whereabouts on these Thursdays in January: the 11th, the 18th and the 25th.'

Jack relaxes a little. He thinks he'll skate this exam. He won't. 'I would have been at home. Lisa takes a college class, and I stay in.'

'Alone?'

'Of course. And you can look at my phone locations if you like; they'll show I didn't go out.'

Levinson twitches, and I'm not surprised. 'Actually, Jack,' I say, 'we've done that, and your phone was in your house on those dates but that doesn't mean you were. And for completeness, we checked your Sky box too. It was showing Eurosport on all three evenings, but it could have been playing to an empty room. Not a corroborated alibi, in my opinion.' I lean forward and tap the list of texts. 'These messages all relate to the three Thursdays I've asked you about.'

He folds his arms, tight. 'Like I said, I know nothing about them.'

I move on. 'When was the last time you drove your vehicle?'

He gazes up at the light. 'Thursday. I drove home from work. About six, six fifteen.'

'And you haven't driven it since then?'

'Correct.'

'You didn't drive it on Friday?'

He sighs. 'No. I took a day off. I've just finished a long job, four months renovating a tenement in Stockbridge.'

He's talking about an area that's close to his house, and not all that far from Inverleith and St Mark's Woods. 'Has your wife driven the pickup since Thursday?'

He folds his arms. 'I keep telling you, it hasn't moved from Glenogle Road since I parked it there after work.'

'And no one else drives it?'

'No.'

'Work colleagues? Friends? Relatives?'

'Fuck's sake, no! Only me and Lisa.' Levinson lays a hand on Jack's right arm. He shakes it off.

'Have you ever driven your vehicle and parked it at St Mark's Woods, adjacent to Warriston Crematorium?'

He gives us a quizzical look. 'No. Those woods are only about five minutes from our house. If I was going there, I'd just walk.'

Andrew picks up several sheets of A4, stapled together. 'This is a report from our Computer Crime Unit. It concerns the satnav installed on your pickup. My colleagues have downloaded the GPS coordinates for all the journeys it made in January this year.'

Levinson speaks for the first time in a posh West of Scotland accent that goes nicely with his suit. 'I wouldn't pretend to be an expert in automotive electronics, DS Young, but I wasn't aware satnav possessed that capability.'

Andrew slides a copy of the report across the table. Levinson casually spins it round, plucks what appears to be a silver cigar case from an inside jacket pocket and slides out a pair of folded spectacles. He snaps them open, pops them on the end of his nose and settles back to digest the report.

When Jack's vehicle arrived at the lab, one of the first things Greg examined was the satnav. Some criminals are incredibly adept at concealing their tracks while others are firmly anchored to the dumb end of the scale. Only a few weeks ago, one of my colleagues managed to stop laughing for long enough to tell me about a housebreaker who had targeted a series of rural properties to the south of Edinburgh. This particular dimwit had used satnav to plot his route, so the postcodes for all the addresses he'd burgled were sitting there, waving at us, and calling out, '*Arrest this idiot. It's for his own good*'. But Greg was stunned when he discovered that Jack's satnav listed, it seemed, a history of every journey the vehicle had ever made. He called Bob to ask if she could enlighten him.

Bob too was mystified, but something was ringing a bell. A trawl through her unit's knowledge database threw up several articles, but they were all marked *Classified*. Now with a bee in her bonnet, she contacted a friend who is, 'Something in the Foreign Office'. Apparently the two of them had a thing going, back in the day. I watch Levinson tweak his lower lip while he reads about a range of vehicles manufactured in Korea and Thailand that were fitted with a souped-up version of satnav, allegedly created by a consortium of Japanese designers, and capable of logging, storing, and analysing thousands of individual journeys. The devices were also programmed to report summary data back to the intelligence agencies in their respective countries using built-in Wi-Fi. Quite simply, these agencies were using the technology to spy on their own citizens and once they proved it worked, the Japanese hawked it around the intelligence community and, unsurprisingly, found many willing buyers. Bob's friend refused to confirm whether British Intelligence were aware of its existence, or how many vehicles might be driving on our roads with the upgrade installed.

Jack's Mitsubishi was designed in Japan and built in Thailand. An ex-demonstrator, he bought it several years ago with fewer than a thousand miles on the clock. We can't imagine Jack knew about it but Andrew asks him anyway.

'You're kidding, right?' he says. 'I'm a plumber, for God's sake. Who the hell cares where I drive to?' Levinson's eyebrows lift imperceptibly, he's telling us to get on with it. But Jack is clearly bemused, wondering where we're going with this. He doesn't have to wait long.

Andrew flicks to the second page. 'On Thursday the 25$^{th}$ at

22:03, three days ago, your pickup was driven from Glenogle Road, which is where you said you'd parked it, to St Mark's Woods. It was stationary at that location for fifty-six minutes then it was driven back to Glenogle Road. And it hasn't moved since.'

Now we can see the whites of McCafferty's eyes. Andrew continues, 'You are aware, because DI Cooper told you, that Rachel Fuller's body was found in bushes overlooking the Water of Leith, behind lock-ups off Powderhall Lane. But are you also aware that Edwin Fuller's car was discovered, abandoned, in the car park at St Mark's Woods? The very same woods that *your* satnav places *your* pickup at approximately the same time Rachel was murdered?' Andrew rattles the papers once; they make a snapping sound. 'The analysis of the mobile phone discovered in Mr Fuller's car and the mobile phone discovered in your pickup shows they communicated by SMS. Plus, their location data shows they were both within one hundred metres of St Mark's Woods at the same times.'

I leave a tiny gap, no more than a couple of heartbeats. 'Care to explain, Jack?'

The silence in the room is broken only by the sound of Levinson's trousers crinkling as he adjusts his position. Jack's eyes are fixed on the table top as if they're connected to it by miniature zip lines. He breathes in through his nose. Then he replies in a flat monotone, slowly and deliberately. 'I had nothing to do with Rachel's murder. I did not drive my vehicle on Thursday night. And I certainly was not in St Mark's Woods.' Now he speaks directly to me. 'Please. I'm telling you the truth.'

Then he stops. Battles with himself before he dares utter his next word. 'Lisa?'

I shake my head. 'No. Mrs McCafferty has told us at that

time, she was in a pub in Stockbridge with colleagues. And several witnesses will corroborate that.'

Jack nods. A little smile. He's relieved, but he slumps back, clearly under pressure. I place my palms on the table, let them slide towards him. I'm down at his level, looking him in the eye. 'This is our problem, Jack. You say you didn't drive it. Lisa couldn't have. And no one else has the keys. So, how did it make that journey?'

'I ... I don't know.'

I sit back, flick to another page. I tell him it made the same journey, at similar times, on the 11<sup>th</sup> and the 18<sup>th</sup> of January. Again, he denies driving it. His wife was out, he was in. *Home Alone: Two* and *Three*, and Lisa has the same cast iron alibi.

I change tack. 'When was the last time you walked or drove to St Mark's Woods?'

A puff comes from his lips. 'In the summer. August, maybe?'

I pretend to think. Then say to Andrew, 'August wasn't a bad month in Edinburgh. Dry for most of it as far as I can remember.'

Andrew plays along. Raises his index finger. 'I do believe you're correct. And I'm sure we could prove it if we had to.'

Ralph Levinson sighs extravagantly. 'How terribly droll, Detectives. But I imagine you have a point to make.'

I reach down to a plastic evidence box that's positioned between Andrew and me. Lift out a sizeable bag and lay it on the table. 'Recognise these, Jack?'

He leans forward. 'Are they my work boots?'

'They are indeed, Jack. One of our Crime Scene Examiners found them in your vehicle.' I point at the chunky tread that's visible through the Cellophane panel. 'See that mud? It's an exact match with a sample we collected from St Mark's Woods this morning.'

Levinson leans forward. 'Seriously, DI Cooper? And might I not be able to gather identical samples from any of the parks and woods in the Inverleith area?' He pauses. 'Of which there are several.'

He has a point, but I don't intend to concede it. 'We also found traces of the same mud in the cabin, on the leading edges of the front seats. I wonder if they were missed during an attempted clean up.'

Levinson leans back, steeples his fingers. Smirks, but doesn't comment.

I lift another bag, lay it on the table. It has a similar Cellophane panel. 'Are these yours, Jack?'

He peers at the bag. 'I can't tell. What are they?'

'Waterproof trousers. In fact, your waterproof trousers. Also found in your vehicle. Also caked in mud.' I point at the boots. 'The same mud.'

I lay two more evidence bags on top of the first two. 'We found these, also inside the cargo deck.' I lift the first one. 'This, as I'm sure you're aware, is electrical earth cable. Now, I'd always thought this would only be used by an electrician but now I've learned plumbers use it too. To provide an earth for copper pipes and suchlike. But hey, I'm stating the bleedin' obvious here.' The cable is about a metre long and I use a pen to point at a marked section near the centre. 'As you can see here, the PVC sheathing has a couple of nicks out of it. The pathologist extracted traces of this PVC from beneath Rachel Fuller's fingernails. She and my crime scene colleagues are of the same opinion; whoever murdered Rachel strangled her with this cable and, in her panic to escape, she grabbed at it, made the nicks with her nails and scraped the skin on her throat at the same time.'

I lean forward and hold his gaze. 'But she didn't break the skin, Jack. Do you know why?' I pick up the second bag and stick it in front of him. 'This, Jack, is a cotton pillowcase. But it's not just any cotton pillowcase. This is a top-quality cotton, with a high thread count.' I tap the bag. 'Being specific, five hundred threads per square inch of fabric.'

He slaps his hands over his mouth; for a second, I think he'll throw up. I wait to make sure he doesn't. He moves his hands, his fingertips pull his cheeks down, revealing the insides of bloodshot lower eyelids. He doesn't say anything, just shakes his head. Over and over and over.

'This morning, despite your wife's protestations, we searched your house. And upstairs, in your airing cupboard, low down in the pile, we found a single pillowcase. An exact match for this one. I expect you know high quality bed linens are one of Lisa's things, don't you?'

He slides his hands down from his face, clasps them, and rests them on the table in front of him. 'This is terrible, I have absolutely nothing to do with any of this. Not the mud on my boots, the phones.' He points at the pillowcase. 'That.' He turns to Levinson. 'You believe me, don't you?'

Before Levinson can answer there's a light tap on the door and Tobias joins us. I pause the interview while I read the note he's handed me. We share a glance and a smile before he leaves again. Andrew leans over and I angle the paper towards him. He doesn't react.

I restart the interview. 'Mr McCafferty,' I say. 'The DNA swab you provided this morning has shown a positive match to DNA materials discovered on Rachel Fuller's underwear and her body at the time she was found. Specifically, her stomach, groin, thighs and buttocks. Can you account for that?'

The solicitor glances at the statue that's sitting to his left then turns to me. 'Give us everything else you have, DI Cooper, if you wouldn't mind. Then I can advise my client how we should proceed.' He leans over and murmurs in Jack's ear. Probably something along the lines of, *Keep schtum, and leave this to me*.

His request seems fair to me, so I explain about DNA found in the cabin of Jack's pickup and how Rapid DNA analysis proves Rachel had been inside. If Jack's wife had given Rachel a lift, it's reasonable we would find her hair and fingerprints, which we did. But we also found her DNA on the back seat, and this DNA was extracted from mucus. Vaginal mucus, at that. 'Were you having an affair with Rachel Fuller, Jack?'

'Detective Inspector.' Levinson stops short of wagging his finger at me, but I guess it was close.

I go on to relate how, when we found Rachel's remains, she was wearing cotton joggers. A greasy stain was discovered on the back of the right leg. The lab report identifies it as silicone sealant, and this time I do know it's a staple in a plumber's toolkit. And there was a caulking gun containing a partly used tube of sealant lying in the rear footwell. On the floor of the driver's seat, we found one particle of gravel. There were two more particles embedded in the front offside tyre; it's known as self-binding gravel, apparently. And guess what, typical of the paths and parking areas in and around St Mark's Woods.

Levinson inhales. I throw up a hand before he speaks. 'Yes, I know, and on other paths too. Circumstantial, but not half adding up, eh?'

Then I show them two photographs. 'You may be familiar with the signposts used on most of Edinburgh's leisure walkways – along the Water of Leith walkway for example. I've learned the whole Inverleith area, all the paths, cycle lanes, you name it, had all the signposts renewed two years ago. If I can draw your attention to image one, it shows the sign at the vehicular entrance to St Mark's Woods, which doubles up as the exit. As you can see, low down on the sign a sizeable gouge has been taken out of the post. Image two is of a series of scratches on your front nearside bumper. Our lab tested the paintwork and reported traces of industrial strength resin-based wood treatment. The same treatment used on all those signposts.'

I finish up by handing over a composite report, detailing the text messages and location data from the two burners, along with GPS data from Jack's satnav. Dates, times, content and locations all match. 'Mr McCafferty. All the evidence I've described – biological and digital forensic evidence, and circumstantial evidence – all combine to place you and Rachel in the same locations at the same times, and they put her in your vehicle where I believe she met her death.' I pause to give him time to gather himself. 'So, returning to the question I put to you at the start of this interview, did you murder Rachel Fuller in St Mark's Woods during the late evening of Thursday 25th January?'

He folds his arms, leans well back, glares at me, tries to be all ballsy about it. He's terrified, so it doesn't come off. Not even close. But give him credit, he holds it together for long enough to say: 'No, DI Cooper. I most certainly did not.'

# CHAPTER THIRTY-ONE

*WHY THE HELL has Lisa not called me?* He was gutted she hadn't been in touch.

Edwin hammered his fist on the kitchen worktop but caught the rim of a tea plate, which spun up in the air and smashed on the tiled floor. Both of his cats flew off their beds and clambered all over each other, desperate to get through the cat flap first. The bottle of vodka was still on the worktop, now about two thirds empty. He tried to ignore it but failed. He sloshed some into a dirty glass, raised it to his lips, then threw the liquid into the sink.

He took a deep breath and moved over to the window. The garage roof wore a heavy rime of frost, as did the next-door neighbour's shed. Pepper appeared. She popped up onto the timber fence that separated the two gardens, assessed the risk of leaping across the gap onto the shed roof then performed the manoeuvre with aplomb. She sauntered to the apex, sat down, tucked her tail in, and surveyed her domain. Edwin flinched as he recalled the time he'd carried her into the garage, while he'd been testing out whether he was capable of killing small animals. In his mind, a cat had been highest on the chain. He'd stood just inside the garage door, supported his pet in the crook of his left arm, and encircled her neck with his right hand. Then he had asked himself, *Honestly and truthfully, if I absolutely had to, could I actually do this?* At that point, he knew he could, and that satisfied him. He'd stepped back outside, kissed the top of her head, and let her bounce down onto the grass where she set off in failed pursuit of a bumble bee.

Back in the present, he was brought back on an even keel as he watched the casual athletic movements of the little black cat, centre stage in the tranquil winter's scene. He had been ready for this, for these feelings of pressure, anxiety, nerves. They had to happen. He had murdered his wife; he wouldn't be human if he didn't suffer a reaction. And here it was. Now. But because he'd always recognised this would surface at some point, it hadn't come as a surprise, and he was able to rationalise how he felt.

On one level, he remained shocked at what he'd done. A couple of times he'd begun to panic at the idea of being caught. And if he was caught, there would be nothing he could do. Que sera sera, and all that. But what would happen to him? What did *life* actually mean? How old would he be when he was eventually released from prison? Then the anxiety, the emotions, subsided. He'd done it now and he couldn't go back, couldn't unkill his wife.

*Unkill. Was that a word?* The random thought amused him. *There. Feel better now.* But he knew these feelings would recur. Next time, would they be less or more severe? He didn't know. Time would tell, but he'd be ready.

He wondered again about Lisa and Jack. Had Cooper not arrested Jack after all? Had she made the arrest, but they were still interviewing him? If, say, 05:00 had been the shock and awe hour, that was about eleven hours ago. Surely that was enough time, especially with all the evidence Edwin had left for them to find. Or had the evidence failed? Had they seen through it? Did they believe a third party had murdered Rachel? And not Jack? No. That wasn't possible.

As part of his research, he'd read that criminals who frame other people, especially for serious crimes, often overdo the planted evidence. 'Biological forensics'. That's why he'd left only three pieces of gravel, not a handful. One tiny smear of sealant. Two strands of hair. Brief, infrequent text messages, not screeds and screeds of gooey love talk. That was for teenagers and lovestruck adults who should know better. There were other things he could have planted, other steps he could have taken but he didn't want Cooper's suspicions to be aroused.

He was desperate to speak to Lisa. *Desperate.* But he couldn't. It was vital that he held his nerve. He breathed in and out through his nose. Settled down now. Calm.

Edwin struck a deal with himself. *I will call her, but today is not the right time. I'll call her first thing in the morning.*

*I'll be able to hold off till then. Won't I?*

# CHAPTER THIRTY-TWO

'Do I need a solicitor too?'

We've asked Lisa McCafferty to come in to the station to help us to corroborate, or otherwise, some of her husband's statements. I tell her she doesn't require legal representation because I don't suspect her of any involvement in the murder of her friend, not least because you could smash a wrecking ball into her alibi, and it would survive without a scratch. 'I want to take you back in time, Lisa, to Boxing Day evening. Where were you around nine o'clock?'

'In my bed,' she replies without the slightest hesitation. 'We had langoustines for Christmas dinner and mine violently disagreed with me. I was in bed for three days straight.'

'And did Jack go out that evening?'

She screws up her face. 'This is one of these situations, isn't it? You ask if he went out. I say no, he didn't. You ask how I can be sure, because I was ill in bed at the time. Well, I'm pretty sure he didn't go out ... but I can't be certain.'

I nod. Can't say fairer than that. 'Jack and Rachel were friends?'

She gives a tiny shrug. 'Not exactly best pals but friendly enough.'

'Were they ever romantically involved?'

She snorts. 'That's a bit Mills and Boon, is it not?'

'Maybe, but the reason I ask is because, at your flat, you both hesitated when I asked if Rachel was having, or ever had, an affair.'

Lisa inspects her fingernails. 'We've always suspected she'd had the odd fling, but we don't know for sure. That's why we were a bit awkward.' She looks up again. 'But to answer your question, no, my husband was never romantically involved with Rachel.'

Andrew and I have already agreed there's no need to tell Lisa about her husband's DNA being present on Rachel but, as bombshells go, it might come in handy later on. I write down the dates Rachel and Jack might have met at St Mark's Woods. Spin my pad round. 'Did you drive Jack's pickup on any of these dates?'

She checks them against her calendar. 'They're all Thursdays, so definitely not.' She stretches her spine. 'As you probably know, during term time I teach an evening class at college. When the class finishes, we sit around for a while and discuss local politics. Then we go to the pub, and I'm never home before twelve.'

'That's late for a school night,' says Andrew.

'Not really, I stick to water. City councillor, on a night out, pissed, and caught on social media. A modern-day cliché, don't you think?'

'And what does Jack do on Thursdays?'

'Stays in. He enjoys the time to himself. So he chills out, plays music, watches football, has a couple of beers, stuff like that.'

I tap the list. 'On any of those dates, when you got home

was Jack out?'

'No.'

'Are you certain?'

'I'm sure I would have noticed if my husband was still out after midnight. Wouldn't you?'

I guess politicians can be as sardonic as the rest of us. I could respond but instead I hand over to Andrew. 'Have you ever given Rachel a lift?' he says.

'Yes, loads of times.'

'Would she ever have sat in the back?'

'Not unless I cleared it out first, it's almost always full of crap.'

'Would your husband ever have given her a lift?'

'Why are you asking that?'

Andrew smiles. 'Would he, or not?'

Her eyes narrow. 'Let's go for not. But again, why are you asking?'

'Simply corroborating your husband's statement, Mrs McCafferty. That's all.'

She opens her mouth to speak but stops herself. Maybe she's scared her answers and Jack's don't match up. I let Andrew continue. 'When was the last time you were in St Mark's Woods?'

'I never go there. I hate forests. Creepy places.'

'What about Jack, would he go there?'

'He might, I suppose, if he was out for some exercise.'

'Would he drive there? Park in the car park?'

Lisa focuses on each of us in turn. She doesn't ask why we want to know. Just says, 'Not as far as I'm aware.'

Andrew sits back. My cue to jump in. I show her the burner we found in the pickup. 'Have you ever seen this phone?'

She leans forward. Keeps her hands folded in her lap. Studies it. 'Don't think so.'

Then I show her two identical evidence bags. They both contain one pillowcase; they too are identical. I point at one of them. 'This pillowcase was discovered in your airing cupboard this morning, quite far down in the pile. Do you recognise it?'

She peers at it through the Cellophane. 'It's hard to tell, can I touch it?'

'I'm afraid not. But tell me, how would touching it help?'

She flushes as she searches for the right words. 'All our bed linens are, em, quite expensive. One of my little foibles, I'm afraid.'

I tap the bag. 'Analysis shows it has a five hundred thread count.'

Lisa's eyebrows shoot up. 'Oh. Maybe it is mine.' Then she points at the pillowcase in the other bag. 'Did you take that from the house too?'

'No. We found that in Jack's pickup, and the two are almost certainly a matching pair. But here's the thing, Lisa. It has significant traces of Rachel's DNA on the inside. Hair, skin oils, tears, mucus, saliva.'

She jams her hand across her mouth, plants the other one on the table to steady herself.

'So, the key question for you, Lisa, is – can you think of any reason why your husband would have murdered Rachel Fuller?'

# CHAPTER THIRTY-THREE

LISA'S GONE HOME; the poor woman's in a hell of a state. Andrew is off to round up the rest of the team, while I pop in to see Jeff to bring him up to date. He stands up, says, 'I'll join you. Save you repeating yourself.'

Now I'm in front of the wallboard in the incident room. 'Folks, some news. I've arrested and cautioned Jack McCafferty on suspicion of Rachel's murder. My plan is to check a few things, tick some boxes, and if nothing changes, I'll be charging him later today.'

I'm running through all the evidence that was found in Jack's pickup when Jeff pipes up. 'Sorry to interrupt you mid-flow, Mel, but I would certainly find it helpful if you listed everything under two columns – hard and circumstantial. Then it'll be easier to see what's what.'

'Good idea.' I pull a tablet closer, log in, and begin tapping away. A few minutes later, I have two lists compiled on the board.

## Hard Evidence

- Pillowcase – high thread count – in Jack McCafferty's (JM) vehicle
- Matching pillowcase recovered from McCafferty home
- Rachel Fuller's (AW) DNA inside pillowcase
- Length of PVC earth cable in JM's vehicle – nicks in sheathing
- PVC earth cable sheathing – deposits under AW's fingernails
- AW's DNA in JM's vehicle
- JM's DNA on AW's underwear and lower body
- 2 x burner phones (SMS, location data, dates and times – all match)
- Satnav location data from JM's vehicle matches above
- AW's burner at SMW on 11, 18 & 25 – matches JM's satnav data
- JM's prints on burner in his vehicle
- Broken signpost (matching resin on JM's vehicle bumper)

## Circumstantial Evidence

- Reel of PVC earth cable (similar to above) in JM's vehicle
- Mud on JM's boots and waterproof trousers, found in his vehicle
- Gravel in JM's vehicle, and in tyre tread

- Sealant from AW's joggers matches tube in JM's vehicle
- MS Word doc on AW's PC – suggests affair

I watch Jeff as he studies my lists. He tweaks his lower lip with his thumb and forefinger. Then he asks, 'What's McCafferty's position?'

'He denies any knowledge or involvement in Rachel's death. Doesn't recognise the phone despite his prints being on it. Maintains he didn't drive to those woods on any of the dates that match the location data. Wasn't having an affair with her and hadn't had sex with her.'

'Alibi?'

'Ah. Nothing that can be corroborated. At home, on his own, on all the dates in question. His wife was out, a regular commitment, can't confirm whether he was home or not.'

'Motive?'

'Tenuous. There's a suggestion he had the hots for Rachel when they were students. I've asked the McCaffertys, together and separately, if Rachel had ever had affairs and they said possibly, but they couldn't say for sure.'

Andrew puts his hand up. 'But remember, Boss, their reaction was definitely a bit odd.'

'He's right,' I say. 'But we've pushed them both on this and they're sticking to their guns. However, Bob is fairly certain the Word document she found on Rachel's PC had been deliberately hidden in a folder that only held jpegs. If Rachel was the author, it appears to suggest she and Jack had sex in his pickup on the first two dates, and she expected they'd be having another go on the day she was killed.'

'Is anyone else in the frame for this, Mel?'

Well, that was left-field. I take a long pause, stare into middle distance, feel everyone's eyes on me. 'The factual evidence against McCafferty says no.'

'But?'

Another pause. 'I have to admit, something is niggling at me.' I tiptoe around my words. 'Think of all the damning pieces of forensic evidence we found in McCafferty's pickup. How did they come to be there? Pillowcase, earth cable, the phone.' I stop; I've made my point. 'When I asked him for his consent to look inside, he agreed. Straight off the bat. And that's what's niggling. Why would he do that, knowing what we'd find? In fact, why would he leave all that evidence there at all? For three days?'

'Maybe he knew the game was up, Boss,' says Andrew.

'Nah. He could have got rid of it over the weekend.' I slap my hand on the table. 'Never mind about the weekend, he told me he took the Friday off. Just finished a big job. Lisa was at work. He didn't lack opportunity.'

My team stays silent. Jeff steeples his fingers, touches them to his chin. 'We both know criminals, murderers, make stupid mistakes. Maybe he thought he still had time to ditch all the evidence. Believed we had no reason to investigate him. Maybe he was scared to get rid of it or couldn't figure out where or how. Then you showed up on his doorstep. But that's all supposition on my part.' He takes his glasses off, polishes them, sticks them back on. 'Ever been winter mountaineering, Mel?'

The fuck did that come from?

He takes my silence as a no. 'In my younger days I was out on the hill most weekends. One time I remember, we were coming down off a peak. Next minute, total whiteout, blizzard conditions. We became disoriented. I was certain we should be heading off to our left, but my climbing partner checked his compass and he said, "No, straight ahead". So, we stopped while we figured it out. I still thought we should go left. He said, "The compass says straight ahead, and the compass never lies". Then, as quickly as it came on, the snow stopped falling and the sky cleared.'

'And if you'd gone left, you'd have fallen to your doom,' says Steph.

Jeff smiles. 'A compass doesn't respond to gut feelings or supposition. It points towards magnetic north. Just like the compass, the evidence points to McCafferty being our murderer. And that's where evidence trumps supposition. Every day of the week. So, we proceed, based solely on evidence and leave the court and the lawyers to sort it out.'

He's right. Of course he's right. But there's one aspect of this investigation that's still bugging the life out of me: how the hell did that burner suddenly switch itself on?

# CHAPTER THIRTY-FOUR

Six Weeks Later

I RARELY THINK about the Rachel Fuller case these days, it was a long time ago in police terms. New cases come along, old ones fade into the background unless something bubbles up or new evidence comes to light. Of course, when they're about to be heard in court our involvement ramps up. But for Jack McCafferty that's about six, seven months down the line.

He pled not guilty, just as I expected. Lisa hired a woman to defend him. Someone told me she was *shit hot* and, actually, I'm pleased about that. No matter, she's taken on a tough job; the weight of forensic evidence incriminating Jack would sink an aircraft carrier. And I don't imagine the prosecutor will need to rely on the circumstantial evidence; it's merely the support act.

Lisa did contact me not long after Jack was charged. 'Surely, in your heart of hearts, you don't believe he's guilty. After all, he opened his vehicle voluntarily, he had no idea all that stuff was there. Besides, I know my husband. He doesn't have a violent bone in his body and there's no way he was screwing that woman.' It's noticeable Lisa didn't say 'Rachel' or even 'her'.

So, I listened. I let her rant. Then I explained the role of the police is to investigate. To gather the evidence and present it to the Procurator Fiscal. To explain, the Scottish legal system is different to our English counterpart. The independent public prosecution service for Scotland is the Crown Office and Procurator Fiscal Service, or COPFS. There are offices of the Procurator Fiscal in every major population centre. They receive and review reports of criminal offences from the local police and determine not only whether there is enough evidence to press charges but that a case can be successfully prosecuted.

Leo Contini is our Fiscal, and this case is as close as they come to a slam dunk. He listened, politely, while I presented my evidence but admitted I could have stopped halfway through, and he'd still have agreed to prosecute. A date has been set, and the process lumbers on.

Crissi and Ella have gone back into the pool and, last I heard, they were working on separate investigations. They were sharp cookies; terrific additions to the team. I'd have no hesitation in asking them to join us again when I need some extra help.

Then there's Lawrence. He's still part of my team, but I just don't rate him as a detective. He doesn't do anything that would be identified in a performance review as a major issue so, for the moment, I'm stuck with him. I guess I've been spoiled. Andrew, Steph and Tobias are all top-notch, they never give me a minute's grief and because they have a terrific work ethic, and are willing and able to use their initiative, I only have to provide guidance when it's necessary. They get on, they work hard, and they always do their level best for victims of crime.

But Lawrence doesn't quite fit in, despite the others trying their best to include him. He's a couple of decades older but his age isn't the issue. It's all down to attitude, which is possibly because of the example he was set as a young detective, at a time when the dinosaurs weren't quite extinct. But I remain hopeful I can turn him, if not around, then at least by a few degrees. Time will tell.

Edwin Fuller wrote me a letter. Thanked me and the team for our 'Sterling efforts'. Much appreciated, and all that jazz. He didn't think he'd be able to rest easy until Jack McCafferty was convicted, but he wouldn't be attending court apart from if and when he was summoned. Out of respect for Lisa, he said.

I didn't reply. I thought that was the end of it but then he started phoning, asking for updates. I was sympathetic at first. That didn't last.

After all the formalities were completed, including an examination of Rachel's remains by a pathologist appointed by the defence, her body was released for burial. I didn't hear anything about the funeral. We moved on.

Except.

Except not fully. Not completely. Not one hundred per cent.

Because the one aspect of this case that wouldn't go away, that I found impossible to cast aside, was the mysterious self-switching-on phone. Jeff and I sat in the pub one night at least two rounds after home time and debated the merits and demerits of the *Copper's nose*. Because that's all this was. Nothing factual, simply a conundrum that might never be resolved.

Did that phone somehow have no signal for God knows

how long then, all of a sudden: bingo! *Hello, network.* Or did it have no power, then a gust of wind rocked a vehicle weighing about the same as an adult hippo and caused a hammer or a wrench to settle inside the cargo deck and miraculously seat the USB cable fully into its slot. Power up: bingo! *Hello, network.*

Or was it the phone signal fairy? Probably about as feasible as my other theories.

No. I'm beat. Give it up, Mel.

So I did.

# CHAPTER THIRTY-FIVE

RACHEL FULLER's funeral had been and gone. As soon as he'd arrived home from the funeral tea, Edwin placed his copy of the order of service centre stage on the mantelpiece. The photo on the front was Rachel on her wedding day. Her gaze followed him around the room in that creepy way photos do but he rarely caught her eye now. No one who came to the house realised it was only there for show. There were days he was tempted to turn it face down but there was always the possibility someone might visit unexpectedly.

Rachel's mother and sister had stayed at a cousin's house out of town. From there, they were heading to Susannah's place in the Lake District. They said they'd be back in about a week to help him, 'Sort things out'. Edwin would rather have walked through a graveyard with the Grim Reaper. But he couldn't put them off for ever without arousing their suspicions, so he played the grieving widower card and asked them to leave it for a while. When he eventually relented, they turned up, but he adopted such a morose *Woe is me* air, they made their excuses and left as quickly as good manners dictated. If he had his way, he'd have kept them at a long arm's length from that point on.

He knew it was vital that he behaved naturally, like a recently bereaved husband. The point was to illustrate the role but not come on too strong. Neither manic depressive nor court jester, more like a mix of the two in short bursts. At other times he remained quiet, introspective, thoughtful. He pretended he cared about other people, so he put aside his antipathy for the coven and their other halves and invited them for drinks and nibbles. The occasional sniffle, his arm around a shoulder, encouraging smiles and a tastefully upbeat persona. All false, and as soon as the door closed behind them, he poured himself a large one and flopped down on the sofa. Job done.

He was well aware of the sage advice, 'After you're bereaved don't do anything in a hurry. Don't move house or take a world cruise, and especially don't throw all her worldly possessions in a skip'. So he left everything as it was until he worked out what wouldn't attract unwanted attention. He contacted her boss who drove up from Newcastle, delivered sincere condolences and packed all her work stuff into his car. That included her PC, her phone and, curiously, her chair. The man hesitated before wheeling it away and it was all Edwin could do not to laugh as he dabbed at his eyes while waving the man off.

Edwin did bin a few of Rachel's things but only what other people couldn't use. Cosmetics, deodorant, personal items like that. More to keep himself occupied than for any other reason, he weeded out items of her clothing that no one would remember – faded underwear, beat up trainers and other items she hadn't worn in years. But he made sure to keep all her jewellery, decent outfits, dress shoes and handbags. Eventually he reached a point where his gut feeling said stop.

He listened.

# CHAPTER THIRTY-SIX

'JESUS! WHAT DOES HE WANT NOW?'

The phone was buzzing away on her desk, but Lisa didn't pick up. When the ringing stopped, the screen faded to black, but Edwin didn't leave a message. Not this time.

She pushed her chair back, sauntered over to her office window and gazed out on a vista that never ceased to amaze her. She was on the third floor, to the rear of the City Chambers building on Edinburgh's High Street, and because the land on the old town escarpment dropped away like a stone, she had Princes Street Gardens and the new town in the forefront, the Forth Estuary in the middle distance, and the Kingdom of Fife as a backdrop. On a clear winter's day, she could pick out snow-capped mountains above Loch Tay, about fifty miles to the northwest. She and Jack had enjoyed several sailing holidays on the loch; she wondered if they'd ever go there again.

She leaned forward and rested her forehead on the cool glass. She sighed. Edwin. He didn't phone her every single day, but it wasn't far off. At first she'd answered his calls, but it wasn't long before she let voicemail do its job. Sometimes he'd left messages, but rarely now. She hoped he would eventually take the hint. She didn't have the energy to deal with him too. When your husband is accused of murdering his alleged lover, who also happens to be your best friend, he becomes your prime focus. Rachel's death and the needs of her increasingly demanding widowed husband paled into insignificance.

Edwin had tried to rope her into helping him with the funeral arrangements, but she'd turned him down. At the time she thought she'd been polite but later, she realised she'd snapped at him. Men don't often pout but he did. In normal circumstances she'd have ripped the piss something awful.

She took compassionate leave while she researched defence counsel. Ralph Levinson would have been her first choice by a distance, and she was devastated when he declined, citing impending retirement. He did recommend a few alternatives, but they all turned her off through a combination of their fancy offices, flashy suits and outright flannel, although she did reject one out of hand quite simply because his PA was a stuck-up bitch. The key for Lisa was this: could she work with them? The answer came entirely from her gut. Then she met a woman who explained in language that bordered on blunt that she didn't concern herself with the issue of Jack's guilt. If, despite her best efforts, the prosecution could prove their case beyond a shadow of a doubt then, no two ways about it, Lisa's husband was a murderer. Lisa hired her on the spot, and the fact she was blind mattered not a jot.

# CHAPTER THIRTY-SEVEN

EDWIN STARED at the knuckles on his right hand. They hurt. The skin on the most prominent one was split, he feared he'd broken a bone. *Next time you punch a wall, idiot, pick one that's not loadbearing.* It might have been comical if he hadn't been so bloody furious.

He hurried through to the kitchen and stuck his hand under the cold tap. It stung but he left it running. He stood there, fuming. His carefully constructed plans were beginning to fall apart.

Once Jack had been charged, Edwin thought he'd have been able to enter a delicious period of Schadenfreude that, in truth, he hadn't foreseen while he was planning to murder his wife. It had been a by-product, a tasty little extra to enjoy at his leisure.

But people were letting him down, not behaving in ways he imagined they should. He'd envisaged regular chats with Cooper, who'd keep him updated on progress. His in-laws would disappear off the scene, never to be heard of again. He'd visit Jack and act all magnanimous with his 'friend'. And then there was Lisa. Beautiful, sorrowful Lisa. He would take her for long walks, stop off for coffee, have deep and meaningful heart-to-hearts, before eventually ...

But absolutely none of these things panned out as he'd envisaged. The fourth or was it the fifth time he phoned Cooper she was terse with him. 'Mr Fuller. Nothing more will happen until the trial. And no, we won't be speaking to Jack McCafferty again unless new evidence comes to light, or he changes his plea. If either of those things do happen, I will contact you.' Then she told him she had to go and hung up.

Rachel's mother and sister: they were the complete opposite, never off the phone. Could he look for this, could he send them that? Could he track down an emerald and diamond cluster ring that had been handed down to Rachel from her grandma? Is her will sorted out yet? Have you been tending her grave? Edwin answered yes to all of these, albeit through gritted teeth. He only answered no to one question: 'Can we come to visit?' He was surprised they'd even asked.

But his frustration levels skyrocketed when Jack declined his request to visit. He was kicking himself about that one because he'd held off for far too long. If he'd asked in the first couple of weeks Jack would probably have bitten his hand off. Edwin had imagined sitting there, making all the appropriate noises and faces, while reassuring Jack that, 'No, of course I don't think you killed Rachel. There must be some mistake'. But he'd misjudged it, given Jack too much time, and missed a gilt-edged opportunity for a spot of quiet gloating.

But Lisa was the bamboo shoot under his fingernail. How could he have misinterpreted the signals so badly? From the day Rachel introduced him to Lisa and Jack, her boyfriend at the time, he'd always felt there was a special relationship between them. They'd make eyes when their other halves were niggling at each other; Lisa would trickle light fingertips across his arm when Rachel was being particularly nasty to him; and he always hugged her a fraction too tightly when they all separated at the end of a night out. Lisa didn't mind that. In fact, she'd encouraged him. Hadn't she?

*No*, he realised. *She bloody well hadn't.*

But that would all change when her precious husband was convicted and put away for a long, long time.

# CHAPTER THIRTY-EIGHT

THE THING WAS, Jack McCafferty knew he was innocent. *So why*, he thought, *did no other bugger?* Except Lisa. She was sticking by him. She knew Jack had the hots for Rachel when they were all freshers. But that was once upon a time, before she and Jack became a solid item. Rachel had changed; way too toxic for his liking, and Jack was a one-woman man. And that woman was Lisa, no question.

Sitting on a bench one day in the outdoor exercise compound at the remand centre he tried to work out, for only about the one thousandth time, who had framed him and, more importantly, why? It must have been Edwin. Who else was there? Jack was perfectly well aware he wasn't universally popular – his reputation for being a grumpy old bastard saw to that – but he genuinely couldn't think of anyone else who would have such a serious axe to grind. Professionally, none of his plumbing contracts had ever turned belly up. No serious customer complaints, never been taken to the small claims court, not even any minor issues raised with his trade body. The odd moan here and there from impossible to please customers but he'd always resolved any problems without quibbling, even if he ended up a few quid out of pocket.

As a businessman, Jack was switched on. Word of mouth was vital for a company like his and he relied on it. His order book was full for months ahead and his two employees had promised to keep things ticking over. 'Until they get a better offer.' And that was fair play as far as he was concerned. Lisa earned a decent salary and they'd paid off their mortgage; she wouldn't starve.

He'd tried to talk her out of hiring the blind lawyer – *How the hell will that work?* – but she'd been adamant. Told him he couldn't stop her even if he wanted to. Jack had complained he didn't like the woman, far too direct for his tastes. Lisa told him that wasn't the point. Subject closed.

Jack rose from the bench and performed a brief stretching routine. He'd lost weight and some muscle definition, but he felt well. He joined the circuit behind two of his fellow inmates and followed them round at their pace. His thoughts returned to the perennial subject: Edwin Fuller. The downtrodden husband who'd murdered his wife and framed his innocent friend. Jack had had visitors including Lisa, his mother and his sister. But his so-called friend had stayed away. *That's a dead giveaway, you bastard.* Time, too much time, had passed *then* Edwin asked for permission to visit. Jack told him to take a hike.

But the answers to the key questions, why and how, utterly eluded him. He could only hope the cops would come up with something, while he kidded himself on they were still trying.

# CHAPTER THIRTY-NINE

EDWIN WAS LOSING IT, and he knew it. But this time it was genuine, not manufactured. He sat bolt upright in his armchair, nails digging into the material, staring into the fireplace. A partly scorched log, shades of brown grey and black, lay amongst the previous evening's ashes. A mug of coffee with a sheen of scum on the surface stood untouched on the coffee table. He felt a tic in the corner of his eye, but blinking didn't stop it, so he let it go. He needed to suffer the tension, to feel wound up.

These emotions had their roots in experiences he'd had as a small boy, maybe nine or ten years old. He and his mother had been visiting his grandma. He was lying on his stomach on the carpet, his feet kicked up behind him, concentrating on a colouring-in book. He was always incredibly careful to stay within the lines.

He'd just turned to a fresh drawing when his grandma said, 'There's something I'd like you to do for me, darling. Come and I'll show you.' On the table, resting on a mat, lay a fine silver pendant chain that she'd managed to tangle into a series of tight knots. 'I can't undo it, but I'm sure you'll be able to. You've got nimble little fingers, not like my stiff old ones.' She showed him her hands, but they seemed perfectly normal to him. No matter, he loved doing things for his grandma, so he sat down, picked it up and set to work.

He pored over it, trying to figure out which end to start with. For several minutes he winkled away at the knots. At first, he thought he was getting nowhere but as he tweaked away at the chain, gradually the free ends lengthened until he realised he only had a few loops to untangle. And that was the moment he stopped enjoying the puzzle – when it was almost complete. Impending triumph morphed into disappointment, but he didn't understand why.

His grandma cuddled him and cooed, 'You're such a clever boy, I would never have managed that. Come through to the kitchen, let's see what's in the biscuit tin.' But not even two custard creams revived his spirits, and he was uncharacteristically quiet for the rest of the visit.

On another day she'd brought him a ball of white wool that looked as though a dozen cats had fought over it. Forgetting what had happened with the silver chain he settled down, concentrating, ready for the battle. But he was aghast when, after tugging at no more than three or four tight connections, the whole thing fell out in his hands. As usual, his grandma fussed over him. He forced himself to smile as she crushed him in a tight hug, when what he desperately wanted to do was scream. At the top of his voice. He'd never felt so frustrated. Never.

Just like now.

He realised he'd made things far too straightforward for the police, giving Jack up so quickly. Despite all his planning, he'd totally misjudged things. He should have leaked the evidence in a drizzle, not a deluge. That would have created more interaction between him and the police, more conversations, more questions that would give him the opportunity to drop into downtrodden martyr mode: 'I honestly don't know. I'm sorry, I'm not much help, am I?'

By moving too fast he'd missed the opportunity to outsmart them: Detective Inspector Mel Cooper and her snappily dressed sidekick, whose name he couldn't remember. They would have been floundering, chasing their tails. There hadn't been enough time between each stage to savour them, like he would a single malt. He could have enjoyed the buzz generated by staying on his game for much longer than a measly few days.

The killing.

Her body.

Interviews.

The evidence.

An arrest.

A few tugs at loose ends and the tangled ball of wool was no more. 'Such a clever boy'.

*No. Stupid, stupid boy. How could I have judged it so badly? Well, I will just have to fix it. Regenerate the buzz. But how?*

He sat in the chair for hours, 'til long past dark. Mulling things over. Then, a glimmer of an idea. He let it float around in his head until finally, he knew what to do.

Now rejuvenated, he pushed himself upright, stretched, then trotted upstairs to find his handbook. He was ready to make another plan.

# CHAPTER FORTY

Moisture dripped off Edwin Fuller's eyebrows, the tip of his nose and the point of his chin. He was uncomfortably warm and light-headed. He supposed if he were a woman he'd be surrounded by scented candles and there would be a gin and tonic close at hand. He might even be reading some trashy novel. But personally, he'd never seen the attraction of reclining only half submerged in water that was either way too hot or cooling rapidly. *Give me a shower any day of the week.*

He hadn't had a bath since the first time he'd attended the gym, when he overdid it and seized solid for days afterwards. But this was a necessity. The doctor in A&E had told him the bruising might take a few days to fully develop but a bath and daily doses of paracetamol would help. He glanced around as if to make sure he wasn't overheard before suggesting that if Edwin believed in homeopathy, Arnica tablets were just the job. But he should consider himself incredibly fortunate to have emerged unscathed.

What the doctor didn't know was that a strategically posi-tioned folded ski jacket and two cushions had mitigated the effects but, in the interests of authenticity, Edwin couldn't avoid taking an exploding air bag to the face. To make absolutely sure he didn't suffer any injuries to his feet and legs, he'd engineered the collision so the passenger side absorbed most of the impact. However, he had failed to anticipate the car would bounce, spin and roll over, coming to rest in a clump of bushes on the opposite side of the road.

He wasn't sure the farmer had accepted his apology while he was being lifted into the back of the ambulance, but he'd offered it more for effect than for any altruistic reason. The wall would mend. He imagined the farmer might also be wondering how the crash had happened, especially with the road being straight as a pool cue. Edwin wasn't concerned, his insurance would cover it.

There was no doubt the action he'd chosen had been extremely risky, even downright foolhardy. But essential, like the bath he was taking. So far there had been only two downsides: he was far more shaken than he'd expected, and Hayley had insisted on coming through from Glasgow to take care of him.

But the major upside was, sometime in the next week, a significant piece of evidence against him would be no more.

# CHAPTER FORTY-ONE

One Week Later

Wednesday Evening

I REVERSE INTO OUR DRIVEWAY. Our house is just off-centre at the head of a cul-de-sac. The security light comes on as I pull up in front of the garage door and turn the engine off. I hear the clank as the latch of the automatic gate engages with the lock. We live in a lovely area of Edinburgh, off Queensferry Road, but our neighbours on both sides have had cars stolen or damaged in the past year so my husband decided we should have extra security. As a police officer I could hardly argue with him although I grudged the money it cost.

I don't move. Eight o'clock, and it's been a long day. Another one. Do criminals never go on holiday? Take a few days off to spend time with the wife and kids? I sigh. Fat chance.

I should move. Get out of the car and go inside. My

husband, my son, and my dinner are all in there. But I'm shattered and I'm finding it impossible to shift my backside. Callum messaged earlier; he's produced some sort of Thai chicken thing with jasmine rice and some crispy accompaniments. Luckily he's a whiz in the kitchen, because I'm definitely not. I'll pop upstairs to Conor's room first, give him a cheeky wee hug just to annoy him, then downstairs for a larger dose of the real thing with his dad. Maybe even a glass of white. Then couch, TV, and bed. Might have a bath before I hit the sack.

I step out onto the gravel, close the door and blip the locks. Then I hear a voice from over on my left. 'Evening, DI Cooper.'

On that side, a lane runs along the edge of our garden. It joins up with a cycle path, part of an extensive spider's web that serves the north of the city. It's known as the *Edinburgh Lanes and Paths Network*, or ELPN. Most of the paths run along disused railway lines that once transported goods trains that hauled freight between places like Leith Docks, Newhaven Harbour and the gasworks at Granton. I see a figure standing under a lamp post between two trees at the entrance to the lane. I'm perfectly safe as he's on the other side of a four-foot fence but still, I take only a few paces towards him then stop. There's light rain falling, turning the streetlight into a hazy arc, like a night-time rainbow.

The man is wearing a bicycle helmet and glasses. He has that peculiar stance which suggests he's astride his bike. Then I recognise him. 'Edwin? What brings you here at this time of night?'

'Oh, I only wanted a quick word.'

'What – now?' I shake my head. 'It's late. I need to go in to see my family.'

'It'll only take a minute.'

I move another step closer. 'What do you want?'

'You arrested Jack McCafferty for Rachel's murder. I'm here to tell you, you've arrested the wrong guy. Jack wouldn't have killed Rachel, he's always been besotted with her. Bloody sap, mooning over her all the time.'

What the hell? 'Sorry. But outside my house in the dark is neither the time nor the place to discuss this. Now, if you'll excuse me, I have to go. Good night.' I'm uneasy so I begin to edge away. The security light goes off.

He puts a hand up. 'You're wrong there, DI Cooper. This is the perfect time to discuss it. Because there's something you should know.'

'And what might that be?'

'Like I said, you've arrested the wrong man.'

My bag is over my shoulder, and my phone is in the front pocket. There's a magnetic catch on the clasp. Aiming for casual, I lift my hand. 'Why do you say that?' I snick the catch, but it makes a sound like a rifle shot.

He leans forward over his handlebars. Points at my bag. 'Don't even think about it, or I'm off.' I let my hand drop away. He grins, waves an arm around. 'It's funny, you know. Only three of these posh expensive houses have CCTV cameras, and none of them are directed at this lane. Not even yours. Tsk tsk, DI Cooper.'

'No, Edwin. It's the garage and the house we're protecting.' I take a step to the side, but the security light doesn't play ball. Bloody thing stays off. And why hasn't Callum come out? He must have heard me parking. I play for time. 'So you don't believe Jack killed her?'

'No, I don't.'

I shrug. 'So who did then?'

He gives out a harsh laugh, utterly devoid of humour. 'Me, you stupid woman. It was me!'

I gawp at him. Did someone just slap me in the face?

He reaches out, grabs his handlebars. 'Yes, I killed her. How on earth could you even imagine Jack could be capable of such a thing? Jeez, you're even dumber than I thought you were.' Then a light appears behind the glass panel in our front door. He glances at it, drags the front wheel of his bike round in an arc. 'So yes, I did it. And do you know the best thing? You'll never prove it.'

The front door lock clicks. Edwin slings one more look in my direction. 'Night night, plod.' Then he cycles away along the path, accelerating down the slope towards the ELPN.

———

I'M MOMENTARILY STUNNED, and it takes a few seconds before my brain kicks in. I open the car, jump in, hammer the heel of my hand on the steering wheel while the bloody gate takes an interminable age to slide open. The instant the gap is wide enough I squeeze through and shoot off down the street. In the rear-view mirror, I spot Callum framed in our doorway; he probably thinks I've lost the plot. The hands-free eventually sorts itself out and I dial Andrew. 'Where are you?'

'On my way home.'

'Yes, but *where?*'

He tells me. *Shit!* He's closer than I am, but not by much. 'Edwin Fuller's house. Get over there now! If he comes home, stop him outside. If he's in, keep him there. I'll be with you in eight, ten minutes.'

The route is fairly direct and apart from a hairy moment at a roundabout I arrive in one piece. Andrew's car is outside, hazards winking. He's standing on the pavement, scrutinising the front of the house. I run up to him. 'Is he here?' I slip a little as I stop, the paving slabs are greasy from the rain.

'He hasn't come home since I showed up but that was less than thirty seconds ago. The living room and kitchen lights are on, and his car's not here. But what's this about? What's happened?'

I give him the highlights. He doesn't ask if I'm joking; definitely a point in his favour. I march up to the front step and jam my thumb on the door bell. It's hardwired and we hear the traditional ring. When it begins to hurt, I drop my hand. 'Back door.' Andrew steps smartly to the side to avoid being mown down.

As we approach the garage, I spot a sliver of light where the up-and-over door meets the ground. I stop. Wait. Hear a clanking sound from inside. I crash my hand three times on the metal door. 'Edwin Fuller! Police!'

The mechanism rattles and the door squeals open to reveal Fuller standing there. He's wearing dark blue gym kit and holding a hefty dumb-bell in his right hand. Sweat droplets are falling from his nose and chin. He glares at us. 'What the hell's going on? You scared me half to death, battering on the door like that.'

'You know damn fine why we're here, Mr Fuller. To continue the conversation you and I were having at my house about ten minutes ago.'

His jaw drops. 'What are you talking about, your house?' He turns to Andrew. 'Is she on something, or what?' Then to me. 'I don't even know where you live.'

'You were at my house. We had a conversation. I was in my garden. You were on your bike, at the top of the lane.'

He bends down, places the dumb-bell on the ground. Rises again, takes his time about it. Folds his arms, rocks back on his heels. 'DI Cooper. I have absolutely no idea what you're talking about. I've been here all evening, and for the past hour or so I've been working out.'

Andrew points at Fuller's bikes, hanging from their hooks. 'May I?' he says.

Edwin turns sideways, sweeps an arm behind him. 'Be my guest.' As Andrew strides past him, Fuller winks at me.

You fucker! I glower at him but that's all. I don't want to give him another opportunity to suggest I'm a fruitcake. There are two bikes hanging from the rafters. Andrew swings each of them back and forth. Shakes his head.

'Are they dry, Detective ...' says Edwin. 'I do apologise, I can't remember your name.' Andrew ignores him; he's too smart to rise to the bait.

I take half a step towards Fuller. 'Would you care to repeat what you said to me at my house?'

He holds his ground. 'I wasn't at your house, so there's nothing to repeat.'

Now I'm closer, I can make out livid marks on his right cheekbone. 'What happened there?'

He raises a hand, touches the area with his fingertips. 'Fell off my bike.'

Good. I hope it hurts. Then I jerk my thumb over my shoulder, indicate the empty driveway. 'By the way, where's your car tonight?'

'A friend borrowed it. Not that that's any of your business.' He reaches up, takes hold of the garage door. 'Now, if you would step back, please. I've had enough of this nonsense, and I'd like to get back to my workout.' Then he slams the door down.

I'm so tempted to hammer on the metal again, but I desist. We walk to the street, stop on the other side of the cars. I take a deep breath. 'The cheeky bastard winked at me, you know. While you were checking out his bikes.' My colleague's eyes widen. I stare past him at the house. 'Thanks for believing in me, Andrew. Appreciate it. But I'll need to take some time to think about what Fuller said tonight—'

'And why.'

I nod. 'Yes. And why. Then I'll give Jeff a ring. Have a chat. Because this is beyond weird.' I pause. 'I suppose it's not particularly unusual to loan your car to a friend, is it?'

Andrew makes a face. 'Not really. A bit convenient though.'

'As you say. It most certainly is.'

# CHAPTER FORTY-TWO

EDWIN STOOD behind the garage door until he heard the cars driving away. Then he relaxed but, to his surprise, began shaking. Probably a mixture of high energy expenditure, relieved tension and the chill inside the garage. He wiped one forearm across his face, then the other. The drops still fell to the floor. He grabbed a sweatshirt and put it on. *A shower will sort me out.*

Later, dressed in boxers and a towelling robe, he sat at his desk skimming the pages in his Murderer's Handbook. He'd added a number of new items once he'd decided to move the project onto the 'Confess to Cooper' phase. He still wasn't exactly sure what had motivated him to take such a drastic and exhilarating course of action, but it hadn't half raised his spirits and made him feel there was nothing he couldn't achieve if he set his mind to it.

He ran through his plans again, point by point, and was satisfied he hadn't made any mistakes. The police would be back, he knew that. *But they have nothing. Nothing they can hang me with.* He chuckled at the unintentional pun as he made his way downstairs to find the vodka. It was a new bottle he'd opened a couple of nights previously, and already it was approaching half empty.

Drink in hand, he moved through to the sitting room and dropped into the armchair. This was a time to enjoy himself, to savour the pleasurable feeling of winning. Not quite victorious, but certain he had a healthy lead.

# CHAPTER FORTY-THREE

'SLOW DOWN, DARLING,' says Callum, in my ear. 'What's this guy's name again?'

'Edwin Fuller.' My words are muffled because I'm speaking to Callum's collarbone, my hands clasped tight behind his back. It's the first time my husband's heard about Fuller. I rarely discuss work stuff at home, and certainly not murder cases. I've been a detective since before the kids went to school and in this house, it's not only the walls that have ears. But I do give Callum the gist of the plot, he deserves that.

'Did he threaten you?'

I shake my head, meaning my nose rubs back and forth across his shirt. But *I will not cry* – I'm still too pissed off for that. I reach up and kiss him properly, tighten my hug for an instant then drop out of his grip. 'I need to phone the boss. This changes everything.'

I turn away, stop, turn back. Give him another kiss. 'Thanks, darling. Oh, and by the way, that was from Bob.' He smacks me on the bum, and I head upstairs.

_____

'You'VE nothing on him to justify bringing him in, Mel,' says Jeff. His voice is tinny, I have him on my phone's speaker. It's propped up against a dictionary. I'm in our study at home. My dinner is keeping warm in the oven and my husband is still waiting for an explanation. Luckily he's a patient chap. He'd have to be.

'I know, I know.' I grab fistfuls of my own hair. 'God, this is so frustrating. I can't question him because he'll just tell me to get lost, and claim harassment if I don't. Can't go into his house, or his garage, or even his bloody car.' I fall silent. Every possibility I come up with is either illegal, unethical or would prejudice any prosecution of Edwin Fuller in the future.

My phone buzzes. 'Hang on, Jeff, it's Andrew on the other line.' I switch calls, listen to what Andrew has to say, thank him, and bring Jeff back in. The only word I utter is, 'Damn!'

'Damn what?'

'The time between Fuller cycling away from here, and Andrew arriving at his house was no more than nine minutes. Ten, absolute tops. Andrew brought his bike over, we calculated the fastest possible route, and Andrew tried to replicate the timings.'

'He's a fit lad, did he manage it?'

'No. It took him a full two minutes longer. The poor boy sounds knackered. And seriously pissed off.'

The line goes silent. Then Jeff says, 'Andrew definitely used the quickest route?'

'As far as we can tell.'

'Maybe it's simply that Fuller's fitter. A faster cyclist.'

'I'd find that hard to believe, he's twelve years older.'

'You've already ruled out Fuller's car; could he have jumped in a taxi?'

'It's possible. But he set off on the ELPN at the back of my house, he'd have to go a fair distance before he hit a road. What are the chances of picking up a cab, and one that's willing to take a bike? I'll check it out but I'm not hopeful. Apart from that, both his bikes were dry.'

'He could have another one hidden away.'

'My head's beginning to spin here, Jeff. I need to slow down, think this through.'

'Fair enough. I'll contact Leo Contini and arrange to meet with him tomorrow, as early as he can manage. For the moment, let's leave things where they are, and it goes without saying that we don't go anywhere near Edwin Fuller until Leo give us some guidance.'

'It might go without saying, Boss, but you just did.'

He chuckles. 'I'm perfectly well aware of that, Mel. Goodnight.'

# CHAPTER FORTY-FOUR

Thursday

'THE MAIN ISSUE FOR ME, Mel, is the case against Jack McCafferty is solid,' says our Procurator Fiscal, Leo Contini. 'Forensically, we have—'

'I know what we have.' *Shit!* I hold up my hands. 'Sorry, Leo, I didn't mean to snap.'

It's the following morning. Jeff and I are in the Fiscal's office, at a meeting table that's drowning in paperwork. I have a lot of time for Leo. We worked closely together during an investigation last year. Tragically, his teenage son died in terrible circumstances that related to the case.

He waves away my apology. 'When you brought McCafferty to me I didn't need much convincing, simply because of the evidence. But, what Edwin Fuller has said to you, that it was he, and not McCafferty, who murdered his wife – well, I've been Fiscal for eight years and this is completely new territory for me. So, let's take this one stage at a time.' He pulls a notepad towards him. 'Do you think Fuller is making it up? An attempt to garner attention for some obscure reason.'

'No. The way he said it was utterly chilling.' I go on to explain Edwin's demeanour at my house and how he winked at me in his garage when Andrew's back was turned.

'At any stage in your investigation did you suspect him?'

'No, I honestly can't say I did. I always thought it was weird he didn't phone her after she stormed out the house but everyone we spoke to confirmed that's how they were. And he was in a hell of a state in the early days – breaking down in tears every five minutes. Jeff and I discussed it at the time; all I had was a niggle, but it was never that strong, and there was absolutely no evidence to back it up.'

Leo jots down a few notes. 'McCafferty – and leaving aside the evidence for the moment – were you one hundred per cent convinced he was guilty?'

I pick my words carefully. 'I was never fully convinced but, as you said, the forensics were solid. Not much room for doubt.'

Leo lifts his glasses onto his head and studies me. 'Yet you do have some? Doubt, that is.'

Of course I do. 'When I asked him if we could see inside his vehicle, he said yes without a moment's hesitation. Didn't ask why, just picked up his keys. When we found the evidence: phone, pillowcase, DNA, everything – he was stunned. And then, when I arrested him on suspicion, he didn't tell his wife to contact a solicitor. That's not standard behaviour. Not for a man who's under suspicion of murder.' I pause, look at both Leo and Jeff. 'But those are only my feelings, and evidence beats feelings hands down.'

'McCafferty didn't have a clear motive either, did he?' says Jeff.

Leo pushes his pen away, sits back. 'The issue of motive is tricky. In days gone by, it had a far higher weighting than it does now. Sometimes a person is killed, and there isn't a specific reason for it. The fact they're dead is enough for a prosecutor although defence counsel might try to make more of the why.' He flicks through the file, looks up at me. 'What did you have?'

'Nothing solid. The document we found on Rachel's PC, where she – assuming she was the author – suggested she was about to break off a sexual relationship on the very evening she was murdered. If that relationship was with Jack, and he didn't want to break up, then maybe he snapped and killed her.' I shrug. 'But even I don't believe that because the pillowcase and the ligature indicated premeditation. Plus, now I think Edwin wrote it and left it for us to find.'

'Ah, yes. The document.' Leo sighs. 'I'll tell you something for nothing, I won't even be referring to that in court. As you said, we have no proof she wrote it, and Jack McCafferty isn't named. Defence would have a proper go at me, and they'd be quite right. I'd do the same.'

Jeff stands up to stretch. 'Speaking of the defence, might they raise points like why would he be stupid enough to use one of their own pillowcases? Why would he kill her in his vehicle then not clean it out? Why would he leave incriminating evidence there for over forty-eight hours and not get rid of it?'

Leo smiles. 'You've answered your own questions there, my man. All those actions would indeed have been pretty stupid. But, murder is not a sensible thing to do and murderers are almost always under tremendous pressure. I wouldn't bat an eyelid if they did ask those questions, and neither would a judge. Which brings me back to Edwin Fuller. Why, totally out of the blue, would he tell you he was the murderer? Assuming we believe him, that is. What's changed in his life? Has he snapped? If he did kill her, is the pressure building to such an intense level that he can't handle it any longer? Or is he playing some kind of twisted game?'

'I don't know,' I say. 'But I certainly don't think he's snapped. I spoke to him on two separate occasions last night and both times he was completely in control of himself. Especially at his house although we still don't know how he got there before us. But he was all set up, working through an exercise routine to give him an excuse for being sweaty – how convenient. And all in stark contrast to his behaviour at once after the murder. So now it's obvious that was all an act.'

'Even the tears?' says Jeff

'That's a harder question to answer, Boss. But I have a friend who's an actor. Or is it actress? Who knows these days?' I pause. 'Where was I going with that? Oh, yes, she's an actor and I asked her one day about how she manages to cry convincingly. Does she drop vinegar in her eye or something similar? But she said it was easy enough, she simply imagined a terribly sad event, especially if it was one she'd experienced personally. So, with Edwin, maybe that was it. He found it easy enough to bring on the waterworks because, after all, he had killed his wife and before that he was an honest upstanding citizen. An ordinary Joe. So, my vote goes with your other idea, Leo, he's playing with us.' I pause. 'Or, actually, with me.'

Again, we all lapse into silence 'til Jeff pipes up. 'Where does that leave us, Leo?'

The Fiscal picks up his pen with both hands, rotates it between his fingers. 'Jack McCafferty is on remand, with a date set for his trial. If Fuller did kill his wife, then McCafferty's innocent. But what Fuller said to you, he said in private. Deliberately, I expect. You've no audio or video evidence, no witnesses to corroborate your version of events, so it's your word against his. I can't do anything about McCafferty as things stand; the legal process will have to play out. If I were to drop the case, he would have to be released. And if he turned out to be the murderer after all, society would be at risk. So, rightly or wrongly, McCafferty stays where he is.'

Leo hasn't said anything I didn't expect. I splay my hands, signalling he should continue.

'But this thing with Fuller is difficult. He's told you in private that he killed his wife, but he's denying it in public. You can't arrest him on that basis, especially as you've never suspected him, there's nothing on file, and you have no evidence. I don't see you have any choice but to investigate him further. However, you will have to be careful. You'll have to do it without driving a bulldozer through his rights; there's no way you'll get a warrant as I doubt any sheriff would support such a request. So when you bring the case back to me, and I sincerely hope you do, make sure it's rock solid – like it was with Jack McCafferty. I would not want Edwin Fuller set free on a technicality.'

'Don't you worry about that, Leo,' I say. 'I fully intend to make damn sure that doesn't happen.'

# CHAPTER FORTY-FIVE

A͟L͟L͟ ͟M͟Y͟ ͟T͟E͟A͟M͟, plus Jeff, are with me in the incident room, and Dave Devlin, Bob Summers and Greg Brodie are on standby in case I need them. Jeff and Andrew were already up to speed, and I've just run through the whole story with the others. Lawrence is here too; he's just finished reading up on the case notes.

'In a nutshell,' I say, 'we have to consider everything that's come out of Edwin Fuller's mouth up until now is a lie. Even if something he's said in the past or will say in the future actually is the truth, we should still be highly sceptical.'

'What is it they say, Boss?' says Andrew. 'Keep the lie as close as possible to the truth.'

I nod. 'And I think that's what he's been doing. So now, I want us to work through this case again, point by point, paying particular attention to the actions and statements of the people who appear to be the four main protagonists: Edwin Fuller, Rachel Fuller, Jack McCafferty and Lisa McCafferty. But one thing we'll have to keep right at the front of our minds is although Leo has encouraged me to investigate Fuller further, it's absolutely vital we respect the man's rights at all times. We require at least two solid pieces of evidence, or an over- whelming array of circumstantial evidence before we can formally change the focus of our investigation from McCaf- ferty to Fuller.'

I fix my attention on each of my colleagues. 'So, if you have to go to the loo, or grab a drink or a bite to eat, now's your chance because this next session could be a long haul. We need uninterrupted train of thought on this.'

Appreciating the urgency, nobody faffs around, and we reconvene within ten minutes. 'Let's go right back to the start, deal with the whole investigation in chronological order. But this time, our job is to prove Fuller is our murderer. Lawrence, I'm hoping you'll be able to provide a fresh pair of eyes. Now, as questions or issues arise, we'll address them if we can. If not, we take them out there and find answers. Make sense?'

'It does,' says Jeff. 'As long as you're certain Edwin Fuller isn't simply pulling your chain.'

'Trust me, Boss, I've thought of nothing else since he showed up at my house last night.' The wallboard is already powered up. I tap my tablet and four bullet points appear:

- Edwin Fuller – why confess now?
- Jack McCafferty – evidence – too convenient?
- Jack McCafferty – reactions to evidence
- Edwin Fuller – mocked me in private.

'Taking these in order, why has Fuller chosen this moment to make this bizarre confession that he killed his wife? We had all the evidence we needed to convict Jack McCafferty but now it looks like Fuller framed him. Why would he do that? Jack was supposedly his friend. But Jack is married to Lisa, and Lisa is remaining loyal to her husband. She doesn't believe he's a murderer.' I pause for effect, and to steady myself for a potential blast from my boss. 'So this morning I called her.'

Jeff's eyebrows shoot up so fast I'm surprised they don't fly off the top of his bald head. I raise both hands, palms out. 'Don't panic, Boss. I made it sound like a friendly chat. Asked her how she was, about Jack, that kind of stuff. I let her blether on, but then she told me Fuller's been sending her messages, leaving voicemails. "Would you like to meet for a coffee or a drink – support each other?" Stuff like that. She put him off, but he kept trying, really coming on strong. Eventually she ignored everything from him, and he stopped.'

'So, he's been stalking her?' says Lawrence.

'I wouldn't put it quite like that, but certainly verging on desperate. The question is, did he kill Rachel, then frame Jack to clear the way for a longer-term plan to strike up a relationship with Lisa?'

'Lisa says she isn't playing ball,' says Steph. 'But did she ever give him any encouragement? Make him think it was even a possibility they'd get together?'

'It's not something I've ever asked her. Hasn't been any need.'

'But Mel,' says Jeff. 'If that was his motive, why would he suddenly claim responsibility and deliberately drag our focus back onto him?'

'That, I don't know. Maybe he had this carefully conceived plan, in some way it hasn't come together the way he intended, and he's lost the plot. Even temporarily. And for all I know, having confessed, he's now kicking himself up and down the street for being so stupid.'

'That's maybe pushing it, Mel. But let's move on to the evidence we found in Jack's vehicle.'

I don't argue. I can spot a stretch with the best of them but it's all I have. 'The forensic evidence we found now seems all too convenient; I'm even beginning to wonder about Jack's DNA being found on Rachel. Then we have a burner that apparently connects itself to the network after three days of silence, containing SMS conversations with the burner we found in Fuller's car. Traces of earth cable under Rachel's nails; a pillowcase from his own house with her DNA on it; his vehicle chockfull of incriminating forensics that he doesn't get rid of, despite being off work for the weekend. No, I don't buy it.'

'Hate to rain on your parade, Mel,' says Jeff. 'But you bought it before.'

'Hands up, you're right. And I bought it because we followed the evidence. I can't sit here and say I've always thought Jack McCafferty was innocent, but what I can say is there's always been a niggle – probably because we caught him so easily.'

Jeff switches his attention to the others. 'I'd rather not be the bad guy all the time so does anyone else fancy trying to punch holes in Mel's hypothesis about how Fuller might've planted the forensic evidence?'

Several hands shoot up – traitors, off with their heads. Andrew speaks first. 'Talking about niggles, here's one. If the burner from Jack's pickup wasn't his, how did his prints get on it?'

I think for a few seconds then turn to Tobias, who's sitting on my immediate left. I move my phone so it's between us, but closer to me. 'Jack said he and Edwin occasionally met up for a pint. In this scenario, I'm Edwin and Tobias is Jack, and we're in the pub.' I stand up, take a couple of steps away, stop, pat my pockets. Turn back, point at my phone, say, 'Oops. Jack, pass me my phone will you?'

Tobias picks it up and offers it to me. I take it and pretend to walk away. 'You see?' I say. 'Simple.'

'Ah,' says Andrew. 'But now your prints are on it too.'

'Not if I'm wearing gloves, they ain't.'

'Nice demo, Mel,' says Jeff. 'So that puts a little dent in the evidence we have against Jack and shows how Fuller might have planted it. What else is there?'

Andrew again. 'We haven't been able to come up with one rock solid reason why that burner mysteriously switched itself on, so do we assume Fuller did it? If he did, he had to gain access to the vehicle somehow, and that would give him the opportunity to plant all the forensics. But how? How did he break in? Because according to the McCaffertys, no one else drives it. Or has a key.'

'I'll ask Lisa about the keys although there's never been any mention of them losing or even mislaying one. But then, would she know if their spare key went missing because I wouldn't have a clue where to look for ours.'

Tobias raises a hand. 'We all know there are devices that can clone a key's radio signal, and they're not difficult to source. Fuller might have one.'

'He might, but I'd be surprised if we were able to prove it because there's no way he'd have bought something like that with his own credit card. I'll log it as a possibility, but could you go through his transactions, and see if you can find anything. Check back at least twelve months, please.'

Steph's next. 'We have to check, but let's face it, Tobias won't find anything on Fuller's credit card, so how would he have paid for it? Not PayPal, that's for sure. I wonder if he's in possession of a stolen card?'

I give that some thought. We know stolen or cloned credit card numbers are freely available on the black market and that it's possible to buy one that already has a credit balance. Criminals know that people who want one of these are desperate and are willing to pay well over the odds, so an *arrangement* fee of double or even treble the balance is not unheard of. Fuller could easily have bought the legitimate version, like the cash cards we take on holiday but then he'd have had to provide an address and ID, and I don't believe he'd have opened himself up like that. 'Yes, Steph, he might have a stolen card, and I guess my only question is how he would have sourced it. There's nothing to suggest he mixes with the type of people who'd sell him one, which doesn't mean anything but it's yet another possibility.'

I add it to the log then switch to Lawrence, who's wearing the same crumpled brown suit. It looks like he's got something to say, and I for one am dead keen to hear it. Whatever it is. 'I want to ask about the burners, Rachel Fuller's personal phone, and this pickup belonging to McCafferty. How could it be that the location data on all those devices matches every time Fuller and McCafferty were supposed to have been shagging at St Mark's Woods?' I spot Jeff's hackles rising at that, but he stays quiet as Lawrence continues. 'McCafferty swears blind he was in his house when the pickup was supposed to be at the woods, but as you've said, nobody else has a key.' He pauses; knows we don't have the answer. I'm wondering if he's just trying to score points here when he picks up again. 'Is there any way Fuller could have moved McCafferty's pickup without him knowing?'

'I very much doubt it,' says Andrew. 'He parks it in Glenogle Road because it's the closest he can get to his house. There are only about a dozen spaces, and it's nose to tail down there. It's central Edinburgh after all. The chances of moving it for what, an hour, then being able to park it back in the same space are practically non-existent.'

Lawrence nods. 'Does McCafferty keep a mileage log? So he can claim it back against tax?'

'No idea. Why? Where are you going with this?'

Lawrence sighs, shakes his head, puts on a sour expression. Now my hackles are up too. But then he says, 'My brother's a painter and decorator. He's completely anal about recording his business mileage, so even if he drives to the local shops he puts that against personal miles because he's terrified the taxman will somehow find out. So, when he comes home after work he logs the mileage, then when he sets off in the morning, he logs it again. Even if his van didn't move.'

I perk up at that. 'Now I see. If Jack McCafferty does the same thing, we might be able to work out if the pickup was moved by checking his logged journeys on each of the Fridays. Good idea, Lawrence. I'll follow that up with Lisa.'

'No worries,' he says. 'Surprised you didn't think of it yourselves, actually.'

I tap my nail on the table to attract his attention. 'Enough of the smartarse comments, Lawrence.' He doesn't reply, just blinks a couple of times. I hold his gaze for a fraction longer than is necessary before opening up a new topic. 'Moving on, I want to talk about McCafferty's reactions to what we found, and to being arrested. Naturally, he denied everything – don't they all? But from my point of view, his behaviour appeared to be completely natural throughout. This morning I met with a DS trained in interpreting non-verbal communications. I showed her footage of my interview with McCafferty, plus some from Dave Devlin's bodycam when we opened the pickup. She didn't mince her words. Didn't quite say, "And why the hell have you charged this guy?", but not far off. Then I took her through all the evidence against him and, being fair to her, she admitted the sheer weight of the forensics would blow her input away. But the fact remains, in her opinion he was genuine in his denials.'

'Which makes it all the more likely Edwin Fuller is our man,' says Jeff. 'But it still beggars belief he'd run the risk of goading you, even if it was in private, and dragging our attention back onto him.'

'Couldn't agree more, boss, but obviously he's set out to challenge us. Or me, more likely. "You'll never prove it", he said. Then, in his garage while the boyo's back was turned, he winked at me. The bastard. But as you would expect he denies he was even at my house, so before we go anywhere with this we'll have to prove he was. We have to go after him – the question is how hard.'

Jeff sighs, uncrosses his legs. 'This is the type of thing that makes me uneasy. I have to be absolutely certain that whatever we do in pursuit of Fuller, we must make sure anyone connected with him is not placed in any danger. And Mrs McCafferty is top of that list.' He pauses, drums his nails on the table top. 'Statement of fact: Fuller told you he murdered his wife. Is he now trying to provoke you into investigating him? And, if so, what will his reaction be if you don't? Because if this man is a killer, we should be extremely careful how we proceed. So my first question is, what do you plan to do about him while you're conducting this investigation?'

Five pairs of eyes focus on me while I digest that. One thing that pisses me off about working with Jeff is he asks damn good questions that put you right on the spot. And if you don't have the right answers, you might as well close the case file. However, to be fair, if you come up with the goods he backs you to the hilt.

'I could ignore him,' I say. 'But that might antagonise, push him into doing something stupid. So that's a no. Or I could go and speak to him, keep things calm, totally non-confrontational, but explain that if he is making a genuine confession he should come in to make a formal statement because I have no legal right to investigate without a valid reason. From there, he can only do one of two things. Tell me again he did it, in which case I would ask him to give me one piece of evidence about the circumstances of his wife's death that I haven't already shared with him. Or he admits he's been playing a stupid game, brought on by stress for all I know. In which case I apologise, tell him there's nothing I can do, and walk away.'

'Making sure you avoid any use of the word "nutter",' says Steph.

'And where's the fun in that?' Then I smile. 'Or I don't go at all. I send one of my underlings—. And before you lot get all stroppy with me, that's how Fuller would perceive it. I, of course, would never use such a derogatory term for any valued member of my team.'

'Well, we'll have to do something,' says Jeff. 'Because all we have is circumstantial evidence, and none of it is compelling. If we had better digital forensics, we might be able to keep pushing. But we don't.'

Jeff leaves that last part hanging. We all know the subtext, and it relates to an infamous case in Edinburgh a few years ago where a successful murder prosecution was brought against a man whose ex-girlfriend had been reported missing. Despite extensive searching, the poor woman's body was never found but the sheer weight of digital forensic evidence based on phone and car GPS, all of which was circumstantial, convicted the killer. But Jeff's right, we don't have anything as powerful to take to Leo, and the big questions, the most important being how the location data always matches up, remain unanswered.

I smile again, wider this time. 'Actually, there's another possibility.'

And then I explain what this possibility is, and how it might encourage Fuller to make a mistake. Because, no question, we need him to.

# CHAPTER FORTY-SIX

EDWIN FULLER IS SITTING in the interview room, calm as you like. He knows there are at least two cameras on him; he's stared directly at the lenses several times. Relaxed, hands clasped in his lap, casually checking out the space. It's as if he's waiting for an old friend to drop in for tea.

The door opens. He turns to his left. A man enters. If the lintel was even a couple of centimetres lower, he would have had to duck. Fuller angles his head to see if this man is on his own. He's not. A woman follows him in and closes the door behind her. She's significantly smaller with a blonde ponytail; an air of barely suppressed energy about her. Fuller's demeanour has altered markedly. Now he's bolt upright in the chair, glancing back and forth between these two people and the door. But there are only two chairs on the other side of the table and now they are taken.

'Where's Cooper?' he says. 'It's her I came to see.'

'Good morning, Mr Fuller,' says Jeff. 'Thank you for coming in at such short notice. May I address you as Edwin?'

'DI Cooper. I'm here to see DI Cooper. Not you two.' Now he's glaring across the table, his hands flat on the surface.

'I'm afraid Detective Inspector Cooper is otherwise engaged. I'm her superior, Detective Chief Inspector Jeff Hunter, and this is Detective Constable Zanetti. Again, thank you for coming in to see us.'

Fuller slumps back, folds his arms. 'I just told you, I'm here to see Cooper. *She* asked me to come in so it's *her* I want to see. And ...' He leans forward and jabs a forefinger at the two officers, 'If I can't see Cooper, I'm leaving.'

Steph opens a file, lays it on the table. 'Edwin—'

'It's Mister Fuller.'

She smiles. If there was an Olympic event for feigning sincerity towards suspects, Steph would have a stack of gold medals. 'As you wish.' She lifts a page from the file. 'DI Cooper has reported that you visited her home last evening at approximately eight o'clock. She says you—'

'Now you listen to me—'

'Mr Fuller. Please,' says Jeff, with a most un-Jeff-like smarm to his voice. 'I would much prefer if we could maintain civil tones, which, if you don't mind me saying, would definitely be to your benefit.' He pauses, but Fuller doesn't butt in again. 'DI Cooper's reported conversation with you, last night, at her home, contains an extremely serious allegation. She alleges ...' He thrusts out his right hand, keeps his attention on Fuller, snaps his fingers a couple of times. Steph practically jams the page in his hand. She glares at him, but he blanks her. Slick choreography. 'DI Cooper alleges that you admitted to murdering your wife, Mrs Rachel Fuller, during the late evening of Thursday 25th January. She also states she and her colleague, DS Young, spoke to you at your home later the same evening, where you denied this allegation.'

Ever so gently, Jeff lays the paper down in front of him.

'Now the reason you're here, Mr Fuller, is to ask you if the conversation at DI Cooper's home did actually take place, and also to confirm whether you did indeed admit to the murder of your wife. Because if these two allegations are true, I will have no choice but to arrest you for that offence and to release Jack McCafferty from custody.'

Gradually, Edwin raises himself to an upright position, shuffles a bit, leans forward and rests his elbows gingerly on the edge of the table. 'I most certainly do deny these ridiculous allegations, DCI ...'

'Hunter.'

'DCI Hunter. And I have absolutely no idea why your subordinate would have accused me of such things. Perhaps she's ...'

'She's what, Mr Fuller?'

Fuller flaps a hand. 'Nothing. Doesn't matter.'

Jeff peers at him but doesn't respond. 'So, for the record, you didn't go to DI Cooper's home last night.'

'I did not.'

'And you did not confess to murdering your wife.'

'And that I most certainly did not. You have already proved my friend, or should that be ex-friend, committed the murder so I'm pleased to say you have the right man in custody.'

'In which case, Mr Fuller, that's all I needed to know.' He sighs extravagantly. 'Regrettably I must now have a rather serious conversation with Detective Inspector Cooper. On behalf of Police Scotland, I do apologise you've had to come in to deny these allegations.' He rises from his chair. 'Good day to you.' He turns to Steph. 'Zanetti. Escort Mr Fuller to reception.' Then he marches out the door without a backward glance.

Steph pulls the file together, barks, 'Please come this way,' and leads Fuller out the door. Even though she crosses in front of him, the movement of his elbow indicates clearly what he does behind her back.

He performs a fist pump. Tiny, but a fist pump nevertheless.

———

'You FELL FOR IT, you pompous arrogant fool,' I say, just as Jeff sits down beside me at the bank of monitors. I stand up and bow, like some sixteenth century French courtesan.

Jeff smirks. 'That should lower our Mr Fuller's defences for a while, don't you think?'

'I do indeed, Lord Olivier. Now I can start investigating him properly.'

'The bugger's definitely guilty, Mel. So, kid gloves, please.'

# CHAPTER FORTY-SEVEN

'COULD you repeat that for us, please, Andrew? For posterity, you understand.' Oh, I'm definitely going to enjoy this.

Andrew does his best to act nonchalant but is some way from pulling it off. 'I said, I've been a bit of a dimwit.'

The team are back around the table in the incident room. Jeff's off to help one of his other teams; an Emirati businessman and his wife have been kidnapped from their suite at the Sheraton, apparently. I fan my fingers across my bosom, flutter my eyes, gawp at my colleague. 'A dimwit, you say? Pray tell.'

'I know how Fuller managed to cycle between your house and his place last night – in nine minutes.'

'Oh,' says Steph. 'When you couldn't, you mean?' But she's sporting a grin that would accommodate a sizeable courgette. Sideways.

I call a halt before things completely fall apart. 'Let's hear it then.'

'We've been working on the basis he must have cycled,' says Andrew. 'Because he didn't have time to change to a faster mode of transport and besides, his car had supposedly been borrowed by a friend. So, he was on a bike, but I think it was an ebike.'

'Could he have travelled quicker on an ebike?' says Tobias.

'I've never tried one, but I've been doing some research. In theory, in the UK, the motors on these things are speed restricted by law to twenty-five kilometres an hour. At twenty-five, the motor cuts out and if you want to go any faster, you're on pedal power only. But if you drop back below twenty-five, the motor cuts in again.'

'You said, "in theory", Andrew.'

'Yes. From what I've read, it's dead easy to either raise the limit to higher than twenty-five or derestrict them entirely. I've recalculated the figures, and for Fuller to travel the four miles from your place to his, in nine minutes, he would have been cycling at an average of forty-one kph.'

I do the maths. 'So that's about twenty-five, twenty-six miles per hour. What was your speed?'

He grimaces. 'I averaged just above twenty, and I couldn't have squeezed out another five miles an hour if my life had depended on it.'

'Are these things expensive?' says Lawrence.

'It depends,' says Andrew. 'The cheap option is to retro-fit a conversion kit to a standard bike, or you can spend stupid money on a top-of-the-range model.'

'How stupid is stupid?' says Steph.

'£13,000 was the highest price on a website I looked at earlier.'

Steph's not the only one whose eyes go wide at that. I cast my mind back to last night and picture myself standing outside Edwin's garage. 'When you checked out the two bikes, they were definitely dry.'

'Definitely.'

'Is it safe to say neither was an ebike?' says Tobias.

'Correct. A racer and a hybrid.' Andrew turns to me. 'When we spoke about this before, you said you didn't actually see the bike he was on. But when he cycled away, did you hear a motor whirring or buzzing?'

I contemplate the ceiling. 'I can't say I did, no.'

'Ah, wait. The lane by the side of your house, it runs downhill before it hits the ELPN, doesn't it. So he probably wouldn't have had to switch the motor on until he was on the ELPN.'

'I'll take your word for it, but it does give us something to work on.' I wake up the wallboard and create two new lists: Items to prove, and, Edwin Fuller's method. I begin typing. 'Three things we have to prove. One, he was at my house; two, the route he took home; and three, where he stores this ebike.' I look up. 'It wasn't in the garage last night, so he must keep it somewhere else.'

Next, under his method, as well as possibly using an ebike, I log that he pretended to have been exercising in the garage to disguise that he would have been sweating from his cycle ride. I tap my screen a few times, bring up a map on the board with Fuller's house in the centre. I zoom in, switch to street view. I trace a laser pointer along a main artery of the ELPN; it passes close to his house. I stop the pointer on a blurred area. I've seen this effect before; the satellite view is obscured by foliage, usually trees or mature rhododendrons. 'Anyone know what this is?'

Lawrence rises out of his chair and peers more closely at the image. 'That's near the defunct Newhaven railway station on Craighall Road. The building's still there, it's been subdivided to house small businesses. From memory, when they were constructing the ELPN, they provided pedestrian and wheelchair access down to the paths from old stations like this one.' He points at my tablet. 'Can you make that thing zoom in closer?' I make to hand it to him, but he blushes and jams his hands firmly in his pockets. 'No, probably easier if you do it. Fingers like sausages, me.'

I don't say anything as I don't want to embarrass the man but that was awkward. I know he's a bit of a dinosaur but surely he knows how to use a tablet. No, he'll have to learn. Computing technology is a vitally important tool that we use every day, and I can't have a team member, particularly a DS, unable to use it. I'll speak to him later but in the meantime I swipe and pinch the screen to zoom in as close as I can before it pixelates. They're not particularly clear but I point out the access paths. 'So, to reach his house from that junction on the ELPN, Fuller would have had to cycle up the path and across Craighall Road. Ah-hah! There we are.' Between two houses we can see the entrance to what appears to be a lane. I zoom out again and now we can see it runs along behind Fuller's house.

I slap the table top. 'Now we're in business. Andrew, go and check if that lane gives access to Fuller's back garden. Take a look around. Could he have stashed the ebike anywhere nearby? And find out if there's any CCTV on the station buildings or on the houses on either side of the entrance to the lane. Steph, can you create a detailed map of the most direct routes from my house to his. Concentrate on the ELPN but widen the search to include any adjacent streets that might provide a short cut. There must be CCTV somewhere along the route, so we need the footage. I know it was dark but if we can pick Fuller up anywhere on the ELPN at just after eight last night, he has some explaining to do. Tobias, could you help her with that.'

'Do you want me to see if I can find footage of him approaching your house too?' says Steph.

I snap my fingers. 'Excellent idea. Yes, do that.'

'How was he dressed, Boss?'

I close my eyes. 'Yellow Hi-Vis, dark clothing, glossy black helmet, glasses.'

Andrew raises a hand. 'And there's nothing you can tell us about his bike?'

'No. He was standing on the other side of our garden fence. Now, Lawrence, Edinburgh cycle shops. Where does he buy his bikes? Does he put them in for maintenance? We know he owns two, does he also have an ebike? But you'll have to tread carefully, I don't want him to know we're investigating him. Or not yet anyway.'

Andrew taps the table. 'One thing before I go, Boss. If Steph and Tobias do catch him on CCTV then, apart from proving he was at your house, he's possibly dropped a clanger.'

'Do tell.'

He holds up his tablet. 'While you were speaking, I've been checking the wider area – Leith, Craighall, Inverleith. The ELPN isn't just comprised of old railway lines, it's connected to paths that cross or skirt all the parks in the area too. And one of them, the Warriston Path, connects the ELPN to the Water of Leith Walkway. So ELPN arteries run close to every major location related to Rachel's murder – their house, the McCafferty's house, St Mark's Woods and the lock-ups at Powderhall Lane. I think Edwin Fuller's been using the ELPN and the parks to make sure he can travel around the area relatively unobserved.'

# CHAPTER FORTY-EIGHT

EDWIN HAD BEEN ENJOYING his day; two hours at the gym and feeling on top of the world. Truth was, the rigorous exercise regime he'd been pursuing during the previous nine months had given him exactly what he needed so there was no real need for him to maintain it. But it might have seemed suspicious if he'd dropped all his normal routines, and since he'd become much fitter and stronger he looked forward to his twice-weekly sessions. He felt healthier now than for years, probably since he was a teenager. As was his routine, he'd enjoyed a full cooked breakfast that morning but between the gym and his cycling he expended plenty of energy, so the calories weren't an issue. He'd often wondered if the café owner, a friendly chatty woman with no rings on her left hand, was coming onto him. But when he paid particular attention, he realised she used the same patter with all her male customers. No matter their age or appearance she called them all 'honey'. So that was fine by him – he had to leave the door open for Lisa.

Lisa. He hadn't worked out what to do about her. How to

get her back onside. After she'd been short with him a couple of times, and then when she stopped replying to messages, he backed off. He'd never been fly-fishing, but it was an accurate analogy. If he was patient, preferably waiting 'til she contacted him, as long as she didn't drop off the face of the earth, he'd rekindle their friendship. Then, in time, he'd crank things up a couple of notches. Or maybe more.

After all, Lisa was a people person. She'd want the company. Would she wait for Jack to come out of prison? Edwin didn't know. But also, would the deputy leader of a major city council with political career aspirations still want to be married to a convicted murderer? He imagined not but he couldn't be certain. But he did know it would be down to him to undermine her relationship with her husband, and he'd have to do so carefully and with subtlety. *Softly, softly, catchee monkey.*

He recalled the interview with DCI Hunter and that female officer. She was a looker, but he'd resolutely kept his eyes off her. He hadn't rated Hunter at all. Too wishy-washy. Edwin doubted the DCI would have his serious conversation with Cooper, more of a 'Let it slide' man from what he'd seen. So, all things considered, he was in a relaxed contented mood that morning.

Then the doorbell rang.

When Edwin swung the front door open and saw who was standing on the doorstep, his first reaction was, *Oh shit!* Followed hot on its heels by, *What the fuck do you want?*

When this woman had been a little girl, a year older than him and all pigtails and skinned knees, Edwin reckoned she was a brat. As a teenager she became intensely dislikeable, while adulthood developed her into an odious, miserable crone. Quite an achievement for a young woman in her early twenties. Even Rachel, who, just for kicks, would take some form of perverted pleasure from socialising with the terminally unpleasant, commented one day, 'Maybe her fanny's healed up, and that's what's wrong with her.'

This was his next-door neighbour's daughter, Diane. Edwin hadn't called her by name since first year in secondary school. It was most unlike him, but he had been genuinely concerned the other kids might think the two of them were friends. He needn't have worried. Throughout school, she was an utter bitch, spreading lies and gossip whenever she saw an opportunity, culminating in the day she told a teacher that Edwin had forced her to have sex with him one afternoon after school. Unfortunately for her, at the time this was supposed to have happened the accused was sitting in the dentist's chair. Her parents were appalled and humiliated and withdrew her from school that very day. She hadn't long turned sixteen and had failed most of her exams. She remained at home for nine years after that, sponging off her family before she eventually found a job and moved out.

On the other hand, her mother was an absolute gem. Olive had stepped in when his parents died, supporting him and Hayley both practically and emotionally. He'd hardly seen the old dear since the start of winter, but she was over eighty now, rarely ventured outside and was too deaf to use the phone. Whenever he bumped into one of her carers, he asked about her, but they didn't give much away. Her daughter showed up once in a blue moon and now here she was, crowding him like a one-woman herd of cows.

She stuck her hand out. 'You've got my mother's keys and I want them back. I put her into a home this week and the house is on the market. I know you've been storing stuff in her shed, although God knows why. It's not as if you're short of space now your wife's dead.'

Edwin didn't move a muscle. *That was blunt, even for her.*

But she hardly missed a beat. 'Give me the keys. I'll open the shed door, and you've got an hour. Anything still in there after that will end up in the skip. It should be here soon. In fact, it better be. I don't want to hang about here all day.'

Edwin turned away, strode through to the kitchen, and plucked a fob from a hook. Back on the doorstep he handed over the keys. 'Will I be able to go and visit her?'

'I couldn't tell you. I haven't seen her. Been up to my eyes sorting the house out.' She was halfway down the path before she shouted over her shoulder. 'Go and see her if you want, I don't care. But you'd better hurry up. If she isn't dead by the end of the week I'll be surprised.'

Edwin had no intention of visiting the old woman but still, he couldn't believe Diane had been so callous. As she marched away a heavy vehicle came clanking round the corner into the street. It pulled up outside his house then reversed into Olive's driveway. He watched as the driver dumped an enormous skip in the front garden.

Retrieving his 'stuff' from next door's shed wouldn't take him anything like an hour. *But where the hell will I put it?*

# CHAPTER FORTY-NINE

As Andrew and Lawrence leave, I move over to the water cooler and top up my drink. I pause for a sip while I figure out what's next. Jeff, Tobias and Steph also take the opportunity to move around.

'I want to concentrate on Rachel Fuller for a while,' I say. 'For example, Edwin told us she was in a mood that Thursday when she came home from work. But was she? We only have Edwin's word so did he make it up? Her client in Livingston, didn't they say she was in good humour?'

'That's right, Boss,' says Steph. 'They'd just signed off on a contract.'

'Okay, let's go back to the start. Edwin told us they'd had sex, but he says it was interrupted. Then she was supposed to have driven off, not in the best of humour, to meet Jack. According to the Word file Bob found on her PC, they'd met twice – on the 11th and the 18th of January. She wrote, or somebody wrote, that the next time was to be the last. Because she intended to finish it.'

'Do we think the document and its content are a little too convenient?' says Tobias.

'Well, I certainly do now. I doubt she wrote it but unfortunately we have no proof that Edwin did.'

'And there's no mention of them meeting on Boxing Day either.'

I rake around in the file for the document. Scan it quickly. 'You're absolutely right, Tobias. There isn't.' I tap the sheet on the table. 'So, what does that mean? Nothing happened, so she didn't consider it worthy of note – or has he made a tiny mistake?' I sit back. 'For now, let's assume she and Jack were not having an affair, but Fuller set it up to appear as though they were. Let's also assume she was killed either in her bedroom or in Jack's pickup.'

'Bearing in mind we still don't know if it actually was driven to St Mark's Woods that night,' says Steph.

'We don't, and until we confirm that for certain, the pickup remains a possible murder site. But bear with me while I work this through. Fuller killed her while they were having sex. According to Klaudia, he was behind and above her, probably kneeling, and he strangled her with a piece of electrical cable on top of a pillowcase.' I pause, glance at the others. 'I can see all that being possible on a bed. Easy to hide the pillowcase under the duvet then whip it out when it's needed. That's realistic.' I pause again, give them time to paint the picture. 'But on the scruffy back seat of a tradesman's vehicle?'

I recall with a mixture of mortification and amusement the one and only time I had sex in the back of a car. An early model two-door Volkswagen Golf, and a tall boyfriend. I lost two buttons off my favourite top but gained a crick in my neck that took days to recover. Total disaster. My next two boyfriends had motorbikes, and then I met Callum, who didn't drive. Thank the Lord.

'To me,' says Tobias, 'Fuller has attempted to convince us it happened in the pickup. McCafferty arrives in the car park, climbs into the back seat, she joins him, her clothing is casual to make it easy to remove – although perhaps that's too obvious. But then he ends up behind her, produces the pillowcase and the cable from somewhere, and kills her. I have seen the space in that vehicle. There is probably enough for willing partners to have sex, and possibly even enough to commit such a murder, but would there not be significantly more forensic evidence while she attempted to save her life? I was thinking about upholstery fibres beneath her nails or fingerprint smudges on the windows. But now I've realised there is a major element missing.'

He hesitates, so I give him a nudge. 'Go on, Tobias.'

'I'm sure you will all know this but in the period immediately following her death, it is highly likely Mrs Fuller's body would have experienced primary relaxation of the muscles. And that includes the sphincter. So surely if she died in the pickup, there would have been at least some biological evidence in the form of bodily fluids. If he actually killed her in their bedroom but wanted it to appear as though she was killed in the pickup, I wonder if he forgot to falsify that piece of evidence.'

I lean over and tap his arm. 'Oh my God, Tobias, you're absolutely right.' I leave out slapping my forehead as I don't do melodrama, but I can't help wondering how we missed that; it wasn't in Greg's report covering Jack's pickup. 'I do believe our man might have made a significant error. He killed kill her on the bed, then probably gathered up all the bedding and slung it in the washing machine without thinking.'

I add this item to my list of evidence, reluctantly placing it in the circumstantial category. We still haven't proved where Rachel died but I think it's safe to say it wasn't in Jack's vehicle.

I'm acutely aware that any lawyer defending Edwin would declare this merely a hypothesis. Pure conjecture. And I guess if I were on the jury, I'd be inclined to agree.

'Boss, can I make a point too?'

'Be my guest, Steph.'

'I've never had an illicit affair – although it is on my bucket list – but if I'd just had sex with my partner and I'd stormed out in a huff to drive off to a car park to meet my lover in bloody awful weather, would I jump in the back for more sex?' She turns to Tobias, as if he's principally responsible for this hypothetical situation. 'No, I bloody well would not. I'd sit in the front with him and bend his ear for half an hour bumping my gums about my sod of a boyfriend or husband or whoever the hell he is. Sex? That'll be flaming right.'

This is a serious investigation, so I resist the urge to roar with laughter, especially at the somewhat apprehensive look on Tobias's face. 'Thank you, Steph. I have to say you do have a point, but sadly it's yet another opinion – it doesn't put a solid tick in the "Fuller killed his wife" box. But I'm sure Tobias is grateful for your valid insight into the female psyche.'

She leans to the side and elbows her colleague in the arm. 'Might be different if I was pissed, though.'

I was checking my tick list when Steph said that. But her comment stops me dead. 'What did you say there?'

She looks at me, puzzled. 'I said it might be different if I was pissed.'

Now I'm grinning. 'Steph, my dear, it's possible you've just punched a big fat hole in this case.'

# CHAPTER FIFTY

WHILE MY TEAM are off doing their investigative stuff, I call Greg to ask why his report covering the pickup didn't include reference to the possibility of biological evidence from Rachel's body as a result of her dying in there. There's silence on the other end of the line, then he says, 'But I remember writing it up, and I'm sure I covered that. Two minutes, while I check.' When he calls back, the first thing he says is, 'Sorry, Mel, this is my fault. We found no evidence of that nature. It was in the draft, but it was missed off the final report. An error of omission and it's down to me. I should have spotted it. Apologies again.' I tell him not to worry. The lack of that piece of evidence didn't cause me too many problems and I do appreciate him taking it on the chin like that.

Now I'm on my own I have time and space to think. I open an A4 notepad and begin scribbling thoughts and ideas that justify our view that Edwin Fuller is the guilty man, not Jack McCafferty. Jeff's advice about attacking this chronologically is sound so I force myself to keep my butterfly tendencies in check.

As there were no signs of a violent struggle, plus no biological evidence to support Rachel died there, and the clothes she was wearing were comparatively clean, I'm sticking with the assumption Edwin killed Rachel in their house – and almost certainly in their bedroom. The method seems straightforward, he strangled her from behind while they were having sex. Fuller admitted the act was incomplete as it would be if you throttled your partner halfway through. He said they argued but I still can't imagine many circumstances where normal people would interrupt a pleasurable conjugal activity in favour of having a domestic. It does explain the empty condom in the bin, but did he deliberately leave it there? And why would he have done that? That's still a puzzle.

A key component of the murder kit is the pillowcase, which he must have stolen from the McCafferty's airing cupboard. I wonder how many pairs are in there, to make it more likely its disappearance would go unnoticed. It's another question for Lisa but I can't have her blabbing, so I'll have to be circumspect about how I broach the subject. But, then again, she's a politician; surely she can be trusted. The irony of that assumption amuses me, but I move on.

The Fullers' car was driven away from the house, and I remember Dave Devlin saying the CCTV footage was inconclusive as to who was driving. It must have been Edwin, although he's not much taller than Rachel was. Something occurs to me about that. I leave my desk, wander over to the window, gaze down and through a gap between two buildings, where I can see traffic passing by – one flash of colour at a time. Then a double-decker bus stops across the gap, my reverie is interrupted, and I pick up the thread again.

A man might be taller than a woman but is there still a height difference if they're both sitting down? The ratio of leg length to body length can make a difference, as can body shape.

A thin person might fit better into a car seat, meaning they sit lower. I'll have to compare Edwin's build with Rachel's because I've only ever seen the woman hanging upside down in a thicket. I wonder if Lisa has photos.

Another thought sashays in like a model on a catwalk and pauses long enough to be admired. I pick up the phone. 'Greg. This is a bit of a long shot but is there anything to suggest the driver's seat in the Fullers' car had been lowered, then returned to its original position?'

'I've actually come across this before.' He goes silent for a few seconds. 'Aye, sorry, was just trying to recall. There's a possibility the adjuster might still have had the factory grease from when the car was new so if it has been lowered as you suggest, the movement could have pushed the grease down and left a clean spot. Couple of things worth bearing in mind though. First, the Fullers both drove it so they might have been in the habit of adjusting the seat. In which case, we'd never be able to tell.'

'They're of similar heights, so maybe not. What's the other thing?'

'From memory, the car's just over two years old so hopefully it hasn't been back to the garage too many times. You know what mechanics are like for changing stuff, even though they only drive it a few metres.'

'Yeah. Like switching the radio to some crappy commercial channel. And me a Radio Four girl too.'

He chuckles. 'I can't be certain we checked for it, but we would have filmed and photographed the interior in detail so let me come back to you. Fingers crossed.'

I'm still waiting for an update from Andrew but it's Greg who calls first. 'I'm not phoning with good news.'

'Let me guess, the seats don't adjust for height.'

'Ah, well. I discovered the driver's seat can be—'

'But you didn't catch it on film.'

A sigh comes down the line. 'No, Mel. Our log says we filmed the whole floor and underneath the seats but—'

'Shit. It hadn't been adjusted, had it?'

This time he exhales so loudly and for so long I'm surprised he doesn't pass out. 'Mel.'

'What?'

'Is there any chance I could finish my story?'

'Sorry. Lip firmly buttoned. Go on.'

'Thank you. Before I trawled through all our films and photos, I wanted to check that model of Focus had the facility. Turns out it does.'

'Damn! Fuller will never let us examine it more closely.'

'This is what I've been trying to tell you. We can't do anything with his car. It's been written off.'

That makes me blink. 'It's been what?'

'When I typed in the reg to find the model, a DVLA notice popped up to say the Focus had been classified as Category B, Cannot Be Repaired. Written off, to you and me.'

I have a tiny squirmy feeling in my stomach. 'What happened?'

'Apparently he crashed into a two-foot-thick stone wall out in East Lothian.'

'When?'

'Ten days ago.'

'Well, that explains a couple of things.'

'Like what?'

I tell Greg about how Fuller said a friend had borrowed his car, clearly a lie, and about the marks on his face. He said he'd fallen off his bike; I'm betting they were caused by an airbag deploying. 'Where's the car now?' I say.

'It was scrapped. I spoke to the dealer; the chassis, the whole front end and almost all the bodywork were totalled so they stripped it down for parts. The rest went through a crusher and was sold on to a scrap metal merchant. So if you had any notions of bringing in a cadaver dog ...'

Damn again. That's exactly what I had been thinking but before I have the chance to dwell on it, my phone beeps. I check the screen. 'Greg. That's Andrew ringing with news, so I need to go. Thanks for following that up for me. I'll be back in touch.' I switch calls and say, 'Andrew.'

He speaks, I listen. He explains the CCTV in and around the old Newhaven Station is a non-starter. The only camera is focused on the front of the building. The exit from the ELPN connects with the street about thirty metres away, directly opposite the lane that does indeed pass behind Fuller's place. The houses on either side of the entrance to the lane don't have CCTV either, so we'll have no way of telling whether he used this as a route. The lane has a base of hard gravel, back gardens to either side, some of which have gates. There's no access into his garden but his neighbour's gate is relatively new. 'It's about six feet high,' says Andrew. 'Solid, recently varnished, with a shiny new mortice lock. And she has a garden shed.'

'She?'

'Yes. An elderly woman in her eighties. I sneaked round and spoke to two of her neighbours but they're both relatively new to the street and they don't know much about her. Apparently, she's confined to the house and carers visit a few times a day. I've put a call out to social services to see if I can find out more.'

'Ah. Could the ebike be in the old woman's shed?'

'It's possible. He could easily lift it over the fence between his garden and hers, it's not all that high.'

'But wouldn't he be seen?'

'Not if he was careful because none of the houses nearby, with the exception of this woman's, appear to have a clear view into his garden. His garage borders the wall on the other side, and the rear fence is screened by high conifers. So if he did cart his wife's body through his garden and into the garage via the side door at ten o'clock on a stormy January night, there's precious little chance anyone would have spotted him.'

# CHAPTER FIFTY-ONE

EDWIN STOOD at his kitchen window, staring at the roof of Olive's shed. 'Fuck!' He turned away, trod on one of the cats' soft toys and kicked it across the room. Then he stormed after it and stamped on it several times. He knew he was being pathetic, but he couldn't stop himself. 'Fuck. Fuck. FUCK! I can't believe this is happening.'

He didn't give his elderly neighbour a passing thought, only that her total bitch of a daughter was about to screw up his meticulously constructed plans. Back at the window, he placed his hands flat on the worktop and drew in a deep breath through his nose. It was a bright sunny day, people were out in their droves, washing their cars, pottering in their gardens, kids zooming up and down the lane on a variety of wheeled toys. The place was like Piccadilly Circus. 'What the bloody hell am I going to do?' He glanced at his watch; twenty minutes of the allotted hour frittered away already. He knew there was no way he could move his ebike from Olive's shed to his garage without being seen by half the people in the street. *Think, Edwin. Think.*

Another fifteen minutes flew by, and he'd morphed from simply being in a temper into a state of escalating panic. He slumped down on the floor, his spine against a cabinet door. He dropped his head into his hands, ground his knuckles into his temples and clamped his teeth shut to suppress a scream that was raging to escape. *What the fuck was going on in my head?* He had allowed his frustrations to run away with him and that had driven him to taunt the police. He'd stuck them with a hot poker. He checked his wrist again, not much more than twenty minutes left. He'd have to do something about his bike and pray no one saw him. It had turned one o'clock, so he still had about six hours 'til darkness fell and although he was fairly certain the police had no grounds to search his property, he had no idea what they'd been doing in the background. Then he recalled winking at Cooper while her sidekick was distracted. *Jesus. What a stupid prick. She will not let that go.*

Edwin realised wallowing in self-pity wouldn't solve his problem. As he dragged himself up off the floor an idea began to form. He paused, then shook his head. *No. Don't be ridiculous. That can't be the answer. There must be something else.* But it was in there now, impossible to shift no matter how many alternatives he came up with. He tried once more to banish it. It wouldn't go. He closed his eyes. Jammed them shut. Marched up and down. He stopped. Could he? Maybe. Now his watch said five minutes, and his hour would be up.

He ran to the living room window, pressed his cheek against the glass in a vain attempt to squint into next door's garden. He needed to know if she had closed the front door, establish where she was in the house. He could see the skip was still empty, but he couldn't hear any noise. What to do? He'd run out of time. He didn't want the bitch coming back to speak to him, causing a scene that would draw attention.

He had to move. Now. Take control. So he left the house,

forced himself to saunter down the path to his gate, lifted an imaginary leaf and sneaked a glance at her door. Closed. He returned inside at the same pace; his muscles screaming at him to *Get a bloody move on*. He rushed through the house, into his back garden. No sign of her anywhere. She must still be inside.

Was she alone? He had no idea. She wasn't married. *Would a horrible cow like her even have a partner? Not a chance on earth.* He knew she had no siblings, therefore no nieces or nephews. And probably no friends either. Yes, on balance, he decided she would be in the house on her own.

It was now or never. He listened. He could make out the sound of someone cutting a hedge, but they were a few gardens away and they'd be concentrating on the job. He checked out the trees bordering the lane. It had gone quiet. No one anywhere in sight.

Now!

He ran at the fence between the houses, half-vaulted half-scrambled over, and sprinted to the kitchen door. He tested the handle. Pushed the door open. Stepped inside.

He closed the door firmly behind him and turned the key in the lock.

And further along the terrace, the hedge trimmer fell silent.

# CHAPTER FIFTY-TWO

I'M MAKING my way along the Cowgate, a deep cleft that's one of the oldest thoroughfares in the city. It runs parallel to the High Street, way up to my right. Dating back five hundred years, traders drove their cattle from pastures to the south and east of Edinburgh through the Flodden Wall, along the Cowgate and into the Grassmarket, a wide flat area tucked in underneath the castle rock. These days the Grassmarket is packed with tourists, not cattle, but in some instances, they're treated the same.

I turn a corner into a cobbled street no wider than three cows and spot the café where I'm to meet Lisa. It's quiet, locals only. She goes there because none of her colleagues ever do, even though her office is no more than fifty metres as the crow flies.

I walk in, scan the room and quickly reach that point where I can't pick her out and feel that every person in there is staring at me. Then I practically fall over her as she rises from a table that's right under my nose. We say hello, she indicates we should order at the counter, so we squeeze past the other customers and join a short queue. 'Something to eat?' she says.

These trousers used to be a much easier fit round the waist so my immediate reaction is no thanks, I shouldn't. But when she tells me the scones in here are orgasmic, my negligible restraint flies south for the winter. 'In that case,' I say, 'we both should have one.'

A few minutes later I dust a few crumbs off the table and onto my plate. 'You were dead right about the scones, Lisa. That was delicious.' I dab my napkin against my lips, hoping for no tell-tale smears of jam. I wait for Lisa to finish her last mouthful. 'Did you have any trouble getting away from the office?'

'None at all. It's becoming claustrophobic in there. I was glad to escape.'

'Why's that?'

'I'm being gradually frozen out, and challenging people all the time is wearing. Truth is, they can't possibly have a senior member of the council married to a convicted murderer. So now we have too many bloody politicians playing their little power games instead of doing their jobs and serving the public. I was blind to it before but now it's as clear as day.'

'So are you under pressure to resign?'

'Hah!' She checks the tables around us, but everyone's locked into their own conversations. Still, she leans forward. 'My colleagues are hoping I'll do the decent thing, but they can fuck right off. If they had the balls, which they don't, they'd make it happen. Cowardly bastards.'

I nod. 'And how's your husband?' That causes her to start, probably wondering why I haven't used his name. But in here I have no intention of using names, and I'd prefer she doesn't either.

She looks away. 'Struggling badly. He knows he's innocent

but nobody else believes him. Apart from me and his family, that is.' I wait 'til she remakes eye contact, and send back a signal that, thankfully, she interprets correctly. She'd been about to take a drink, but she pauses, coffee mug suspended in mid-air. 'Is there something you'd like to tell me?'

'There is. But it's important I state I'm not here on official business. This is just two women meeting for coffee and a chat. So before I say one word more, do I have your cast iron guarantee you will not repeat a word of this conversation to anyone. And Lisa, I mean anyone. Not even your husband. In fact definitely not your husband, and especially not his friend.' Lisa smiles. She's caught on. 'And while we're on the subject of his friend, you need to steer well clear, Lisa. Do not become involved with him under any circumstances.'

She drops her voice. 'Jesus. You think he did it.'

'Guarantee, Lisa, or we go back to discussing orgasmic scones.'

'You've got it. Now please tell me why, after all that's happened, you believe my husband is innocent.'

I lift my bag off the floor. 'Tell you what, let me pay for this and then we'll go for a walk.'

———

LISA and I are strolling through an area of parkland called The Meadows, which sits in between the university and student bedsit central. It's not a particularly bright day but she's put on a pair of sunglasses, ruby red with a cream detail. I comment on how cool they are and compare them to the frumpy black ones I wear for driving – and only driving. I gaze around. It's lunchtime. The place is teeming with undergraduates who, naturally, pay no attention whatsoever to two women they probably classify as ancient.

'Right, Lisa, stepping back to where we were in the café, guilty and innocent are not terms I'm prepared to use. For obvious reasons. Let's just say something has happened, and it's made me take another run through the facts of this case, to make sure I haven't missed anything vital. Fair enough?' She nods. Several tiny movements, like a six-year-old who's about to be told the most incredible magical secret. 'First, the pillow-case. On the morning we arrested Jack, you told me that high thread count bed linens are one of your things. But would Edwin have known that?'

'I've been wondering about that ever since it was found in the pickup. There was one night in our house, a good couple of years ago, when Rachel was taking the mickey because I'd just spent hundreds of pounds on new bedding. I won't repeat what she said but it was typically crude. I remember Edwin being totally bemused, wondered what the hell she was on about. Turned out he'd never heard of thread count, so I took him upstairs to the airing cupboard and showed him. It's the sort of thing you do when you're pissed, isn't it?' She pauses. 'If you're also wondering how he could have taken one without me knowing – that's easy. You've been in our house; we only have one bathroom, and it's a house rule with visitors that if someone leaves the table or the living room, they're going to the loo, so everyone stays put 'til they come back. He would have had plenty of time to take one. Plus, we have more bedding than John Lewis, so if he chose one from low down in the pile, where you said it was, it could have been months before I noticed.'

We pause while a short-haired ginger dog moseys up to us, checks us out for treats then wanders on. Its owner doesn't take his eyes off his phone to see what the hound's up to but sadly I can't nick him for it.

'Does that help?' she says.

I rock my hand from side to side. 'It's a piece of useful information, Lisa. A building block. Now, do you have a relatively recent photo of Rachel and Edwin together? I need to compare their body shapes but please don't ask me why.'

My walking companion regards me as if I've grown an extra nose, but she takes out her phone. 'The four of us had a weekend in Budapest last May. So that's about, what, nine or ten months ago. There should be something ... yes, here we are.'

It's a typical city break photo. Dazzlingly sunny day, four grinning adults wearing tee shirts, shorts and shades, two on either side of one of those human statues. This one is absolutely ingenious; a man who appears to be sitting astride an eagle in flight with, apparently, no points of contact to the ground. If I had the time, I'd try to work out how the artist created the illusion. Edwin and Jack are extreme left and right, Lisa and Rachel are next to the statue. The women are not paired with their partners. I scrutinise Edwin, then Rachel. They're both wearing casual shoes, and being a holiday snap, neither is standing particularly straight. Next, I study their build. They're similar; not slim but definitely not what you'd call fat either. I can quite easily see why neither of them ever adjusted the driver's seat. *Damn.* This still means we can't be certain who drove that night.

I recall how Edwin looked, working out in his garage. I point at him in the photo. 'And this is less than a year ago? He was a lot thinner then.'

'I wish I could say the same.'

She looks like the weight's been falling off, so I don't like to contradict her, especially considering the circumstances. I hand the phone back; I can always ask for a copy of the photo if I ever need it. I ask another couple of questions, but her answers don't help. Jack doesn't record individual journeys for mileage purposes; he claims an annual figure that he and his accountant agreed was acceptable considering most of his work is in town. And, unlike me, she knows exactly where the spare key for the pickup is – in her handbag. She carries it around with her because if Jack ends up working later than expected, and she needs transport, she can go to the car and take it without interrupting him. This means she's virtually certain Jack has never lost or even temporarily mislaid a spare key. So that wasn't how Edwin managed to access the pickup and set it up as a forensics hotspot. *Damn* again!

I step off the path to allow a young woman pushing a twins' buggy to manoeuvre past us. Both children are zonked, and their mother mouths a thank you as she passes, as if she's scared she'll wake up one or the other. The pause was useful because my next question is a tad tricky. 'You told me before that Jack and Rachel were just friends, nothing more than that.'

'Yes.' With more than a trace of steel.

'What about you and Edwin?'

She stops dead. 'Edwin is Rachel's husband. He and I are friends too, nothing more than that.' She starts moving again and I have to hurry for a few paces 'til I catch up. 'But that might change if he doesn't stop bugging me.'

'You mentioned that on the phone earlier. Tell me more about that.' So she explains in a lot more detail about Edwin trying to contact her and how she's practically had to blank him to make him stop. And now I'm beginning to wonder if this is a clearer indication of his motive.

I finish with the idea Steph put in my head earlier this morning. 'Rachel's blood alcohol level meant she would have been almost three times over the limit when she drove away from their house. Drink driving: would she have done that, do you think?'

Lisa moves to block my path and leans in to eyeball me.

'No way on God's earth. She was violently opposed to that. Her opinion was drunk drivers should be shot, especially after her accident.'

'Why? Was the biker over the limit?'

'Yes. Didn't you know that?'

I did not. And it's another building block. But a bit heftier.

We're heading back now when Lisa slows her pace, then stops. I stop, half turn, look at her. 'Something's just occurred to me,' she says. 'I've no idea why I didn't think of this before.'

'Go on.'

'About six, seven months ago, Jack was playing rugby at his club. Just a fun thing with the old gits, as he calls them. When he got home, absolutely pissed I might add, he told me he'd lost his kitbag. He thought he'd left it in the taxi, but I phoned the company, and it wasn't in the cab, or in the pub. At the time we joked about whoever opened it would have needed a gas mask. Eventually he replaced all his gear and we just forgot about it.'

'So what brings it to mind now?'

'I said he came home pissed, but he only had a couple at the club then he went off to meet Edwin. They shared the taxi home, and Edwin got out first.'

———

As I'm DRIVING BACK to the Fish Tank I reflect on a successful discussion with Lisa. Maybe I didn't get all the answers I wanted but I'm left with no loose ends and, bonus, I know how Jack's DNA might have ended up on Lisa's body and clothing. Sadly, my self-congratulatory mood only lasts until I take a call from Andrew. 'Yes?'

'I was driving out of Fuller's street when a skip lorry passed me. Something made me watch where it was heading, and it turned out the skip was for his neighbour.'

'The old woman?'

'Yeah. So I went back and spoke to the people who live next door to her, made the excuse that I wanted to make sure nothing was wrong. They let me through their house, and I climbed over the fence.'

'Did you see inside?'

'No. Once I was in her back garden I noticed the shed was open.'

'And?'

'And it was empty. Wherever he's hiding the ebike, it's not in there.'

# CHAPTER FIFTY-THREE

I stop off in the middle of the office and relate the tale of Jack's lost kitbag and his shared taxi home with Fuller. Andrew says, 'How could Fuller have stolen it without Jack noticing?'

'According to Lisa, he was absolutely pissed. But if Fuller did take the bag, it does explain how he could have made it look like Jack and Rachel got it together.' I pause. 'But the key words there are "could have".' I sigh as I turn away, all too aware that it's our job to prove how Fuller set his friend up and nicking a sweaty jockstrap to do it is fanciful to say the least.

———

Steph appears at my office door. 'Boss. Quick update for you.' I wave her in, and she takes the chair in front of my desk. 'With your house being in a cul-de-sac, there are only two ways in. The lane that comes off the ELPN, and the junction at the end of the street onto Queensferry Road. There's a camera at that junction but I checked the footage for two hours prior to eight o'clock and Fuller didn't come in that way.'

'So he must have used the ELPN,' I say. 'And there aren't any cameras on it, are there?'

Steph shakes her head and carries on. 'Regarding Edwin Fuller's bike route between your house and his, there are only three real options. One stands out so we concentrated on that. The others are a fair bit longer; two, even three minutes. Like you say, there are no CCTV cameras situated on the ELPN but a few of the bridges have them. Problem with that is the cameras are six to eight metres above the paths, so we haven't been able to positively identify Fuller using the description you gave us.' She pauses. 'In either direction.'

I'm disappointed but Steph still looks bright, so I reckon there's better news coming. And I'm right. 'But we have captured images of a bike flying past five different points on the route, heading away from your house. And, to confirm the estimate Andrew made earlier, it was travelling at an average speed of twenty-six miles per hour, measured between the first and last points. Tobias noticed the ELPN between points two and three is on a steady incline and the cyclist was still doing bang on twenty-five. So we're pretty certain it is an ebike. Only thing is, the rider isn't wearing Hi-Vis like you said Fuller was, and I can't tell if he's wearing glasses because he has a bright headlamp on his helmet. You described the helmet as being black and glossy, but did it have a lamp clipped on?'

I close my eyes. 'I'd say it didn't.'

'Shame. But it's possible he clipped it on after he left you. Also, it wouldn't have taken him a second to whip off the Hi-Vis jacket to change his appearance. Now, one positive thing we do have is there are no sightings of the same rider on the ELPN either before it reaches your house, or after it passes his. So, it's highly likely he is Edwin Fuller, but we can't prove it conclusively.'

I thank her and she heads back to her desk. Then I say to

the empty room, 'Jeez, could we not find one thing that's hard evidence, and not bloody circumstantial?'

———

LAWRENCE AND ANDREW are next up, with the older man going first. 'There's a few bike dealers in Edinburgh obviously, but only one in Leith so I tried there first. Struck lucky.'

'Seriously?' I say.

'Yeah. The Leith Bike Shed. It's the place Fuller uses. A right old-fashioned shop, for proper cyclists. There's stuff everywhere. I've no idea how the old boy who owns it knows what he's got in stock. Anyway, he knew who Fuller was, called him an arse, says he can't stand the sight of him.'

'Hang on a minute, Lawrence, did you ask for Fuller by name? Because I specifically asked you to tread carefully, we do not want him to know we're investigating him.'

He shrugs. 'Doesn't matter, does it? The guy didn't like him so he's not likely to say anything.'

I don't need to look at Andrew to know he'll be stunned by his colleague's response. 'That's not the point,' I say. 'And well you know it. We'll talk about this later.' I pause, gather myself. 'What did you find out?'

Lawrence appears not to register the rebuke and goes back to his notes. 'The owner thinks he has three bikes: a road bike, a mountain bike and a hybrid. He told me Fuller paid £550 cash for the mountain bike in June last year.'

'Cash? Is that normal?'

'The old guy says he prefers it. Went off on one about card transaction fees and nearly blew a gasket when I mentioned Amex.' He pauses. 'An old-fashioned place, like I said.'

'Back up a minute,' says Andrew, turning to me. 'When we spoke to Fuller in his garage, and I checked the bikes to see if they were wet, there were only two. A racer and a hybrid – no mountain bike.'

'Could the owner have been mistaken?' I say to Lawrence.

'Doubt it. He was whingeing on about having to take "all that cash" to the bank.'

'Hang on a minute.' I stand up and yell, 'Tobias!'

Our German colleague ambles over to the door. 'Jawohl, mein Kommandant.'

I smirk, he can be pretty droll when he feels like it. 'Tobias. Can you look at Fuller's bank accounts again? I'm interested in any large cash withdrawals in the past twelve to eighteen months and, specifically, for five or six hundred pounds. Check the ATM limit for his bank and ask about withdrawals across the counter too.'

'Yes, Boss. Right away.' Now he speeds up.

I turn back to the others. 'With someone else, I'd say a missing mountain bike was no big deal. But not with this man. Lawrence, get back in touch with the shop and ask for a description; preferably with a photo.'

'Will do.'

'But getting back to this ebike, we don't think he owns one?'

'Doesn't seem like it. The bike shop guy says he's never seen him on one and Fuller's never bought anything ebike related or brought one in for maintenance or repair.'

'Question, then. If the rider Steph picked up on CCTV was Fuller and bearing in mind he was travelling at an average of twenty-six miles an hour, it sounds like it probably was an ebike. So where did he buy it from, and where does he keep the damn thing hidden?'

'To be fair, Boss,' says Andrew, 'we only saw inside the garage. Maybe he'd dumped it in the kitchen, knowing you were likely to be hammering at his door any second.'

I shake my head several times. 'No way. He wouldn't take

that risk. We're beginning to see the amount of detailed planning he put into this. There's not a chance he'd want us barging into his house, warrant or no warrant, and blowing all his plans out the water by finding that bike. No, he's stored it somewhere, and close to his house because he'd have had to run the last part to get inside the garage before we showed up.'

Ten minutes later, Tobias reappears, leafing through a few sheets of A4. 'Mr Fuller didn't make any cash withdrawals for the figures you specified, but in a six-month period commencing last April he did withdraw significantly more than normal in cash. £4600, in fact.'

I guess there are any number of perfectly innocuous reasons why a person's cash expenditure would spike for short periods of time. Paying tradesmen, a run of expensive social events or, perish the thought, buying an ebike on private purchase. But Edwin Fuller is far from innocuous, so alarm bells are clanging like there's no tomorrow.

But, yet again, conjecture.

Blast.

# CHAPTER FIFTY-FOUR

WE – that is Andrew, Lawrence and I – are at St Mark's Woods, standing by my car. Until we crack the puzzle of how Fuller moved his wife's body from here to the lock-ups we're completely stymied.

'This arsehole obviously believes he's bomb proof,' says Lawrence.

'Correct,' I say. 'But he also thinks we're stupid so he's wrong on both counts.'

'Is he arrogant enough to believe he's committed the perfect murder?' says Andrew.

'That's an interesting question because, actually, he already managed that. Jack McCafferty was almost certainly going down, and it beats me why Fuller deliberately dragged our attention back onto himself. So that was his first mistake, and it was a doozy. He's slipped up a second time too, don't forget – the complete lack of biological evidence that she died in the pickup. So that's two, and he will have made more, we simply haven't found them yet. Now, I've had to make some

274

calculated assumptions, so challenge me if they don't hold water. Based on what Lisa McCafferty told me about Rachel Fuller's attitude to drink driving, we can be fairly certain Fuller drove the Focus here from his house, with his wife inside, already dead, dressed in the clothes we found her in. So how did he move her from here to the lock-ups? Not in another vehicle because Steph reviewed all the CCTV footage on the surrounding roads and no vehicles made that journey at that time. Did he put her over his shoulder and hike that distance? Three hundred metres; would that even be possible?'

I spread my arms wide, look down at myself. 'Lawrence. I'm a similar size and weight to Rachel. See how far you can carry me before you collapse.'

The DS doesn't possess a lot of natural colour, but I swear he loses a couple of shades. He shakes his head. 'No way I'm doing that.' Then folds his arms and glares off into the distance.

Andrew bursts out laughing. 'Come on, man. Where's your sense of humour?'

I didn't mean that as any form of test, it just came out naturally. But the 'Suss Lawrence Out' questionnaire is filling out nicely. Then, bang on schedule, a white van turns into the car park. I wave, and it alters direction. I can read the logo now: *Scottish Fire and Rescue Service*. The tyres crunch across the gravel as the driver manoeuvres into a space. 'Sam?' I say, as he climbs out.

He grins. 'Guilty as charged.' He walks to the rear doors, opens them and says, 'Okay, Manny, out you come. We have work to do.' He drags a rescue mannequin out and dumps it on the ground.

My two colleagues stare at it, then at me. 'I've asked Sam to help us with an experiment,' I say. I point at the dummy. 'What does he – or she – weigh?'

'Sixty-five kilos, as requested.'

'Spot on. The same weight as our victim.' I indicate the entrance to a path over to my left. 'That heads off in the direction of Powderhall Lane, which is about three hundred metres from here. But the path veers off before it reaches the lane so anyone walking there on a direct route has to hike through bushes and scrub for that last part.' I tap Sam on the shoulder. 'I asked specifically for help from someone of similar build to our suspect. Looks like you fit the bill. So, could you lift your friend there, and follow me along the path. I'd like your opinion as to whether my suspect could have carried her body all the way to Powderhall Lane without putting her down.'

'A dead weight then?'

Black humour: love it. Then I hold up a finger. 'Oops, nearly forgot.' I open my car and lift out a quilted coat. It's one of mine, a similar material to the coat Rachel was wearing when we found her. Its texture means if I sling it carelessly across the back of a chair it will hang there for an instant then slip gracefully to the floor.

I help Sam dress the mannequin then he hefts it up into a fireman's lift, says, 'Ready when you are,' and we set off. Andrew and Lawrence fall in behind.

The path meanders through typical woodland terrain, past bushes and the occasional rock. We have to continually negotiate half-buried tree roots made smooth and slippery by countless pairs of feet, but it's reasonably flat for all that. After one hundred metres I check how Sam's doing. He's breathing a bit heavier than he was at the start. He pauses, adjusts his load, nods at me and we start off again. About fifty metres later he calls a halt, still with Manny over his shoulder. 'The problem isn't the sixty-five kilos, it's this coat. It's sliding about all over the place and I'm struggling to keep Manny on my back. How much further 'til we turn off?'

'Seventy, eighty metres.'

He fine-tunes the dummy's position. 'Not all that far. I can keep going for now.'

But once we're off the path and Sam has stumbled for the second time, he stops and lets the dummy fall. He stretches his spine, rotates his neck and rolls his shoulders. 'Call me a wimp if you like but I'd say we've proved your experiment. In a straight line on smooth ground, I could have carried Manny the full three hundred metres. But unless your suspect is incredibly fit and in the habit of manually transporting heavy awkward weights over long distances, this terrain would be a killer.' Then he catches my eye, angles his head slightly in Lawrence's direction, and makes a face. The DS is leaning forward, hands on his thighs, puffing and blowing. I only walk in places like this when my husband decides to force feed the kids and me some countryside air, and I'm managing fine. I'm tempted to ask Lawrence if he's okay, but I'm not sure it's fair to draw attention, especially as Sam is with us.

But Andrew saves the day when he waves a hand in the air. 'The thing is, Sam, today's not a bad day, weather wise. On the night in question, it was pouring down and blowing a gale. Didn't let up 'til well into the following day.'

Sam drops to one knee and rubs the coat. 'Fabric like this would have caused him problems. It's designed to be warm for the wearer but while I was carrying Manny, my upper body was practically encased in the material.' He points to his tee shirt and lightweight jacket. 'And I'm dressed like this. When was this storm?'

'Late January.'

'So your suspect would probably have been togged up for the weather. He'd have been sweating like a pig and that, along with the rain, would have made the coat even more slippery. Then there's the terrain. As you say, it's dry today but, in the middle of winter, stormy, soaking underfoot ... No. In my opinion, for him to have carried her the full distance in those conditions, without dropping her, is a huge ask. Not impossible, but highly improbable.'

I'm not disappointed with what he's said because his opinion might prove or disprove how Rachel was moved but there is one point I still want to raise. 'We also have to consider lividity in our victim's body. When we found her, she was hanging upside down and the pathologist's report stated the position of the body resulted in permanent levels of lividity in the chest, shoulders and neck. But lividity can be altered by moving a body within thirty minutes of death. The report said there were early signs in the lower back, and on the left side, which fits with how you were carrying the dummy.' I smile. 'Right, Sam, thanks very much for your help. That was a useful experiment.'

I switch onto Andrew and Lawrence. 'Right, you two, do the decent thing and take Manny back to the car park.' Andrew leans down to lift the dummy then realises his colleague hasn't moved. Andrew's an amenable chap but he's no pushover. 'I'm not carrying this myself, Lawrence. Give me a hand here.'

I decide to leave them to it, but a full and frank discussion with my new DS is definitely on the cards. 'Now, Sam. If you were planning to lug a body for that distance, over that terrain, in a storm, what would you do to—' I stop dead in my tracks. 'Oh, wait a bloody minute, he planned it.'

They all look at me as if I'm daft. 'Boss,' says Andrew, 'we already know that.'

'No. Wait. Let me think.'

I recall something Greg said to me. What the hell was it? I try to imagine the situation. Him speaking, me listening. What was I wearing at the time, where was I standing in relation to him, where were we? Gradually the picture emerges, then I have it. Not face to face, it was a phone call. Greg saying, 'If your murderer was waiting for the ideal conditions to hide his tracks, he couldn't have chosen a better time. The rain and wind were not our friends on this occasion'.

# CHAPTER FIFTY-FIVE

BACK IN MY OFFICE, I say to the team, 'We've always known Thursdays were significant. Rachel didn't normally see clients on a Friday so nobody would have missed her, and Edwin doesn't work at all on Fridays. Lisa had her Thursday evenings all mapped out in college term time, and Jack usually stayed in on his own. So, it was the ideal day for Fuller to kill his wife. But not any old Thursday. The weather had to be horrendous, not only to cover his tracks but also to make it less likely there would be other people out and about.'

'But he couldn't possibly have predicted a storm on that particular day,' says Steph.

'No, you're right, he couldn't have. But what if he had the whole thing planned out and was all set up and ready to go? Then all he needed was a bad forecast. Lisa's classes wouldn't have started 'til the first full week in January, so his first option was the 11$^{th}$. He probably calculated there was a decent chance of a bad Thursday sometime during the winter. And as things transpired, he didn't have to wait long before he struck lucky.' I drum my nails on the desk. 'Tobias, check out meteorological reports for bad storms on a Thursday. Go back as far as September. There's no point in looking for anything before that, the nights would have been too light. And match it up with college term times, would you?'

————

TOBIAS IS BACK within the hour and calls on the others to join us. 'I am surprised to find there was only one other Thursday in the period September through to January 25<sup>th</sup> that could be classed as stormy. It was in term time, but the college suffered a power failure, and Lisa's class was cancelled. She and her husband went out to dinner with friends, and I have confirmed that with the restaurant. Mrs McCafferty paid fifty per cent of the bill with her credit card.'

So, yet another piece of circumstantial evidence. They're not half mounting up.

Then I take a call from Sam. He says, 'I've been thinking about your suspect, putting myself in his shoes, as it were. Fire-fighters have to lift unconscious people and extract them from burning buildings, and often they weigh significantly more than sixty-five kilos. Then there's the weight of our uniform and our gear, which isn't exactly light as you can imagine. But we train for that, day in, day out, and in our spare time too. Do you know if your guy's a gym bunny?'

'He does weight training at the gym for three or four hours every week. He also has a gym set up in his garage, and he cycles a lot.'

'So, he's been building his core strength, and the cycling would help with cardio. Does he smoke? Is he overweight?'

'No, on both counts. But going back to the gym, what kit would he work with if he was preparing to carry a body like you did earlier on today.'

281

'Give me a few minutes and I'll email you.'

———

I READ Sam's email and relay the gist to the team. 'Basically, he says gym workouts would all relate to building upper body strength, but he would supplement that by practicing with, "A heavy / awkward weight e.g., two or three twenty-five kilo sandbags joined together in some way to resemble a body".' I read on a few lines and then paraphrase the rest. 'Too suspicious (I guess) to test it outside but if he climbed up and down a ladder inside his garage with a weight on his back, or on and off a bench, it would add more realism. And cycling would help develop all-round fitness.' I look up at Andrew. 'Equipment-wise, what did he have in the garage?'

'A typical home multi-gym, with a bench, and a few heavy dumb-bells. I'd say ten or maybe twelve kilos.'

'What about sandbags, or anything like that?'

'I didn't see any. But we know how careful he's been, so he would probably have dumped them as soon as he was finished with them.'

They all fall silent while I think. We're in danger of being overwhelmed by data, and as things stand, it's becoming increasingly difficult to tell what's important and what's a smoke screen. 'Steph, Tobias. I need you to pull all these locations together on a far more detailed map. Much more wide-ranging this time, so make it a decent size.' Then I explain precisely what I want them to plot.

———

THE MAP I asked Steph and Tobias to produce is up on the wallboard. Hanging off the far left in its own little box, like cartographers often do with Shetland, is my house. On the extreme right is Edwin Fuller's school. Clustered around the centre are three locations: the McCafferty's house, the lock-ups at Powderhall Lane, and St Mark's Woods. Situated further north is Fuller's house. The Water of Leith cuts between Powderhall Lane and the back of the McCaffertys' place, and ELPN routes criss-cross the entire map.

Steph's standing by the board, ready to talk us through it. 'I'll start by saying the solid blue lines indicate cycling routes that Fuller has used or might have used. We've timed them all using an average cycling speed of eighteen miles per hour because as far as we know, Fuller normally uses one of his two conventional bikes, bearing in mind he's stashed the ebike somewhere.' She shines a laser pointer on the board. 'We know he cycles to and from school, and it's "from school" we're most interested in. He travels north through Leith, west along the Water of Leith walkway, north again through Inverleith Park, crosses Ferry Road, then home.'

'Steph,' says Andrew. 'If there's no CCTV on the walkway, how do you know he stays on it all the way to Inverleith?'

'There's a camera right at the start, here, and another one on this bridge where he turns off. The timings don't allow for any deviation to his route. Then, because he uses the ELPN all the way home, and there are hardly any cameras on these paths, we don't see him again.'

I hold up my hand. 'So you think he's deliberately avoiding cameras.'

'I do. But having said that, it is the most direct route.'

'On the 25th, do you have him on CCTV?'

'Yes. We know he left school at 16:00 sharp, his normal time.'

'He doesn't take any extra-curricular sessions? After-school club, nothing like that?'

'Not on a Thursday. Possibly because it's the start of his weekend.' She uses the pointer to drag an icon onto the board from a stack on the right, clicks it, and a grainy image appears. She places it beside the map. 'Here he is, joining the walkway at 16:08. You can see how bad the weather is.'

'Andrew, what bike is he on?'

'That's the mountain bike, the Cannondale.'

'The one that wasn't in the garage?'

'Correct.'

I stare at it for a few seconds. 'Okay. Based on my new-found knowledge of all things cycling, let's see if I've got this right. Of the three bikes he owned until recently, the road bike and the hybrid would be faster than the mountain bike?'

'Yes. Especially on roads.'

'Fair enough, but Fuller also uses the ELPN where the surfaces are a mix of asphalt and hard packed gravel. And therefore suitable for the road bike and the hybrid?'

'Yes. Although in bad weather, like there was that day, the mountain bike would be a safer option. The tyres have more grip.'

'Tobias,' I say. 'You researched the weather, when did that storm kick off?'

He scrolls through his notes. 'Around noon.'

'So when he set off for school that morning the weather was okay?'

'It was, but the forecast said it would deteriorate badly by midday.'

'Yeah, assuming anybody ever believes a forecast. But my question is still, why would he use that bike to go to school when he has two others that are faster? Because let's think about this, if he intended to go straight home after school it wasn't vital that he was on a mountain bike. Now, maybe it was a whim. He didn't care which one he took, and it so happened

284

that particular bike was nearest the garage door. But we know Fuller is a meticulous planner.' I scrutinise the map. 'Steph, what time did he turn off the Water of Leith walkway?'

She pulls over another icon and clicks it to show a still of Edwin cycling across a bridge towards the camera. She points at the time – 16:17. 'Then he would have turned onto the ELPN, so that's the last shot I have of him.'

I'm back on the map, tracing the route he'd have taken if he'd cycled straight home, when Andrew snaps his fingers. 'Ah hah!' He shines a pointer on one of Steph's blue lines; a major artery of the ELPN. 'Look. Fuller's route takes him along the Warriston Path.' Then he jerks the laser over to the right and spins it in circles. 'At this point here, he's only a couple of hundred metres from St Mark's Woods.'

I stand up, walk over to the board and jab my finger where Andrew is pointing the laser. 'That's why he took the mountain bike, with its capabilities, on that particular stormy Thursday. Because he knew that was the day he would kill his wife. This wasn't about his normal bike ride home from school. He needed his strongest bike, the one with the most grip, the one most suitable for wet and muddy woodland paths, while he carried a body over his shoulder.'

Now Lawrence pipes up. 'So you think he dumped his bike in the woods so he could use it later on?'

I nod. 'And if he did, how long would it have taken him to jog to his house? Another, say, ten minutes? So that's about 16:30, which is when he said he arrived home.' I shrug. 'But it doesn't matter what he said because there are no witnesses. To quote Andrew, this is an example of "keeping the lie as close as possible to the truth".'

Tobias is flicking back and forth through his notes but clearly he can't find what he's searching for. 'Steph. Can you please bring up the table with the texts that Bob downloaded from the phones?' Once the table is up there, he moves closer and peers at it. Steph passes him a laser. 'According to the records from Rachel's mobile phone, the timings we have for Edwin's journey coincide with the time she drove home from Livingston.' He shines the laser on the map. 'Her route home, and her husband's, would have intersected here.'

I can practically hear his neurons crackling away so I wait while he puts his words in the right order. 'She supposedly used her burner to message Jack's burner at 16:19 from Ferry Road, at the entrance to Goldenacre playing fields. But actually, her own mobile shows she wasn't far from there at the time.' He raises both arms and clamps his hands on his head. 'But how could Fuller have known where she was?'

Andrew swipes at his tablet. 'I have his phone logs here.' He runs his fingernail down the screen, scrolling as he goes. 'Here we are. He called her, twice. So he knew she would drive straight along Ferry Road; it's the most obvious route. And that would take her past Goldenacre. All he had to do was time it right.'

Tobias points at the map. 'His route along the Warriston Path was virtually equidistant from both the woods and Goldenacre. He could easily have turned off that path and cycled over towards Ferry Road. Then he used the burner to message Jack, but Rachel's position made it appear as though it was her.'

Now we all edge closer to the board. I point at the table. 'Fuller set it up to make it look like she messaged Jack at 16:19. And there's Jack's *reply*, nine minutes later, at 16:28. But Jack didn't send it, did he?'

'Boss,' says Steph. 'I've just checked to see where Jack was working that day.'

I smile at her. 'And by any freak of nature was it close to where the text was sent from?'

'Yeah. He was working in Stockbridge. No distance at all as the crow flies.'

'Is that not a bit too coincidental?' says Andrew. 'Not only is he working relatively close to the woods but also it's not that far from where he lives.'

I shake my head. 'No. Because remember, when we interviewed him, he told us he'd been working there for four months, and Edwin Fuller could easily have known that.' I point at the map. 'Steph, how far is it from Goldenacre to Stockbridge?'

'By the ELPN, a mile or so.'

'Which he could easily have cycled in nine minutes.'

'Definitely,' says Andrew. 'But would that not have been incredibly risky? You know what Stockbridge is like – busy streets, loads of shops, cameras all over the place. No way he wouldn't have been picked up.'

'Maybe not. Where about in Stockbridge was Jack working, Steph?' She reads out the address. We all study the map. I laugh. Point. 'There you go. An offshoot from the Warriston Path runs behind the street where Jack was working. The masts would only triangulate to an approximate area, so Fuller didn't have to cycle all the way into Stockbridge to create the ping.'

'Steph, do you own a bike?' says Andrew.

'I do.'

'Good. Go and fetch it and meet me at St Mark's Woods. I want to test out some theories.'

Steph smirks. 'Are you joining us, Boss?'

I sling her a look that says *Behave yourself, woman*. Although it is telling that neither of them bothered asking Lawrence.

---

Tobias taps on my door. 'I believe we've missed something.'

I shove my mouse away and sit back. 'And what's that?'

He places a printout on my desk; the texts between the two burners plus a couple of others he's highlighted in yellow. 'When we first logged these locations, we were under the impression Rachel and Jack were having an affair.' He points at the two lines he's highlighted. 'Bob lifted these from Rachel's personal mobile. They state that her phone was located in or close to the woods on the 11th and the 18th, at the same times as the burner suggested she was there.' I lean forward, elbows on the table, examine the details more closely. 'But we now believe Rachel wasn't in the woods on those nights, so how could her phone have been there?' he says.

I recall our discussion with Edwin. 'He told us they rarely go out during the week, especially in winter. Rachel preferred to stay in most nights. He said something like, "She would often switch her phone off and veg in front of the TV".' I look up at Tobias. 'So did Edwin take her phone to the woods on those dates to make it appear as though she'd been there?'

'I did consider that but surely if he'd gone out and taken her phone with him, she'd have noticed.'

I stand up, walk over to my favourite spot by the window. Three floors below, the car park is awash with empty spaces. I picture myself lazing about on my sofa, my phone lying on a cushion within arm's length in case I have to google something or communicate with the kids. Even if all my family were at home, and even if the phone was switched off, it would be there or thereabouts. I can't imagine my husband removing it without me noticing. Tobias and I stare at each other. 'I'm stumped. How could he walk off with her phone, two Thursdays in a row, for at least an hour, at exactly the same time, and she's totally oblivious?'

'I don't know either, Boss. I wondered about a second SIM

card, but even if he took out another contract with a different provider, with the same number, they would put a stop on the original SIM. Besides, I checked with her provider, they've never issued a second card or a replacement.' He pauses, scratches at his beard. 'Is there a slight chance he could have taken the SIM out, and used it in another device?'

'No, that's pushing it. There could have been any number of reasons she wanted to use her phone.' We both fall silent, fresh out of options. I sigh. I appear to be doing that a lot lately. 'The bottom line is a phone can't be pinged without a SIM. And you can't fool a mast. Either the phone is in the vicinity, or it isn't.'

Tobias winces, like someone's nipped his flesh. 'There's another thing.'

I don't say, *Jesus. What now?*, although I'd love to.

'Until Edwin saw a weather forecast that included the 25th, he couldn't have known there would be a storm that day. So, he must have left the house on the two previous Wednesdays to set up all the mobile phone hacks, on the off-chance the weather deteriorated.'

'You're right. But he had the perfect cover. After all, he'd been acting the part of fanatic cyclist and fitness freak for the best part of nine months. All grist to the exercise mill.'

I give up. I've no choice but to admit I have no idea how Fuller achieved all these things. Fortunately, I know a man – or woman – who does. Time for me to go and speak to Bob.

# CHAPTER FIFTY-SIX

'WELL, Melissa, my dear. I had intended going out on the pull tonight, but I may have to put that on hold.' Bob leans her elbows on her desk, rests her chin in cupped hands and gazes at her monitor. 'These are two interesting puzzles you've brought me. Very interesting indeed.'

She talks to the screen and me at the same time. 'On one hand we have a mobile phone belonging to Rachel Fuller that appears to have moved from her house to the car park and back, on two separate occasions. Consecutive Thursdays, around nine o'clock in the evening, and you believe she didn't leave her house.'

'She may have left her house, but she didn't go to that car park.'

'But you think her phone did.'

'We're certainly being led to believe it did.'

'And you can't imagine her husband was able to remove the phone from the house without her knowing.'

'No chance.'

'It's fair to say you've covered the obvious options – a new contract, or even a second SIM. But you're right, they're not the solution. Hmmm, so what is?' She rattles around in a tray on her desk for a paperclip and, while she's thinking, she twists it out of shape. 'Let's leave that one for now. Problem number two, the GPS on McCafferty's pickup stated it was driven to locations it may not actually have visited. The data suggests McCafferty drove the vehicle to meet Mrs Fuller in the afore-mentioned car park, three Thursdays in a row.' She flicks the mangled paperclip into the bin. 'But you believe it didn't move from its parking space on any of those dates. Correct?'

'Correct.'

'And would it be fair for me to suggest that you are utterly clueless about how this could have been achieved?' I don't answer right off the bat. Instead, I hit her with my hardest glower. It has about the same effect as Minnie Mouse landing Mike Tyson with her best left hook. 'I'll take that as a yes,' she says.

But she doesn't follow that up. She says silent, chews her lip, glances around. Shit! She's as clueless as I am. I feel mildly nauseous. A sense of rising panic. Bob always, always bails me out.

But there's a set to her mouth. Her spine appears a little straighter than it was even one minute ago. 'How,' she says, 'did Rachel Fuller's phone ping a mast when it very probably didn't leave the house? And how did McCafferty's vehicle roam around the Inverleith area while its gearbox remained reso-lutely in neutral.'

Then she beams out a smile that would give a searchlight a decent run for its money. 'Same as you, Melissa, I have abso-lutely no idea. But, also same as you, I do love a challenge.'

# CHAPTER FIFTY-SEVEN

Steph was cycling through Inverleith Park, heading for the agreed meeting place at Goldenacre playing fields. She spotted Andrew in the distance, leaning his bike against a fence that formed the boundary between Goldenacre and Ferry Road. As she approached, she hopped her bike over a fallen branch and pulled up beside Andrew, who had just hooked his helmet on his handlebars.

Steph compared the two bikes. Hers resembled a small motorcycle; suspension front and rear, big fat chunky tyres, and caked in mud. Andrew's was altogether more elegant, and so shiny his colleague wondered if he'd bought it earlier that same morning.

'How do you do it, Andrew?'

'Do what?'

'Stay so flaming clean.'

Andrew chuckled. 'As a kid, if I ever came home dirty my mum used to freak. I guess she must have passed it on.' He was already holding his phone. 'Okay. This is where we believe Edwin was when he used Rachel's burner to message Jack. So send me a text, and hopefully I'll be pinged by the same masts as that burner.'

Back in the office, Tobias was monitoring their location. Within a minute he messaged Andrew:

You have a match – identical masts / cell towers

The two detectives jumped on their bikes and followed the ELPN to the point on the Warriston Path, where it passed behind the tenement in Stockbridge that Jack had been renovating. Andrew checked the time. Without racing, they'd covered the distance in less than seven minutes, well within the nine that Fuller had left between his two burner messages.

Again, they tested the ping. Tobias sent a similar message:

Success – another match

Andrew dropped his phone into his pocket. 'So far so good. That replicates what we think Fuller did. Set up the two messages so it looks like Rachel is asking if Jack wants to meet her for their regular Thursday evening assignation. But this time, Jack says no. Then, supposedly, Rachel's pissed off and goes home in a bad mood. She and Edwin have their evening together, spot of sex, marital tiff, she storms out. Then, supposedly again, she messages Jack and drives to the woods to meet him. Only she doesn't drive, Edwin does. Because she's already dead.'

'Makes perfect sense, Andrew, but the one thing I don't understand is why he would have made up a tale about them having sex and her leaving the house in a bad mood. What was the point in that?'

'The way I see it, Edwin needed to instigate sex with her to set up the kill. How far it went, who knows? Because then it appeared as though she'd had sex with Jack before he supposedly killed her. Edwin had to say she was in a bad mood because that gave her a reason for storming out the house.

Because it's the sort of thing she did; the whole world agrees on that.'

'But what if she'd turned him down? "I don't fancy it tonight, I've got a headache" or whatever.'

Andrew hitches a shoulder up. 'Don't know. Expect he'd have had a backup plan of some sort.'

'Or maybe he'd have called the whole thing off.' Steph adjusted the straps on her helmet. 'Okay, where to now?'

Andrew nodded over to their left. 'I'd intended to go to St Mark's Woods next, but we'll cross the Warriston Path on the way so let's take a detour along there. Check out where he might have dumped whatever he wrapped her in.'

The pair cycled almost all the way to Fuller's house, turning back when they reached the old Newhaven railway station. They took note of potential sites with communal waste bins and visited a couple of commercial premises with skips outside. The manager of one company told them the waste was uplifted on a Friday. 'The bugger thought of everything,' muttered Steph as they climbed back on their bikes.

When they reached the woods, Andrew lifted a tablet out of his backpack and typed in the access code. Steph slugged water from a blue plastic bottle, while her colleague attempted to reconfigure the map he had on the screen to show a suitable view. Andrew shook his head and flipped the lid closed. 'There's not enough detail, and satellite view is useless because of the trees. Let's see if the interpretive board is any better.'

The board was built into a wooden structure in the shape of an inverted 'V', attached to two posts. The map was protected by a Perspex sheet, which was worse than useless as it was pitted with scratched declarations of love by the area's teenagers. The finer detail of the map was difficult to make out through the scars, but they were able to see the woods had three trails: one circular, marked in yellow, and two loops in blue and red. They all merged with each other at various junctions to form trails of different lengths.

Andrew tapped the Perspex. 'I wonder if there's an unmarked path that gives access to Powderhall Lane. If so, it would be somewhere off the bottom of the circular. I'll go round that, you take the blue route, and we'll meet up somewhere in the middle.'

Minutes later, Steph braked to a halt when she spotted Andrew heading her way. 'Anything?'

'Nope.' Andrew jerked a thumb over his shoulder. 'The area of scrub that fireman Sam tried to cross is back there. We should go over it again in case there's a path we missed.'

After only a few minutes the two officers ruled it out as a possibility. They couldn't see any way that Fuller could have used a bike to transport a body through the trees without churning up the mud and leaving rutted tyre tracks. Steph had grumbled more than once about tree roots being a hazard, even with mountain bike tyres. They were forced to accept that no matter how much care Fuller had taken, he'd likely have fallen at least once, and dropped Rachel's body. No, he hadn't taken that route.

'Change of plan,' said Andrew. 'If we can't find our way to the lane from the woods, how about we try it the other way round?' This time the online map did help. They found two different routes by road, so they took one each and set off in opposite directions.

No more than five minutes later, Steph phoned Andrew. 'I'm on the road, just down from the crem. I've found something. It could be what we've been looking for.'

Andrew was there in no time flat.

Warriston Crematorium, as one might expect, stands on a huge slice of ground but the road that takes mourners to the site was constructed in the days when cars were scarcely wide enough to seat two people side by side without clashing elbows. Directly outside the gates, at a push it's two lanes wide, immediately turning into double bends running downhill one after the other; not particularly handy for manoeuvring a hearse. To add to the degree of difficulty, on one side a high rough stone wall hugs the kerbstones, while the other is guarded by trees and banks of hulking rhododendrons. If there was a road equivalent of Nepal's Lukla Airport, this one would be it. Andrew found Steph near the entrance. She was standing with one foot in the gutter and the other on the grass, ready to leap back into the safe clutches of the surrounding foliage at the merest hint of an approaching vehicle.

'What've you found?' said Andrew.

Steph showed him. Andrew chuckled and clapped his hand on the junior officer's shoulder. 'Kudos, my friend. Let's call the boss.'

———

'I HAD no idea this was here,' I say. 'It's totally invisible from the road.'

Behind the trees and the rhododendrons is an unsurfaced pavement. I suppose it was created for people who walk to and from the crem but the building's so far off the beaten track that most folk drive, hence the astrodome-sized car park. In trying to find a route from the woods to the lock-ups, we'd been searching for one that was either short or direct. Coming down this pavement makes it a good bit longer, but if Fuller had been able to mount his bike in the car park, with Rachel in a fireman's lift, he'd only have had to turn the pedals a few times and he'd have reached this pavement. It follows the road, which slopes down. So, all he had to do was roll the bike and stay upright, and he'd arrive at where we're standing now, at the entrance to a path that's guarded by one of those offset gate things. Designed, ironically, to stop cyclists.

One thing this does explain is why, on the night Rachel was killed, the Focus was driven only as far as the woods, and that Steph's CCTV research was right – the car didn't travel down the road past the crem. And the illusion Fuller created, of his wife meeting Jack in the car park, stood up to scrutiny. Which makes it even more bizarre that Fuller chose to shatter it himself – something I plan to quiz him on, first chance I get.

At this point I picture Fuller dropping his bike, readjusting his load and staggering through the gateway where, a few metres further on, the gravel path changes to smooth asphalt and merges with the end of Powderhall Lane. I stand there shaking my head at the simplicity of it. I turn to Steph. 'The lock-ups are just along there. What is it, a hundred and fifty metres?'

'Tops. And although Sam proved that was possible for a professional, Fuller's super-fit and he'd have been awash with adrenaline.'

'So, he dumps the body, goes back to his bike, and cycles off home.' I look at Steph, expecting her to agree with me but she's wearing a look I'm familiar with. I exhale, louder and for longer than is strictly necessarily. 'Come on, then. Spill.'

'Well, I wonder if he did cycle home. He's demonstrated over and over how clued up he is on biological forensics. Remember that talk we went to, the one about botany and soil samples and stuff like that?'

I do remember. Palynology: how microscopic grains of pollen can help with an investigation if the plant is restricted to a particular location or environment. Thought it was going to be like watching paint dry, but it was utterly fascinating. 'Yes, what are you getting at?'

'Well, no matter how thoroughly he cleaned that bike,

there would have been traces of these woods all over it. He couldn't take that chance, so I reckon he dumped it somewhere then walked home.'

'And that's why it's not in his garage.' I nod to myself. 'Nice one, Steph. Sounds logical to me.'

Then Andrew appears, and I explain Steph's theory about the mountain bike. 'Makes perfect sense,' he says. 'Good thinking.'

Then he goes on to tell us he's been taking photos and filming the route. 'I've timed it. Fuller would only have been exposed for three or four minutes. But he took an enormous risk, it was always possible he could have met someone. However, as we've said a thousand times, it was late, the weather was totally shit, so he got away with it.'

I sigh. 'I suppose there had to be a risk somewhere, he couldn't have mitigated it fully.' I take a few seconds to think. 'Andrew, as soon as we get back, I'd like you to apply for a warrant to search both his house and his garage. Unlikely I will admit but it's always possible that mountain bike is in his house somewhere. Assuming it's granted, I want to move on him as quickly as possible.'

'What are our chances, Boss?' says Steph. 'Of getting a warrant, I mean.'

I shrug. 'Fifty-fifty. Here's hoping the Sheriff's in a good mood and isn't too hidebound by protocol.'

We're standing in the middle of the lane, but I walk back 'til I reach the pavement. Stop. Look over towards the crem. The pavement isn't as winding as the road, but it is on a down-hill curve. 'Andrew. Steph. I've never carried anyone in a fire-man's lift, but I watched how Sam did it. He used one arm to hold the dummy's leg and wrist, so it didn't slip, and he used his other arm like a counterbalance. How could Fuller have managed that while cycling a bike? Because there were no signs that Rachel was tied on by a rope or a belt. No fibres, no rips in the coat, nothing.'

Andrew is wearing an expression that fits neatly into the smug category. But it's Steph who speaks. 'We were talking about that while we were waiting for you.' She digs her colleague in the ribs. 'Go on. Tell her.'

'Ah, well,' he says. 'My guess is he didn't use a rope. And he didn't leave any fibres of his clothing, or at least none that would stand out.'

I squint at him. 'You'll have to explain that one to me, young man.'

So, he does.

# CHAPTER FIFTY-EIGHT

Friday

THE PREVIOUS EVENING, Lisa had been in her kitchen. The only illumination in the room came from electrical appliances. The temperature LEDs high up on the fridge-freezer, the digital clock on the oven, and a single blue neon that betrayed the position of the kettle. The only change was when she lifted her phone, which she'd done several times in the past hour since the message had arrived.

Hi Lisa. It's been ages since we spoke and I have to say I'm missing you. We're probably both in a bad place right now and I feel we should support each other. After all we've been friends a long long time. Would you like to come over for dinner either this Saturday or next? Let me know please. Take care, love, Edwin xx

The text had freaked her out. Or at least the timing had because minutes before her phone chimed she'd been rooting around in a drawer for a measuring tape. Instead, she'd come across a key fob, which she held in her fingers for a few seconds before she fell apart: big time. It was a tiny silver metal Eiffel Tower, a souvenir of the first trip she and Jack ever made abroad. She hadn't long graduated, and he was an apprentice plumber, so they were strapped for cash. The fob held one single Yale key. It was for Edwin's house; Rachel had given her a copy years earlier – 'Just in case'.

Lisa sat at the kitchen table, a box of tissues at her elbow, the fob clutched in the palm of her left hand. For the umpteenth time she reached out and tapped her mobile. She read the text yet again. Most of it was the same soppy blurb he'd used in previous messages and voicemails: 'missing you; in a bad place; support each other; friends a long long time'. That he saw it necessary to repeat the word 'long', stank of desperation as far as she was concerned.

Two things were bothering her: how she'd be able to say no without sounding dismissive, because she didn't want to go at all, never mind this Saturday – only forty-eight hours away. And his choice of words and comma placement in 'Take care, love, Edwin xx'. Was he being cute – 'Take care, love'? Or was it simply 'Love, Edwin'? Either way, she didn't welcome the attention.

She recalled DI Cooper's instruction, 'You need to steer well clear, Lisa. Do not become involved with him under any circumstances'. But she had a major problem with that. Her husband was suffering an enormous miscarriage of justice. Being held on remand was bad enough, but what if he was convicted and sent to jail? She knew that outcome was almost certain because the weight of evidence was overwhelming, especially as he was the prime and only suspect. But now she had an alternative. And, more importantly, Cooper had an alternative.

The fact was, Lisa hadn't ever suspected Edwin. Not for one single second. But ever since her conversation with Mel, she'd been wondering if he could he have done it. And because there wasn't a speck of evidence against him, she always came back with the same answer: no. And prior to their walk in The Meadows, clearly DI Cooper didn't have any evidence either. But now it seemed she did.

'So, what does she have?' Lisa blew her nose. Stood up, padded over to the bin, pushed the pedal down carefully with her toes. Normally the lid crashed back against the wall but not this time. It lifted – nice and smooth. She took that as an omen. She dropped the soggy tissue inside and turned towards the kettle. 'Sod it.' Instead, she opened the fridge and lifted out an unopened Sauvignon Blanc. She nodded. 'More like it.'

———

Now IT WAS six o'clock on Friday morning. Last night, Lisa had poured herself a large glass then put the wine away. She'd moved through to the living room and flopped down on the sofa. She kept the room in darkness to help her think.

DI Cooper obviously hadn't been flying a kite when she asked to meet up, her questions were too focused for that. There was her interest in Edwin's and Rachel's body shapes, and how he'd changed over the last year; the relationships between the two couples or, more specifically, between the individuals in each pairing; whether they'd ever lost or mislaid a key to the pickup; and would Edwin have known about the high thread count of Lisa's bed linens. Then, the clincher – would Rachel have driven while under the influence. *No. Cooper's on to something. Definitely*.

Lisa sipped her wine; let it float over her tongue. As her vision adjusted, shapes gradually made themselves known in the room. A red neon lit up on the Sky box; a programme began recording. She had no idea what – probably sport. She hadn't been able to bring herself to cancel any of Jack's series recordings. Her brain refocused. *I bet Cooper wants into Edwin's house. She thinks there's something in there that'll implicate him. But she doesn't have sufficient grounds for a warrant.*

She squirmed around, pulled one leg underneath her, moved a cushion to support her back. The change of angle meant the red neon was now glinting off the miniature Eiffel Tower. She'd stood it on the coffee table before sitting down. She kept her eyes on it while she pondered Cooper's predicament.

*The police can't access the house. But I can.*

# CHAPTER FIFTY-NINE

LISA HADN'T SLEPT WELL, too many thoughts and questions buzzing around in her head. She'd worked out a plan, but it would only work if Edwin was out. *Friday morning – did he still go to the gym? And, if so, what time?* She knew he was an early riser, and a creature of routine. He worked out for a couple of hours then had breakfast at a café somewhere; always the same one. But she didn't know what constituted early in Edwin's world so now, here she was, driving towards his house at 06:20. On the way, she called her PA and left a voicemail to say she was taking the day off. She didn't imagine she'd be missed.

She'd visited her friends often enough over the years to know that when Edwin cycled away from his house he'd hang left out of the drive, left again down the side of his garage before turning onto the lane behind the house. So Lisa drove a circuitous route and parked where she could watch him leaving, tight in behind a grey Fiat 500 and away from any street-lights. The height of the cab meant she could see over the top of the car in front. She anticipated Edwin might take a glance to the right as he was going left but he'd never spot the pickup, simply because he wouldn't expect it to be there.

Almost two hours later, the sun had cleared the rooftops and was shining directly into the cab. A combination of her sunglasses and pulling the visor down had helped her maintain a vigil. Eventually, she spotted his garage door flipping up. *At long bloody last*. She'd been cursing herself for her lack of preparedness. No flask of hot tea, and totally inappropriate clothing for a stakeout on a March morning in Scotland. But all that was forgotten as she watched him taking the route she'd expected. 'Ace,' she said, slapping the heel of her hand on the steering wheel.

Then, 'Fuck!' when the horn sounded. But Edwin had disappeared behind the garage and didn't come back. 'You stupid cow,' she said, her hand flat on her chest. She'd already decided she would wait ten minutes before she approached the house. She had been concerned she'd chicken out, but the stakes were far too high; she wouldn't have that luxury. But, once inside, what would her excuse be if he came home and caught her? She'd been worrying about that all morning and, hands up, she had no valid reason for being in his house. However, she imagined she'd be in such a state she'd easily be able to burst into tears and wail something about desperately missing her friend or some such bullshit. Edwin would fall for it; she was certain of that.

And if he didn't, she'd throw herself into his arms and deal with whatever happened next.

But striding down the street, what she couldn't get out of her head was DI Cooper's explicit instruction: 'Steer well clear, Lisa. Do not become involved. Under any circumstances.'

---

EDWIN HAD PASSED the glass frontage of the gym and stepped inside before he realised all the interior lights were out. Three instructors were lounging about in the gloomy reception area. One screwed the top down on his water bottle and smiled. 'Sorry mate, we're closed. Power cut, I'm afraid.'

'Aw,' said Edwin. 'Any point in hanging around?'

'Probably not. We've been told at least two or three hours.'

'What a bummer.' Edwin reached for the door handle. 'Might as well go over to the café for some breakfast.'

'You're out of luck there too. It's not only us, the whole street's out.'

# CHAPTER SIXTY

'I'M ANNOYED the Sheriff didn't side with us, Mel,' says Jeff. 'But I can see why she didn't grant the warrant.'

We're sitting in his office. He'd called me first thing this morning, asked for an update, and I told him about the warrant. Or lack thereof. Sadly, I'm pretty sure I know what's coming next, and he doesn't keep me waiting.

'It's hard for me to be too critical because you and your team have worked hard. You've done a cracking job of proving how Fuller *could* have murdered his wife, and how he framed Jack McCafferty into the bargain. But, like I'm sure you're sick of hearing—'

'Yes, I know. And our evidence may all be circumstantial, but we do have a significant amount of it.'

'I don't dispute that, but it's all evidence that Fuller's defence would have no difficulty in rebutting. And although you've also put together a number of worthwhile hypotheses I'd bet my last pound they'd all be thrown back in your face, along with the words "pure conjecture". When we last spoke to Leo he made it clear that if we take the case back to him it must be rock solid.' I open my mouth to speak but he holds up a hand. 'Hold your horses, Mel. We're not giving in, not yet. So, tell me, which aspects of the investigation are you still working on?'

'We believe Fuller drove the Focus from his house to the woods with his wife's body in the boot. But, oh so conveniently, he smashed up his car and it's been scrapped. Thing is, his planning has been so detailed I can't imagine he simply threw her in the boot, he'd have wrapped her in heavy duty polythene or something similar. Where he sourced it, and where he dumped it are unanswered questions. And we assume he's been buying electronic items, probably online.'

'Such as?'

'He was able to break in to Jack's pickup to plant evidence, but Lisa says they've never lost or mislaid a key.'

'So he used a key cloner?'

'Probably. Now, he could have bought that from criminal sources and paid cash for it. Problem is, we don't know if he has those connections so the alternative would be buying it online.'

'Meaning he has a credit card we don't know about.'

'Again, probably. But it won't be legit, or we'd have tracked it down.'

'Well, no matter which card he's using, if he bought any items from a reputable source, there would be an order history, a delivery address, and therefore a courier. But if he's paying by cash to some dodgy dealer, or using a stolen card, you don't have much chance of tracing it.'

'Yeah, I know.'

'Nothing you've told me sounds like it'll come to fruition, Mel. Do you have *anything* we can hang our hat on?'

'Bob's working on a couple of things—'

'And they are?'

I explain about how Rachel's phone was tracked to St Mark's Woods on the key dates but that I'm virtually certain she didn't take it there. And also that Jack's satnav says it was at the same location, at the same times, while logic states it could not have moved from its parking place in central Edinburgh and somehow magicked back into the same space one hour later. On three different nights.

Jeff puffs out his cheeks. 'Well, if anyone can find out how he did it, Bob can.'

I nod, but don't admit my IT friend isn't entirely confident she'll be able to figure it out. 'That just leaves me with Fuller showing up at my house with his so-called confession. And that's at an impasse. We have footage of a cyclist on the ELPN at the right time, but we can't prove it's him. And before you ask, it's unlikely we'll be able to.'

'Define unlikely.'

'Not a fart's chance in a whirlwind.'

'Okay, on that, there's one more option available. There's a risk attached but we have no choice.'

Then he explains what he wants me to do.

# CHAPTER SIXTY-ONE

Lisa was in uncharted territory. She was inside Edwin's house searching for ... what? This was as far as her plan, such as it was, had taken her. So she was wandering aimlessly from room to room on the hunt for evidence that would implicate Edwin and free her husband. With absolutely no idea what that evidence might be.

Downstairs, there were only three rooms including the kitchen and there wasn't anything lying about that jumped up and shouted, 'It's me! I'm what you're looking for'. A couple of magazines on the floor next to the TV, a dark blue woollen jumper over the back of a chair, a few items on the kitchen work surfaces. She opened the cupboard in the hall. Coats and jackets on wall hooks, two pairs of shoes on the floor, a rucksack and a Dyson. As she was closing the door, she heard footsteps outside, but unless Edwin had taken to wearing heels, she had nothing to worry about.

In the kitchen she opened a couple of drawers, a few cupboards, and the fridge. She'd just reached the conclusion this was a pointless exercise when there was a rattling sound behind her. As with the footsteps, she was unconcerned. She turned to find one of the cats halfway through the cat flap, checking it was safe to enter. But when he saw Lisa, he eased his hind legs under the plastic and strolled across the floor. 'Hello Chilli, where did you spring from?' She laid the house key and her sunglasses on the table, picked up the animal and pulled him in tight for a cuddle.

When Edwin had named this cat, Lisa thought he was being ironic. Because Edwin hated spicy food. It was always a pain when they were out for a Chinese or an Indian, searching the menus for something he would eat. Lisa nuzzled into the cat's fur. 'Come on, Chilli, let's take a look upstairs.'

———

As EDWIN CYCLED along the lane behind his house, he spun the pedals a few times then freewheeled round the corner and along the side of his garage. Then he hit the brakes. Hard. His front wheel was level with the front of the concrete building, so he put one foot down and pushed himself backwards. Now he was only visible from the opposite side of his street, and from a narrower one that ran perpendicular.

Parked a short distance up that street in clear view was a black Mitsubishi. Jack's pickup. Edwin recognised it straight away; Jack had stuck a decal of the Scotland flag on the underside of the visor, which had been left down.

'Lisa.' His first reaction was a flash of joy that transformed instantly into suspicion. *Why has she parked so far away?* He leaned against the garage wall, unclipped his helmet and hooked it on the handlebar. *I can't see her,* he thought. *She must be in the house.*

But he didn't know what to do. Maybe he should just walk in the front door, shout, 'Lisa!'. She'd say, 'Hi,' and then they'd have a coffee and sit down for a chat. But it only took him a second to jettison that as an approach. *It's Friday morning. She must know I'll be at the gym. She's obviously chosen to come here while I'm out.*

He wheeled his bike in a tight arc and jumped on the pedals. He sped round to Olive's back gate, unzipped his fleece pocket and pulled out his keyring. Although he'd handed keys over to the old woman's daughter, he'd kept the spare key for the gate – which he'd installed. As he dragged his bike inside, his helmet fell off the handlebar and bounced away from him. He ignored it. He let the gate slam behind him, but it didn't close properly. Then, bent double to keep below the top of the fence between Olive's garden and his, he scurried in close to the building and sneaked a glance through his kitchen window. The room was empty, but he spied Lisa's keys and sunglasses on the table. He vaulted the wall and took a couple of steps to his kitchen door.

Seconds later he was inside.

# CHAPTER SIXTY-TWO

ON THE WAY back to my office I drop in past Bob's cave. As I approach her desk, I'm tempted to tell her she looks like shit but in the same instant I realise she's wearing the same clothes as she was yesterday.

She lifts her head, removes her glasses, and rubs her eye with the back of her hand. 'I was on the point of phoning you.'

'You were?'

'No. That was a fib.' She grabs a water bottle, takes a slug. 'Pull up a chair.' Then, 'Your man, Fuller, is he tech savvy?'

'It's hard to say but I guess he'd need to be, or his pupils would run rings round him. Why?'

'Because if my suspicions are correct, he's probably bought a number of electronic items, which would have cost a packet and would require IT expertise not only to operate them but to buy them in the first place.'

'For example?'

She takes another swig. 'If he didn't nick an actual key for the pickup, then he cloned it or used a device to intercept the signal. Either way, the kit wouldn't have been cheap.'

'Being fair, we already had that in mind but where would he have sourced it?'

Bob rocks her head from side to side. 'Online. Obviously. Unless he has connections of the nefarious variety, and then he could have paid cash.'

'That's not impossible but I've no evidence to suggest he has.'

'Online it is, then. Which bring me to my next point – I don't believe Rachel's phone was physically at St Mark's Woods without her knowledge.'

'You don't?'

'No, but her SIM card was. Or, at least, a copy of her SIM card.'

I scratch my forehead with my index finger. 'We did think of that, but how the hell did he copy it? I know it's straightforward to order a duplicate SIM from a provider but there would be a record and usually their first step is to cancel the original so there aren't normally two copies of the same card on the go.'

'You're right.' She reaches for her mouse. 'But take a gander at this.'

She clicks a minimised window and up pops an advert on what appears to be an Amazon page, but on closer inspection it's a facsimile. The ad is for a device that resembles a payment handset of the type restaurants use, only neater. It has a rectangular screen at the top and below that are two tiny slots; the bottom edges of two white SIM cards are visible in the slots. Below that are four coloured buttons: red, yellow, blue and green. The image shows the green button illuminated and the screen displaying the words: *Success – Card Copied*. A banner headline across the top of the advert declares it a *SIM card Replicator*, with an offer price of $199.99.

'I take it this isn't legit,' I say. Bob smiles and shakes her head. 'So where did you find it?'

'On an e-commerce site where everything is priced in US dollars, but who knows where it's based.'

'Well, that device is a solution but assuming he does have one of these, how the hell did he even find out it existed? Because I take it you didn't just google it?'

'No. I didn't. And as to how he found it, I'm beginning to wonder if he discovered the dark web.'

I groan and drop my head into my hands. If Bob's right, this cranks things up more than a few notches. The dark web is a sizeable and hidden part of the worldwide web which isn't accessible to people using popular browsers such as Firefox and Chrome, and pages aren't indexed by search engines like Google. Users need a special browser; Tor is probably the most well-known. The dark web has a reputation for being a dangerous part of the Internet, where all sorts of shady dealings take place, and one of these is the ability to purchase goods and services that are not freely available from legitimate vendors. This piece of kit is a perfect example.

'Jeez,' I say. 'If he wasn't a murderer, I'd be inclined to admire him for the amount of planning he's put into this. But enlighten me, how would he have accessed it without being traced?'

She contemplates the ceiling. 'Download an anonymous browser to a mobile phone or a tablet then go online via a public network with a low level of security. A café, or somewhere like that. To further conceal his tracks, he might even have created temporary disposable email addresses or bounced his online activity through proxy servers in places like Romania or Russia. But that's adding layers of complexity that would be beyond most people's expertise. Assuming he kept things simple, his Tor browsing history would be hidden and there wouldn't be any cookies stored on his device that our investigations might uncover.'

'But where would he learn how to do all these things? An article in *Computer Monthly*?'

'Actually, that's not as bizarre as it sounds. I've seen lots of features in computer magazines that explain in detail how a theory or a device works, and then it's a question of research. And while we're on that, do you know much about online bulletin boards?'

'I've heard of them, obviously, but I'm no expert. Do tell.'

Bob stands up, moves her upper body in a series of stretches then glances at her chair, but doesn't sit down. 'Back in the 80s and early 90s, before the Internet kicked off commercially and years before websites took off, people used to post stuff on an area of electronic storage called a bulletin board. So, if you were a devotee of, let's say rock climbing, there would be bulletin boards published by climbers, where they shared info about new ascents, weather, stuff like that. Incredibly primitive in comparison to these days but they worked. I've recently discovered they're experiencing something of a renaissance, and apparently, they never really became extinct because the diehards kept them going.'

'Do you reckon Fuller's possibly using bulletin boards on the dark web to learn all this stuff, and also as a source for illegal pieces of kit?'

She nods. 'Yes. I do.'

I think for a second. 'I've just been talking to Jeff about this – if Fuller's buying gear online, he must be using a credit card. Most likely a stolen one, maybe even with a preloaded balance. I'm assuming he could have bought that from a dark web source.'

'He could.' She chuckles. 'You're about to ask the chicken and egg question, aren't you?'

'I am. How do you buy a credit card online when you don't have a credit card to pay for it?'

Bob sits and drags her chair in close to the desk. 'I found this earlier, and you won't believe it.' She brings up another window, angles her monitor so I can watch. 'This is a site that sells stolen cards.' She clicks on various dropdowns as she's talking. 'I can choose the card type, so let's say VISA. Do I want it preloaded? Yes. Denomination? Pounds Sterling. Amount? Five hundred quid.' She focuses on me. 'And this is where it definitely becomes interesting. I've seen loads of stolen card sites – but never anything like this. Watch.'

Gradually, my mouth falls open as she clicks an icon labelled *Choose my location*. It brings up a map showing our office address, then asks her to refine it by postcode and building number. When she clicks *Go* I am truly stunned.

Under the heading *Vendors near you* is a list of email addresses, all @Hotmail.com or @Yahoo.com. She clicks on the first one, and a new page appears. It has all the details she specified on the left, and on the right is the price: £1000. Below that are two buttons: *Add to basket* and *Purchase now*. And finally, a text box with the heading *Message your vendor*. With a *Send now* button.

I gawp at the screen. 'You are kidding me on.'

'I wish I were.' She lets out a sigh. 'I don't intend to, naturally, but if I did fill in that box and click send, I imagine I can set up a meeting with a local Mr Fixit, then pop along with my one grand in cash and become the proud new owner of a dodgy credit card – preloaded to the tune of £500.'

We look at each other. 'What bloody chance do we stand?' I say.

Bob doesn't reply; her face says it all.

I pick up again. 'So now he can buy his electronic gizmos online. A foreign vendor, maybe?'

'Yes. And if I had to guess, most probably in China or Taiwan. Delivery might not be the quickest, but they would never reveal their customer data to Western law enforcement authorities. He could have arranged drop off to any number of collection points in Edinburgh. He cycles there, uses the ELPN or back streets – you'd be lucky even to find the haystack.'

I shake my head for probably the hundredth time. 'So now we know how he sourced a credit card, meaning he could then buy a key cloner and a SIM card replicator. That only leaves one thing.'

She leans back in the chair. 'Ah. You want to know how he put false journeys on Jack's satnav?'

I smile. Nod. Expect my friend and colleague to enlighten me one more time.

'You've got me there, Mel.'

'Come again?'

'I've been searching all night and I have absolutely no idea. None whatsoever.'

# CHAPTER SIXTY-THREE

LISA HESITATED before opening the door to Edwin's bedroom. As she crossed the threshold, Chilli squirmed out of her arms and landed on the carpet without a sound. The duvet had been turned down and a single pillow was propped up against the headboard. An open window made the room feel cool.

She padded round to Edwin's side, slid open the bedside cabinet drawer. On top was a pack of condoms. She lifted it out; same brand as she and Jack used. She stared at it for a few seconds, shrugged, and replaced it. The drawer only held a few other items; nothing of any consequence. She pushed it shut and knelt to check the open shelf below. A magazine and a novel – a historical thriller. She pushed the book aside to read the title of the magazine. This was the first thing she'd found that struck her as odd. *Since when was Edwin into computing?*

She was still puzzling that over as she left the bedroom. The room opposite was Edwin's office. She glanced along the landing to the bathroom, deciding to leave that 'til last. By far, the office was the untidiest room in the house. A teetering pile of Rachel's clothes sagged into one corner, lumpy black bin bags holding dishes and utensils, two holdalls containing assorted bric-a-brac, and a sizeable cardboard box that had been taped shut. *Rachel stuff* was written on the side. Clearly Edwin was planning a number of charity shop runs.

On the floor to the right of his desk were several boxes, all of which had once held half a dozen wine bottles. She was surprised to find they were packed full of teaching aids, notebooks, textbooks and reference materials. Yet, on his desk there were none. She scanned the shelves around the room. Nothing anywhere to do with school. *Isn't he going back to work?* She dropped into his swivel chair. To Lisa, this was a conundrum. *Edwin loves being a teacher. Working with kids. Helping them.*

While she pondered, her gaze tracked lazily along the rows of books on the shelves. At either end, about a dozen had been arranged in two stacks. Again, she thought this was curious. Why stack books on a shelf when there was plenty of space to stand them up? Then one in the stack on the right caught her eye. She recognised the logo at once. Distinctive fonts in black writing on a yellow background, there was a *Dummies' Guide* for anything and everything. The book was second from bottom and upside down, so she had to lean sideways to read the title.

'Excel Formulas for Dummies! What the fuck?' She laughed out loud. If there was any book that had no place on Edwin's desk it was a reference manual about Microsoft Excel. Rachel was the spreadsheet buff, and Lisa knew Edwin wouldn't recognise a formula if he found one in his soup. He was always banging on about how overrated spreadsheets were and reckoned anyone with more than a passing interest in the application was a nerd.

She eased it from the stack, flipped it over and reread the title to make sure. As a senior officer in the Council, Lisa didn't have to design or build her own spreadsheets – her PA did all that. But she did have to interpret data and often devised formulas to help her do that. Nothing terribly complicated, but she was one of the more clued-up members of the senior management team. She opened it and thumbed through the pages, more out of interest than anything else. She didn't have her reading glasses with her, so she swivelled the chair through ninety degrees to catch light from the window. Now her back was to the door.

The content of the manual was arranged in order of complexity: simple examples first, working through to complex. The first few sections covered formulas she was familiar with. She noticed Edwin had pencilled annotations on most of the pages. His writing, even made up of capitals and numbers, was highly distinctive. She remembered Rachel describing it as cartoony; yet another topic she would use to belittle him.

After a few pages, Lisa spotted something that appeared out of kilter. Edwin had rewritten an example of one of the simpler formulas; one she used often. But the syntax was all wrong, it didn't make sense. On the next page there was another annotation and again, the format wasn't correct. Both would have thrown up error codes had they been entered into Excel.

The next few pages held several more, and Lisa was beginning to feel she was missing the point. Perhaps the examples that Edwin had noted down were more complex than she realised, or she wasn't quite as smart as she thought she was. She was on the point of closing the manual when she spotted one more example. And then she got it. Now she could see exactly what these formulas really meant. And they had nothing whatsoever to do with Excel.

She turned to the desk, laid the book flat out, lifted her phone from her back pocket, and photographed the annotations from several pages throughout the guide. They all related to formulas she had used, and she could explain precisely what was wrong with them.

*This is the evidence DI Cooper was searching for, and I've found it. Now she can arrest Edwin, and Jack will be free.*

She snapped the camera twice more, locked her phone, and closed the book.

Then a voice behind her said, 'Hello, Lisa. What a lovely surprise.'

# CHAPTER SIXTY-FOUR

My team are clustered around my desk. Or, at least three of them are. Lawrence called in sick this morning, and I'd be a liar if I said I was surprised. Maybe he's realised he's on thin ice but, whatever, his feet won't touch when he comes back. Assuming he does, of course – I should be so lucky.

I've just outlined Jeff's plan for what we should do next, and Andrew says, 'Pushing Fuller that hard will be risky, Boss.'

As a team, one of their main strengths is their ability to remain upbeat in the most demanding of circumstances. But I've laid it on the line, we're fast running out of options. I'd explained the results of Bob's all-nighter but when I dropped the bombshell – that she hadn't been able to prove how Fuller fooled Jack's satnav – any positivity that had been in the room evaporated. It's very possible we've lost our last chance of securing firm evidence to convict him.

'To make sure I understand,' says Steph, 'we bring him in, hit him with a mountain of circumstantial evidence, and hope it spooks him into confessing.' She glances at Andrew and Tobias. 'Is it just me, or does that not sound like we're becoming a tad desperate?' Her two colleagues don't exactly back her up, but they don't shout her down either.

I spread my hands. 'Can't argue with that, Steph. But Leo Contini is quite clear, we do have a mountain – to use your word – of circumstantial evidence, but it's not strong enough to take the case against Fuller to court, never mind gain a successful prosecution. But leaving that aside, Jeff says to bring him in. We can detain him for twelve hours, and Jeff can autho- rise up to twenty-four if necessary. But let's not be in any doubt, folks, we have to shake some hard evidence out or we are up a certain creek without the necessary hardware. As Andrew has suggested, and the boss said the same thing, we run the risk of showing all our cards and still having to fold.' I make a face. 'But we don't have any choice.'

I stand up, push my chair back, and pick up my phone. 'So, let's get organised. It's, what, 09:23. I want to be out of here by 09:30 – latest.'

# CHAPTER SIXTY-FIVE

EDWIN BATTLED TO MAINTAIN A RELAXED, friendly demeanour, when he was actually dying to lean over and scream, straight in Lisa's face, *What the fuck are you doing, snooping about in my house?* But Chilli saved the day when, out of the corner of his eye, Edwin spotted him in the bedroom curled up on top of the duvet. 'Now, puss-puss, you know you're not allowed in there. Silly daddy must have left the door open.'

But cats being cats, his pet blanked him completely, so Edwin stepped over to the bed and scooped him up in his arms. On his way out he pulled the door closed, making sure it clicked solidly into place. He smiled at Lisa. 'The catch is a bit iffy.' He diverted his gaze deliberately onto the Excel manual, then to Lisa. 'Fancy a coffee? I'll go down and put the kettle on.'

He placed the cat carefully onto the carpet and set off down the stairs.

———

LISA WAS TERRIFIED she might collapse if she rose out of the chair, so she stayed where she was. *No, I have to move.* She pushed herself upright, coughed to clear her throat, gathered herself, then called out as confidently as she could, 'Edwin. I'll just wash my hands. Be down in a minute.'

In the bathroom, she locked the door, leaned back on it and shut her eyes. He'd seen the manual open on his desk, but had he watched her taking photos? She didn't know. He hadn't been angry or upset. Instead, he'd been calm. Or was it all an act? She thought it probably was. Then she realised she was tying herself in knots, and furthermore, she couldn't stay in the bathroom much longer. She flushed the toilet, washed her hands, and headed downstairs. When she reached the bottom step, she hesitated. Was she in any danger? She glanced at the front door. It wasn't too late to run.

'Sorry,' said Edwin, appearing from the kitchen. 'I can't remember – milk and sugar?'

'Oh. Neither. Just black, please.'

'Sure.' He pointed into the living room. 'Go and make yourself comfortable and I'll fetch the drinks.' But he didn't move until she did, and her opportunity was lost.

———

WHILE EDWIN WAS ORGANISING the coffees, he fought hard to suppress the rage that was threatening to derail him. Lisa hadn't discovered the Excel manual by accident, he thought. She'd obviously searched the house for it. But how could she possibly have known what to look for? She must have checked all the rooms; Chilli's presence in the bedroom was proof of that. But now he was kicking himself because the manual was the only item in the house that connected him, even tenuously, to Rachel's murder.

No, he'd have to play things with a straight bat. She'd clearly discovered his annotations and worked out what they meant. And she hadn't taken the photos for her own amusement, she obviously intended to share them. And no prizes for guessing with whom. Detective Inspector bloody Cooper. Well, no way could Edwin allow that to happen.

But his choices were limited – that much was obvious.

'Sorry I let myself in, Edwin,' said Lisa. 'I came across Rachel's key. Thought I'd better return it.'

Edwin flapped a hand in her direction. 'Oh, you didn't have to do that. I'm happy for you to have a key; never know when it might come in handy, eh?'

Lisa didn't know how to respond to that, so she blustered on. 'When I opened the door to the kitchen the cat ran up the stairs, so I went to fetch him back.'

*Two things wrong there, darling Lisa. I always leave the kitchen door open, and the bedroom door closed. Chilli's a highly intelligent creature but breaking into rooms is definitely beyond him.*

'Then,' said Lisa, 'I wasn't feeling well, and I'd just sat down for a minute when you came in.'

Edwin leaned towards her and patted her arm. *Utter bull-shit. But I suppose it was the best you could do at such short notice.* 'That's a shame. Are you feeling better now?'

'Oh yes. It was probably that I haven't been in the house since Rachel ...'

*Was murdered?* 'Well, I'm glad you're here. It's fantastic to see you, it's been way too long.' He snapped his fingers. 'In fact, now you are here, maybe I could ask a favour. I have some boxes of stuff to take back to the school. My car was written off, so would you mind driving me over there?'

Lisa's brows shot up. 'Oh, I'm not sure. I have to—'

'Honestly, it'll only take five minutes. I'm only dropping off, and I can always walk home if you have things to do.'

———

LISA DIDN'T SEE how she could legitimately refuse. She watched him fussing over the coffees, dripping spots of milk on the table and then nearly overflowing his mug. *You're as jittery as I am, Edwin. If not more.* That encouraged her, lifted her confidence. Had she misread the jottings in his manual? She tried to recall a couple, but couldn't; not with any accuracy. 'I'll happily run you down to the school if we can go right after our coffees. I have an appointment with Jack's defence team, and I can't be late.'

'I suppose it's dress-down Friday,' he said, pointing at her jeans and trainers.

*Shit!* She put her drink down. 'I'll, em, have to go home first to change.' She jumped to her feet, made a big deal of checking her wrist. 'In fact, can we go now, please?'

He drained his mug. 'Sure. Suits me down to the ground, as it happens. It's just gone half nine, so we'll be there before morning break.' He caught Lisa throwing him an odd look. 'Sorry, but I'd rather not meet any of my pupils. You know what kids are like, they'll ask questions, and things are still far too painful.' He grinned. 'Don't want to embarrass myself.' He stood. 'I'll bring the boxes down.'

Lisa followed him into the hall, glanced at the front door. Edwin had been a bit creepy when he'd spoken to her upstairs, but now he seemed to be behaving quite normally. Maybe she had been mistaken after all. He'd left her there, she could walk out whenever she liked. *I'm better off outside, more space to run if I need to. And I can always scream my head off if I'm scared. Besides, as soon as I appear in the doorway an entire battalion of curtain twitchers will be following my every move.*

She stepped to the door, opened it, called over her shoulder, 'I'll bring the car over to the drive.'

His feet appeared on the top stair. 'Okay. Just coming.'

Out in the fresh air, Lisa felt so much better, in control of the situation. *I'll be driving. He can't threaten me, and if he does I'll just hit the horn. I can stick to busy main roads all the way so there's no chance I'll end up down a side street. And, come on, we're going to his school. I couldn't have chosen a safer place. Then, as soon as I drop him off, I'll go straight to the police station. It's two minutes away. Tops.*

Five minutes later, Lisa climbed into the cab and patted the top of her head as she gunned the engine. *Damn. My sunglasses. I've left them in the kitchen.* Fleetingly, she was tempted to go back for them, but she felt much safer in the car. She jammed the gearbox into *Drive* and pulled away from the kerb. Behind her, the cardboard boxes creaked as they settled. Edwin had stacked most of them on the back seats but had placed one inside the cargo deck. Lisa was sure it would have fitted in with the others, but he'd insisted it was likely to topple over. All Jack's tools were still in the back; Lisa hadn't wanted to move them out until she absolutely had to. While she was driving, Edwin was quiet and that suited her perfectly.

Ten minutes, and she'd be home free.

Morton Street Primary is housed in a magnificent sandstone building that dates back to 1898. It's sixty metres long, four storeys high, and faces onto Leith Links. Lisa had never been inside, but she'd passed it many times, and knew the main entrance was off to her left. So she was taken aback when he directed her to a single blue door, down a short flight of steps near the corner of the building.

'This door's closer to the storerooms,' he said.

Lisa glanced along the street. Whenever she passed here on a weekday, parking spaces were like hens' teeth, but today she could have docked a cruise liner. She turned to comment on how quiet it was, but Edwin had hopped out. He appeared at the door behind her, pulled one of the smaller, lighter boxes off the pile and held it out for her to carry. She waited while he selected a much larger one, before flipping the door closed with his elbow. Lisa checked up and down the street. It was deserted and she wondered why he was being so security conscious about a few cardboard boxes when the access door was only a few steps away.

As they crossed the pavement, they passed beneath some scaffolding that was fixed to the side of the building. She reached out and touched the metal. 'Subsidence,' said Edwin over his shoulder, as he approached the door. He leaned a knee against the wall to support the box, fished about in his pocket for a bunch of keys and turned a mortise in the lock. 'Could you get the door, please? This weighs a ton. The light switch is just inside on your left.'

Lisa opened the door and switched on the light. No more than two metres in front of her was another door. She checked with Edwin who nodded, so she opened the second door. The space ahead was in total darkness but again, the switch was on the left. As she clicked on the lights an alarm began to beep. She hadn't moved from the doorway but instantly she recognised what was happening. She dropped the box, but as she turned she was confronted by Edwin charging across the gap between them. Before she had the chance to react he barged into her, knocking her through the door. She fell backwards and surely would have smacked her head off the concrete floor had she not landed on the box she'd been carrying.

He followed her through the door, slammed it closed, ran to the alarm control panel, and keyed in a code. The alarm beeped twice more then fell silent. Lisa had been shaken by her fall but managed to scramble to her feet. She looked around to find they were in what appeared to be a long corridor. Only the first couple of ceiling lights had come on, meaning the corridor vanished gradually into the gloom. Then Lisa spotted stairs that headed upwards to the left and realised they must lead up to the ground floor. But before she could take a step, Edwin grabbed her wrist, and jerked her towards him.

Lisa screamed. A short scream first, then a much longer one, and several decibels louder.

Edwin crossed his arms and inspected her as if she were a particularly unusual specimen. 'Lisa. We're in the basement. This building's over a hundred years old. Make as much noise as you like. No one will hear you, not down here.' Then he smiled. 'In fact, even if there was anybody in the building, which there isn't, they probably still wouldn't hear you.'

Lisa's eyes were popping. 'It's Friday. What do you mean there's no one in the building?'

'Oh. Did I forget to mention? Today's a staff in-service day, but everyone's out on a team building event. Or a jolly, depending on how you look at it.'

He smiled again but this one stayed well away from his eyes. 'So, darling Lisa, we're all alone. Just you and me.'

# CHAPTER SIXTY-SIX

I THUMB Edwin Fuller's doorbell for a second time then take a couple of steps back and check out the upper floor for any sign of life. Andrew is peering through the living room window. 'Can't see him,' he says.

I hear footsteps crunching on gravel, and Tobias appears. I'd sent him and Steph round to the rear of the house in case our man legged it. He holds out a black bicycle helmet. 'This was in the lane.'

It could be Fuller's, but I can't be certain. 'Stay here, Tobias,' I say. 'Andrew. Come with me.'

We jog to the lane. Steph is waiting at the neighbour's gate. She points into the garden. 'The gate was open, and his hybrid bike is here.' Although the wheels are on the grass, the handle-bars and seat are jammed in the hedge. I cast an eye at the wall between the two gardens, but high jumping's never been my thing. My sidekicks, however, have youth on their side. 'You two – that way, I'll go round by the garage.'

By the time I puff into the back garden, they have their

faces pressed against the kitchen window, hands up to shield the glare. I join them. 'Anything?'

'If he's in, he must be upstairs,' says Steph. She points. 'The place looks neat and tidy apart from a key lying on the table, with a metal thing as the fob. Can't make out what it is though. A pair of sunglasses too.'

I see them: ruby red with a cream detail. 'They're Lisa's. She was wearing them when I met her.' I glance sideways. 'Is the door locked?'

'Yes,' says Andrew.

I take a few backward steps 'til my heels hit the grass and look up – more for inspiration than anything else. I take out my phone, find Lisa's number, dial. 'Damn! Voicemail.' I think for a few seconds. 'This could all be perfectly innocent, but I want to make sure Lisa's safe. I didn't notice if her vehicle was parked outside anywhere; if it is, we'll break in to the house. And we don't need a warrant for that – person's life possibly in danger, and all that.'

It only takes us a few seconds to confirm the pickup isn't anywhere on the street so we can't start throwing bricks at windows. Not yet anyway. 'Steph,' I say. 'Call the Control. Lisa's phone went to voicemail, so it's definitely switched on. I need to know where it is. Then you and Tobias go back to the Fish Tank and start searching for her vehicle. It's always possible she walked here but Andrew and I will go to her house and see if it's parked anywhere nearby. If we find it, I'll let you know.'

'Are you concerned about Lisa's welfare, Boss?' says Tobias.

'Damn right. And just how concerned I am will depend entirely on what we find out in the next hour or so.'

# CHAPTER SIXTY-SEVEN

Every muscle and tendon in Lisa's body was primed to explode but she concentrated on remaining composed and tried to stay focused on Edwin while she processed what he had said. 'So, darling Lisa, we're all alone. Just you and me'. The year Lisa became deputy leader of the council, she had championed a personal safety initiative aimed primarily at female employees who might find themselves under threat. One of the key principles put forward by the speaker was any woman in that position should make every attempt to manage the situation, not the aggressor.

Edwin appeared relaxed, waiting for her to react, so she willed herself to dial down from panic mode into a state that was more considered and logical. Gradually, her stance softened. She was still ready to run but now she was able to think. *I've been friends with this man for twenty years, why would he want to hurt me?* Then she remembered about Rachel. *But then, 'darling Lisa'? Where had that come from?* At that point she realised it was the situation that was scaring her, not the man standing in front of her. *Manage the situation, Lisa.*

Edwin held his hand out. 'Can I see your phone, please?'

'Why?'

'Because you took photos of that manual you found in my office, and I would prefer you didn't share them with anyone.'

*Manage the situation.* Lisa didn't speak, she handed him her phone.

'The code, please.' She told him.

While Edwin swiped and tapped, Lisa glanced back at the flight of stairs. *Five metres. If I run, now, while his attention is distracted, can I make it up to the ground floor before him? No. This isn't TV. He's fit, I'm not. I can't outrun him. Manage the situation.*

'Thanks,' said Edwin. 'I think I'll hang on to this for a while.' He dropped the phone into a pocket in his fleece and pulled up the zip. 'Oh, and by the way, I noticed your photos are backed up to the cloud, so I got rid of them too.' Then he took a step towards her.

Lisa put both hands up and moved back.

Edwin stayed where he was. 'I'm not going to hurt you.'

'Then why did you bring me here?'

'I don't know. I needed to be somewhere we could talk, without being interrupted. The house wasn't suitable, you'd have wanted to leave.'

'I *want* to leave here Edwin. I'm scared. I can't handle enclosed spaces. Can't we go outside? We can talk out there.' Her confidence was growing but she couldn't let him see that. *Manage the situation. Be patient. Wait for your chance.* She dragged a tissue from her pocket, dabbed at her eyes. Sniffed a couple of times for good measure.

'We'll talk first, then we can leave,' he said. But he didn't meet her eyes.

Lisa also looked away. *I don't fucking believe you.* She hesitated. Deliberately. 'Okay, what do you want to talk about?'

335

'Do you think I killed Rachel?'

*Shit! Wasn't expecting that.* This time the hesitation was real. 'I know Jack is innocent.'

Edwin shook his head. 'No, darling. He isn't. The evidence proves it.'

*Darling? Shit! Manage the fucking situation!* Lisa let herself crumble. 'Oh, Edwin. What am I going to do?' Then she spread her feet slightly apart and threw her arms out.

His expression lightened as he stepped towards her. Lisa knew what she was about to do, and she was ready. She slipped her arms around his waist. Naturally, his response was to wrap his arms around her shoulders. She pulled him in tight, and deliberately squashed her breasts against his ribcage. Her final move was to change her stance so she could rub herself onto his thigh. He responded automatically, moving his left leg to accommodate her.

Edwin Fuller may have murdered his wife, but he'd never been a fighter. So, when Lisa took half a step back, paused for an instant to steady herself, then smashed her knee up into his balls, he collapsed as if his spinal cord had been severed. Before he hit the floor, she was sprinting along the corridor towards the stairs. She turned the corner and leapt up the steps. It was a short flight that led to another door. Her only thought was, is it locked?

She skidded into it, grabbed the door handle, hauled it down and crashed her shoulder against the door.

It didn't open.

———

LISA THUMPED her shoulder into the wood again, and when she bounced off it, still gripping the handle, it opened towards her. *Idiot!* She shot through the gap, grabbed at the edge of the door and slammed it behind her.

She found herself in the main ground floor corridor. Lisa's school had been a new build, so she was momentarily taken aback by the scale of the space around her. The corridor was long, wide enough for half a dozen kids to pass shoulder to shoulder and flooded with sunlight that blasted through pairs of massive internal windows to her left. The glass panels stretched from shoulder height to the ceiling, easily three metres above her head. A wide staircase, whose treads had witnessed a million passing feet, disappeared up to her right. Its mirror opposite loomed at the far end of the corridor. The sense of space was cavernous, and as high as the likelihood of Edwin catching her with ease if he came through the door any time soon.

She checked the door. Although it had a lock, there was no key. But, standing in a metal frame that was side by side with a drinks vending machine, was a red fire extinguisher with a cream panel marked *FOAM*. Lisa knew how to operate these things; she'd been an office fire warden in the Council for several years. She dragged it from the frame, popped the locking pin out, and manoeuvred it so the hose faced the door. But it was too low for her purposes, so she hauled a chair away from the wall and lifted the extinguisher onto the seat. She adjusted her grip and stood there, waiting. And shaking.

Seconds later, the door crashed open to reveal Edwin framed in the gap. His eyes lit up – until he realised her intention. Lisa aimed the hose directly at his face and squeezed the lever. It made one hell of a racket. She struggled to control it but kept on firing. The foam blanketed his face and chest and trying to evade it, he slipped and fell heavily. He landed face forward, smacking his head on the tiled floor. Lisa didn't stop, she emptied the fire extinguisher all over his skull, his back and his legs. Then she dropped the hose, turned tail, and ran.

She knew the main entrance was on the left, halfway along the corridor. Her trainers slapped on the ceramic tiles as she raced towards it. She slithered to a halt at a pair of double internal doors, several feet taller than her. Both doors had quick-release emergency exit push bars. She slapped the nearest one with the heel of her right hand and threw herself against the door. Nothing happened. She hit it again with both hands this time; still it didn't budge. Lisa screamed at it and was moving over to try the other door when she spotted the sign made from a sheet of laminated A4 taped to the glass.

Due to building works, Main exit currently out of commission – use West exit door instead.

'Fuuuuuck!' She read the sign again; the words seemed to swim around on the page. 'Where's the fuck's the west exit?' But whoever had made the sign had slipped up – they hadn't included a directional arrow. Lisa had no idea which end of the school was west. But she couldn't turn back towards Edwin, even if that was the right way. She had no choice but to head for the other staircase.

Off to her left, she heard Edwin groan. He was trying to stand up. He had one knee on the floor but when he tried to push off with his other foot, it slid away from him. He crashed face first back into the foam and Lisa heard the crack of bone on tile as she took off in the opposite direction.

She charged on and passed another pair of high internal windows. Now she noticed the lower halves were made up of frosted decorative glass. A classroom. She reached the door and shoved it wide open. The windows facing her were just as high as the ones that led onto the corridor. She sprinted through the chairs and tables, belting her knee off the corner of one and scattering a few more as she dodged her way through. She scanned all around the window frames for a release catch. But there were none, the windows were fixed. She took a step back, looked up. The top pane could only be pulled down with a hook on the end of a long pole, but even if she could have opened it, she knew she'd never be able to climb out. *Find something to smash the glass.*

She whirled round, but the miniature tables and chairs made it obvious she was in an infants' classroom. There were twenty or more chairs. All about eighteen inches high. And all plastic.

She weaved her way to the door, paused, squinted past the edge for Edwin. She gasped and leapt back. He was upright. She edged forwards again. He was rubbing at his eyes with his sleeve. Shaking his head. *The foam. He can't see.*

She ran on a few paces to a single door with a frosted glass panel. An office. Locked. She passed two more classrooms before reaching the staircase, meaning now she was able to read a wooden sign suspended from the ceiling by two black twisted wires. *East Stairs.* Her legs wobbled as she realised the temporary exit was the one they'd come in earlier. Lisa was at the wrong end of the corridor. And Edwin was in between her and escape.

Her gut instinct was screaming at her to keep running but she didn't; she forced herself to stop and concentrate. *Up these stairs. Along the corridor. Down. And out.* Logical, and she would be moving, her fate in her own hands. She looked up. The height of the ceiling meant each flight was long – fourteen, sixteen steps to a half landing then it turned back on itself. 'No choice, Lisa. Shift yourself.' She grabbed the heavy wooden banister and began to climb. When she reached the half landing, she spun herself round the balustrade and glanced back.

Edwin was still struggling to clear the foam from his eyes. At that, he raised his arms like a demented preacher and roared into the airspace. 'You can't go anywhere, you bitch! The whole place is locked up. And I will fucking find you.'

Lisa sprinted up to the next level. At the top step she stopped, searched for a hiding place: a solid door she could lock behind her. She had no idea if there was another way out. Then, from below, came a horrendous screech of metal crashing off tiles, and glass breaking.

That gave her a shock, and again she fought to suppress the rising panic. *Manage the situation.* She started running again, heading for the first door she could see. Then she slowed. Stopped. And realised precisely how she could escape from the building, and from Edwin.

———

EDWIN POURED one last bottle of water down his face, shook his head and blinked his eyes. Bleary, but he could see.

He checked the door they'd come in. It was still closed. He knew Lisa hadn't stepped over him while he was thrashing about in the foam, he'd heard her running away from him. No question, he had to trap her inside the school, so he moved to lock the door to the corridor. He'd used a master key to get into the school but when he rummaged around in his pockets, he came up empty. He scanned the floor, but it was covered in foam, water, glass, and the contents of the vending machine he'd toppled over. So, he pulled the door shut and manhandled the smashed cabinet across the floor to block the exit. She'd probably be able to move it – but he'd hear her. Now he had time to work out what to do.

A few years previously, Edwin had been involved in a root and branch security review following several damaging and costly break-ins. He knew the important doors on this floor would be locked; the offices, and the double doors by the side of the east staircase that led down to the cafeteria, kitchens, toilets and the exits to the playground.

He was standing by the west staircase. There were two floors above him, running east to west with classrooms on both sides. He could easily see the east staircase was clear, so he darted a few steps up the west stairs, leaned over the banister and looked up. There was no sign of Lisa. He tore back down and slowed when he reached the corridor. *She can't escape*, he thought. *This'll be like catching a spider in a bath.*

There were six classrooms on the ground floor. The frosted glass panels prevented him from seeing inside but that didn't bother him. One look through the door would tell him if she was there. These classrooms were for the youngest pupils so everything inside was sized accordingly. Throughout the school, classroom storage space was built-in so there was nothing for her to hide behind. And if the packed cabinet in his room was any guide, there would be no space inside either.

The door to the first classroom was open, and a few chairs skittled off to the sides made it clear she'd run in here first. All the windows in this building were vast. The top panes opened on the tilt, using the window poles, but the lower panes were fixed. He stepped out into the corridor, saw the vending machine was still blocking the exit then checked all the other classrooms were empty. They were.

He ran back to the west stairs and up to the half landing, checked the east one more time, then charged up to the first floor. The corridor was clear, but he sprinted back down to the half landing to make sure she wasn't playing hide and seek on the east stairs. He bounced up the remaining steps to the first floor.

He paused for a breath. The layout of each floor and the shuttle search pattern he was following meant he was utterly confident he'd find her. Even if she did slip past him, he was much faster. Plus, she'd have to drag the vending machine out of the way.

He'd finished checking most of the classrooms on that floor and was heading back to the west stair when he heard a noise. He stopped, listened. Then he heard a different sound. Glass tinkling.

He ran for the stairs. He knew exactly where she was, and what she was doing. And he laughed like a maniac because he was certain he'd catch her now.

*Because Lisa, you stupid bitch. You've trapped yourself.*

# CHAPTER SIXTY-EIGHT

'THERE IT IS,' says Andrew.

He's referring to Lisa's pickup, it's parked outside the school. Transpires that between tracking Lisa's phone, and the fact she used main streets all the way from Fuller's house, finding it was a breeze.

I park behind it, and Andrew hops out. Steph drives past with Tobias, stops in front and now all four of us are at the pickup. I glance up and down the street. Usually it's packed with cars during the day but today it's quiet. It's not a local holiday so the school must be closed for some other reason. Tobias crosses the pavement to an open gate in the fence, while Andrew tries the driver's door. It opens. He sticks his head inside, shrugs at me, then moves to the rear door and opens that too. The seats are stacked with boxes. I'm on the point of asking myself if this is innocent after all when, from high above us, we hear glass breaking.

We all take a step back and scan the upper floors. There's another loud noise, like a heavy metal bin being bounced off a stone floor. And then a scream – definitely a woman.

'Boss!' Tobias is standing next to a single door set at the corner of the building. He's holding it open. He disappears inside, and we charge after him. We go through a second door into a partially lit corridor. Tobias has disappeared but then he shouts, 'I'm up here!' We run up a short flight of steps to find yet another open door. Tobias is leaning over a vending machine that looks as though it's been toppled end over end. He drags it out of the way, and we squeeze past.

The hallway in front of us is a disaster area, and a fire extinguisher lying on its side with the hose uncoupled tells us what's happened. 'There!' says Steph, pointing. A trail of wet greasy footsteps leads away from us along the corridor. The sunlight on the floor tiles shows them changing direction, stopping at several doors, and coming back this way. Now we can see they head up a staircase to our right, becoming fainter as they dry out.

'Those are a man's shoes,' I say. 'Up here.' Then I watch as Andrew and Steph sprint up the stairs with Tobias labouring in third. Shame there isn't a lift.

———

FROM THE STREET, the rows of windows suggest the building has four floors, including the basement. But as I drag my feet up what I believe to be the last flight, I realise there's an additional floor. Eventually, as my legs are about to go, and my lungs prepare to wheeze their last, there are no more stairs. I totter across a hardwood floor and through a set of double doors, following the sound of Andrew's voice. He's speaking in low, even tones – but he doesn't appear to be in the room.

I take my cue from him and walk casually into a huge studio, flooded with natural light from a couple of skylights, and picture windows on three sides. As I pick my way past a few easels and low tables and chairs, I realise one of the window frames has no glass. Steph and Tobias are standing in front of this aperture, staring out. Tobias has his left hand out and down, fiddling with a lock. There's a door on that side.

Andrew is outside, on what appears to be a terrace, facing away. He has his arms out in front of him, palms down, gently patting the air. About three or four metres away, Edwin is restraining Lisa, both arms tight around her upper body. She's thrashing from side to side, kicking her heels at his shins. But she's wearing training shoes, and he has her pinned. Gradually, her energy subsides. She slumps, her head falls forward and down, like a rag doll. Edwin glares at Andrew, glances down at the top of her head. Even from here I can see they're both soaked through with what appears to be greasy water. He doesn't relax his grip.

Steph moves aside and allows me through. Now I can see more of the roof. Close behind Edwin and Lisa is a stone parapet – four feet high, no more. Over to my left, there are maintenance gangways with handrails, running horizontally across the slates; an aluminium staircase gives access to the clock tower. I take a deep breath through my nose, experience a rush from the oxygen boost. There's no point in hurrying now. I must keep this slow and steady.

I try to keep my voice gentle but firm. 'Edwin. You remember me, Mel Cooper. I'm so relieved to find you both unharmed. Now, if it's okay with you, I'll climb out there and join you. It's not easy to hold a conversation through a window.' He doesn't object, so I sling my leg over the sill. I crunch through shards of broken glass, and neatly body swerve a fire extinguisher lying on its side. 'Heavens, that was a struggle—'

But before I can launch into my admittedly limited hostage negotiation spiel, Lisa tenses her legs, drops her head another couple of inches and whips it back into Edwin's mouth and nose. The crunch, and the blood spatter, momentarily turn my stomach.

Edwin's arms slacken automatically, and Lisa tries to wriggle free. She almost succeeds, but as her feet scrabble for purchase on the wet flagstone floor, he slides a hand down her arm and locks tight on her wrist. At the same moment, Lisa's trainers find some grip on the stones, and she bursts forwards a few steps. She reaches the point where both their arms are fully extended but she fails to break free, and her momentum whiplashes her round in a tight semi-circle. Her body is now moving faster than her legs and she begins to lose her balance. Edwin sees what's happening, swings his other arm round to grab her, but as he alters his stance in an attempt to cushion her weight and speed, his foot slips and he loses his grip. Lisa flies off at a tangent, out of control, and hits the parapet like a gymnast on the asymmetric bars.

She doesn't scream. She makes no attempt to arrest her fall. She topples over the coping and vanishes from sight.

Edwin gasps, freezes solid. Andrew tackles him low and hard. They both go down.

I charge towards the parapet, and I don't pause when I reach it. I grab the top with both hands, lean right over and stare down.

'Oh, sweet Jesus!'

# CHAPTER SIXTY-NINE

I'M with Jeff in my office. We're sitting side by side, thighs practically touching, concentrating on my monitor. He says, 'Let me see that last part again, please.' I check my index, key in the time, and press *Play*.

Edwin Fuller appears on the screen. He's at the interview room table, facing the camera. The film quality isn't brilliant, but it doesn't have to be. The strapping across his nose, pushed tight by the swelling, two black eyes and a badly split upper lip are all clearly visible. He exhales. 'Like I told you, God knows how many times now, I thought she was about to jump off that roof, and I was trying to stop her.'

My voice comes from off screen. 'Tell me how you both came to be in the building.'

'It was all completely innocent, I asked her to give me a lift to the school with some boxes of teaching materials—'

'Why did you need a lift? Why didn't you just drive your own car?'

He stares at me. Does he know I know? He tries anyway. 'My car's out of commission just now.'

'By out of commission, do you actually mean it's been written off and subsequently scrapped after you smashed it into a farm wall out in East Lothian?'

'I ... em ... yes, that's right.' His ears turn a scorching shade of crimson.

'But nine days after your *accident* you told me, at your house, that a friend had borrowed your car. Why did you lie about it?'

'I was embarrassed.'

I don't believe that for a second and my face probably shows it. But I don't care. 'Did you own a mountain bike up until recently? A Cannondale, purchased from The Leith Bike Shed for £550?'

He sits back, levels his gaze at me. 'If you have all that information then clearly you know I did.'

'But you don't own it now?'

'No. It was stolen from the row of shops at Granton about a week before my wife was murdered.'

'Did you report it?'

'No point. I couldn't claim against my insurance because I know I forgot to lock it.'

'A scrapped car and a stolen bike? Lucky I'm not a cynic, eh, Mr Fuller?' I've no need to push this further; I've made my point. 'Tell us what happened after you and Mrs McCafferty entered the school.'

He hesitates for a second, picks up the threads. 'As soon as we got inside, she came on to me. I didn't want that, not with Lisa, so I said no. I tried to push her away as gently as I could, but I was maybe a bit heavy-handed and, I didn't mean to, but I hurt her. She went crazy. Kicked me in the nuts, attacked me with that fire extinguisher and ran away, crying. I searched all over for her, heard the window smashing up in the art department, found her out on the roof, and I was doing my best to calm her down when you arrived. And you saw what happened, I was holding her, just trying to keep her safe 'til your colleague, DS Young, could restrain her. Then she attacked me again.'

'Pause it there, Mel,' says Jeff. He points at the screen. 'Fuller said all he was doing was holding Lisa, trying to keep her safe 'til Andrew could restrain her. Then she attacked him again. Is that what you saw?'

I take a few seconds to answer. 'I've discussed this at length with the others. What we all saw was open to interpretation. Either he was holding her because he was concerned she was going to harm herself. Or, she was struggling to escape from him because she felt she was in danger.'

'Did it appear to you that he was trying to harm her?'

'I couldn't say that for sure, Jeff. No.'

My boss sits back, claps his hands behind his head. 'And the only person who could say for sure is poor Lisa.'

The rest remains unsaid.

# CHAPTER SEVENTY

Saturday

'WHY? WHAT DOES HE WANT?' It's just after six on Saturday morning, and I'm driving along gloriously deserted streets on my way to the custody suite at St Leonard's police station on Edinburgh's Southside. It's ridiculously early, but I need the maximum amount of time with Fuller before I have to release him at 10:04, twenty-four hours after he was arrested. We questioned him under caution 'til late last night, then I was legally obliged to allow him time for some sleep. Human rights – bah!

But now I have the Custody Sergeant, Bryan Fraser, on hands-free. Apparently, Fuller's been creating a ruckus for about the last hour, demanding to see me. 'He won't tell me what he wants,' says Bryan. 'He'll only talk to you.'

Well, this is curious. Maybe he's going to confess, but something tells me that's not likely. I glance at the clock on the dash. 'I'm not far away now, Bryan, and Andrew's on his way in too. We'll see you soon.'

We're running out of time to continue questioning Fuller, just less than four hours, and being my own harshest critic we're running out of ideas too. Lisa and Edwin were the only witnesses to the wrestling match on the roof and, perhaps more importantly, what had preceded it. We all saw what happened before Lisa tumbled over the parapet, but the cause of her fall, and whether Fuller could have prevented it are, like I said to Jeff, almost entirely down to interpretation. Plus, we only have Fuller's side of the story.

As I approach the station, I wonder again what he wants.

———

LAST NIGHT, when we left him, Fuller was marginally less cocky than he had been, but I put that down to him being uptight about spending a night in the cells. I still detected an arrogance about him, possibly because he knew time was on his side. All through yesterday, he continued to toe his own party line: 'She came with me to the school voluntarily. She freaked out when I spurned her. She attacked me. I followed her to the roof. I was trying to calm her down, keep her safe. And you saw what happened.'

But this morning, chalk and cheese isn't even close; the man's practically bouncing. He won't stay seated, I fear for the bones in his right hand because he's smashed it down on the tabletop at least half a dozen times, and I don't need a doctor to tell me his blood pressure is up there with the eagles.

'10:04?' he yells. I've stopped counting how many times he's quoted the time back at me. 'Are you seriously going to keep me in here for the full twenty-four hours? I've nothing more to say. You're asking the same stupid questions over and over 'til I'm sick of hearing them. What's the bloody point?'

'So I should simply release you, Edwin?'

351

'Yes!'

I'm surprised his eyeballs don't ping out and bounce around on the floor. 'Why?'

'Jesus! Because I haven't done nothing.'

A double negative? That knocks me back in my chair. Edwin Fuller has lost the plot.

I turn to my sidekick. 'DS Young. A word outside, please.'

# CHAPTER SEVENTY-ONE

Two hours later – 08:30

I'M WATCHING – and waiting. The thing is, I've no idea what I'm waiting for. And, as for watching, so far there's nothing to see. It's two hours since Andrew and I left Fuller in the cell at the custody suite. Two hours: I needed that amount of time to set things up. To get all my ducks in a row, as the terminally verbose are wont to say.

I'm in a nondescript pool car with Steph, three houses along and on the other side of the street from Fuller's place. There are two PCs in another pool car watching his front door and his garage from a street opposite. I have two patrol cars stationed at each end of Craighall Road, the main road that serves this area. And Tobias, Andrew, Dave, and a couple of his heftier colleagues are hunkered down behind hedges and gates in the lane behind his house.

And all based on a hunch that I explained to Jeff by phone from St Leonard's. Andrew backed me, so my boss agreed I should follow my instincts and see what transpired.

Forty minutes ago, once everyone was in position, I called the custody sergeant and he released Fuller.

Fifteen minutes ago, a lackey from his solicitor's office collected their client from outside St Leonard's and set off to drive him home. We knew this because we were tracking them.

Two minutes ago, one of the patrol cars announced they'd turned into Craighall Road.

And less than sixty seconds later, Fuller jumped out of the car and sprinted to his front door, where he jammed his keys in the lock and disappeared inside. I alerted all units to sit tight. Now I'll find out if my hunch was correct.

I've hardly stopped speaking when Andrew announces that Fuller has appeared in his back garden.

Twenty seconds after that, Andrew tells us where Fuller is now, and what he's doing.

And no more than a minute after that, Tobias announces we have him, and I hear Andrew in the background summoning an ambulance. As an emergency.

Then Fuller's neighbour's front door opens, and Tobias appears, waving. The sort of wave that says, *Get in here, Boss. Right away.*

———

As JEFF DRIVES into the street, he pulls over to allow the ambulance to pass. Then he parks in the space it's just vacated and walks over to where I'm standing, next to the skip in Olive's garden. Seconds later, we hear the siren, but we don't speak until it cuts out again.

'The neighbour's daughter?' he says.

'Yes. Diane Palmerston. As soon as Fuller arrived home, he went straight into Mrs Palmerston's house by the back door. We found him with the daughter; it looks like he'd locked her in the cupboard under the stairs at some point. He's not talking, and obviously neither is she at the moment, but my guess is she'd been in there without food or water for maybe forty-eight hours.' I touch the skip. 'This was delivered Thursday lunchtime, and she signed for it. She'd just phoned the company, bawled them out because it was late.'

'How is she?'

'The medics said severe hyperglycaemia, but they've stabilised her. They're confident she'll regain consciousness, but she might already have suffered damage to organs and suchlike. Steph's gone with her to the hospital. I'll let you know once I hear from her.'

'Did Fuller know she was diabetic?'

'Says he didn't. I don't know if I believe him, though.'

'And where is he now?'

'On his way back to the custody suite with Andrew and Tobias. I've arrested him on suspicion of culpable and reckless conduct towards Diane Palmerston. Only time will tell if that will be upgraded to culpable homicide. I'm going over there soon; Dave will tidy up and make the place secure.'

'I've got to say congratulations, Mel. Your hunch played out.'

Yes. My hunch. In the corridor outside the interview room, Andrew had asked me what I was thinking. I explained I couldn't understand why Edwin Fuller was so desperate to be released that he was practically demanding I did so. It was in his best interests to stay where he was, let the clock run down, and then I'd have to release him. And furthermore, I couldn't bring him back in on the same charge for more questioning without new evidence coming to light. So, there had to be a compelling reason why he couldn't wait even four hours.

I could only imagine that reason was either related to evidence he was keen to supress, or to a person involved in the case. But all the major players – Rachel, Jack and Lisa – were, one way or another, out of the game. If there was someone else, it had to be someone we didn't know about. And there was no question, he was definitely losing it in there. My rationale was if we let him go, he wouldn't all of a sudden regain all equilibrium. He'd charge off at a hundred miles an hour and lead us to whatever was driving him so nuts. Besides, I had absolutely nothing to lose, and everything to gain. I had been about to release him anyway, so I'd still have the remaining three or four hours up my sleeve.

Lucky for me, my winning numbers came up and it made dragging myself upright at half five in the morning all the more worthwhile.

———

WE'RE BACK at the custody suite, same interview room, Edwin Fuller sitting across the table from Andrew and me. Only this time he has his solicitor for company. I've met her before. Keira Quinn, a petite Irish woman whose languid demeanour and benign style disguise the legal equivalent of a Venus Flytrap. I'll need to be on my game today.

'Mr Fuller,' I say. 'Why were you so desperate to be released from the custody suite this morning?'

'No comment.'

'When you got home this morning, why did you immediately climb over your garden fence and enter your neighbour's house via her back door?'

'No comment.'

It takes a monumental effort, but I don't sigh. Whoever came up with the bright idea that a suspect doesn't have to answer questions from the police in an interview situation needs their brain examined for signs of intelligent life.

I then ask a range of questions including how long he'd known Diane Palmerston, about the last time he'd been inside her mother's house, did he imprison her in the cupboard under the stairs, and why did he go straight to that cupboard the minute he'd entered the house. As I expect, he replies 'no comment' to them all, but these are all preamble – the warm-up act. I have to cover all the bases; lay things out properly.

Then I kick things up a gear. 'We found Diane's phone in a drawer in your kitchen; did you put it there? Your fingerprints were on the phone; did you handle it? When you were observed entering Mrs Palmerston's house by her back door, you didn't close it behind you, yet your fingerprints were on the handle on the inside; how could that be? Your fingerprints were found in various places, specifically the stair cupboard door and the woodwork surrounding it; how could that be?'

Fuller gives the same reply to all of them: no comment. At this point, he's leaning back in his chair, arms folded casually, his gaze on me. Keira Quinn is quiet too, but there's a set to her expression. To be fair, she's a lot more streetwise than her client, and she can probably sense trouble a mile off.

So now I move on to the crux of the matter. 'Mr Fuller, did you know Diane Palmerston suffers from Type 1 Diabetes?'

Quinn starts at that. She tenses, her lips part by a few millimetres, then she figures out several ways he could have known, and all quite innocently. She relaxes again.

'No comment,' says Fuller. His arms are still folded, but perhaps a touch tighter.

I check my notes, but that's overkill; I know what I'm talking about. 'Type 1 diabetes, in case you don't know, requires daily insulin injections to keep the condition under control. Daily, Edwin.' I pause to let that register. 'Now, she could probably have missed one day's medication without suffering too badly, but longer than two and she'd have been in a bad way. Unfortunately, no one knew where she was. And worse, no one else had keys to her mother's house.'

Now Quinn speaks. 'Your point, Detective Inspector Cooper?'

'My point, Mister Fuller, is during last night, while you were in custody, did you realise Ms Palmerston would very probably still be trapped in that cupboard?'

'No comment.'

'And is that why you were demanding to be released from custody, so you could return home as quickly as possible to find out if she was still alive?'

He unfolds his arms, sits up dead straight, jams the heels of his hands on the seat. 'No comment.'

'I will ask you one more time. Did you lock Diane Palmerston in the cupboard beneath your neighbour's staircase, sometime after noon on Thursday – two days ago?'

'No comment.'

I stop there. I'm done asking questions. 'Last I heard, Ms Palmerston had been admitted to hospital having suffered a hyperglycaemic emergency known as diabetic ketoacidosis.' He's staring across the table, willing me to let him off the hook. But there's zero chance of that. I stare right back. 'At this stage I don't know if she'll recover. Therefore, Edwin Fuller, you remain under arrest, under suspicion of culpable or reckless conduct.'

I pause. 'At least.'

# CHAPTER SEVENTY-TWO

Monday

As I WALK towards Jeff's office, I have the distinct feeling this will turn out to be a bittersweet morning. An innocent woman has suffered a terrifying ordeal. Imprisoned inside a tiny, dark cupboard, with no food or water, minimal chance of rescue, and fully aware that without her medication, her time was limited. Doesn't bear thinking about.

I'm sure we can make the culpable and reckless conduct charge stick but I'm less confident Fuller will serve a lengthy term inside. It's almost certain he locked Diane Palmerston in that cupboard, but the woman was a virtual stranger to him, so it's unlikely he knew she was diabetic. Therefore, he didn't anticipate the potential consequence of his actions. She could have died, but he didn't deliberately set out to kill her. There is no manslaughter in Scottish criminal law, but its equivalent is culpable homicide: 'The killing of a person in circumstances which are neither accidental nor justified, but where the wicked intent to kill, or wicked recklessness required for murder, is absent'. I guess the footnote is I would rather not speculate what the poor woman's fate might have been had Edwin waited out his twelve hours until he was released. Would he have gone to the house and killed her anyway, to guarantee her silence? We will never know.

Jeff sees me coming and waves me in. He's set up a video conference call with Leo Contini, and I can see the Fiscal on the TV screen on my boss's wall. He's behind his desk shuffling through paperwork. We're here to discuss Rachel Fuller's murder. Specifically, was she murdered by her supposed lover, Jack McCafferty, or by her husband? Long before Leo gives his verdict, it's obvious the pendulum has swung back to bitter. Sweet is out to lunch.

Leo spreads his hands. 'Sorry, Jeff, Mel. But materially, nothing has changed. Yes, you've amassed a wealth of circumstantial evidence but a significant portion of it is borderline conjecture. We have no hard evidence to shore up our case, and Edwin Fuller's defence team wouldn't need to be John Grisham to discredit a lot of what we do have. We can't conclusively place Fuller at any of the scenes, and we have nothing to prove Jack McCafferty's innocence. And those two things, folks, are showstoppers.'

Nobody says anything. We let that hang.

'Mel,' he says. 'Anything new?'

'We're still chasing up a couple of leads.' I feel pathetic even saying that.

'On a scale of one to ten, how confident are you they'll come through?'

I don't answer. He's a good man, Leo. One of the best. What he says next is not a surprise. 'I'm calling this now. Charging Edwin Fuller for murder just will not fly.' He doesn't have to say the case against Jack has already sprouted wings. 'But, as I've already confirmed, I am willing to proceed with the charge of culpable and reckless conduct in relation to Diane Palmerston.'

This is followed by a few minutes of procedural chit-chat but I've long since zoned out. Only good manners and my respect for Leo and Jeff are keeping me here. Once Leo has dropped out of the call, Jeff closes out the discussion calmly and professionally. He's not the type of guy to say something banal like, 'Can't win 'em all, Mel'.

I go back to my team and tell them precisely what they expected to hear. 'Unless new evidence comes to light or we are instructed to take another look, I'm sorry to say the investigation into Edwin Fuller is closed. The Fiscal will be proceeding with the murder charge against Jack McCafferty.'

Nobody complains. Nobody says, *but that's not fair*. Nobody stamps their little feet. Nobody writes to their MSP.

No. We close the file, and we move on. We have other high priority cases to deal with.

# EPILOGUE

Three weeks later

A PERCENTAGE of the population would probably disagree but we, the police, are only human. We're fallible, the same as other people. We have our frailties, and yes, we make mistakes. Some of these are significant and innocent people suffer, or criminals don't get their comeuppance. Some mistakes are comparatively minor and can be easily recovered. And with others, fortune smiles on us and we dodge a bullet. No damage done.

Occasionally, luck is on our side. It shouldn't be a major weapon in the detective's armoury, but we are grateful for any rub of the green that comes our way. I can only speak for myself and my close colleagues, but we work hard, do our best, put ourselves through the ringer. Time after time after time. On balance, we deserve some luck once in a blue moon.

In the later stages of our investigation into Rachel Fuller's murder, we dropped the ball. Notice I don't say 'clanger'; I would class our mistake as understandable.

In the period right after Diane was rescued and Fuller was

arrested, we searched the house. Not inch by inch. Not like we suspected several bodies might be acting as foundations for a newly constructed patio. Because after all, we caught Fuller before he did whatever he was going to do to the woman, and she recovered well enough to leave hospital a few days later. She also described how Fuller had barged into the house that day, threatened her, and when she told him to go to hell, he manhandled her into the cupboard. Our search was thorough enough to find Fuller's prints in various incriminating places despite, clearly, his best efforts to wipe them clean. One shouldn't believe everything one sees on a TV crime drama. We checked the skip, the garden, the shed, and the recycling and landfill bins. And every room in the house, including the loft. We even found Diane's phone in a drawer in Fuller's house. And once we thought there was nowhere else to search, and the crime scene team had packed up and gone home, we released the house back to Diane Palmerston.

I questioned Diane while she was still recovering in hospital. She came across as an angry embittered woman, who said she wanted 'that bastard to swing for what he did to me'. When she told me her mother had died during her period of enforced incarceration, I felt incredibly sorry for her. But less so when I heard she'd sold the house with what might be termed indecent haste.

A few weeks later, the new owners moved in and decided their number one priority was to replace Olive Palmerston's archaic kitchen. A local company came round to quote and went in search of the mains stopcock, and to check if there was lead piping to be replaced. The rep explained his company had installed kitchens and bathrooms in many other houses in the area and the stopcock would be under the hatch in the vestibule.

That would be the hatch we missed during our search.

When the rep opened it, he lay on the floor, popped his head into the shallow void created by the foundations, and turned on his flashlight. He was quite surprised when, as well as the stopcock, he discovered a bicycle jammed in underneath the flooring joists. And not some ancient boneshaker that had been dumped there halfway through last century; no, it was a relatively new ebike.

The householder, an honest chap, called Diane to ask if it was hers. She said it wasn't, but then she called me. She remembered that right after Fuller locked her in, she heard him crashing about somewhere near the front of the house.

I don't immediately confront Fuller with that little nugget. I'm not quite ready yet.

———

A DAY OR SO LATER, I'm in my office with Steph. Fingers crossed; she's come up with the answer to a problem that's defeated us for weeks. I'm distracted by the sight of Bob heading across the room, wafting a sheet of A4. As she passes the back of Andrew's desk, she trails the paper over the top of his head, leans in, and murmurs in his ear. My sidekick might be Joe Cool most of the time, but whenever my red-headed friend appears on the scene he transforms into a gibbering wreck. And well she knows it, so she rarely misses an opportunity.

She leans a shoulder on my door jamb. Smiles. 'Do you have a minute, my dear?'

'Only if you promise to stop razzing up the male members of my team.'

She flutters her eyelashes. 'I was simply saying to the delectable Andrew that if he doesn't have a hot date this week-end, my diary happens to be clear.' Then she saunters in, slides into a chair, places the paper on my desk and spins it round. 'After weeks of hard graft by yours truly – on your behalf I might add – this just landed in my inbox.' She prods it towards me with one red nail and folds her arms. The word that best suits her expression is triumphant.

I read the document. Then read it a second time. I glance at Steph and Bob in turn. 'Two pieces of good news in one morning. Is it my birthday?'

———

IT's LATER the same day and, yet again, I'm in an interview room sitting opposite Edwin Fuller and his solicitor, Keira Quinn. Jeff's with me, the others are watching through a live feed.

While I'm working my way through the introductory formalities, Fuller is scratching at his ankle and tutting. I don't know if he's trying to make a point: 'Woe is me. I have to wear this dreadfully uncomfortable electronic tag on my leg'. If he is, he should look somewhere else for sympathy. I'm fresh out.

'I've brought you here to talk about how you murdered your wife—' I glare at him. 'Please don't roll your eyes at me, Mister Fuller. At least, not until you've heard what I have to say.'

Quinn taps him on the arm; legal sign language for, *Not a smart idea to piss this woman off. Not today.*

I start with the key question, might save us all a lot of time and trouble. 'Edwin Fuller, did you murder your wife, Rachel Fuller, in your home, during the late evening of Thursday 25th January then dispose of her body in undergrowth behind lock-up garages off Powderhall Lane?'

'No comment.'

I sigh. 'I will admit that, to date, much of the evidence we

365

have against you is circumstantial. I've even been accused of dealing in pure conjecture. But that's about to change. For you to have achieved what you set out to do, i.e., murder your wife and lay the blame on Jack McCafferty – meaning you got away with it – you needed a number of electronic devices that "a", had to be purchased online, and "b", had to be supplied illegally. In the UK at any rate. And for those, you needed a credit card.'

On the top of my sheaf of papers, I have the sheet Bob gave me. Tobias has made copies of all the documents, and I pass this one to Quinn. 'Have you ever bought a stolen credit card, pre-loaded with a cash balance?'

Now, I'm pretty sure if someone asked me that, I'd say, *What?*, and look at them as if they were stupid. Instead, Fuller replies, 'No comment.' I find that interesting.

'Have you ever used a stolen credit card to purchase electronic items from online retailers based in these Chinese cities – Guangzhou, Tianjin or Shanghai?'

Fuller appears to have developed a peculiar fascination for the nails on his left hand. He grunts out a 'No comment.'

My next document is ready to go across the table. 'Perhaps China has more than its fair share of villains, and there's no doubt as a regime they suffer a bad press from time to time, but they are also impacted by the same crimes as the rest of us.' I hold the document up. 'This came into my possession this morning. One of my colleagues tapped into an international alliance of collaborating law enforcement agencies, whose ranks have recently, and most unexpectedly, been swelled by intelligence units from several Chinese cities, including from Guangzhou, Tianjin and Shanghai. I doubt we know how long our Chinese friends will remain with the alliance, or how serious they are about collaborating, but the good news is they appear to be handing information over quite freely at the present time.'

I hand the papers to Quinn. 'As you'll see, these are invoices from online retailers in the three cities. They include your client's customer details, order details, dates, shipping information, delivery points. The works, really.' I give her time to scan the information before I add, 'The same credit card number is listed on all of them.'

'That isn't my credit card, and well you know it,' says Fuller.

I let that go – for now. 'The first invoice is for a device that captures and records the signal from a car key, a practice known as cloning. This device is also illegal in the UK. Did you purchase this device from an online retailer based in the city of Guangzhou?'

'No comment.'

'Did you use that device to gain access to Jack McCafferty's vehicle, to enable you to plant evidence that would lead to him being charged with your wife's murder?'

He's examining his nails again, affecting nonchalance. 'No comment.' He did squeak a little that time, I have to say.

'Now, Mr Fuller, while I'm on the subject of planting evidence in Jack McCafferty's vehicle, there was one thing you missed.'

'That would be *allegedly* missed, DI Cooper,' says his solicitor.

I tilt my head slightly, and paraphrase Tobias. 'In the period immediately following death, and especially if a person dies in sudden and violent circumstances, there is what's termed primary relaxation of all the body's muscles – including the sphincter. That means it's likely there would have been significant traces of bodily fluids at the location where death occurred. But there were no such traces in Mr McCafferty's vehicle, so it's highly unlikely your wife died there. Did you murder your wife in your bedroom and wash all the bedding afterwards, thereby destroying vital biological evidence?'

Fuller leans forward and takes a sip of water. 'No comment.'

Next I pass over a copy of the online advert Bob showed me in her office all those weeks ago. 'The second invoice is for one of these devices. It replicates SIM cards and is also illegal in the UK.' I address Fuller once more. 'Did you purchase this device from an online retailer based in the city of Tianjin?'

'No comment.'

'Did you use that device to create a duplicate of your wife's SIM card, which you temporarily installed in your phone, thereby creating the false impression that she was with Jack McCafferty in St Mark's Woods on the evenings of $11^{th}$ and $18^{th}$ January?'

'No comment.'

'I'm sorry, Mr Fuller, I didn't hear that.'

He lifts his eyes. 'No comment!'

I smile at Keira, who raises an eyebrow in return. 'Mr Fuller,' I say. 'Were you aware that certain vehicles imported to the UK from Thailand have satnavs fitted that are capable of logging, storing and analysing thousands of individual journeys?'

He freezes for a moment before, yet again, 'No comment.'

'Were you aware that Jack McCafferty's Mitsubishi L200 pickup, manufactured in Thailand, incidentally, happens to be fitted with one of these upgraded satnavs?'

'No comment.'

I slide another sheet of paper off the top of my file. 'This final invoice,' I say, 'is a corker.' I hand Quinn a screenshot of another online advert. Then I'm back on Fuller. Or, at least, the top of his head. I'm so tempted to rap the bald bit with my knuckles. 'Mr Fuller, have you ever used a satnav hacker?'

'No comment.'

'Did you purchase this device from an online retailer based in the city of Shanghai?'

'No comment.'

'Do you know what they are for, and how they work?'

'Fuck off.'

I lean over towards my boss. 'A quaint deviation from the litany of no comments, wouldn't you say?'

'I'd like to know,' says Jeff. Keira Quinn sighs, but I suspect she's angling for an explanation too.

'Apparently, these things are brand new on the black market. They work through an app and are built around world-wide mapping software ripped off from Google Maps, or so I'm told. So, let's say Jack McCafferty's vehicle is parked on Glenogle Road, and it doesn't move all night, but I want to make it appear as though it did move. From where it was parked, to the woods, and back. On three consecutive Thursdays. Working from my PC, I can use the app to create the fake journey, complete with GPS coordinates, dates, and times. Then I copy it to a USB drive, break into the pickup using the cloned key, plug the USB into the vehicle, and upload the fake journey to the satnav. I can either insert the fake journey anywhere into the vehicle's history or I can replace an existing, genuine one. Totally undetectable, even to us.' I open my eyes wide, build up the tension. 'But not to our multimedia boffins at the Scottish Crime Campus down in North Lanarkshire, who helped us prove that several journeys Jack McCafferty was supposed to have made were conducted solely on the app, and not on the mean streets of Leith.'

'Wow!' says Jeff. 'Blow me down, but I've never even heard of such a thing.'

Fuller doesn't have quite the same colour in his cheeks as he did when he was brought in, but Quinn isn't taking this lying down. 'If, as you say, these items are illegal in this country, how do you suggest my client was able to source them in the first place?'

I'm not fazed. 'In my opinion, how he sourced them is irrelevant. I'm more interested in the fact he purchased and used them to commit this crime.' I don't bother mentioning the dark web – that would take me dangerously close to the land of conjecture. She doesn't respond, so I move on.

'My next item involves a piece of film.' I tap an icon on my tablet and bring up an image on a TV monitor on the wall to our left. Three of us concentrate on it – no prizes for guessing who doesn't. 'One thing that's always puzzled me is why there were no traces of fibres on your wife's clothing that could have come from you. But what I am clear about is the exercise and strengthening regime you've been pursuing for the last year was specifically designed to enable you to physically transport her body from the woods to the lock-ups, and I believe you used your mountain bike to assist you in the task. Oh, and that would be the mountain bike which was conveniently stolen a few days before Rachel died.'

'Detective Inspector,' says Quinn. 'If I recall correctly, there was no evidence of mud on Mrs Fuller's outer clothing. So even if my client was able to lift his wife's body, and carry her that distance, would he not have had to lay her down from time to time?'

'One would think so, but I believe after your client murdered his wife, he dressed her in the clothes she was found in – generic grey cotton hoodie and joggers, and the coat he gave her for Christmas. I also believe he used an extra pair, or pairs, of joggers to harness her body to his, meaning he only had to support her weight.' Quinn begins to speak but I hold a hand up. 'Furthermore, I believe your client wore matching grey cotton hoodie and joggers, so even if Mr Fuller had been forensically examined at the time, any transference of fibres from him to her would have been easy to explain. As would his DNA. After all, he says they had sex together before they argued, and she left the house.'

Quinn taps her pen on her notepad. 'I wasn't able to count the number of times you used the words, "I believe", in your explanation but the Fiscal will require more than your beliefs to pursue this.'

I hold up an index finger and address my next question to Fuller. Andrew came up with the original idea while he and Steph were waiting for me outside the crematorium, and Steph produced the goods this very morning, just before Bob came into my office. 'At any time in the past year,' I say, 'did you purchase a minimum of two casual outfits, hoodies and joggers, all in grey cotton material?'

No question he's rattled. But he manages to recover enough to squeeze out another no comment.

'I'll wager, Mr Fuller, that you believe there is no record of you buying these items. But, unfortunately for you, I have evidence you bought them from a trader at the monthly car boot sale that runs on Sundays at Ingliston Showground. That's out by the airport, in case it's slipped your mind. You thought you were safe – a cash transaction, goods that might be, let's say, dodgy, no receipt provided, therefore untraceable. But you'd be sadly mistaken.' I swear he gulped when I said that. 'Now, I've no doubt there are traders who are less than scrupulously honest but most of them are hardworking citizens doing their best to earn extra money. During our investigations, we learned there's a high level of unreported theft at most of these weekend events, and not only at Ingliston. Understandably, the traders became totally fed up with all the thieving, so they set out to protect themselves. These days, at most of the markets, they have a network of stalls with webcams that connect to a central server. At Ingliston, the server is in the showground office.'

I tap my tablet, and Quinn does likewise on her client's arm. Grudgingly, Fuller turns to the screen, and I hit *Play*. The quality of the footage isn't brilliant but it's certainly good enough to see Fuller handing over some cash and stuffing a fat pile of grey clothing into a backpack before retreating into the crowd.

'Is that you in the film, Mr Fuller?'

'No comment.'

I don't even consider how pointless a response that was – the footage shows him full face on to the camera. Then I lift an evidence bag from down by my side. 'Mr Fuller. Earlier in the interview you stated that the credit card on the Chinese retailers' invoices didn't belong to you. Do you stand by that?' He doesn't answer – I don't care. 'We contacted Morton Street Primary about the boxes of materials you intended to return to the school. They were all sealed, and your prints were on the packaging tape, which matched a roll we found in your office. Your head of department was present while we searched them for anything that didn't belong to the school. We found this item in the only box you'd put in the cargo deck.' I hold it up so he and Quinn can read the title: *Excel Formulas for Dummies*. 'Throughout the manual there are pencilled notations in your handwriting, which is quite distinctive, isn't it? Now, I don't know much about Excel but it transpires one of my team here is a bit of a whiz. He checked out all these notations and told me they're gibberish. Said if you typed them into a formula, they'd throw up error codes.' I tap my tablet, point at the TV. 'This is supposedly an example called *Info*. I have no idea what it does, but I'm told that all formulas begin with the name, in this case *Info*, and then there are various parameters that must be entered for the formula to work.' I point up at the screen. 'Do you recognise the four blocks of four numbers that are shown as parameters of this formula?'

'No comment.'

'Is that your handwriting?'

'No comment.'

'Fair enough, Mr Fuller. It is your right to reply no comment to all my questions. However, this book has your fingerprints all over it. It was in a box you carried into the school. A police graphologist has advised me there is a strong likelihood that the handwriting inside is yours. The four blocks of four numbers I've just shown you match the credit card number on the Chinese retailers' invoices. Furthermore, throughout the book, there are annotations that are meant to look like parameters but, in reality, they are names, dates, times, phone numbers, GPS coordinates, item codes for all your online purchases.' I lean forward on my elbows. 'Need I go on?'

The glare he sends me would strip paint.

'DI Cooper,' says Quinn. 'If I may have some time alone with my client, please?'

I shut down the TV monitor and begin to gather up my papers. 'You may indeed. But before I finish, you might want to ask him how many bicycles he currently owns. And if he says two, ask him if that includes the ebike we found concealed below the floorboards in his deceased neighbour's house. The one we have film of him riding away from my house, which has his DNA all over it, and that's been modified to derestrict its top speed.'

Fuller sits back, places his hands on his knees, and lifts his chin. But I have one more card to play. It's overkill but I can't resist. I lean down, fiddle about inside my bag, then rub at my eyes. Within seconds there are tears streaming down my cheeks. Jeff's sitting back, so I turn my head to let him see. His brows come down and he reaches for my arm. 'Mel. What's wrong?'

When I burst out laughing he jerks his hand away. I blink several times, and rake about for a pack of tissues. 'Jeez. Think I overdid it.' He stares at me as if I've completely lost the plot. I pull a bottle of chilli oil from my bag and plonk it on the table. 'Instant tears, Boss. If you ever need to play the grieving husband, this stuff is just the job.'

I dab my eyes with a tissue. 'But it doesn't half sting, so you have to be really careful to clean your hands properly.'

Then I produce, of all things, a lemon. I hold it up between thumb and forefinger and look across at my murderer one final time. 'One of these does the trick, though. Doesn't it, Mister Fuller?'

———

The following day

It's late morning. The sun is shining, and I have quite the spring in my step. This has nothing to do with the transfer request I received first thing from DS Lawrence Ratcliffe. I wish he'd accepted my offer to continue in the team, but I can't say I'm heartbroken he declined. Hey ho.

When I reach the house, I climb the flight of stone steps and knock on the door. It won't be answered quickly but I'm happy to bide my time. I glance towards the road but there's no sign yet of the vehicle I'm expecting.

The call I was desperate for came through from Leo less than an hour ago. Before I'd even said thanks and goodbye, I hit

*Send* to request an authorisation that I had already lined up. And thanks to Jeff, it was granted in minutes.

The door opens. I smile. 'Still on crutches, then?' I have to admit as pointless questions go, that one was right up there.

'Afraid so. But more as a precaution than anything else.'

I shake my head while I look her up and down. 'I still can't believe it, Lisa.'

When she fell over the parapet she landed flat on her back on the highest tier of the scaffolding. When I'd leaned over, I couldn't believe she was staring up at me from only three metres below. But just as I called out, her eyes closed, and we suffered an anxious couple of minutes while Steph and Tobias clambered down. I'd clasped my hands together when they yelled she was still breathing. It was several hours later before a surgeon had called me. The medical terms, 'Fractured skull, cranial bleed, emergency op, induced coma', terrified me. And they still do.

She eases herself into an armchair, and I trundle off to make tea. She sips at her drink. Winces. Hopefully because it's too hot and not that it tastes like crap. She puts the mug down. My vote's on crap.

'I love your suit,' she says. 'New?'

I look down, rub my fingertips over the material. It feels, what, luxuriant? 'Thanks. Yes, it is. My daughter helped me choose it. Online, a shop I've never used before.' I make a face. 'Cost a bloody fortune – but I rather like it.'

'It looks great on you. You should buy more from places like that, you deserve it.'

'That's what my husband says.' We both giggle at that.

We chat for a while longer then, during a brief lull, I reach down, lift the Excel manual from my bag and show it to her. 'Seen this before? It was inside one of the boxes that Edwin took to the school.'

She looks at it. Rocks her head from side to side. 'Rings a wee bell but I'm not sure why. Things are still a bit hazy. Sorry.'

I flap a hand at her and put the book away.

We chat for a few minutes, then I say, 'One thing I've been meaning to ask you. Did you really go out onto the roof, intending to climb down the scaffolding to escape from Edwin?' I know she does remember that part of the whole school episode, we spoke about it not long after she was discharged from hospital. She told me she'd known about the restoration works from her position on the various Council steering committees.

'Oh, yes. Definitely,' she says, laughing. 'I'm only mildly nervous of heights but Edwin's absolutely scared shitless. No way would he have followed me down there.'

We both glance up when there's a hearty knock at the door. Lisa is surprised – but I'm not. I lift my bag and cross the floor. Put my hand on the door handle. 'Mel,' she says. 'You're not leaving already, are you?'

There are two men on the doorstep. The one in uniform grins, throws me a wave that might have been a salute, and trots off down the steps. 'Thanks, Dave,' I call, and switch my attention to the other chap.

I step forward, and he moves aside. 'Hi there,' I say. 'It's great to see you.'

Clearly he's a bit lost for words, so I help him out. 'Don't mind me, I'm just leaving.'

I pause on the top step. 'Go on, then. Your wife's inside. She's ... em ... not expecting you.'

# ACKNOWLEDGMENTS

It's said writing is a solitary pastime, but my experience is that's far from the case. So many people have read my books – some whom I know and some I don't – they've encouraged me, offered positive and unsolicited feedback and been wholeheartedly supportive. Every single time it happens it makes me happy, makes me feel part of a community, and for that I am incredibly privileged.

Many other wonderful individuals have helped to bring this latest work to life by giving freely of their time, expertise, advice and opinion. I can only apologise if I've forgotten anyone, but these include: my niece Dr Anna Wight, Dagmar Grant, David Stead, Hilary Sidgwick, Klaudia Monkiewicz and Nikki Tierney.

Of course *Yes, I Killed Her* is a work of fiction but I've tried to make it as accurate and realistic as possible, particularly in relation to Police Scotland activities and procedures. Without tremendous help and advice from Duncan Smith and Stuart Murray, that would have been extraordinarily difficult so thank you, gentlemen. Any errors or inconsistencies that remain are entirely down to me.

I'm also indebted to Andrew Crosbie of www.crime.scot, his amazing guide to Scottish criminal law, and my fellow Hobeck author, Brian Price, whose work *Crime Writing: How to Write the Science* did precisely that.

I also enjoyed my guided tour round my old school, Leith

Primary, so thank you to the teachers who took time out to refresh my memories and give me such a treat.

One of the stars of this story is Leith itself. People who are familiar with the areas I've described will have noticed I've taken a few liberties with the geography and invented a few places and settings to make the story fit better. On that, I'm grateful to Maurice Dougan for allowing me to use his images of the Water of Leith on the cover.

An enormous thank you to my friend, Chris Livingston and my cousin, Joyce Nisbet who have worked with me on all my books by reading and critiquing the later drafts. Chris finds technology and technical holes in the plot – which I have to rewrite, and Joyce offers guidance and advice on the creative aspects of my writing – which also leads to rewriting. But neither is a chore because both result in significant improvements to the story. Chris, Joyce, you've no idea how much I appreciate your contributions.

To Rebecca Collins and Adrian Hobart at Hobeck Books – thank you for continuing to display faith in me and my writing, for all the work you do in the background on promotion and marketing, and for assessing and checking the final drafts. And to my editor, Helen Gray, whose detailed and perceptive comments make so much sense, and who is an absolute joy to work with.

And finally – as always – my amazing wife, Shiona. There's so much I have to say thank you for. Reviewing the first draft; your creative input; unwavering encouragement and support as I waded through several revisions; and for helping me, page by page, to polish the final version. There are so many unseen aspects of getting this book out there, and I couldn't have done it without you. For everything, quite simply: THANK YOU. I love you. HTM.

# ABOUT THE AUTHOR

Harry Fisher is a native of Leith (the port for Edinburgh) so, mainly, that's where his crime thrillers are set. Write about what you know, and all that.

Prior to self-publishing his debut, Harry had never written a word of fiction. So he just launched in – cold turkey for authors. And now he's written three books.

*Way Beyond A Lie* is a standalone crime thriller set in Edinburgh and Prague with bang up to date themes: identity theft and cybercrime. During two free book promotions in 2020, it was downloaded 2,700 times over five days.

*Be Sure Your Sins* is #1 in the DI Mel Cooper Series. "Six events that happen to six people that destroy six lives". There's a serial blackmailer – and an interfering boss. But Mel takes no crap, not even from the bad guys.

*Yes, I Killed Her* is Harry Fisher's audacious follow-up crime thriller starring DI Mel Cooper. It's the story of the perfect murder. But with omnipresent CCTV, digital and biological forensics, and electronic footprints like a Yeti's, is that even possible? The killer thinks it is. Mel disagrees. Game on.

Harry loves chatting about crime writing. Covid meant Zoom became the norm, but he'd far rather meet people face to face. He lives in Aberdeen with his wife, Shiona. They share their home with their crazy Hungarian Vizsla – his job is to stop them seizing up completely. It's sort of working.

# ALSO BY HARRY FISHER

Way Beyond a Lie

The prequel to the DI Mel Cooper Series.

**Your wife goes missing. She leaves no trace.**
**You have no idea where she's gone.**
**How would _you_ try to find her?**

When Ross McKinlay's wife, Carla, vanishes during an afternoon shopping trip he's left bewildered and grief stricken. As Ross uncovers the reasons for his wife's disappearance, his life begins to unravel. He's determined to find her. He needs answers. But the deeper he delves, the more confused he becomes and the closer he edges towards danger.

As Ross is soon to discover, he isn't the only person looking for his wife.
One man wants the truth.
Another wants blood.
**Who will find her first?**

The prequel to the DS Mel Cooper Series, Harry Fisher's fast-paced story of love, friendship, fraud, intrigue and murder will keep you guessing until the last page.

'Bl**dy brilliant!' *****

'This book is worth every penny and keeps you entertained for literally hours.' *****

'Well Mr Fisher, you are now well and truly on my list of favourite authors.' *****

'It wasn't a case of wanting to know how the book ended, I needed to know.' *****

'A great story line with good twists and turns and some fantastic dry humour.' *****

'Told with impressively forensic detail and credible, natural dialogue.' *****

'Harry Fisher spins plates of plot to maintain your attention and keep you cheering on his improbable hero.' ****

'A clever scam which could happen and a great wee twist in the tale.' *****

Be Sure Your Sins

The first book in the DI Mel Cooper Series.

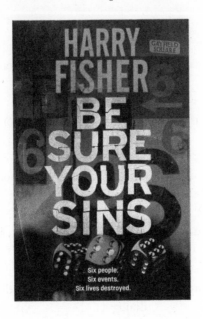

**Six people
Six events
Six lives destroyed**

**What is the connection?**

Detective Sergeant Melissa (Mel) Cooper has two major investigations on the go. The first involves six apparently unrelated individuals who all suffer inexplicable life-altering events.

Mel is also pursuing a serial blackmailer but just as she's about to prove the link between this man and the six bizarre events, she's ordered to back off.

So why are her bosses interfering with her investigations? Who are they trying to protect? And how far will they go to stop her?

The answers come from a totally unexpected source.

**The first in the brilliant new crime series by Harry Fisher introduces Edinburgh's DS Mel Cooper. She doesn't take any crap – not even from the bad guys.**

'Be prepared to read well into the early hours!' *****

'Loved the style of writing and the original story line.' *****

'This is a humdinger of a crime story.' *****

'Superbly plotted storyline, red herrings, misdirection, and some of the wittiest writing I've read for a long time.' *****

'And just when I thought it was all neatly wrapped up there was yet another revelation!' *****

'An intricate web that kept hold of me to the end.' *****

'Harry Fisher would give many a top name crime thriller author a run for their money.' *****

'A lot of different threads, cleverly interlinked.' ****

# HOBECK BOOKS - THE HOME OF GREAT STORIES

We hope you've enjoyed reading this novel by Harry Fisher. *Way Beyond A Lie*, the prequel to the series, and the first book in the series *Be Sure Your Sins* are both published by Hobeck Books. If you would like to find out more about Harry's writing please visit his website: **www.harryfisherwriter.com**.

If you enjoyed this book, you may be interested to know that if you subscribe to Hobeck Books you can download *Crime Bites*, a free compilation of novellas and short stories by the Hobeck team of authors: **www.hobeck.net**.

Included in this compilation are the following:

- *Echo Rock* by Robert Daws
- *Old Dogs, Old Tricks* by AB Morgan
- *The Silence of the Rabbit* by Wendy Turbin
- *Never Mind the Baubles: An Anthology of Twisted Winter Tales* by the Hobeck Team (including all the current Hobeck authors and Hobeck's two publishers)
- *The Clarice Cliff Vase* by Linda Huber
- *Here She Lies* by Kerena Swan
- *The Macnab Principle* by R.D. Nixon
- *A Defining Moment* by Lin Le Versha
- *Saviour* by Jennie Ensor

Also please visit the Hobeck Books website for details of our other superb authors and their books, and if you would like to get in touch, we would love to hear from you.

Hobeck Books also presents a weekly podcast, the Hobcast, where founders Adrian Hobart and Rebecca Collins discuss all things book related, key issues from each week, including the ups and downs of running a creative business. Each episode includes an interview with one of the people who make Hobeck possible: the editors, the authors, the cover designers. These are the people who help Hobeck bring great stories to life. Without them, Hobeck wouldn't exist. The Hobcast can be listened to from all the usual platforms but it can also be found on the Hobeck website: **www.hobeck.net/hobcast**.